The
Scrapbook
Quests

sands press

The
Scrapbook
Quests

Dennis Stein

sands press

sands press

A division of 3244601 Canada Inc.
300 Central Avenue West
Brockville, Ontario
K6V 5V2

Toll Free 1-800-563-0911 or 613-345-2687
http://www.sandspress.com

ISBN 978-1-988281-26-1

Copyright © Sands Press 2017

Cover Design by Kristine Barker and Wendy Treverton
Original Cover Art by Sharon Stein
Edited by Katrina Geenevasen
Formatting by Renee Hare
Publisher Kristine Barker

1st Printing September 2017
To book an author for your live event, please call: 1-800-563-0911

Sands Press is a literary publisher interested in new and established authors wishing to develop and market their product. For more information please visit our website at www.sandspress.com.

For the children...

Part One:
The Heart of the Raven

Preface

The Thousand Islands area of Ontario is full of local legend and lore, and is rich with a unique history like few other places in the world. Loyalists and the Native people who lived here long ago have stories to tell.

The idea for this story arose while I was writing historical articles for local newspapers and was focused when my son took an interest in finding a geode. Although we have yet to discover one, I did quite a bit of research in an attempt to learn how to locate and identify a geode. In doing this, I came up with a great idea for a story; one that plunges the characters of my son and youngest daughter into an adventure to find a legendary crystal, to help avert disaster in their family. My mother and father are also characters in this tale, and everyone who reads the story will know who Dad is supposed to represent. Although The Heart of the Raven is fiction, many of the characters are based on real people and it is set in my hometown: Brockville, Ontario, Canada. The legend of the Heart itself may be fictional, but it mixes with real places and real stories from the Native people who have inhabited this area since long before European settlers arrived here.

1

Nana's art room was full of interesting things, from sketches and paintings in progress, to figurines and sculptures. Large bookcases covered one whole side of the room, filled with books, papers, and curious trinkets from all over the world. Alex and Valerie loved this room and always listened intently as Nana told stories about strange and wonderful things. The room was Nana's personal space, and contained all the things she loved. It had large windows at its end that allowed in lots of light. Grandpa rarely entered the room, except at his wife's personal request to critique a painting or sketch she had completed. She loved to have Valerie and Alex here, allowing them to explore their own artistic sides. The children's father was working today and Nana had brought them to her house for some art time. Grandpa watched television in the living room as the three of them painted and talked.

Valerie was using some pastels to colour a picture she had drawn under Nana's expert supervision: an old barn on a snowy day. She loved to draw and paint, and Nana had shown her many tricks to help make her artwork look more realistic. Her long brown hair hung down almost onto the paper on which she drew, and her matching brown eyes focused on her work. Her slender form was seated at Nana's drafting table; her pretty face set in concentration. Valerie had turned fourteen this year and had just begun her first year of high school. She had a bracelet on her wrist made of coloured beads on a leather strap, another artsy project Nana had come up with. Valerie had always held a fascination for the beads that Nana kept in a large box. They looked like jewels to her, being a myriad of colours and shapes.

Alex was busy with some watercolour paints, working at his grandmother's easel. His artwork was somewhat abstract: a combination of colours and patterns. To Valerie it looked like a mess. Nana reminded her that art is in the eye of the beholder. Alex frowned at his sister from behind a paint-streaked face. Unlike Valerie, Alex had sandy blond hair and grey-blue eyes like his grandfather. He was a fairly quiet and reserved boy who usually stuck very close to his sister. Alex always had a well-worn backpack with him, in which he carried everything that he thought he might need. Presently it rested a short distance away from him in the studio, and was never far from reach. He was about a foot shorter than Valerie, and four years younger. He enjoyed the time he spent at his grandparents' home, as his grandmother always had something fun for them to do, or at least, a great story to tell them.

Today, the children were about to hear a special story. Nana brought out a scrapbook containing newspaper clippings that she had saved over the years. Nana coughed for a long time and took a moment to catch her breath. Both of the children exchanged a worried glance. She had not been well over the last few weeks, but carried on, ignoring the looks of empathy from her grandchildren. Placing the scrapbook on a large table at one end of the room, Nana adjusted her glasses and flipped through it, searching for one story in particular. The pages were filled with pictures and interesting articles, and they crinkled as she turned them.

"I remembered a story that might interest the two of you," she said, turning another page.

Valerie looked up from her pastel, waiting. The stories Nana told them were always fascinating, and the two hung off of every word. Their older sister, who was now grown and away at college, had shared some of Nana's stories with them when they were very young. Nana told each story as if it were some kind of major event, and drew them into all facets of it. The children felt like they were part of the adventure. Nana had a definite flair for storytelling, at times just making it up as she went, especially when around a campfire. Any family gathering was a great opportunity for her to get the children involved in a new tale.

Nana finally produced an old newspaper article from the pages of the book, and her mouth moved silently as she looked at it. After reading the article again to refresh her memory, she began to tell them the story. It was always fun to listen to her and, like in her artwork, she painted a picture for them with words. This story, from the newspaper clipping on the table, was an old, native legend about a crystal that the ancient people believed had special healing powers.

Back when the New World was young and the white man had only just arrived, the Native people had hidden the crystal from them. The legend describes a great raven that took the crystal from the ancient people and clutched it to its breast as it flew away. It held the crystal so tightly that the bird and the crystal became one. The raven was finally captured and hidden away, far from the reach of the invaders. Many years passed, and the story of the crystal and its power became nothing more than a whispered myth. It was said that the glowing purple crystal could cure illness and even death if used in the presence of those who held no malice and were pure of heart.

Nana looked over her glasses at Valerie as she put the news clipping back in the scrapbook.

"Kind of neat, eh guys?" she asked.

"Very cool," replied Alex with enthusiasm.

"Yeah!" Valerie agreed eagerly.

"There is a very old book," Nana began again. "It is called History of the Thousand Islands. It tells more of the story of the Heart of the Raven: what it could do and where it went. Very few copies of this book have survived, but I think there is one in the library down the street from your house!"

Nana pointed to the children as she emphasized the last of her words. She turned, picking up the scrapbook, and placed it back amongst the collection of things in the bookcase.

"Really?" asked Alex, his paint-smudged face breaking into an excited grin.

"Yes, dear heart," said Nana, returning his smile. "Imagine a crystal that could heal sickness!"

Valerie's eyes were wide and her hands were frozen in mid-air. Her thoughts drifted as she replayed the story in her mind. Nana had told them many stories before, but for some reason, this one intrigued Valerie more than the others. She was lost in her thoughts.

"Yeah, that would be something!" she said dreamily.

~~~~

The following week at school, Valerie was still daydreaming. She had always wanted to go on an adventure and Nana had basically handed her one. But how could they ever hope to find the Heart of the Raven, and did it really even exist? Nana was now in the hospital. Her father had gotten the call that morning, before they had gone to school, and every time Valerie thought about it her heart ached. Why did bad things happen to good people?

That familiar pain came on again as she thought of her grandmother lying in a hospital bed. Cancer. She had the very same disease that had claimed Valerie's mother's life.

Suddenly, Valerie's cheeks filled with blood, and she was angry. She pledged that she would get Alex after school and they would somehow find the Heart. She had no idea whether the legend was simply a myth or whether it was all true, but she was determined to find out. Valerie pulled back her long brown hair, tucking the loose strands behind her ears as she shook the deep and sorrowful thoughts from her mind. It was a motion she made often since her hair had grown long.

She snapped back to the history lesson at hand, and was conscious of the teacher's voice once again. She certainly didn't want to be singled out for not paying attention, and Mr. Thatch could be unpleasant at times. He was reading a lesson about the woodland Natives and their involvement with early settlers from their textbook. She almost chuckled as Mr. Thatch read from the text. Had he ever met one of the Métis, the Mohawk, or the Mi'kmaq? She knew as well as anyone else in the school that he had aboriginal roots. All one had to do was look at his straight black hair, dark brown eyes, and tan skin to know it. Did he realize what his people had sacrificed to help the early British settlers of this country? These were the lessons and stories Nana had handed down to her. The Native people of the country had been forced to give up control of the New World, and, thus, became a minority on their own land.

A pause came in the lesson. Valerie suddenly felt the urge to put her teacher on the spot. She raised her hand, distracting his attention from the textbook.

"Yes, Valerie?" he asked.

"Mr. Thatch, do you know anything about the Heart of the Raven? The story told by the Mohawk about a healing crystal?"

There was silence in the classroom. After the look Valerie received from her teacher, she almost regretted asking the question. Mr. Thatch looked at her with a gaze that told her that the question was out of bounds. It was immediately apparent to her that he knew a lot about it. His deep voice boomed in the classroom.

"What is it you want to know?" he wondered, looking at her intently. She shrugged, not knowing what to do and feeling silly for asking.

"I suppose the story is not too far off from the topic of the early Loyalist settlers who we have been discussing here today."

Mr. Thatch began to tell the story almost exactly as Nana had told it. He watched Valerie's reaction as he spoke, and she could feel his gaze upon her as he paced back and forth at the front of the classroom.

"It is a legend among the indigenous tribes of the Mohawk community. More of the legend is described in a book that was written many years ago; a book that people claim is carried in our very own library. However, no one seems to have seen this mysterious copy for years."

He ran through the very basics of the legend and Valerie listened intently, searching for any clues in his words that might provide a glimmer of real truth to the story. As she listened, she was amazed at how well he could unfold the entire tale with no text to refer to.

Just then the bell rang, signalling the end of class. Valerie breathed a sigh of relief. She gathered her books quickly and escaped out the door of the classroom with the other students, still feeling Mr. Thatch's eyes on her. She shuddered as she made her way through the waves of students, all hurrying to their lockers for a brief break before the next class.

Her locker was at the very end of the hallway where it intersected with the lobby and the entrance to the gymnasium. She held her books under her arm and grabbed the combination lock on the door of her locker. Suddenly someone grabbed her arm, and she turned with a start, dropping her books. Valerie's mind had been on other things: Nana, the native legend, and her next class, all swirling in her brain like a nest of hornets. She certainly was startled by whoever had grabbed her.

"Ha, got ya!" said a friendly voice.

It was Robert Bradley, the young custodian and maintenance man. He wore a dark blue golf shirt with his name embroidered on the breast pocket and beige work pants with a brown leather belt. His brown hair was almost long enough to be in his blue eyes. He wore dark brown work boots that had seen better days, and he leaned on a long-handled broom. He gave Valerie a wide grin.

"Thanks, Robert! You scared me to death!" Valerie exclaimed. "Don't you have work to do?"

She swatted him on the shoulder as he playfully tried to dodge her. Robert always seemed to be around when she finished her first class, and at times, she found him to be a bit of a nuisance. Since the beginning of the semester, he had seemed to enjoy bugging her at every opportunity. Most of his stories made Valerie laugh at some point, and then he would leave, strolling down the hall with a bit of a limp. He had said it was an old injury from a car accident, and walked as though he were much older than his young age of twenty-five.

Valerie bent down to pick up her books.

"Yes, sorry about that!" said Robert, in his best Sean Connery impression. Valerie grinned as she scooped up her texts and tossed them onto the shelf in her locker. She retrieved a new one, along with a notebook, and gave the door of her locker a kick to close it.

"Hey, easy on the hardware, eh?" he said, pretending to look mad. "I have to fix all this stuff, you know!"

Valerie closed the combination lock, spinning its dial and dropping it before letting it smack against the metal of the locker door with a smirk. This action produced another gap-mouthed look from the young custodian. Just then Katie, Valerie's best friend, showed up and grabbed her arm to get her moving, not wishing to enter into a drawn-out conversation with Robert. The two girls hustled off down the hall, and Valerie turned back to Robert for a moment.

"Just consider it job security!" she hollered after him.

~~~~

Valerie and Alex had been out all evening, wandering the bicycle path, when their dad stepped out on the back deck and called for them. It was a school night, and he wanted to get them fed and off to bed at a reasonable time. The two of them were difficult enough to get up in the mornings without the late nights. It was a pleasantly warm evening, and the chirps of crickets could be heard over the urban sounds of traffic and dog barking. Fireflies began to flash in the tall grasses beyond the back fence as night dropped its dark veil over the neighbourhood.

The children heard their father's loud call and began to head home. It had been a long day, but the two kids were loath to come in for the night. They had been out looking for any kind of clue regarding the mysterious treasure that Nana had spoken about. But with no clues and no real direction to head in, Valerie was not surprised that they had come up with nothing. It suddenly made her aware that this feat would not be an easy task to accomplish. It was going to be like finding a needle in a haystack.

"Well, that was a waste of time!" said Valerie.

"Yeah, but it was still fun!" exclaimed Alex, pausing for a moment to rifle through his backpack for a small flashlight.

It was dark now and finding their way had become a little more difficult, even though they knew the path like the backs of their hands.

"We need a real clue," replied Valerie.

Alex clicked on the small light and the two continued along.

"I guess it is a little crazy to think that this Raven's Heart would be right out here on the bike path," said Alex.

"It's the Heart of The Raven," Valerie corrected him.

"Whatever!"

"Well, we will have to go to the library right after school tomorrow and find that book Nana was talking about," said Valerie.

"Aye-aye, Captain!" Alex said, faking a salute.

Valerie ignored his sarcasm. They continued to walk along the path with the creek flowing silently past beside them. As the summer had gone on, the water level in the creek had dropped a lot, but there were always small fish in there that they enjoyed catching during the summer to put in the garden pond that their dad had built in the backyard.

They stepped off the asphalt of the path and walked up into the yard through a gate in the fence. As their dad saw the beam of the flashlight coming he stepped back into the house. He didn't like them being out on the path after dark. They were getting a little older, but he still preferred them home before dusk. The days were slowly getting shorter and the evenings coming sooner.

Valerie and Alex walked across the yard, looking at the warm glow of the lights from the house spilling out onto the darkened lawn. Crickets continued their night song as the children hurried up to the house and climbed the wooden steps of the deck. Valerie took one last look at the backyard as she walked and watched the flash of the fireflies in the darkness. The kids stepped into the kitchen and were greeted by the aroma of something warm and tasty. Their eyes brightened as they saw the large cardboard box and the plates set out neatly on the counter. It was pizza night!

2

One particular floor of the library was still using a card catalogue system - paper index cards that revealed the location of a book - while the newer sections had all been converted to a computer-locating system. The main library room was huge, very old, and smelled of wood and paper. It was full of dark wooden bookcases that reached almost to the ceiling. Valerie and Alex went to the chests of small drawers, and Valerie scanned the labels on the front. She crossed her fingers and slid open one of the drawers. The old paper cards sat neatly in the drawer, organized and debossed with the ink from an ancient typewriter. Valerie began to flip through, skipping large sections of cards. If they could find the book, it may help them find the Heart of the Raven, she thought. Alex watched her as she searched, glued to his sister's flying hands.

"Can I help you children find something?" asked a voice from behind them.

They spun around, startled by the voice. It was Ms. Stone, the librarian, to whom all the children in the neighbourhood referred to as "old stone-faced Stone." She looked over the tops of her glasses at the two of them and waited patiently for an answer.

"Uh, no thanks, Ms. Stone, I was just amazed at how neat and organized they all are," Valerie replied shyly as she slid the drawer closed slowly behind her.

"Very well then," Ms. Stone said, not changing her expression. She lingered a moment longer. Valerie grabbed Alex's arm; her brother was still looking up at the woman with wide eyes. She dragged him quickly away, and the two headed to some of the rows that were farther back in the library. Ms. Stone observed them as they went, and Alex watched her nervously as he was pulled. He didn't like the woman; she was mean.

Past rows of tables and chairs, they turned into one of the aisles of shelving. The books all looked very old, and were mostly hardcover or leather-bound with that peculiar smell of oil and paper. Alex took one last peek quickly around the corner of the aisle. Ms. Stone was gone. He sighed in relief and then turned back to Valerie.

"How are we going to find it now?" he asked, shrugging his shoulders.

From her left pocket, Valerie produced a single index card.

Alex gasped and held a hand up to his open mouth.

Valerie made a quick motion with a finger to her lips to shush him.

"Keep watch while I look!" she said quietly.

As Valerie began to search through the books in the huge wooden bookcase, Alex crept back to the end of the bookcases and peered out at the rest of the vast room. People were seated here and there at a few of the tables, heads bowed and reading. He gave a thumbs-up to his sister. Valerie was already tracing her way along the shelves, looking for the old book. There were books of all types in these cases: some were very old with hard, leather spines and lettering in gold and silver. She went down a few shelves. Alex suddenly saw Ms. Stone emerge at the far end of the room, gazing around. She must be looking for them, he thought.

"Hurry up!" he whispered to Valerie. "I just saw her!"

Valerie dropped down one more shelf as she ran her fingers across the book spines. She stopped suddenly. It wasn't there! She quickly checked the card again. She was right where it should be. Now frustrated, she pulled the book out that she had her finger on. She pulled another, but the title wasn't even close. Then she saw a book behind the others that was lying on its side. She moved enough books to retrieve it. In gold letters on its hard cover the title read: History of the Thousand Islands. She smiled. It had been hidden away.

"I found it!" she exclaimed. Quickly she replaced the other books and stood up to show her brother their prize. It was a fairly plain-looking hardcover book that was reddish in colour and appeared very old.

"Good!" he replied hastily. "Now let's get out of here!"

"We have to sign it out or we will really get in trouble," Valerie stated.

They walked quickly toward the front desk. Valerie was carrying the ancient tome in a death grip. Ms. Stone was there, and the two tried to look as innocent as possible as they presented the book to sign out. Ms. Stone looked over her glasses at the book and then at the two children in front of her desk. Alex swallowed hard and held his breath for a moment. Valerie simply smiled and handed over her library card. After another long moment, Ms. Stone withdrew the book's card for Valerie to sign and watched as the young girl carefully filled in her name and the date.

"This is a very old book, you know?" the woman stated dryly, looking at the two of them with no real expression.

Both children nodded and Alex took a small step closer to his sister. Ms. Stone pulled a rubber stamp out from under the counter and blotted it on an inkpad on her desk. She still had her eyes fixed on the children. Alex shivered and looked away. Like a chef with a meat cleaver, the librarian slammed the stamp down onto the card so quickly and violently that both Valerie and Alex jumped slightly.

"Don't forget the due date," she said in a serious tone.

~~~~

Valerie awoke late the next morning. Since it was Saturday, her father had let them sleep in. She was still holding on to the book, and she closed it and fumbled to place it on her nightstand. She stretched long and hard before flinging the covers aside. The sunshine was already bright on the carpet in her room and she knew she had to wake her brother. Their next great adventure had begun, and with the weekend at hand, she decided it was best not to waste any time. Alex could sleep with bombs going off overhead, she thought, and she wasn't about to let him delay the plans that were already brewing in her mind. She threw on her housecoat, struggling to get her arms through the sleeves, and tried to put her feet into slippers at the same time. Valerie grabbed for the old book, cradled it like a newborn in her arms, and headed down the hall quietly to Alex's room.

Opening the door a crack, she peered in and saw Alex's sleeping form lying spread-eagle on the bed. She pushed the door open some more and slipped inside. She simply could not resist. Picking up a small flag from the shelves opposite the bed, she settled just beside her brother and leaned over him. She touched his ear with the end of the miniature flag. Nothing. She grinned as she did it again. Alex swiped sleepily at his ear and then rolled over on his side. Stifling a desire to giggle, Valerie moved in again and tickled his other ear. Alex swatted again, but this time he opened his eyes to see his older sister holding the flag with her hand over her mouth in an attempt not to laugh.

"Get lost," he mumbled sleepily.

"C'mon, get up!" she replied, her voice brimming with excitement.

"Mmm…" he murmured, and rolled away from her.

She jumped up onto his bed and bounced until Alex nearly fell off onto the floor. Now he was definitely not amused. He grabbed the comforter on the bed and yanked it hard, just as Valerie landed one of her bounces. She yelped in surprise as the blanket was ripped out from beneath her feet and she landed with a thud on the mattress. This action made her brother laugh uncontrollably. A brief pillow fight ensued, until their father hollered for them from downstairs and caused a hush to suddenly fall over the two.

He had called for breakfast, and as if on cue, the smells of bacon, pancakes, and syrup filled their young noses. They dropped their pillows and ran down the stairs like a herd of buffalo. They ate ravenously, and their father urged them to slow down with a reminder that there would be a lot of food left if they wanted more. They loved Dad's weekend breakfasts that were filled with bacon, eggs, pancakes, and enough syrup to sink a battleship. When they finished, they cleared their plates and put them into the dishwasher to help out their father.

They got dressed quickly with the smell of the warm, autumn air flowing into the house through open windows. The sounds of birds singing their morning songs could be heard and the smell of fresh cut grass hung in the air. The children hurried down the stairs and Valerie carried the old history book under one arm.

It was another warm, sunny day. They went out to the backyard and climbed the steps into the tree house. It was private in there, and Dad was occupied with the weekend edition of the newspaper. Valerie and Alex looked through the pages of the old book, hoping something would lead them to the crystal. The words were cryptic and difficult to understand, but they knew that the path to the crystal was written in there somewhere, waiting to be discovered - waiting to be found. The pages had that feeling of old: they crinkled when turned, and smelled of wood shavings. The two could feel something in the writing and sense the power of the crystal; they simply needed the book to tell them where it was.

Valerie began to read the passage that told the ancient Mohawk legend of the Heart of the Raven. She read it aloud to her brother who sat next to her. At ten years old, he could already read very well for himself, but Alex enjoyed it when his sister read to him. Valerie usually just took control of whatever situation was at hand, a fact that sometimes caused arguments between the two siblings. Valerie continued to read the text and stumbled upon a riddle:

"Along the paths of the forest we go,
To the rip in rock and earth.

In the belly of the world in darkness,
Is the resting place of the Raven.
Deep in the Raven's nest,
Lies the Raven's egg,
The keeper and protector of the
Heart."

She read it again and tried to make meaning come from the words as she emphasized each in her mind. The riddle's hidden secrets eluded her, and she sat in silence for a short while. Their father's call roused her from her thoughts and she poked her head out of the doorway of the tree house. Dad was on the back deck, motioning for her to come over. The two kids climbed down and sprinted across the lawn to the steps at the side of the deck.

"I am going to see Nana in the hospital. Do you guys want to come, too?" he asked, already sure he knew the answer.

"Not really, I hate seeing her sick like that," Valerie replied shyly, her brother shaking his head as well.

"You'll have to go sometime; she may not be around much longer, and she loves to see you two," their father stated matter-of-factly. He didn't wish to force the issue today, however. "Ok, don't go too far. I will only be an hour or so. Stay in the neighbourhood, right?"

"What can we do, though? I'm bored," Alex demanded.

"I don't know Bud, why don't you both go for a hike or something? Along the old trails? Just not too far."

Valerie thought for a second, and she grinned as realization dawned on her. That was the starting point from the riddle! It was as if her father had read it, and uncovered the clue for her. She hugged her father around the waist, not paying any attention to his confused look.

"You're a genius!" she exclaimed.

3

The forest was cool and dark as they walked along the path, with sunlight tracing shadows of the leaves above onto the ground. Birds sang in the trees, and the sound of crickets along with the constant high pitch of cicadas could be heard. Valerie held the tattered page she had photocopied from the book as they went, looking here and there for clues as to where to go. Alex pulled at the straps of his backpack, adjusting it. The path wound through the trees and down amongst ancient clumps of granite. As they walked, the path entered a large ravine, with steep rock walls rising high on each side. There were ferns here, huddled between the rocks scattered everywhere. It was still very warm, even for September, and very few leaves on the trees had even begun to change. The two children were dressed fairly lightly in their t-shirts and jeans. Still, they were sweating slightly as they made their way along the trails. Valerie and Alex had no real idea in what direction to go, as there were many smaller trails leading off the main one. They spent an hour or two simply exploring.

Suddenly Alex stopped, and Valerie nearly slammed into him. The sounds around them had ceased. They had emerged into a small clearing, where the path dropped away into a long crevasse, disappearing into the darkness of the undergrowth. The two children looked at one another with worried faces. Neither of them wanted to take another step. Barely visible in the tangled growth was a narrow opening in the seams of rock.

"You mean we have to go in there?" asked Alex with a shudder.

"That's what it says..." replied his sister, checking the paper in her hand. She looked down into the dark passageway with an expression of distain. Reaching forward, she pretended to give Alex a shove, instead giving him only a slight nudge. He gave her a swat back.

"Knock it off!" he exclaimed. "You go first!"

"Don't be a baby. We'll go in together," she suggested.

"All right," Alex replied.

They started forward, taking a few small unsure steps into the void and trying to be careful on rocks that were slick from condensation. Brushing the thorny growth aside carefully, they entered the crevasse. A cool, damp waft of air struck them and they paused just inside the entrance. A sound began to emerge, like many birds chirping. It was quiet at first, as if distant, but quickly became louder, building in a noisy crescendo. Suddenly the air became a black cloud of small leathery wings, spiralling around in the dark and zooming out of the cave entrance. Bats, Valerie realized, ducking down low. Alex cried out for a second, but he had barely gotten the sound out of his mouth before they were gone.

"Whew!" he breathed, looking at Valerie with wide eyes.

"I think they are all gone," she said softly.

They continued slowly, feeling their way along the walls in the darkness, which was only growing thicker. Small streaks of water flowed down the granite in the passageway, and the air was stale. Alex and Valerie almost tripped several times while moving along.

"Oh! I almost forgot!" Valerie exclaimed unexpectedly. She fumbled around in the pockets of Alex's backpack, and produced a small LED flashlight on a keychain. She turned it on and illuminated the cave. It wasn't wide - maybe two and a half feet across - and became slightly narrower farther on.

"Sure, you remember it now..." Alex said with more than a hint of sarcasm.

"C'mon, let's go!" Valerie replied enthusiastically, ignoring the jab.

On they went, until they had to walk in a single file and scrunch down a bit to avoid a bump on the head. They both became slightly nervous; it was getting tight. But after a few more feet, the crevasse began to open up again, and they finally emerged into a room carved in the rock. It was almost perfectly round, and the granite walls were smooth, as if the room had been made by someone. As they entered, it became clear that someone had been here before - long ago. The walls had faint paintings on them: native artwork. And in the centre, near the back of the small cave room, was a large painting of a raven. Valerie and Alex looked around in awe. In the floor in the middle of the cave there was a small pool of clear water - clear, but deep. Valerie crept closer to look, shining her light into the water. She pulled the page from her pocket again and read it over.

"I think this is 'The Raven's Nest'!" she exclaimed, peering down into the pool once again, and trying to get her light to shine to the bottom.

"Doesn't look like any kind of nest to me; looks like a hole full of water!" her brother chimed in.

Valerie shot him a quick frown and returned to her reading. The riddle was beginning to make a bit of sense now.

"Deep in the Raven's Nest, rests the Raven's Egg, the keeper and protector of the Heart," she repeated from the text. They both looked down into the pool again with slight frowns, then at one another. If this was the resting place of the Raven's Egg, it certainly wasn't very inviting. The water was clear and deep, and the two children paused. Uncertainty unleashed its grip on them, and they sat looking into the water for a minute more.

"No way am I reaching my hand in there!" Valerie finally stated.

"Yikes!" said Alex, concurring with the thought.

"Come on, if you do I'll do the dishes for a week!"

"Not a chance!" he said, shaking his head.

"A month, then!"

He squinted at her suspiciously. He knew his sister was not above pulling a fast one on him.

"You better not be faking!" he said, still eyeing her.

At this comment, Valerie made the motion of an X across her chest. Alex lookd again at the pool, and his sister generously held her flashlight to it for him.

"This is going to suck!" he muttered.

Alex pulled up a sleeve and reached down slowly into the cold, clear water. Valerie couldn't resist. She grabbed his shoulder in a quick motion that made him jump slightly, pulling his arm out suddenly and splashing them both. Frowning at his sister, he regained his composure, and reached in once again. Alex had to lean over to reach all the way down.

"I feel something, like a rock," he reported.

"So grab it!" Valerie instructed.

"I'm trying, but it's slippery!"

Alex fumbled around in the water, almost falling forward on his face in his struggle to get a grip on the invisible object for which he was reaching. Finally, he pulled his arm out with the object in hand: a ball of pinkish rock flecked with colours. Valerie shone her light on it. It was perfectly round, and very smooth, more like a small bowling ball than an egg. She tapped the side of it with the light. It was definitely made of stone.

"Great," said Alex. "We did all this for a rock!"

Valerie looked at it for a moment. Whatever it was must have been important, otherwise, why had it been put there? The rock they had must at least be a marker of some sort on the way to finding the Heart. Its round surface was certainly pretty to look at. She rolled it around in her hands. It was heavy, but not as heavy as it should have been for a rock of its size, she thought. Alex opened his backpack, waving a hand over the opening invitingly.

"Ok, put it in here and let's go!"

Valerie hesitated for a second, still looking at the rock as if it might give up a clue. Finally she deposited it in Alex's backpack and stood up.

"I guess. Let's get out of here," she acquiesced.

The two of them moved toward the tunnel of rock that would lead them out, ducking their heads. It seemed like a very long time before they reached the opening and could see the light of day shining into the passageway. The warm, humid air could already be felt as the two children stepped out into the blinding sunlight coming through the forest canopy. They must have been in the cave for quite a while, they realized, judging by how low the sun was in the sky. But as Valerie's eyes adjusted, she could see something that didn't seem to fit with the scenery. A tall figure suddenly stepped right in front of them, blocking the light from the sun.

"Where is the Heart?" demanded a deep voice. "I want it now!"

Valerie shaded her eyes, trying to see the face of the person standing above them, but the sun was too bright. A silhouette was all she could make out.

"We don't have it; all we found was a rock!" she said shakily.

There was a long pause, and the two children looked up at the figure standing there, feeling terrified.

"Show me this 'rock,'" said the dark figure, a shade of sarcasm in his voice.

Valerie was becoming agitated, and tried to offer an excuse.

"Look, sir, we should be getting home - "

"NOW!" hollered the figure, causing the two children to flinch. Alex was becoming visibly scared, and Valerie wondered who this person was, and how he knew that they were out here. The figure let out what could only be described as a growl, and Valerie grabbed hold of Alex's backpack without further delay, reaching inside. She rummaged around, still not wanting to give up their find. Her hand found the smooth, round rock - but there was something beside it. She rummaged some more, trying to make it look as though she were still trying to find the mysterious prize. Her hand finally closed around another smooth, round object that just happened to be in her brother's backpack: a softball.

"Come on! Give it to me!" the figure commanded harshly, holding out a grasping hand.

Valerie held her breath for a second, focusing on the shadowy form above them. She began to slowly pull her hand from Alex's pack. The figure reached forward, its fingers stretching out in anticipation of the rock. Quickly, Valerie cocked back her right arm, and fired with all her might. For a moment, she felt as though time had slowed as she watched the ball leave her fingers and travel toward the silhouette in front of her. It had launched perfectly, soaring out of her hand. All they heard was the dull thud of the ball as it hit home, followed by a surprised grunt of pain from the person in the path of the sun. He staggered backward, and dropped down onto one knee. Valerie saw their chance, and, grabbing Alex's arm, leapt forward in a flat-out run. The two scurried along the twisting path, often dragging each other in their desire to stay together as leaves and branches whipped at their faces. It seemed like forever before they reached a small clearing and were able to pause, their lungs on fire. The sound of brush rustling on the path behind them spurred them on, until they suddenly emerged from the forest into a rail yard.

Alex pointed to one of the open boxcars.

"C'mon, we can hide in there!" he exclaimed, barely able to breathe.

They sprinted across the gravel, and struggled up into the open boxcar. The door was only open a foot or two, and they squeezed inside, dropping onto the dirty wooden floor. They were sweaty and panting loudly, but Valerie quickly made a shushing motion to quiet her brother. The two slid up against the inside of the door, listening carefully and trying to get their breathing under control. The sound of footsteps on gravel could be heard, and they froze instinctively. Whoever it was had managed to follow them. The children glanced at each other in the gloom of the old boxcar, listening with every fibre of their bodies. The steps paused, then came closer and grew louder. They stopped again, and there was a silence that seemed to last forever. Valerie and Alex remained frozen, not moving a muscle between them. Then the sound of a vehicle could be heard, and the footsteps retreated. They waited. The vehicle was gone now, too. After some time, the light began to fade, rendering the interior of the old boxcar even darker. Alex became restless, crunched up tightly against the cold steel wall.

"Let's get out of here!" he exclaimed. "My legs are starting to fall asleep!"

Valerie needed little urging. They peered out of the car, checking to see if the coast was clear. It seemed to be. Now they could hear the deep sound of a diesel engine, and the car in which they were standing lurched forward suddenly, causing them to lose their balance for a moment. They scrambled down from the car as its wheels gave a great squeal against the rails and it started moving slowly forward. Enough was enough, Valerie thought. She grabbed Alex's hand and led him away from the rails, heading toward home as fast as she could drag him. It would soon be dark, and they had had plenty of adventure for one day.

~~~~

Dad looked down at Nana's sleeping form for a second, checking on her as he had been doing for the last hour. Grandpa had become very tired, and Dad had taken over the vigil. He was reading a newspaper while awaiting the nurse's arrival with supper. Nana had slept most of the day after being administered a primary dose of chemotherapy, the standard treatment in the fight against cancer. He let out a brief sigh. Just then, Nana roused slightly and opened her eyes. Away went the paper, and Dad reached for her hand.

"Where are the little ones?" she asked.

"The neighbour is watching them..." he replied quietly.

This answer seemed to satisfy Nana for the moment, and she moved herself upward on the bed to a better position in which to sit. She waved off Dad's motions with the bed controls, instead stuffing a rather fluffy pillow behind her. Much better, she thought.

"Do you need me to get somebody?" Dad asked.

"No, I am happy to just rest."

"Ok, maybe you can eat something for supper?"

"We'll see. I really don't feel like eating."

"I can imagine, but you should, it will help your strength..."

Nana simply waved at him and rolled to her side. She tried not to be grumpy, but it seemed as though everyone thought that they knew what was best for her. All she wanted lately was to sleep and be left to her thoughts, and anything else agitated her.

"How are you feeling?" Dad pressed.

"Did the kids have fun the other week?" she asked, ignoring the question.

"Yes, Mom, but please stop filling their heads with these crazy adventures, will you?"

At this comment Nana adopted an expression of disbelief and raised her hands in a gesture of innocence.

"Never mind," he began, picking up his paper again. "I can always tell."

He began to remember all of the craziness about buried loyalist treasure. The children had wanted to go hiking along the park trails every evening for weeks. He had come home one particular day to a backyard full of small holes, as the lawn had been made into Swiss cheese by Valerie and Alex digging for the lost gold "treasure." They had begged him for a solid week before he finally agreed to buy them a simple metal detector. It was difficult to keep either of them focused on schoolwork while under the spell of one of Nana's stories. However, he had lost weight going on plenty of hikes in search of the treasure, he thought, grinning slightly at the memory.

Nana gave no reply; she simply offered a slightly sheepish grin. Yes, she had told the children many old stories, about how the local Native people had lived, and of lost gold and ghosts in the Thousand Islands. She grinned wider as she remembered taking the children on a treasure hunt along the hiking trails in the area to try to find that lost gold. Her grandchildren also enjoyed the occasional ghost story around a campfire at the family cottage while wrapped in warm blankets and munching on freshly made popcorn in huge plastic bowls. "The Witch of Plum Hollow" and the story of the Native maiden Tesli Mocca were their favourites. She loved watching their wide-eyed reactions, just like their father and uncle used to experience when they were young.

The nurse appeared rolling the meal cart into the room, and Dad once again folded his paper, stood up, and moved aside to provide more space. The nurse rolled Nana's tray table over her bed while she struggled to sit up a bit straighter.

"And how are we feeling today, my dear?" the nurse automatically inquired as she set the thick plastic tray on the table.

"Well, I'm still here," Nana replied with a shrug.

The young lady in the scrubs smiled, and recited what was for dinner that evening. Nothing very good, in Nana's mind. Soft mushy stuff and bland soup. The only thing she really wanted was the tea in the corner of the tray. Off went the nurse, and Dad sat back down in the chair again, eyeing his mother knowingly. He pretended to read a magazine that he had picked up from the table beside her bed. He could feel her gaze, and tried to keep from appearing worried. He went back to the magazine article.

"I hope you plan on having more than just tea, Mom," he said.

"Oh relax, I ate quite a bit at lunch time," she replied with a mischievous look. The look simply told Dad that Nana was fibbing.

4

The voice on the phone seemed unimpressed, and somewhere in the darkened room, a book slammed into a wall. It fell in a flipped-open mess on the carpeted floor. The woman who had thrown it gave a heavy sigh and paused for a moment to get her anger under control. She thought about what to say next. If she pushed too hard, the man on the phone might become very angry himself, despite being the idiot she was sure he was. Rubbing her forehead, she gripped the telephone receiver with white knuckles and tried to remain calm.

"So, we can safely assume that these two children must have something, even if it is not the actual Heart," she hissed.

"Yes, I think they definitely have something. I lost them in the rail yard or I might have found out exactly what it was."

"Well, this is just wonderful. How are we to know if they even have it on them the next time?" she said, making a fist in her frustration.

"I don't know, but we are going to have to come up with some kind of solution, if they have found it."

"I realize that; I know what this artifact could be worth. You would have done better to get it off of them before they managed to give you the slip!" she screamed into the phone, before hanging it up with a violent bang. Idiot, she thought. How was she supposed to retrieve this precious item working with someone like this? She set her glasses down on the table at which she sat, and put her face into her hands for a moment.

She breathed deeply. The Heart of The Raven would fetch a large cash price from the right collector, whether or not the legends of its healing powers were true. Damn those kids. The phone rang, and she knew it was the man calling back. She ignored it. And when it rang again minutes later, she finally unplugged it from the wall.

She could sense the prize slipping through her fingers. She was tired of living in the same crappy little apartment in which she had resided for the last several years. Her husband had left, running off with a younger - and, in her mind, prettier - woman. She could feel the blood pounding in her temples, and tried to calm herself. They would simply have to try again, and if the situation required being a little less subtle, so be it. She had to find the Heart. It was the key to starting a new life, the way to show everyone that she was not an idiot; that she was highly intelligent and deserved respect. It would change her life back to what it could have been.

She deserved more than this. She had worked hard, all her life. Her former husband had been a lawyer, and made good money. But once he had decided to leave, she had been left with nothing. She stroked back her greying hair, deep in thought. She had been forced to give up everything, including the fancy lifestyle she had enjoyed for years. Now she lived in this tiny apartment, with few things to enjoy, and only a meagre job to support her. She could feel the rage building again, and tried her best to calm down. It was close. If she could just get this artifact and sell it, she would be back to square one. She hated her ex-husband, hated the position in which he had put her. But he was a lawyer, after all, and schooled in how to screw people over. What hope had she had? He had left her destitute, after taking everything away from her.

From across the shadowy room, her gaze came to rest on the book once again. She had studied it for months, hoping to decipher the riddle in the ancient story. She simply could not uncover the location of the Heart from the text. It didn't matter anyway, if those kids had actually found it. The book would be useless to her. It made sense, after all. The trails were rumoured to be ancient native lands, and numerous archeological digs had been done on that piece of land over the years, although she couldn't remember anything ever being unearthed there other than a few trinkets and arrowheads. She glanced up and looked once again at the book. Its gold lettering laughed at her from its resting place on the carpet. *History of the Thousand Islands.*

~~~~

Valerie and Alex returned to their tree house the following day, engrossed in the smooth, round rock. They were a little more secretive, based on their scare with the strange person who had chased after them the evening before. Their father occasionally came out onto the back deck, curious as to what the sudden big secret was, but content with the fact that the children were getting along quietly. He had enough on his mind already. He always kept a close eye on things, and prided himself on his sixth sense regarding when the children may be up to something. Whatever it might be this time seemed innocent enough, and he tried to put it on the back burner of his thoughts. Nana was not well, and he knew it. He made a conscious effort to hide it from the kids, but he was aware that they were far from being fooled. They probably knew more than he did at this point, he thought.

It was another beautiful, warm, sunny day, and Dad took a sip of coffee from the mug in his hand, casting one last look at the tree house before stepping back inside.

Today, Valerie's friend Katie had come over, and was also in awe of the rock. Wondering what it had to do with the legend involving the Heart of the Raven, Valerie searched the old book again and again, looking for some sort of new clue, and trying to discover what they needed to do next. Valerie's pal, Katie, rolled the rock around in her hands, examining its round, smooth texture, while Alex rummaged through his backpack, checking his inventory of "stuff." He found an assortment of small tools his father had given him, including screwdrivers, Allen keys, and, of course, a small multi-tool with a built-in LED flashlight, bubble gum, string, a small plastic mirror, and a pair of binoculars. He had added the tool with the flashlight just that morning, realizing after their trip into the cave that it might come in handy. There was also a small pocketknife that his father didn't know he had, and an old glass lens that was full of scratches, but that still burned bugs very well. Everything seemed to be there, with the exception of one softball.

"So what do we do with this rock now?" he asked Valerie.

"No idea," replied Valerie, sweeping her brown hair back over her ears as she thumbed through the pages again. "We must be missing something."

Alex could no longer resist teasing his sister.

"Or maybe you're just too dumb to figure it out!" he responded with a smirk.

"Whatever, then you find the answer!" she said angrily, slapping the old book shut and roughly heaving the ancient tome onto the floor beside her.

"The keeper and protector of the Heart..." she recited again quietly, looking at the rock in Katie's hands.

It seemed ordinary; just a perfectly round rock. What could be so valuable about a round rock? The pink granite seemed an odd colour in the tree house. It was only dimly lit even on this sunny day, nestled as it was in a flowering crab apple tree near the back of the yard. The smooth surface of the rock seemed to shine by itself, despite the shadowy environment. Valerie looked at it, mesmerized. It looked almost as if it had been polished. What was it for? It was obviously not the Heart itself, so what were they to do with it? And, most importantly, how had that strange man in the forest known they were there, and what they were looking for? Her thoughts returned quickly to the present as she noticed a fine, straight line in the rock. She reached for it and grabbed it abruptly from Katie.

"Hey!" her friend exclaimed in protest. "What gives?"

"Keep your shorts on! Look here!" Valerie pointed at the line in the granite. Both Katie and Alex leaned in to look, studying the rock's surface. The line was there, very faint, extending all the way around its centre. Valerie tried to twist it. Nothing. She pulled on it, but to no avail. The line made it look as though the two halves of the sphere should separate. She struggled with it some more. It had to open somehow! Alex grabbed for it, and the two children wrestled over it briefly.

"Let me try!" the boy exclaimed, trying to wrench it away from his sister.

Suddenly, they both lost their grips on the rock's smooth surface and it dropped to the floor. With a cracking sound, the two halves of the stone separated on the hardwood floorboards, exposing the rock's interior. The room was suddenly bathed in a shimmering purple glow, and watery reflections danced on the walls. The children stared down at the stone on the floor, mesmerized by the purple light. The insides of the round stone's halves were covered in purple crystals. It was a geode that held inside of it the glowing crystal form of a bird with outstretched wings.

Valerie reached forward and gently lifted the crystal bird from its place inside the geode. As she lifted it out, the light faded. She put it back in, and it began to glow again. Alex grinned.

"Whoa!" he said in amazement. "That is the coolest!"

Valerie lifted the half of the geode that contained the bird up to her eyes for a closer look. The small bird fit perfectly among the purple crystals in the geode, and nestled securely in place. It even looked like a raven. The three children stared at it for a long time, caught by its beauty.

"Ok," said Valerie. "Now what do we do with it?"

"We could sell it on eBay!" Alex said with a smirk. His sister shot him an unimpressed look. So did Katie. Alex put on a large, fake smile.

"It would make a cool night light!" he continued in a mocking voice.

The girls simply rolled their eyes. Valerie realized that now that they had found it, things had changed. Someone else was after it, too. And they knew that Valerie and Alex might have it. It was a scary situation, and a shudder crept up Valerie's back, knowing as she did that the person who had chased them might do anything to get the Heart from them. Anything.

5

A group of Mohawk elders sat in their healing lodge, chanting near embers of a fire meant to heat the interior of the longhouse. Stones sat atop the glowing remnants of the fire, and were bathed in water occasionally to raise the level of moisture in the air. The chant was deep, rhythmic, and heavy with the sounds of ancient things, in a language mostly gone from the world. In the centre of the fire pit sat the Heart, carved in the shape of the sacred raven; a glowing crystal bathed in the light of the embers, soaking in the energy of the ancient song. There was a flash of purple light, and a droning sound, the sound of...

Valerie awoke to the sound of her alarm clock, and rolled over slowly to look at it. 7:45 AM. As she shut it off, she wished that she had not set it for so early. With a yawn and a stretch, she rolled herself out of bed, and sat on its edge for a few moments while she became fully awake. Her dreams faded rapidly, and she had already forgotten most of them. Only fragments remained in her memory as remnants of her brain's activity during the night.

Rubbing an eye and letting out another yawn, she stumbled out her door and down the hall toward the bathroom. A breeze ruffled the curtains in the hall window, and the birds could be heard singing a morning chorus. The sun was up, and it bathed the hallway carpet in its early morning radiance. It was a Sunday morning, and the street outside was quiet. The house was quiet as well, as even Dad took advantage of the opportunity to sleep in a bit on Sundays.

Valerie returned down the hall now, trying to step lightly so as not to wake anyone else. She closed the door to her room silently, hoping the door latch wouldn't click too loudly. It didn't. She fumbled under her bed, searching for the prize. Her hands met the cool of the crystals that were the Heart. She pulled it out and gazed into its purple translucence, leaving the cover rock behind. She had experienced that moment while she was becoming fully awake, like deja-vu, and she had wanted to see the Heart again, knowing that they had actually found it.

It seemed impossible, Valerie thought as she rolled it over in her hands. It was more than a story; more than an old native legend. And they had actually found it. She tucked it safely away under the bed again, hiding it in a small beach bag with drawstrings. She was fairly sure that her dad didn't know about some of her hiding places, and if he did, he didn't say a word. It would be safe. She stood up, stretched one more time, and proceeded to get dressed for the day.

Alex was awake now, too, and he rolled over to the sound of the cat emitting a soft noise to alert him that she was there. She crawled forward and shoved her nose under his hand, looking for him to show her some affection, and purring the whole time. She was a fat tortoise shell cat, and had a unique motherly instinct. She persisted in prodding him, rubbing her face against his hand.

"Go away..." he said through layers of sleepiness.

The cat seemed not to care, and thrust her face once more under his neck. She persisted until he finally began to pet her, running his hand across her back while she purred and soaked in the attention. Alex roused, sat up, and rolled his legs off the bed. It was quiet. He could hear the birds singing outside, but the house itself was like a tomb: silent. He got up, realizing that it was time to head for the washroom, where he would go through his morning ritual, handed down from father to son. He had to go to the bathroom, and then he would rub a clean facecloth soaked in cool water across his face and look at his reflection in the mirror. Next, he brushed his teeth, making sure to get at each tooth before spitting and rinsing. A swipe of cool water again across his sandy blond hair, and he was ready for the day.

The breeze blew at the sheer curtain in the bathroom window, making it dance. Alex turned to his own window as he came back to his bedroom and rested his elbows on the white painted windowsill. It was very sunny outside, and the street was quiet, except for the occasional bark of a dog and the incessant song of birds. He could see someone coming down the sidewalk out front. A girl. It was Katie, his sister's best friend. She was obviously not very happy; she was crying and wringing her hands as she approached the house. Alex left the window immediately and quickly headed down the hall to Valerie's room. He didn't make the mistake of forgetting to knock, as that had resulted in a tongue-lashing before. She pulled open the door before he even rapped a knuckle on it, and gave him a questioning look.

"Uh, Katie is here, and it looks like she is upset," he stated.

Valerie opened the door farther and quickly pulled on a pair of sandals. The two went down the stairs, trying to keep quiet so as not to wake their dad and draw attention to anything. At the bottom of the stairs, they arrived in the foyer. Valerie silently turned the deadbolt and slowly opened the front door.

Katie was just stepping up the steps onto the front porch with tears in her eyes. As she made eye contact with Valerie, Valerie drew a finger to her lips to indicate the need for quiet, and ushered her in. Katie was crying, and Valerie knew that if her dad heard, there would be a lot of questions. She led her friend toward the kitchen, Alex following silently, and from there they emerged from the house onto the back deck. The door swung shut behind them, and Alex caught it just before it slammed, pursing his lips as he slid it closed without a sound.

It was shaded on the deck at this time of morning, and cool. The birds sang as they floated from tree to tree in the backyard. Valerie tried to calm Katie down and discern what was wrong. Her friend was very upset, and tears streamed down her face as she tried to tell Valerie what had happened. Her dog had suddenly become very sick. He was a pug named Sparks, and Valerie knew the little canine well. Many times they had walked him through the path in town that connected the various small parks. He had always seemed like a happy little dog, and it hurt Valerie to hear her friend tell the sad tale of how the pet had fallen ill. He was Katie's friend and animal companion, and had been with her since she was very young.

Valerie could feel tears welling up in her own eyes as she listened to Katie describe the situation. Sparks had gotten into a confrontation with one of the neighbourhood cats, and had come out of it badly scratched up. The wounds had become infected, and the animal was now in bad shape.

"If the medicine doesn't work, the vet says he will need to be put down," Katie sobbed.

"I'm sure it won't come to that!" Valerie replied sympathetically. Suddenly, an idea sprang into her mind. She wanted to help her friend, and she and Alex had something in their grasp that might do the trick. She didn't really believe in magic, but at this point, she was at a loss for any other solution. She knew that veterinary bills were very expensive, and had no idea how they might help Sparks otherwise. He was Katie's best friend, and she felt that they had to do something.

"Hey! Let's see if the Heart of the Raven will help heal him!" she exclaimed.

Alex rolled his eyes at this outburst, not sure what his sister was thinking. Some rock they had found on a hike through the trails was going to help this dog? Really?

Katie's eyes brightened a little at the thought. It could work, couldn't it? Maybe there was some truth to the old native legend. Valerie practically jumped up off of the chair on which she had been sitting and ran back into the house. She climbed the stairs quickly, then suddenly remembered that her father was still sleeping and tried to make her steps quieter. Into her bedroom she proceeded, closing the door silently behind her. She practically dove under her bed and retrieved the crystal raven from its hiding place, along with the book. She tucked it under her arm as she reopened her door and glided back out into the hallway. She had taken only one step back down the stairs when she heard a voice that stopped her in her tracks.

"Valerie, what's going on?" asked her father with a certain tone in his voice.

"We're just going down to Katie's for a while, Sparks is sick, is that okay?" she inquired, trying her best to keep her response innocent and simple.

"Yes, but if he's sick don't be touching him without washing your hands after, and tell your brother the same thing."

Their dad was always concerned about germs, and continuously made them wash after getting dirty. Valerie agreed to tell Alex and continued down the stairs without another word, hoping that her dad didn't think that she was up to something. He must have been just getting up, and Valerie wanted to be out of sight before he emerged from his bedroom. She knew he would probably make a stop in the washroom, and then head downstairs to make a coffee. As she made her way through the kitchen toward the back door, she checked the electric kettle, lifting it slightly to ensure there was adequate water in it, and then clicked it on to boil the water. She figured that this action might please her father; either that or make him more suspicious.

Valerie burst out onto the back deck again, motioning for her friend and brother to hurry. Down the deck steps she headed, with the others now in tow. This way, they could get away without having to risk going back through the house, she reasoned. Valerie reached up and unlatched the fence gate, and they emerged onto the driveway. They headed toward the front of the house and out onto the sidewalk. Just when they thought that they were in the clear, the voice sounded again.

"Don't be too late, kids. I am making spaghetti tonight."

Valerie turned and saw that her father was standing on the front porch, still in his housecoat. He had the newspaper in his hands, and Valerie realized suddenly what she had missed in his schedule. She nodded quickly with a murmured "okay," as did her brother, and off they went down the street.

~~~~

Sparks lay on his blanket in the living room, comfortable but obviously not well. He let out the occasional doggy groan as he shifted his fat little body around in an attempt to become more relaxed. The children watched him anxiously, knowing the poor dog was not feeling well at all. The day passed slowly, and they sat and watched television while they waited for their opportunity. Katie's father was now home, and the family scrambled about, making supper and performing the various tasks that required doing in the evening. Valerie looked at her watch, knowing that her dad would already be tapping his foot and wondering where they were. If Katie's dad would leave the room for a short while, it would be easy. Or so she thought.

She thumbed through the pages of *History of the Thousand Islands* to keep herself occupied. Katie's father was a mechanic who owned his own garage, and he liked to watch television when he finally finished his day, especially sports. It wasn't as though he didn't like or care about Sparks, but tonight he was engrossed in a baseball game.

Now dinner was on the table. Katie's mom called for them, asking politely if Valerie and Alex were going to have some as well. Katie assured her mother that her friends would be off in a few minutes to have their own dinner, and she winked at Valerie on her way toward the kitchen. Katie's father finally rose from his recliner and headed there as well.

Valerie knew they had little time. She looked at Alex, who returned her glance and motioned for her to hurry, knowing that Dad would soon be looking for them. Valerie pulled the crystal from its hiding place in the beach bag and placed it next to Sparks on his blanket. He lifted his head just enough to sniff at it with his pushed-in nose, and then lay back down with a brief whimper.

At first, nothing happened. Then, slowly, the Heart began to glow: softly at first, then brighter and brighter, until the living room was filled with a shimmering purple light. Sparks whined for a moment, and Valerie hoped no one would notice, even though she was mesmerized herself. She could hear a sound resembling faint drums as she watched Sparks intently. He seemed to relax and become comfortable on his bed. Finally the glow subsided, slowly fading away until the light was all but gone again. Sparks still lay on the blanket, and moved his head slightly to look at Valerie periodically. Had anything happened? She stood up, rolling the crystal over in her hands and wondering.

At that moment, Katie's mother poked her head in the room.

"You guys sure you don't want some dinner?"

"No thanks, we had probably better head home. Our dad will be wondering where we are. Just tell Katie I will see her in the morning."

Valerie ushered Alex toward the front door, scooping up the book and her beach bag along the way. She took one last look back at the little pug that was laid out on his blanket and frowned, wondering what would happen to him and whether the Heart had done anything at all.

6

Grandpa put on his glasses as he picked up Nana's medical folder, which contained her chart. He tried to read the scrawled writing on the papers inside and grimaced in slight disgust. The writing on the papers before him made no sense; either he couldn't understand the words, or they were scribbled so poorly that they were senseless anyway.

"You would think that after going to school for so many years, these doctors would learn to write better!" he complained sarcastically.

Nana looked up from her novel and over the tops of her glasses at him with a slight grin.

"Maybe they are writing in code so that nosy folks like you can't read it."

"Well seriously," he began, "have you ever seen a doctor's writing that is actually legible? I can hardly read any of this."

"It says I'm sick…" she sighed, returning to her book.

Grandpa slid the folder back into its plastic holder on the end of the bed and removed his glasses once again, putting them in his shirt pocket. He hated the hospital. He always felt restless there, and didn't know what to do with himself. And he hated that "hospital" smell. Still, he tried not to complain, as he didn't want to upset Nana. After all, he could come and go, but for the time being, Nana had to stay here.

It was nearly 8AM; almost time for breakfast. The very thought of food made Grandpa's stomach growl, and he paced over to the window.

"When did they say this doctor would be here, anyway?" he asked.

Nana looked up at the clock in the room unnecessarily.

"Within the hour," she replied.

Grandpa gave her an exasperated look, so she told him to go down to the cafeteria to have something to eat. She wanted to ensure that he went, and asked him if he would bring her back a nice cup of tea. He obliged at once, happy to actually do something, and shuffled off down the hall. She smiled after him. Idle hands were the Devil's playground, she mused in her thoughts.

Fortunately, no sooner had he left than the doctor walked into the room. It had worked out perfectly in Nana's mind, as she knew what the young man in the white smock was going to say, and she didn't want her husband to hear all of the details until he had to.

"How are we feeling this morning?" the doctor asked as he looked over some papers that he had brought in with him.

"About as good as can be expected, I guess," she replied, setting her novel aside.

"Yeah, the chemo is nasty stuff. Sorry about that."

"Oh, it hasn't been as bad as I expected, really."

The doctor placed the papers in the folder at the end of her bed.

"There you go, some people react to it differently than others. How has your sleep been?"

"Crummy," she replied. "A lot of bad dreams…"

"Yes, I have heard that reported many times from people. It will pass." He looked at her with an apologetic expression and folded his hands together in front of him.

"The news is not good," he started. "It has spread. I would like to urge you to undergo radiation, and possibly surgery if that does not work."

Nana removed her glasses and set them on the table next to the bed. She looked down at her hands for what felt like a long moment, trying to decide how to articulate her thoughts. Finally, she looked back at the doctor.

"My good man, I have been through several procedures, and none of them have rid me of this foul disease. I have no wish to be in my casket looking like a dried up skeleton, but if this is what you recommend, then I will do the radiation. But… I will decide what happens after that."

She watched as he lifted his hands, and gave him the kind of look she would give to a mischievous child. He knew there would be no use in trying to argue against any decision she made.

"And," she began again, pointing to him, "I wish for my husband and my son to know as little as possible unless I tell them."

"Very well. If asked, I will simply state that we need to run a few more tests," he said.

Their conversation was interrupted as the breakfast cart was wheeled in by a young lady in flowered scrubs. As she was placing the tray on the table, Grandpa suddenly returned, nimbly carrying a tea. He rolled his eyes when he saw the fresh tea that the young lady revealed as she lifted the top from the plastic meal tray. He set the one he was carrying down next to it and cast Nana an agitated glance. The doctor swiftly left the room, telling Grandpa that they had more tests to run and giving Nana a quick wink as he went. Dad now appeared, strolling in and handing Grandpa the day's newspaper. Nana looked at him, surprised by his sudden entrance.

"I didn't expect you here this morning. Where are the children?" she asked in alarm.

"Relax, Mother. They usually meet Katie out front, and walk Alex over around the corner on their way to the high school."

"Okay," she said simply, grinning at him. "It is nice to have my men here to keep me company."

"Well, hopefully you won't be in here too much longer..." he replied, smiling.

~~~~

The following day, Alex stood with his elbows on the windowsill, looking out the hallway window at the tree house in the backyard. It was another warm but rainy fall afternoon, and he had just returned from school. He moved on, going into his room to find something amusing to do. Raindrops fell against the window, making the world outside his room seem very wet indeed. His backpack was on his bed, and he was trying to decide what to do to have some fun. He never ventured too far from home without his pack, which was getting a little worn out looking these days. It held everything a young boy needed, and then some. His schoolwork was last on his list of essentials; it hung out of the front pocket, stuffed in almost as an afterthought.

He circled the room idly, tracing a finger across the spines of the books on a shelf across from his bed. He certainly didn't feel much like reading today. Valerie was the bookworm, not him, although he liked a good comic book now and then. He looked around again, indecisively. His grey-blue eyes came to rest on his backpack. He knew everything that was in there, and there was nothing with which he wanted to play right now. He could hear the television blaring downstairs and knew that Valerie was engrossed in a show, probably some teenager stuff, he figured. Alex's thoughts turned to the crystal bird again, and of how it had glowed when they had brought it close to poor, sick Sparks. It must be magic, or how would it have done that? It wasn't like it took batteries!

His oldest sister Jorden was home from college that day for a visit, and she was looking after the two younger children while Dad was working, with Nana being in her current condition. He thought about venturing down to see Jorden; maybe bugging her to make him something good for a snack. But he wasn't really hungry, either. What he really wanted was to do some more painting in Nana's art studio. He felt sad that she was sick, and hoped she would get better soon.

Finally Alex decided he might as well play some games on the Xbox, and reached for his television remote and the well worn-in controller that sat on the shelf. He sat down on his bed, getting ready for some combat action as the screen came on. The sounds of machine gunfire and explosions ensued as Alex began to play. It would be better than watching Valerie's lame show about teenage vampires, and definitely more fun than listening to his oldest sister go on about her new boyfriend. Yuck.

7

Valerie and Alex were stunned the following morning. They looked down the street with their mouths hanging wide open. Here came Sparks prancing happily down the sidewalk on his leash, his curled tail wagging, and his bright pink tongue hanging out in stark contrast to his small black face. Katie was walking him, beaming. It looked as though nothing had ever been wrong with him, and he strained at the leash upon seeing Valerie and Alex.

"Isn't it amazing?!" Katie called out excitedly.

Valerie jumped up and down with joy, and Alex rushed down from the front porch of the house to greet the little pug, which reached up and licked at his face.

"Cool," exclaimed Alex with a broad smile. "He's perfectly fine now!"

Valerie came down and gave the excited little dog a pat, rubbing his back and head. He jumped and strained at his leash, soaking in the attention. Valerie watched him, fascinated. The Heart did this, she thought. It works. The old stories were all true. Somehow this artifact that they had found was able to do magical things; to heal sickness. As these thoughts ran through her mind, she felt a little jolt of fear, as well. They would definitely have to be careful now. Whoever had chased them the other day either knew about the legends, or how much money the artifact could be worth. Either way, this person was serious about getting the Heart away from them for their own gain. It was safe in her bag upstairs, inside the sanctuary of her bedroom.

Katie ran back home with Sparks, returning a short while later with her schoolbooks. The three of them headed off around the corner, and the two girls dropped Alex off at his school before continuing on to the busy high school across town. It took about fifteen minutes to reach the large red brick building if they travelled through the city's bicycle path. Valerie and Katie chatted all the way there, but Valerie's thoughts kept returning to what had happened the previous evening. The crystal had shone with a purple glow like a miniature sun, and then this morning the little dog was right as rain, despite having looked like he might die at any time the night before. Her mind raced. If it could cure Sparks, maybe it could help save Nana!

The two girls finally arrived at the school. Some of its massive, outdated windows were open, leaking the sounds of young people chattering and rushing around. They hurried through the steel double doors and said a quick farewell to one another. Valerie made her way down the hall past the main office to her locker. She squeezed in between the other students and grabbed the basics that she needed for first class. As she turned to head to class, she almost put the old history book in her locker, but decided to keep it close instead, hoping she may have a few minutes to leaf through the old native legend again. Closing her locker, she headed off just as the first bell sounded.

Valerie had trouble concentrating that morning on anything remotely like academics. Her English class was spent perusing the text of the old book. She read about the Heart again and again while trying not to give away the fact that she was not really following along with the lesson in class. Finally the bell rang, and she headed back to her locker. As she approached, she knew something was wrong. The door to her locker was open slightly, and the lock was hanging through the hasp. Looking inside, she visually confirmed that nothing was missing. Had she accidentally left it open? She tried hard to remember the events of the morning. At least none of her things were gone, luckily.

Valerie changed books for her next class, holding the old book tightly in her grasp. This time she made a conscious note that it was locked, and spun the face of the combination lock once it clicked. Glancing around her, she became aware of the fact that Robert was not bugging her as per normal. Strangely, she almost wished he were. The uncertainty about her locker made her uneasy. She was sure she had locked it.

The uneasiness continued as she sat through her next class. Mr. Thatch was away and had been replaced by a substitute teacher. In all the time she could remember, he had never been away. Valerie shuddered as she visualized the look he had given her when she had asked about the Heart a few days before. She managed to settle down during the afternoon, but the itching thought that something was wrong would not completely go away. As the final bell rang, she gathered her things, not even waiting for Katie, and started to head straight home. Valerie's pace was quick, and she tried to calm down. She was just being foolish, she told herself. Everything was fine, and her mind was playing tricks on her. Rounding the corner to the house, Valerie looked up toward home, and her breath caught in her throat.

~~~~

The two police vehicles were parked with their wheels up on the sidewalk, facing the wrong direction for the side of the street they were on. It didn't really matter, as there was plenty of room for the minuscule amount of traffic that came down this particular street. The flickering blue and red strobe lights were blinding even in the full light of day.

Inside the house, the blare of an officer's portable radio could be heard, and two policemen stood in the destroyed living room, talking to Dad. He was obviously very angry, and was waving his hands at the ransacked mess that lay all around the main level of their home. The upstairs was equally trashed. Valerie's father was understandably upset, and was hollering about what he had discovered upon coming home. As Valerie walked in, he saw her and immediately toned it down a notch.

She looked around. Everything had been pulled out of cabinets and drawers. The first thing she noticed was that the flat screen television was still in its place, even amongst the chaos. Why would thieves not take it? Valerie felt icy fingers crawl up her spine as she quickly realized that these were not thieves. Not in the conventional sense, at least. Whoever had broken into the house had been looking for something specific. Valerie felt nauseous. She knew exactly what they were looking for.

"Valerie, can you go sit with your brother out on the deck for a while, please? He's a little shaken up," said her father.

She didn't hesitate, but waded through the mess and out to the back door. The deck was quiet at least, and shaded in the afternoon. Alex sat on a patio chair, tears in his eyes, holding his backpack. Valerie pulled a second chair over beside him and plunked down into it.

"They busted my Star Destroyer," Alex said as he began to cry. "It took me two weeks to build that thing…"

Alex put his hands over his face. His sister put her hand on his back and rubbed it gently. She could feel her own emotion welling up inside her chest, and tried not to cry too. Her little brother had loved Star Wars Lego for the past few years, and the big Star Destroyer kit was what he had always wanted. She started to feel angry. Who did these people think they were? Just because they wanted this amazing artifact did not give them the right to mess with other people's lives! Alex composed himself. The back door opened, and their

42

father emerged onto the deck. They both stared at him with haunted looks.

"Everything is fine," he began. "But I think you guys should sleep someplace else tonight until I clean up the mess."

"Who did it, Dad?" asked Alex.

"I don't know, son… Looks like some kids did it; nothing is really missing!" Dad said. "You guys will go out to Grandpa and Nana's tonight, and I'll get this stuff under control."

He told them to try to find some clothes amongst the mess of the bedrooms, and they headed upstairs. Valerie knew what she must look for first, and practically dove under what remained of her bed. It was gone. The bag, the Heart… Gone. She felt panic grip her as she rummaged farther underneath, finally pulling the whole mess of a bed aside. There was nothing: some old running shoes, a few board games, and plenty of dust, but the Heart was gone. This wasn't some random break-in, she knew. Whoever was responsible had come here looking for the Heart of the Raven and nothing else. Valerie could already feel the tears welling up in her eyes. Her father peeked in, and after taking a brief look at her, he tried to console her.

"It's okay, Valerie. I'll get the mess cleaned up while you guys spend the night with Grandpa, and everything will go back to normal."

She nodded at him, tears streaming, not knowing how she could explain to him that this was all her fault.

8

The Mohawk and Algonquin people inhabited this area long before the arrival of French and English settlers. At that time, they led a simple life, taking what they needed from nature, and living in the woodlands surrounding the Manitonna, or "Garden of the Great Spirit."

A region formed while the world was young. The Thousand Islands, as they were later called, were comprised mainly of pre-Cambrian rock that was slowly shaped over millions of years by retreating glacial ice and the flowing St. Lawrence River. Several parts of the area were rich with mineral deposits, including veins of amethyst. Carved by Native artisans, one particularly large piece of purple crystal took on the shape of a bird. A bird sacred to these people: a Raven.

~~~~

Nana groaned slightly as she struggled to sit up further in the bed. All this lying around had begun to cause her to feel a little bit tender in places. She wanted to be up and alert this evening, because the children would be visiting along with Grandpa this time. It simply would not do for her to look like death warmed over, even if she did feel awful.

Dinner was out of the way, and she had become a little bored. Reading had lost its appeal to her, and she was hoping her company would arrive sooner rather than later. Time seemed to slow to a crawl in this place, and Nana felt at times as if everyone on this ward was simply waiting their turn to die. She would never say these things aloud, however, as she was quite conscious of the fact that what she said sometimes upset Grandpa, and her son. And she certainly knew enough not to worry her grandchildren. Her thoughts were interrupted suddenly as Alex poked his young, round face into the room.

"Hi Nana!" he said with a shy smile.

"Well hello!" she replied, trying her best to look perfectly fine.

"We brought you some new art books, in case you get bored," he said happily as he put two large hardcover books on her table.

"Where are Grandpa and Valerie?" she asked as she picked up one of the books to look at.

"They stopped to talk to the nurses; I think they are coming in a minute," he replied, plunking down in a chair at the side of the room.

He had his famous backpack with him, as usual. Nana knew that he went nowhere without the tattered old pack, and smiled as she looked at it, knowing it contained everything that her grandson needed.

After a few moments Grandpa and Valerie appeared, and Nana noticed the haunted look on her granddaughter's face immediately. She smiled and opened her arms to Valerie, who hugged her briefly but did not say anything. Grandpa gave Nana a quiet look, indicating that maybe something was up. Nana pretended not to notice, and opened up the big art book as Valerie sat on the edge of the bed.

"Thank you for the gorgeous books, sweetie-hearts!" she said. The term was truly an invention of Nana's own making. She had called all of the children that name since time immemorial. Even her son was familiar with the term. She had referred to him by the affectionate moniker many times, and it had been a customary greeting of hers for a long period of time.

Nana leaned back for a moment and looked at Valerie again. Whatever was troubling her granddaughter was deeper than this visit to her bedside in the hospital. She could read it in Valerie's face.

"Grandpa, would you two men be so kind as to get me one of those yummy fruit bowls from the cafeteria, by chance?" she asked politely.

"I think we could handle that, eh, Alex?" he stated with a knowing look in Nana's direction.

Alex nodded, and the two headed out and down the hall on their sudden mission, Nana having successfully removed them so that she and her granddaughter could have a little "girl-time."

"So," Nana started, taking Valerie's hand. "What's wrong? I can see the trouble in your face."

Tears began to fall immediately, and Nana's warm expression became slightly worried. Whatever it was that had Valerie upset was obviously something of great importance, she realized. Nana waited patiently for the young girl to start explaining what was wrong. She gave her a comforting pat on the back.

"We found it, Nana! And then we lost it again!" Valerie stammered. "The Heart of the Raven!"

Her grandmother looked at her in confusion, then grasped her and pulled her in for a hug. This legend was nothing but a story from an old newspaper clipping, stored away amongst the scrapbook. How could it be that Valerie was now telling her that they had gone out and found this artifact? Her mind raced as she looked again at Valerie.

"What are you talking about, dear? You found what?" she asked, bewildered.

Valerie sat back up, looking at Nana with tears streaming down her face.

"The Heart of the Raven!" she exclaimed again. "We actually found it, and it healed Katie's dog, too! He was dying, and it healed him! And if it wasn't stolen, we could have used it to heal you too!" she cried, collapsing back into Nana's arms.

Nana was speechless. Was it really possible that the two children had found this artifact? It was a story, a legend, one of Nana's fanciful tales told by the firelight. She picked Valerie up by the shoulders and looked at her with a level gaze. She smiled at her, wiping away tears. She certainly didn't want to make things worse by saying that what they had found, whatever it was, could not possibly be the real Heart of The Raven. It was just a legend, after all. She thought of something better to say.

"Well, don't worry; if you found it once, you'll probably find it again. Besides," she added as she gave Valerie a wide grin, "there's no cure for old!"

9

Mr. Thatch quietly examined the old photos of family on his desk in his home study. It had been no mystery as to why the high school had snapped him up directly out of teacher's college. He was of Mohawk descent, and a history major. He understood more about local history than just about anyone else alive, and knew many handed-down native stories that he enjoyed sharing with his students. They seemed to appreciate these story sessions, and he thought it was a valuable part of their course studies.

As he held a photo of his great grandfather, a black-and-white window showing Native people wearing full ceremonial clothing and gathered in front of the main buildings in their village, he thought of those stories. One in particular was his favourite, because it told of a certain animal, and how it had become what it was. It was a very simple and entertaining legend about a particular species of turtle. It tied in nicely with his fellow science teacher's ecology program. The story of the Blanding's Turtle went as follows:

One day an evil person came and stole the sun from the sky above. He took it and hid it in his home, holding the sun prisoner and keeping its light and warmth for himself. A lone turtle came from the woodlands, knowing that none of the people could do anything to rescue the sun. The little turtle snuck into the house of the evil person unnoticed, hid in the shadows under a table, and disguised itself as a rock. When the evil person left the house for a short while, the turtle grabbed the sun under its chin and took it back to the woods. When they got to a safe place, the turtle released the sun, and it floated back up into the sky. The turtle was left with a bright yellow patch under its chin from holding the sun, and became what it is today.

Mr. Thatch looked again at the photos. One story had come back to him lately, brought on by one of his students. This mention had been a surprise to him. He thought about the prophecy that young Valerie had spoken of in class. It was a centuries-old legend. Why was she interested in it? How had she discovered the story? Did she have an idea where the Heart was?

He had seen the book, tucked in with the texts on her desk, despite her attempt to conceal it. He now reached forward, picked up a plain notebook, and flipped it open. It contained notes and native stories; various works he hoped to someday assemble into a book of his own. He flipped to a section where he had scrawled notes about the Heart of the Raven. In the folds of the pages was a large black feather. He picked it up and turned it in his fingers. A raven feather. If the children knew about the legend, they might actually look for the Heart. What was the possibility of them finding it?

He dismissed the thought. It would probably amount to nothing at all. How could they find it? Even he had no idea whether or not there was any truth to this story. It was a legend from his own people, buried in history, but he could still sense something about it in his mind. It was like an itch that he could not scratch. The possibility that this crystal made of amethyst actually existed made his thoughts race as he turned the feather over in his fingers.

He remembered his reaction to Valerie's mention of it in class, and his own doubts as to the truth behind the ancient story. He tried to imagine the legend becoming a reality, and contemplated the possibility that the Heart could actually be found. He could almost hear the sound of the drums; the chanting of the dances echoed from the pages in front of him as he thought about the purple crystal shaped like a sacred bird. It would be an amazing thing to uncover the Heart, and he knew that he would be made famous by it. He could elevate his status amongst his own people, and become more than simply a history teacher. He grinned at the feather in his hand greedily, thinking of the money it could bring him as well.

~~~~

On Sunday afternoon, the children arrived back at home, where their father was waiting after cleaning up the mess. Once again there was a policeman there, giving Dad a copy of the report about the break-in and making a few minor notes on his laptop to finish up. Grandpa had left quickly, knowing that things were now okay. Valerie and Alex looked around in amazement. It was almost as if nothing had happened. Everything was back in its place, the exceptions being the odd vase or picture frame that had been broken.

Alex rushed off to his room, lugging his beloved backpack full of supplies up the stairs with him. Valerie went to the kitchen to grab a few cookies, able to put her schoolbooks on the hallway table now that it was back where it was supposed to be. She tuned in to the conversation in the living room between her father and the officer as she absently opened and closed the fridge, hanging off of each exchanged word. The policeman figured that the break-in was the work of kids looking for money or maybe alcohol and tobacco.

Valerie exhaled. She knew very well that she could say nothing to Dad about the Heart; that she would get a huge scolding for following another one of her grandmother's flights of fancy. He might give Nana trouble too, sick or not. She fumbled in the cookie jar, which was thankfully intact, taking as long as she could so as to be close enough to listen. She wished she had kept the Heart with her, and not left it under her bed. She could feel herself getting upset again as she thought about what had happened with Sparks, and what she might have been able to do to help Nana. She forced herself to settle down and focus on what was being said as she took a bite of a windmill cookie.

"We have some video footage of a young person leaving your driveway around the time it happened. We got it from a neighbour's home security camera," said the officer.

Valerie's eyes widened. She slowly walked out to the living room and made her way toward the bookcase on the far wall, to a position where she might be able to see the laptop screen on the coffee table.

"I'll see if I can freeze it," the policeman stated, focusing on the computer. Valerie picked up a National Geographic from the bookcase and idly thumbed through the pages. She swept her brown hair from her face, pretending not to be interested in what the two men were doing.

"There! There's the young lad we are looking for. Know him?"

Dad paused for a long moment, watching the screen and looking carefully at the person frozen in the video footage. It angered him that anyone would have the nerve to set foot on his property with the intention of breaking in and that this invasion of their privacy had upset his children. But he slowly shook his head, not recognizing the figure on the screen.

"No," replied Valerie's father with a serious tone. "Never seen him before around here."

Valerie raised her brown eyes from the magazine toward the screen. Her mouth fell open and she could feel blood pounding in her ears. Her palms were already sweaty as she stared at the scene on the policeman's laptop. There on the screen was a slender young man with brown hair hanging into his face. Worn work boots were on his feet, and faded work clothes made up his attire.

As the police officer let the video resume, Valerie had to fight not to gasp. He walked quickly away from the house in the video on the glaring computer screen, with a slight limp...

10

She stared at it as it lay on the table, her eyes filled with greed. It was the answer to all her problems. Regardless of any foolish legends, it would fetch a fortune. Someone who knew the legends, however, might make it priceless. She had to contact the collector and set a price for it. He would have to pay what she wanted in the end anyway; it was inevitable. She had it, and he didn't. If he wanted it, he would have to pay a handsome — no, obscene — price. Enough for her to escape the feeble little existence she was attempting to eke out.

She had already decided to tell any prospective buyer the story of its creation anyway, to make it an easier sell. It sat there, looking back at her. She could do nothing but stare at it, and roll the idea of it over and over in her mind. This sale would have to be done very discreetly, however. It was, after all, an artifact. If the wrong people found out that it had been discovered, there would be a frenzy of interest, and demands for it to be handed over to a museum for posterity. She knew she had to liquidate it for cash quickly. If she were discovered with it, there would be too many questions.

The man with whom she had chatted via email was very interested in the Heart, and for whatever reason, didn't seem to be too concerned with the price. It sat there on the table in front of her, gleaming. It seemed to have an energy, a life, something tangible that she could feel even as she gazed at it. She reached out to touch its purple crystals, wondering how these ancient people could carve something so beautiful without modern tools. She could almost hear the drums of some ancestral ritual as the Heart seemed to throb under her fingertips. Her trance was interrupted by the sudden waking of her computer screen, which displayed a message with a request to chat. The cursor flashed slowly in the chat window, and she squinted at the bright light from the monitor and clicked Accept. It was him, she realized quickly. It just might be payday. Let's make a deal, she thought.

~~~~

It was getting late, and Robert limped down the walkway from the housing project. He stopped at the sidewalk briefly, looking around. It was quiet tonight; the only sound on this street was the hum of the streetlights overhead, and the occasional bark from a dog in the distance. He threw on his hoodie and walked away, heading down the street past the hedge bordering the property.

It was awful living in that place, he thought. It could have been a nice complex to live in, but the property managers had long ago given up on try to keep the place looking good. Robert shook his head slightly as he walked, dismissing his cynical thoughts. It would soon be better, he told himself. If this woman kept to her word regarding the money they would get for the crystal thingy, he would be out of that place in short order. Maybe get himself a condo or something. Anything would be better, really.

He stopped for a moment and looked back behind him. He was sure he had heard something. He surveyed the shrubbery and dimly-lit lawns of the houses along the street. Nothing. Maybe raccoons, he thought. He glanced around for a few seconds more and finally turned back to his walk; back to the pleasant thoughts of a better life. Maybe with some money he could actually find some nice looking chick to date, instead of being alone all the time, and watching movies by himself on his little twenty-six inch Sony. He didn't even have a flat screen, just an old tube TV. All that would change soon, though, and he would have it all. Even if he had to force the old woman to make the deal.

Robert turned the corner and walked down Bethune Street under its towering trees that lined the sidewalks like silent guards. As he approached another small apartment building, he looked at its neatly weeded flowerbeds, clean façade, and windows all aglow with light. He paused at the walkway for a moment. She thinks she has it rough, he thought comically.

He limped up the walkway to the buzzer mounted outside the main doors. As he punched in the number and waited for the resounding buzzing sound that meant he could open the door, he failed to notice the two shadowy forms behind him that were hiding in a grove of trees at the edge of the property. The buzz came to his ears, and he yanked open the heavy glass door to get inside.

It was quiet again outside for a moment, and then a slight rustling sound emanated from the edge of the yard. Two small shapes emerged and crept to the entranceway. As the light from the foyer fell on them, the two children hugged the wall and scanned the names on the entry keypad. After a quick inspection of the entry door, they left hastily and moved on to the side alleyway until they were below the second-floor windows of an apartment in the building. A rusted fire escape stairway led up the side of the brickwork. Quietly, the two ascended the metal stairway and peeked into a second floor window that was shaded by lace curtains.

Valerie pulled down her hoodie and gazed inside. She was looking through a kitchen window, but could clearly see Robert sitting in a plush chair in the living room beyond. It hadn't taken her long to track him down; he had insisted that she accept him as a friend on Facebook weeks before, and five minutes on Google had given her his address. Everything was available on the Internet for someone who knew how to find it, and Valerie and Alex had been playing with their dad's computers since before they could talk. They had followed Robert in the hope that he would lead them to the Heart again. And he had.

Sitting on the table nearby and visible through the holes in the lace was the purple crystal of the Heart of the Raven. They had to get it back, Valerie thought. She became angry as she considered how Robert had misled her and betrayed her friendship. She could feel the hot waves of emotion washing over her body, and crouched down a little farther on the fire escape landing in an attempt to get a better view while trying to remain silent.

Alex was close behind her, clutching the straps of his backpack tightly. They waited. Valerie hoped that their father would not call over to Katie's house tonight; she had lied to him about staying there for a sleepover. She didn't like to lie to him, but considered this to be a special emergency situation.

Valerie and Alex continued to watch Robert through the curtain-covered window. He rose from the chair suddenly, and walked out of the room and out of view. Muffled conversation could be heard through the windowpane, but no words that Valerie could distinguish. Then it became quiet again. Valerie looked down at the table in the kitchen. There it was: the Heart, so close she could almost have grabbed it if the windows had been open. Her thoughts turned to her Nana, lying in the hospital in a room with no one for company, always waiting for the nurses or doctor, who seemed to be unable to do anything for her.

Valerie looked at the frame of the window. It had an old hook and latch mechanism. She dug her fingers in at the bottom of the sill and wiggled it. The outside pane of glass moved up and down slightly. The hasp had shifted a bit. Valerie continued to wiggle the window, and watched as the two metal pieces dropped away from one another. She slid the window up, and it opened just a little. She looked back at Alex, whose eyes were wide in disbelief. He motioned for her to keep going.

She opened it a bit more, listening carefully. There was the sound of fingers tapping on a keyboard: that clackity-clack in rapid succession. A few muffled words could be heard. Valerie now had the window halfway open, and strained in an attempt not to make a sound. She gently pushed the window open still further. Alex moved slightly, rustling just a bit. Valerie turned with a raised finger to her lips and wide eyes, trying to convey how important it was for him to remain silent. She turned her attention back to the kitchen window, sliding it quietly open the last inch.

She took her hand away from it just in time. A woman appeared suddenly from around the corner, striding casually forward and placing an empty glass into the sink immediately in front of the window. There was no time to react, and the two children simply froze. The woman glanced briefly at the open window and reached forward, slamming it shut without a thought. Thunk. Then she turned away and returned to the other room in a few steps.

Valerie and Alex's jaws hung open. Scared stiff, they didn't move for a few moments. Then they looked at one another in disbelief. It was Ms. Stone. The librarian and the janitor had taken the Heart. Well, that was just great, they thought. Valerie could feel the hot flow of anger again, and blood rose to her cheeks as she realized that "Stoneface" could not see them through the curtain. She felt invincible. The kitchen was bare again, and devoid of movement, so Valerie seized the moment. She slid the window silently open again.

Valerie looked back at Alex, pulling on her own belt and offering it to him. He nodded, and grabbed at the back of her pants and belt as she leaned inside. Valerie strained as she reached forward. The Heart was much too far away to grab, but she could just barely touch the tablecloth. Alex leaned back hard to keep her from falling in, and he hoped she was hurrying, because he was beginning to lose his grip. She inched the tablecloth toward her, sliding the purple crystal ever closer.

Valerie tried to divide her attention and listen to the sounds of the conversation in the other room. They were talking about selling the Heart to a collector of rare artifacts. They were on the Internet chatting with him now. If she didn't get it back right now, it would be gone forever. She reached forward, straining harder, and closed her fingers around the crystal. She smiled. She had it.

Valerie told herself deep down that she would never let it go again, despite what might happen. It wasn't that it was hers, but she simply would not let anyone take it from them for something as stupid as money. She began to lean back out of the window again, but just as she did, Alex slipped and lost his grip on her belt. She fell suddenly forward, catching herself with one hand on the wall below the window.

Valerie held the Heart tightly against herself as she quickly recovered and pulled herself back out of the window. She landed with a crash on the fire escape. A head poked into the kitchen once again, its owner curious about the sudden noise. Ms. Stone's usually stoic expression was now a snarl of rage as she realized what she was seeing. The children did not wait to see any more than Ms. Stone pointing angrily out the window as Robert came to determine what was happening. They leapt to their feet and took the stairs down the fire escape two at a time in their panicked retreat. One thing they did hear as they darted off through the hedges, running as fast as their legs would carry them, was the voice of Ms. Stone yelling, "Get them!"

11

Nana had spent that evening, like the last several days, sleeping fitfully. Her normally rosy face had drained of colour, and Dad and Grandpa had been there almost every minute. The doctor had reserved his comments, as per her request, which frustrated the two men immensely. Grandpa knew that the staff wasn't sharing everything with them, and it made him angry. The doctor had simply shrugged and replied that they would be sure to update them as tests came back from the lab. Both men knew that it was bad; that the unspoken truth was that Nana might indeed die from the disease. They would not speak of such things to one another as they sat patiently, trying to pass the time, each in their own way. A newspaper, a crossword book; anything to help the clock tick by in the hope that there might eventually be some good news. But it had not come. It was almost painful to watch nurses stroll by the room, going here and there, without anyone coming in to see how things were. Without any news at all. Both of them hated the situation, and time ticked by extremely slowly.

Dad thought about his earlier days, drifting through memories of when he and his brother were young. Nana and Grandpa were larger than life then, and always seemed to be taking the two of them somewhere. Camping, travelling, competing in sports. He remembered bedtime stories around a campfire at the lake, their eyes wide as they listened to Nana telling stories, their marshmallows burnt in the flames as they anticipated what she might say next. He smiled a bit, unconsciously. The memories drifted through his mind like smoke from the remembered campfire.

He turned his gaze toward her sleeping form, and the expression on his face changed. He felt a deep sadness; the idea that something terrible might be at the end of all of this waiting shredded his very soul with its potential. That his mother could actually pass from this world, leaving him and his father alone to continue their existence without her, was a chilling thought.

He dismissed it immediately and looked up at Grandpa, whose head was now bobbing slightly. He must be tired. It had been another evening of waiting and watching. How would he carry on if Nana succumbed to this disease?

Dad looked at his father, remembering the days when he had helped him accomplish any task that was too much for him. He had been a giant in his mind, and able to do anything. Now, he wondered how Grandpa would survive. He might have to cook for himself every day, do things that Nana had done, and be lonely. The truth beyond all of their sarcastic comments - the bantering between the two of them - was that they were truly meant for one another, and Dad wondered what effect watching his wife die of illness might have upon his father.

He looked away, shutting the door on these thoughts in his mind. It was nearly midnight. He watched the red second hand sweep around the clock face on the wall opposite where he sat. He wished someone would come in. A doctor, a nurse, circus clowns for God's sake. Anything to make that clock tick a little faster. He settled with picking up a National Geographic issue he had already read at least twice, and flipping through the pages in the hope that there might be something new that he had missed. Grandpa bumped the back of his head against the wall and awoke suddenly with a start.

"What's going on?" he inquired groggily.

"Nothing new, Dad."

"Did the doctor come by?" Grandpa ventured.

"Nope."

At this response the old man gave an exasperated sigh, tucked his hands together on top of his belly in the chair, and slumped into a sulking posture. Dad did his best to conceal a slight grin.

"How about a coffee?" he offered.

"That sounds good; I need something to keep me awake! All this waiting is wearing me down," replied Grandpa. Without another word, Dad got up and began the walk down the hall toward the elevator. It would be a long night.

~~~~

Valerie and Alex peeked out from the alleyway in the darkness, trying to decide where to go from here. Still breathing heavily, they had stopped to rest for a minute. Valerie remembered their best hiding places in the neighbourhood from games of hide and seek with the local kids. She considered sending Alex in a different direction, but decided that splitting up might be a bad idea. If Robert would ransack their home, she didn't know how far he might go if he caught them. And right now, that was what scared her the most. Dad's anger at her deception about sleeping over at Katie's was a minor problem compared to the danger they were in right now.

The narrow alley offered perfect cover for them for the moment, but Valerie knew they could not stay there long; eventually, Robert would find them. It was cool and still, and the streetlights did little to illuminate the area. They crept forward and concealed themselves in a large lilac bush near the sidewalk. They stayed for a moment, crouched in the shadows, and Valerie gripped the Heart firmly in her left hand. There was a very slight rustling in the leaves in front of the shrubbery in which they hid. As they both watched, a large toad struggled to hop away, one of its hind legs injured and unmoving. Alex deftly caught him, and cradled the amphibian in his small hands.

"Aww, he's hurt!" he said in pity, as he looked the animal over.

"Probably got hit by a car or something," Valerie stated, beginning to examine the toad herself now.

They had momentarily forgotten the fact that they were being pursued and that they had the crystal, which began to glow purple again in the presence of the injured toad. The Heart's radiance grew to a blinding shine, and Valerie gasped and tried to cover it up under her sweater before it gave them away. It was too late; they began to hear Robert and Ms. Stone's voices from somewhere down the street, and their footsteps hurrying in the children's direction. The toad took advantage of the distraction and hopped out of Alex's hands and into the grass, his leg working just fine all of a sudden.

Valerie yanked her little brother to his feet, practically dragging him up in her haste to run. They exploded from the cover of the lilac and sprinted across the street and through several backyards, avoiding one birdbath and several flowerbeds along the way. Alex held on firmly to his backpack and kept right on Valerie's heels. They could hear Robert following, and the sound of him crashing through the hedges behind them kept them moving as fast as they could. Suddenly they came to a large wooden fence bordering one of the yards, and Valerie knew there was no way they could climb over it. She grabbed Alex again, and escorted him down toward the back of the yard where it bordered on the creek. They kept going, following the edge of the water, and trying not to slip on the algae-covered rocks along the bank. It was almost pitch black here, except for the odd porch light coming from the houses nearby. They stopped for a moment and huddled in the long grasses, catching their breath.

"Now what do we do? Do you know where we are?" asked Alex in a gasping whisper.

"Not sure. Doesn't really matter as long as they don't find us."

As if right on cue, there was a slight splash behind them, followed by some quiet cursing. Robert was still on their trail. They continued on, dodging branches and fighting through the undergrowth. They emerged onto the bicycle path in the dark, and Valerie began to get her bearings again as they ran along the cool asphalt. She slowed as they met a point in the trail where it crossed a street, and shoved Alex into a bush at the side of the path, following closely behind.

A car passed by slowly, and Valerie could see a woman driving it. It could only be one person: Ms. Stone. The car stopped briefly, and the children pulled back farther into the shadows of the shrubbery. At least there were no mosquitoes out this late, Alex thought. Valerie watched the rusty, cream-coloured car pull away, and they darted across the road, trying to put some distance between themselves and Robert. Now that Ms. Stone was in a car, it would be difficult to lose them.

The children kept running, staying on the darkest parts of the path and trying to be as quiet as possible. Robert was now way back by Valerie's estimates; she could hear him in the distance, his limp causing him to drag one foot slightly every once in a while, giving him away. He had found his way out onto the bicycle path, though, and to Valerie, this fact meant they had to get off it as quickly as possible.

A thought came to her suddenly as they reached a fork in the path. One way continued straight, while the other went across a cement bridge toward the grocery store. Valerie yanked on Alex's arm again, prompting him to follow her as she ran toward the bridge. He knew instantly what she had in mind. They often played around this bridge, although it looked different now in the darkness. They had been underneath it only two weeks ago, and had enjoyed catching minnows in a trap their father had given them. It was a fairly large and sturdy bridge, made of concrete instead of the wood from which most of the other bicycle path bridges were constructed. The best thing about it was the fact that the large concrete pillars that supported it created a shelf underneath, which allowed them to sit in its cool shade, hidden from the world on hot summer days or sheltered from a sudden rainstorm.

They crawled quickly and silently down under it, and Valerie boosted

Alex and his trusty backpack up onto the ledge underneath before lifting herself up and out of sight in the shadows of the greenery. It was calm and quiet here, the gurgling creek the only sound in the dark. The rough surface of the cement was cool and dry, offering quite a contrast from the dew of the long grasses surrounding the creek itself. The children lay flat out under the bridge, calming their breathing and listening.

At first all they could hear were the crickets singing their late summer song. Eventually the sounds of someone moving through the path came to their ears. Alex looked at Valerie with wide eyes and froze. She raised a finger to her lips even though she knew it wasn't really needed. Somewhere in the dark above them, the noise paused. Valerie could hear breaths, deep and quick, as the person waited a moment. Robert. She knew he was listening for them.

The children were silent, almost not breathing at all as they waited and listened. If Robert found them under here, they were done. They would not be able to escape quickly from the spot they were in, and they knew it. Long moments passed, seeming like an eternity. Finally they could hear Robert's awkward steps retreating down the bridge and out onto the path again. His steps disappeared, and still the two remained motionless. After what seemed like forever, they stepped back down into the dark green underbrush around the edge of the bridge. They crept slowly back out into the long grasses beside the creek, listening for any sign of unwelcome company. Valerie knew that they had to get to somewhere public right away. But where, at this hour? The light bulb came on in her brain suddenly, and she grinned at Alex in the shadows.

"What?" he asked, shrugging his shoulders.

"Let's get out of here!" she whispered. Grabbing his hand, she led him back up onto the path until he became slightly aggravated at being dragged along. He shook his hand free of hers with a frown that was barely visible in the darkness. Off they sprinted, doubling back the way they had come. As silently as possible, they made their way across the neighbourhood, freezing and melting into the shadows of the path if they spotted a car. Before long, Valerie stopped.

"Take off your backpack for a minute," she said to Alex.

"Why?"

"Because, I want to pack this away in it."

She held up the Heart and gestured toward her brother's backpack with a look of insistence on her face. He slid off the pack, and Valerie wrapped the Heart in a cloth that Alex had inside before stuffing it down into the canvas bag. The boy put the pack back on his shoulders.

"Now it won't give us away, at least!" she stated, and returned her attention to the path. There was no sign of Robert behind them so far. Valerie could only hope that he was still heading away from them, not realizing that they had come back this way. The two continued on, keeping to the darkest parts of the path and avoiding the lights from backyards and streetlamps.

"Where are we going?" asked Alex in a whisper.

"Straight to the hospital, to Nana!" Valerie whispered back.

Alex was not as sure of this idea; showing up at the hospital late at night might get them into serious trouble, if not from Nana, then definitely from their father. But it would be better than being caught by these people who were following them; that much was certain. He knew very little about Robert, but he certainly wasn't fond of mean old Stoneface. He shuddered slightly to think of what she might do to him.

On they went, slowing to a walk when they became winded. The sound of someone's dog barking made them hurry on again. They were both sweating despite the chilly evening air, and Valerie put her hood down in an attempt to cool herself off a bit. They approached a street crossing the path, which was lined with cement flower planters, a bench, and a large garbage bin. She considered stopping for a rest with Alex, but dismissed the thought quickly. It was just too well lit up, and it would be too easy to be spotted under the glow of streetlights.

Suddenly, the cream-coloured car pulled up just as they were preparing to dart across the street. They stopped momentarily, and Valerie looked Ms. Stone right in the eyes. She had no time to make a real decision, but pulled Alex to the left, crashing through a low hedge and into a backyard. They heard Ms. Stone give two brief honks on the car's horn as they sprinted across the lawns: a signal to Robert. Now they would both be back on them.

The children ran across the street well back behind the idling car. Valerie glanced in that direction, knowing that Ms. Stone must have seen them in her rear-view mirror. As they hit the far sidewalk, the reverse lights illuminated and Valerie heard the slight bark of the tires against the pavement. They ran down the street, and moments later the rusty car driven by Ms. Stone roared around the corner behind them to follow.

Valerie led them left again, knowing that they could not hope to outrun a car, and the children took off up a driveway into another darkened backyard. It was pitch black here, and they slowed their pace as they tried to search the darkness for an escape route. They could only see for about a foot in any direction, and Alex raised his hands in front of him to avoid bumping into something unexpectedly. Valerie took each step with caution, feeling ahead with hers shoes in an attempt not to trip.

Suddenly, they stopped in their tracks as they heard what sounded like the large links of a chain being dragged over a ledge of wood. In the darkness there was just enough light for the children to make out a very large, dark shape approaching them, and as it advanced, it began to snarl. It was a dog; a BIG dog.

The kids instinctively stepped back a few steps as their brains registered the danger. Valerie stumbled and crashed down onto the cool grass. Before she could recover, the dog was already leaping toward her. Even through the blackness, she could see the bared white teeth, open and coming straight at her. She closed her eyes - the only reaction for which she had enough time. The big, snarling animal sailed through the air toward her, a blur in the darkness of the yard.

The dog reached the end of its chain just inches away from connecting and was yanked back, away from Valerie. It had come close enough for her to smell its rank breath. Alex let out a slight whimper as he continued back another step. The two did not wait for the dog to try something else, and ran out the side of the yard and away as fast as they could. Fortunately there was nothing in their path, and they sped behind several houses and up a short rock embankment to a small parking lot. Here there was at least some light. Valerie and Alex paused momentarily, breathing heavily. Valerie had lost track of time by this point, but she knew it was very late. They had little choice but to keep going on; it wasn't like they could simply stop running and go home, after all. This was one adventure that they would have to see through to the end.

A car door slammed somewhere close by, and voices could be heard. Ms. Stone must have picked Robert up to bring him back this way, thought Valerie. She knew they didn't have long. The more time they spent out here, the greater their chances of getting caught. They weren't far from the hospital now, but the bicycle path was no good to them anymore, as it veered northward, away from the place they wanted to go. That meant that they would be left dodging from building to building, and finding hiding places wherever they could.

The children hid behind a dumpster in the small parking lot as steps approached. Odd steps: Robert. His shadow extended across the black asphalt of the lot, and he stopped suddenly to listen and scan the area for any hint of the troublesome pair's whereabouts. He was close enough now for Valerie and Alex to be able to hear his breathing. From their concealed spot behind the dumpster, they could still see his shadow, traced on the pavement. He remained still; listening, watching. They remained still as well, not making a sound.

The stalemate seemed to go on forever, and Valerie realized they were trapped there unless Robert decided to move on. He didn't. Minutes crawled by like hours, and the two children crept silently to the edge of the dumpster and carefully peered around the corner. Robert had his back to them, and was turning his head slowly from side to side as he listened.

A new sound slowly emerged in the dark: a deep rumbling, combined with an occasional horn. It was a train. As it got closer it became much louder, and Valerie knew it would help mask any sound they made. This moment might be their only chance to get away. She pulled Alex back slightly and whispered in his ear about the plan forming in her mind.

The train horn sounded again, louder this time. The children could see the large blue "H" sign of the hospital on the side of the building only a block or two away. It was lit up brightly above the treetops, shining like a welcoming beacon in the dark of the night. Valerie could hear the bells starting to ring at the railroad crossing up the street as the oncoming train sounded its horn again. The two were ready, and as the train sounded off they broke from cover, heading across the asphalt of the parking lot, behind Robert, and across the street.

They ran as fast as they could down the side street, and Valerie risked a look back. She saw Robert turn his gaze toward them. They were in the shadows of the houses they were running past, but it did no good. She glanced back again, and Robert was in pursuit, following as fast as he could. The children sped forward in sheer terror as the young man following tried to close the gap. As they neared the next corner, they began to pass over a large gully that ran beneath the street. Just then, the cream-coloured car of Ms. Stone appeared at the intersection ahead. Before Valerie could fully stop, Alex darted left, and he tumbled down the embankment, hollering as he rolled down through the darkened undergrowth, out of control. With little choice left, Valerie plunged down in pursuit, lost her footing in some vines, and fell after her younger brother.

12

Grandpa was very upset. He had been waiting for hours and hours, and no doctor had appeared. Not only that, but no one had entered the room apart from a young man in hospital scrubs who was simply there to clean the washroom and refill Nana's water pitcher. The old man had begun to pace, and was beyond tired. It was becoming very late, and no news was not good news in Grandpa's book.

He paused to look out of the window, and glanced quickly in his son's direction. He had finally given in to sleep, and his head was slumped forward and his arms were crossed in a position that Grandpa could only imagine must be uncomfortable. The old man turned back to the view of the darkened street outside and pondered why this entire ordeal was occuring. His thoughts turned to memories of travel and fun: camping at the lake, trips to the ocean during March break, his boys growing into men, and his grandchildren. Images flashed through his mind in a never-ending stream of events, people, and places they had seen together.

He looked over to Nana, who was sleeping heavily as the IV unit next to her bed ticked, clicked, and whirred. The doctor had ordered a saline solution to keep her hydrated, along with a painkiller. He thought of how peaceful she looked as she rested, free from the burden of pain. He sighed heavily. Suddenly, he asked himself the unthinkable question: how would he live without her? Trying to picture what his life would be like without her in it was almost impossible. He felt a tear forming in his eye, and turned back toward the window, extinguishing the thought.

Outside it looked quiet, and streetlights were illuminating the street and sidewalk. There was a slight mist rising as well, barely noticeable under the lights. It looked cold out, Grandpa thought, even though he knew it would be two months yet before they would see even a hint of winter. He reached into his pants pocket and took out his wallet. Flipping through it, he found a photograph with tattered edges. They both looked so young then, he thought, gazing at the image of him and Nana.

His thoughts were interrupted by a young man in a white coat as he entered the room. Finally. Grandpa glanced at his watch in irritation, and it was not difficult for the doctor to see that the old man was frustrated by the lateness of his arrival.

"I apologize for the wait, gentlemen. It has been a crazy evening."

Grandpa swallowed an angry retort, saying simply that it was fine. Dad roused in his chair and stood up hastily upon seeing the doctor was finally there. The young man cast a subdued look at the two men before him, realizing that the cat and mouse game that Nana had him playing with them had run its course. He would now have to tell them everything. In a last ditch effort to delay the awful news of her condition, he asked if they would rather speak in his office.

"Why don't we just quit wasting time and you tell us what you know?" Dad replied in a serious tone.

Grandpa nodded in approval.

The doctor drew a heavy sigh, then flipped open a file folder and withdrew several x-rays. He described the cancer as if it were some kind of living thing, spreading through vital parts of her body and robbing her of any strength to fight back. It was destroying healthy tissue, and causing acute pain. Other dark film x-ray sheets told the story, and the blotches looked as if they were growing with each new page. Dad suddenly thought of those little books that made cartoon characters drawn on paper become animated if you flipped through them quickly, and of how it would make this horrible disease come to life on the sheets the doctor was handing him. He shook his head slightly to clear it.

"So, what's next? More chemo? Some kind of experimental treatment?" he asked.

The doctor paused a moment, not wanting to proceed.

"We can try some more things, yes, but with your mother's strength fading, I'm not sure if it will do much good." He paused again. Grandpa looked down at the floor as he realized where the doctor was headed.

"I am really very sorry," he began delicately, "but there is not much more we can do."

~~~~

Ms. Stone drove down the side streets, craning her neck into the darkness to each side and looking for the two young children. She was frustrated by their ability to evade her, and she wanted desperately to find them once and for all. She gripped the steering wheel of the car tightly, her knuckles white. She had to find them; had to get her salvation back. Who cared about Robert, really? He was simply a tool to her, a means to an end. She brushed the thought away; she would have time to decide what to do about him later. She needed to get the Heart back first. The buyer would be contacting her soon to arrange the details of the sale, and would not be pleased to find out that she had let a couple of kids take it from her.

He seemed to be a very serious individual, whoever he was, and hadn't been the most pleasant person to talk to on the phone, either. She had only spoken to him twice, but both times she got the sense that he might be a very bad man. Ms. Stone shivered slightly as she remembered the icy tone of his voice, and his insistence that things be done his way. She knew it would not go well for her if she could not find the two children and get the crystal back.

Ms. Stone continued to drive along slowly, examining every bush and empty yard. It frustrated her that Robert had not found the two children by now, and recovered the Heart. Surely he could at least accomplish one thing. How hard could it be to find a pair of young kids at this hour of night? There was no one else out on the streets! She would find them, even if Robert was too incompetent.

~~~~

Alex cried out in pain, and Valerie quickly clamped a hand over his mouth. They lay for only a minute at the bottom of the embankment, far below street level, before Valerie dragged him onward. They headed away from the street, stumbling along through the greenery in the dark. Alex was in obvious pain. There was a deep gash in his knee, and his pant leg was torn open and soaked with blood.

Valerie looked around in the darkened undergrowth as she wiped some dirt and dead leaves from her clothes. She recognized where they were, and helped her younger brother as they made their way north. He limped along, keeping quiet only out of fear of being caught, and letting the occasional whimper escape as they made their way through the tangle of brush and ferns that lined the bottom of the gully.

Out of the darkness rose a large pair of wooden doors against a wall of stone: the old train tunnel. Valerie made her way toward it, supporting Alex as they struggled forward. The doors were clamped together by a chain and large rusted lock, but Valerie knew by looking at them that the doors would still open with the slack of the chain just slightly. Maybe just enough. She set Alex down, and he sat on a large rock and rested for a moment, not wanting to look at the injury to his knee.

Valerie turned her attention to the doors, which must have stood at least fifteen feet high and were half as wide. The ancient wood was rough, but she grabbed hold of the inside edges and pulled hard. Old iron hinges creaked, and the doors came apart just a bit.

"Alex, see if you can fit through!" she whispered hoarsely, straining to hold the heavy doors open. The boy struggled forward and squeezed between the edges of the old wood with his backpack taking the lead. Valerie wriggled into a position that would let her try to follow, and slid slowly in, head last. She picked up two big slivers but managed to fit, falling into a heap on the ground once inside. If it was dark outside, then the train tunnel was like a tomb; it was pitch black within. The two children settled for a moment up against the brick wall of the tunnel. Alex began to cry, and Valerie turned her attention toward her brother.

"It hurts… Bad," he said through tears, trying to be quiet.

Valerie dug around in Alex's backpack for the small flashlight, then tried to use her hand to shield the light so that it could not be seen through the opening in the wooden doors of the entrance. Alex had a deep cut in his left knee. She told him to look away as she examined the wound. It was deep, and she gritted her teeth subconsciously as she gingerly pulled the blood-soaked tear in the pant leg away from it. Alex whined slightly, as if expecting terrible news. Valerie let go of the fabric of his pants and showed him her hands as if to say "don't worry." She knew exactly what to do.

Valerie rummaged around in the backpack again and pulled out the cloth-wrapped crystal. After unwrapping it, she held it close to her brother's damaged knee and watched as the carved raven began to glow. The light cast swirling patterns of pink and purple onto the walls, illuminating the tunnel brickwork. Alex shut his eyes tightly in expectation of pain, but nothing bad happened. He opened his eyes again and stared into the light shining from the Heart.

It was mesmerizing to them, and for the first time they saw some of the fine detail carved into the crystal. There was writing on the underside, which glowed in the shimmering light. The writing was ancient, little more than symbols that they could not read. Alex's face relaxed, and Valerie could see the pain disappear from his eyes. She looked at his knee. There was nothing there; the skin was clean and was left without even a scar. She looked at him with her eyes wide and her mouth hanging open as the light from the crystal began to fade. It was amazing. She shon the small LED flashlight on Alex's knee, unsure whether or not to believe what she was seeing.

Suddenly, Alex grabbed the light and turned it off with a slight gasp. Valerie sat dead still. Obviously her brother had heard something that had escaped her ears as she marvelled at the healing of his injury. She perked up her ears, listening. At first there was nothing. Then she began to hear footsteps through the leaves and brush outside the tunnel. The two of them were frozen in the pitch-blackness of their hiding place, not even daring to breathe. The steps became closer, and more frequent. It had to be Robert, still on their trail. They were trapped as well; the tunnel was sealed a short way down, so the only way in was through the massive wooden doors.

The children remained still. He was just outside the entrance. In the sliver of dim light that came through the opening in the doors, Valerie could see fingers reaching inside and grasping the wood. She held her breath, horrified, as the doors shook slightly. A shadow appeared, blocking even the tiny amount of light from the night sky. Still they did not move. They could hear him breathing, heavily, as he tried to look inside. Valerie knew that he could not see them, but remained perfectly still. There was nowhere they could go, but she was confident that he could never squeeze through like they had.

Again the doors shook, violently this time, making them start. Minutes passed like hours. The fingers were gone now but they could still hear footsteps here and there. Eventually they diminished, and only crickets could be heard. Valerie relaxed a little. She turned to look at Alex, and was instantly plunged into worry; the boy was slouched down, with his chin resting on his chest. He was asleep. She sat back, almost comfortable against the sloped brick wall of the tunnel. She knew that they should keep going and get to the hospital, but these thoughts slowly melded with others. Her eyelids grew heavy as she tried to stay alert and listen. Only the crickets sang their autumn tune as sleep took her down into its depths as well.

13

Ms. Stone pounded angrily on the steering wheel of her car as Robert again confessed to losing the children at the driver's side window. Never send a boy to do a woman's work, she thought. She tried to calm down, even though she could sense that her prize was slipping away, and knew that they must find the two children before they handed the Heart over to an adult. It would then become much more difficult to get their hands on it, and the ordeal would become twice as complex.

Grey light of day began to show in the sky to the east, and Ms. Stone knew that time was running short. Robert stood by the car, not sure what else he could say to her. He had tried to keep up with the children as they had moved through the paths next to the creek. It angered him that he couldn't catch them, and it also angered him that this woman seemed to view him as some kind of idiot. Maybe she should get out of her car and try to find them. He began to wonder if the money she had promised was real, or if she was just dangling a carrot in front of him. It had been the middle of the night, and those two were like ghosts hiding in the undergrowth of the bicycle path. He wasn't some kind of commando, after all. He fidgeted as he waited for her to say something.

"Where was the last place you saw them?" she asked him once again.

"When they went into the gully at the train tunnel!" Robert replied, exasperated.

"Well they simply must be there; maybe they are hiding down there somewhere."

"I checked it all, even the train tunnel, and it's all locked up," he said, pulling off his hood.

"Well, they can't disappear, and they could not have gone far. Go back and retrace your steps. We have to find them."

Robert looked at her for a moment as he crouched next to the car. It was a new experience for him to accept orders from anyone. She had promised him a large payday, however, so he grudgingly turned, replaced the hood of his sweatshirt over top of his greasy dark hair, and walked back down the street the way he had come. Ms. Stone watched him go, resting her cheek against her fist and drawing a long sigh. If they didn't pull this job off, she would remain in her crumby little apartment, struggling to make ends meet and working her thankless job in the public library.

She looked up, suddenly realizing that she was parked oddly, with her foot still on the brake of the idling car. She pulled ahead into a parking spot opposite the hospital building and slammed the gearshift into Park. Laying her forehead against the steering wheel in the dim light, she tried to think of what to do next. Her cellphone sounded, indicating that she was receiving a text. She pulled it from her purse and looked at the small backlit screen. It was the buyer. He wanted to know if things were on schedule.

This was it; things were coming to a close. She could sense it. Ms. Stone was desperate to see this sale through, as it would be her salvation from a life of hard work. She looked at the screen of her phone and read the text again. The buyer was becoming irritated at waiting. She felt a slight panic building inside of her, as she felt unable to do anything to resolve the current situation. Her eyes flared with anger and frustration as she looked at her phone. Two children were keeping her from prosperity; the life she wanted and needed. They would pay.

~~~~

Dad looked across the cafeteria table at his father after a long period of silence. They had barely spoken a word since the doctor had left Nana's room. There wasn't much to say. The two of them sat with cups of coffee in front of them, pondering their thoughts in silence. Neither of them felt like eating. The light of dawn was making the large windows at the end of the room slightly brighter, although it still seemed like night under the florescent lights of the cafeteria. Time ticked by slowly, every minute seeming like an hour. The light was always the same in here, whether it was day or night. It made the two men uncomfortable. Dad's thoughts turned to the children. He hoped that everything was fine, but there was a nagging feeling in the back of his mind that something was wrong; a mental itch that he didn't like. It was far too early to call over to Katie's house to see that everything was okay, so he tried to push the thoughts aside. He looked up at Grandpa.

"So…" he began, then paused and waited for a response.

"So, I don't know," started Grandpa irritably. "Should maybe get a second opinion. These doctors. I think maybe he's just giving up. There's got to be something more that can be done for her."

Grandpa wrung a hand after looking at his watch for the hundredth time, as though he didn't believe the time it was showing him. They were approaching the wee hours of the morning; that strange time when everything seems skewed, and the world plays tricks on your mind. Fatigue was setting in on both of them; a deep, tired feeling that could not be cured by brief naps in chairs or the numerous coffees the two men had consumed. Morning was coming, but all they wanted was closure to the situation. Even though they spoke no further words, it was clear that they only wanted to hear the doctor tell them what was happening. Dad knew that the answer would not be something that he wanted to hear, and he also knew that his father saw it the same way. All they could do was sit here, waiting.

Dad simply remained quiet. There was nothing he felt he could say, and he wanted very much to share his father's optimism. He looked down into the coffee cup, watching as the clouds formed at the top of it and feeling very tired suddenly. This ordeal all seemed like some kind of nightmare from which he could not seem to wake. Only a week ago his mother had been at home, and now this. How would he explain to the kids that Nana might no longer be around? The weekend visits, the stories, the art lessons. They would not take it well. He knew this fact. It went well beyond his powers as a father to protect his children from things that might cause them pain. He could no sooner prevent them from experiencing it than he could himself. All he could do was be there for them, hold them, and console them. But who would console him? And what about Grandpa? Would he be able to go forward, living without her beside him? He shut his eyes, breathing deeply and casting all of it aside. We will have to figure it out, he thought.

14

Valerie shuddered as she awoke in the cold of dawn. She jolted upright, suddenly coming out of the haze of slumber. The memories of what had happened earlier flooded back into her mind like a tidal wave. Looking around quickly, she saw that everything was still okay. Valerie knew that she had slept too long and that time was against them, and she rubbed her eyes, shaking off the groggy feeling of sleep.

She looked over at her brother, still sleeping peacefully, and wondered if what she had seen the night before had just been a dream. His jeans were still torn at the knee, and she could see his unblemished skin in the grey light that was filtering in through the gap in the doors. He was fine. His knee was healed.

Valerie was now fully awake. She stretched in the cool air, and then stood up. She crept to the massive wooden doors of the tunnel and peered carefully outside. Mist covered the floor of the gully in the dim light, and she could not see very far through the undergrowth. It was time to move. Valerie lingered at the doors for a moment, breathing the fresh dawn air. Life had been a lot simpler a week ago. She knew that it had been her who had pursued the Heart; her who had followed Nana's story. Alex followed her, but if it weren't for him, she never would have found it, despite everything. She watched his sleeping form, feeling grateful that he was all right.

The cool of the morning reached into her bones, making her shiver again slightly. She glanced back out the doors, listening to the morning songs of birds in the distance. Valerie thanked her lucky stars that her brother was fine, and that the Heart of the Raven had healed his knee. This adventure was not child's play anymore. She wasn't sure what she would have done if he had been harmed, but it had healed him, and they still had a job to do. Valerie thought about Nana again, sick, maybe dying. She had to get this job done. It was time to go; time to finish what they had started.

Valerie gave Alex a gentle nudge, and he opened his eyes, blinking in confusion for a moment.

"C'mon, we have to get out of here," Valerie whispered.

He nodded, yawning, and slowly stood up before grabbing his trusty backpack. Valerie tucked the cloth holding the Heart into it and zipped it closed. They were set.

Valerie pulled her dark brown hair into a ponytail and tugged her sweatshirt straight with a brief yawn, still slightly sleepy. Alex rubbed his eyes for a moment and tossed his trusty backpack onto his right shoulder. Without a word to one another, they squeezed through the wooden doors and out into the brisk dawn air, then stepped through the leaf-litter at the bottom of the gully. Gingerly, they made their way through the undergrowth.

The air was still but cold in the dim light of dawn as they made their way through the trees. The land sloped slowly upward, and after a few more minutes of walking, the two emerged onto the rough stones of the railway roadbed. Valerie knew it was a short walk down the tracks to the crossing at Ormond Street right next to the hospital, and she pulled Alex forward, stepping between the rails to head in that direction. It was certainly easier than walking through the brush, and the two children hurried along in the grey light, able to see better now. As they went, the crushed stone between the ties crunched under their feet, and the occasional rock that Alex kicked made a metallic sound as it bounced off the inside of the rail. Valerie felt a little more confident as the sky lightened, knowing it would be easier to keep an eye out for Robert and Ms. Stone. She turned to Alex as they walked.

"So your knee is okay?" she asked.

"Yeah," he affirmed. "It's like it never happened."

"What did it feel like when the Heart was glowing?"

"It was hurting real bad, then it started to tingle kind of, and then there was nothing, no more pain!" explained Alex.

Valerie walked along, pondering this statement and looking down at the tracks. They were almost at the road crossing when the red lights began to flash and the bell began to ring. There was a train coming. The children turned to look behind them and were blinded by the bright headlight of a freight train coming down the track toward them. It sounded its horn several times, the blasts almost deafening. The two of them scrambled off the track and up onto the sidewalk beside the crossing before making a fast dash across the street toward the hospital lawn and parking lot while the gates were down for the train.

Valerie looked up at the locomotive as the train went through, its steel wheels emitting a metallic scream against the rails. She could see the engineer clearly, and he was looking down at the two children and shaking his head at them. Valerie knew it was dangerous to be around the tracks, but it had helped them get to the hospital without being caught. She also knew that her father would be very upset if he knew what they were doing. As they ran up the lawn toward the huge sliding glass doors of the main entrance, they failed to notice the rusty cream-coloured car parked nearby. Ms. Stone was watching as they entered the hospital.

~~~~

Valerie felt safer under the bright lights of the lobby and reception area, even though there were very few people around at this hour. She hurried Alex along down the wide main corridor, and smiled briefly at him after nodding toward a lone security guard enjoying a coffee as he flipped through the day's newspaper. They were here at last, and Valerie felt confident. Soon they would be with Nana, and the Heart would heal her. Everything could go back to the way it used to be.

The two of them turned down a narrower hallway with a green line painted down the middle of the polished floor. It was very quiet this morning, and Valerie and Alex tried to be silent as they hurried along. The two always enjoyed a ride in the elevator where they pushed the buttons for every floor, an action that usually drew a frustrated sigh from anyone else who had the misfortune of being on board. They turned the corner and entered another hallway, following the faded green paint on the floor. Around the middle of this hallway they slid to a stop, and Alex pushed the call button for the elevator. While they stood, Valerie tapped her foot as her brother made strange faces at her in the highly polished stainless steel doors.

Finally a small bell sounded, and the doors of the elevator gave a mechanical "thunk" as they opened. Despite the fact that Alex took great joy in pushing the button for each floor once again, the ride to the third floor did not take very long. Valerie watched the floor numbers progress in the panel above the buttons until the bell sounded and the doors opened wide.

Valerie looked up and stepped to the door of the elevator, Alex right beside her. She stopped suddenly, and put an arm out to halt her younger brother as well. Alex's eyes became wide as he looked straight ahead down the hallway. Emerging from the stairway door at the end of the hall was

Robert. He locked eyes with the children, paused as he took a split second to register that it was them, and then began forward as fast as he could with an angry scowl on his face. The children both gasped, and Valerie dragged Alex backward into the elevator car again while slapping at the buttons to close the doors. They seemed to take forever, and she began to panic, rapidly pressing the button as if it would help the process along. Robert was almost there when the doors closed with a "clunk," and then the elevator was in motion. Valerie exhaled deeply.

"How did he find us?" she asked out loud in disbelief. Alex shrugged, his eyes still as wide as saucers.

"I don't know, but let's lose him and get to Nana!"

The doors opened and the kids peeked out cautiously, looking back and forth before exiting and rounding another corner in order to avoid the stairwell. They were back on the first floor, and Valerie hurried along with her brother in tow as she looked for the security guard they had spotted earlier. He was not where they had first seen him; probably making his rounds, she thought quickly. They turned back just in time to see Robert crash forward from the stairway door down the hall. He lurched toward them, and the two children darted down another hallway past a line of wheelchairs.

Valerie knew they were headed toward the emergency department, and hoped that at least it would be busier there. Robert was less likely to do anything drastic with people around. They flew past the cafeteria, not noticing the two men sitting near the back wall having coffee in silence. But the children were certainly noticed by them, and Valerie heard someone call her name as she ran. They didn't pause, pushing open the double doors marked "EMERGENCY" instead.

Once inside, the two stopped in their tracks. The security guard stood talking to a policeman; the same officer who had been at their home several days before. The two turned as the children burst through the doors, and a spark of recognition appeared on the police officer's face as he looked at Valerie. She didn't even get a word out, and was barely able to point behind them while trying to catch her breath. Robert came through the doors in a rage, his face red and twisted with anger. His expression changed, however, upon seeing the police officer. He turned around quickly, and the two men lunged forward to give chase as Robert crashed through the doors again in an attempt to get away. He didn't count on the two men on the other side of those doors, however. Robert ran right into Valerie and Alex's father, bouncing back and landing in a heap on the polished floor. The policeman charged through, grabbed the sweater Robert was wearing, and pulled the hoodie off roughly. He grinned at Dad.

"Look familiar?" he said.

It took the children's father a moment to recognize the young man from the computer screen on the day of the break-in at the house. He glared at Robert as Grandpa looked at them, totally bewildered.

"I - I didn't do anything!" Robert yelled.

"You didn't, huh? How about 'Breaking and Entering,' 'Destruction of Property,' 'Criminal Mischief,' and whatever else I can think up, punk?" replied the officer angrily.

Robert didn't bother answering. He glared at the children as the policeman gruffly thrust his hands behind his back and handcuffed him.

"And don't forget 'Theft'!" said Valerie. Alex held up the cloth-covered crystal, producing it from his backpack and exposing it for them to see.

"Didn't do anything, eh?" the cop repeated to Robert as he and the security guard led him away.

The look on Dad's face told Valerie and Alex everything. There was a lot of explaining to do, and they were in big trouble.

"I want to know exactly what is going on here, young lady," Dad began with a very serious tone in his voice.

Valerie could tell that he was not happy about the fact that it was plain that she had deceived him about staying at Katie's. He gave her the look; the one she knew meant that she was in deep trouble. Her mind raced, trying to find the words to tell him about everything that was happening.

"Dad, I can explain all of this, but first we have to get up to see Nana. Everything depends on it!" she replied meekly.

15

Back on the third floor again, the children went into Nana's room. Dad and Grandpa came in too, taking their respective places in the chairs on which they had been sitting all night. It was dark in the room, except for the one fluorescent light above their grandmother's bed. The children paused for a moment, not wanting to wake her. Valerie stepped forward, not able to contain herself, and hoping that what they had found would somehow help her grandmother.

Nana woke as Valerie and Alex came to the side of the bed. She turned her head toward them and managed a feeble smile. Valerie took her grandmother's hand and sat on the edge of the bed. It seemed cold to her, and she glanced around at the various tubes and monitors connected to her Nana. Alex set down his backpack and rummaged through his collection of stuff until he found a comic book he had been reading. He laid it on Nana's table beside the bed.

"I saved you something to read while you are here, Nana," he said very quietly, as if he might be disturbing her. At this gesture, Grandpa had to look away, for he thought he might begin to cry and he didn't want the children to see him become emotional.

Nana's smile widened as she looked at Alex. She coughed weakly, and Grandpa started to rise to get her water glass, but she waved him off. She looked back at Valerie.

"It's awfully early for you two to be here; what's going on, guys?" she asked.

Valerie took her hand again.

"We've got it, Nana," she said excitedly. "It's here; it will fix everything for you!"

Her grandmother pulled Valerie in for a hug.

"Oh Valerie, Sweetie-heart, it's just an old story. There's not any way to fix me."

Valerie stepped back from the bed with a little smirk and a raised eyebrow. Alex went back into his backpack and pulled out the cloth-wrapped crystal bird. He handed it to his sister.

"Soon you'll see what it can do, Nana… it's real!" she said, handing the cloth to her grandmother.

Valerie held her breath as Nana took the gem from her hand. She watched her grandmother as it settled into her palm, waiting. It had to help her, she thought. Valerie whispered a silent prayer as Nana examined the cloth-covered crystal, curious as to what her granddaughter was giving her. Nana had a look of slight disbelief on her face as she looked at the cloth in her hand.

As Nana unfolded the cloth, the Heart instantly began to glow, building in brilliance with a light so intense it shone right through the protective cloth wrapping. Nana's mouth was agape as she gently pulled the purple crystal from its hiding place and rolled it over in her hands. Purple and pink light bathed the entire room, and even Dad and Grandpa looked in awe at the Heart as its brilliance reached an almost blinding intensity. It glowed like a miniature purple sun in Nana's hand, shooting arcs of lightning into the air around it. Pink flares of light danced down her arm and onto her bed sheets, tracing patterns where they landed.

Valerie could hear the faint, rhythmic sound of ancient drums. The Heart seemed to be alive, and its beauty and intensity were impossible not to look at. They all stared into its purple light, mesmerized by it as it pulsed and glowed. All Nana could do was hold it and gaze into the depths of its light. At last it began to fade, slowly dimming until there was only the crystal, shining in the low light of the hospital room.

No one spoke for what seemed like an eternity. Valerie waited for her grandmother to say something, smiling as she watched her astounded expression. Alex had a big grin on his face as well. Nana finally set the crystal bird down in her lap and lay back deep into her pillow. She turned and looked at her grandchildren, still wearing an expression of disbelief. She finally returned their smiles.

As Nana fell back asleep after a few more minutes, she still had a trace of a smile on her lips, and a peaceful expression that she had not had in years, without the creases caused by pain. Dad and Grandpa were speechless, and were still trying to figure out what they had just witnessed. Whatever it was, it was certainly not something one saw every day, they knew. The two looked at one another with questioning looks, wondering if they should believe any of the events they had just witnessed.

~~~~

The morning sun streamed through the windows of the television room as everyone waited for the doctor to finish examining Nana once again. Uncle Jason had finally arrived, and had brought fresh coffee and some donuts for Valerie and Alex. Grandpa had ultimately succumbed to sleep and was resting his cheek in his hand against a wall, and Dad looked equally exhausted. It had been a very long time since they had heard any news about Nana.

The television played an early morning cartoon, and people and patients shuffled here and there in the hallway. It was a much busier place now that morning had arrived. A couple of people stopped by the television room - an old man in a wheelchair, a lady who had just delivered a baby - all of whom looked just as bored as the rest of them. Time had once again slowed to a crawl, and Valerie was thankful for the cartoons to occupy her mind while they waited, even though her thoughts kept drifting back to her grandmother. Jorden had shown up by now as well, boyfriend in tow. It was like a family event, but for all the wrong reasons. It was a rarity to have everyone together, as the family had become quite spread out over the last few years.

The doctor finally appeared carrying charts and folders, and everyone dropped what they were doing and turned their attention toward him. Valerie stood up suddenly, anxious to hear about Nana's condition. Jorden roused Grandpa, and he jerked awake in mid snore, sputtering as he looked around and confused until he spotted the doctor. Dad picked up the remote for the television and lowered its volume, and suddenly everything became quiet. Everyone in the room was still, waiting for the young man in the white coat to speak. He seemed a bit nervous, shuffling the papers in the folder he held and clearing his throat as he shifted his weight from one leg to the other. He looked up briefly at the group before returning his gaze to some x-rays in his other hand. He was obviously unprepared to speak to all of them.

"Well, doctor?" Valerie said impatiently, ignoring a jab from both Alex and Jorden.

Dad stood up slowly. He was prepared to hear what the doctor was about to say, but was still wound up tightly.

"Just tell us, please," he began. "I think everyone here is prepared for what you have come to say." He looked around at the rest of the group sitting anxiously in anticipation. This would not be a happy day, he thought.

The doctor paused for one more moment, unsure of how to say what it was he needed to convey. He flipped pages and shook his head slightly. He let out a brief sigh. Nothing could have prepared him for what was happening.

"Just tell us," murmured Grandpa. His face had become sullen and sad.

The children waited for the words to come. Valerie reached for the security of her older sister's hand, and, feeling her younger brother clinging to her like a sponge and sucked right in tightly beside her on the couch of the television room, she patted his hand reassuringly. The seconds seemed to last an eternity. She felt ready to burst with emotion.

The doctor finally gave one last exhale, absently grabbed a pen from his pocket, and used it to trace along the paper as he read what it said. He spoke quietly, evenly, trying to maintain his composure.

"It seems that, um, some strange results were acquired in this morning's diagnostic imaging… The anomalies have regressed to the point of… Uh…"

"In English, Doc!" said Dad quickly, startling the doctor. He felt bad for doing it immediately, as he could see that the young man was already a bit shaken up.

"Right," he began again. "To put it plainly, your mother displays absolutely none of the cancer in her body that we detected previously." He flopped the images of the x-rays onto the coffee table in front of Dad. Valerie began to display a very wide grin. Her heart leapt, and she could feel her eyes misting up uncontrollably.

"Well, are you sure about this?" said Dad, picking up the x-rays.

"Very," replied the doctor. "We ran the test three times because we thought there was a problem with the equipment."

"Can you do some more tests to confirm this?" Dad asked.

The children sat forward, both with smiles as big as could be on their faces, awaiting his response.

The doctor shrugged with an apathetic look and another sigh. "She won't let us."

"What do you mean? My mother is sick; just take her down and do it again!" Dad began, raising his voice slightly in irritation.

The doctor extended his hands to signify he could do no more. It was obvious to the group that he had said about all that he was able to say.

"Maybe you had best go and see for yourself…"

16

Ms. Stone watched the police bring Robert out of the emergency entrance doors, kicking and fighting. She had gotten rid of her car, sensing that something was wrong. It would not be spotted where it was. She had parked several streets over, and walked back from a side street.

The woman now sat in the glassed-in enclosure of a bus stop, observing the scene across the street. She was desperately trying to think of a plan, one that would get her inside, close to those meddling children, so that she could regain her prize. Had Robert told the cops about her? Could she slip into the hospital somehow without being noticed? It was doubtful at this point. Maybe if she appeared as a patient somehow... Ms. Stone knew she would gain nothing by trying to sneak in and jump on a gurney, but there had to be a way to get in and not be recognized. Somewhere within the hospital building was the Heart: her salvation from a life thrust upon her, and a means of paying for all of her dreams.

The officers put Robert in the back of a cruiser and slammed the door shut with a finality that told her he was going away for a while. The car fired to life and left the platform that was normally reserved for ambulances and emergency personnel only. As she watched them pull away, she breathed a sigh of relief. She realized at that moment that she would no longer have to worry about splitting the proceeds from her deal; it would all be hers. Once the police car was gone, she looked around the emergency exit for any sign of the children. Nothing. They were in there; she could feel it.

She watched from the cold bench of the bus stop as people came and went to and from the hospital. An old man emerged from the main entrance, wheeling his wheelchair out to enjoy the early morning sun. As Ms. Stone watched him, a new idea struck her. She could go in as a patient, she realized as she spotted empty wheelchairs sitting just inside the sliding doors of the main entrance. That was it.

Her plan began to form in her mind. She got up quickly and headed across the street and up onto the walkway leading to the hospital main entrance, keeping her head down to prevent anyone from seeing her face. She passed several people milling about outside the large glass doors and kept on the move. Only one thing was on her mind as she glanced up, avoiding eye contact with the people she passed: the Heart. She had to get it back. It was her way out of all of this; her way back to a life of comfort. A way to get back what had been taken from her.

Once inside, she followed a sign leading off the lobby and down a narrow hallway that read, "LAUNDRY". Ms. Stone moved quickly, finding the main room of the laundry facility to be abandoned. She threw on a plain blue gown that covered her clothes and made her look like a patient. She strode back out into the hall and claimed the first empty wheelchair she found, shedding her shoes to make her disguise complete. Ms. Stone wheeled herself along, keeping her head down. It wasn't a very large hospital, and finding those two children would not be hard.

~~~~

Valerie opened the door to Nana's hospital room with Alex and the rest of the group close behind. The lights were still dim, and Valerie walked toward the windows on the far side of the room. Grabbing the soft fabric of the curtains, Valerie pulled them open, bringing the sun into the darkened room. She turned and looked toward Nana's bed. It was empty. Valerie took in a large breath and peered around for her grandmother. The rest of the group now entered the room and gazed at the empty bed with confused looks. Valerie examined Nana's bedside table: a book, her half-finished breakfast, and a tea that still had steam rising from its surface. Nana was nowhere to be found. What had happened to her?

Suddenly, the door to the room opened again and Nana walked in, her hospital gown drawn around her. She looked at them in surprise. All they could do was stare at her, wondering what exactly was going on. She simply smiled back at them.

"Well?" she asked. "When are we getting out of here?"

Everyone was silent for a moment, stunned into speechlessness. Valerie and Alex beamed, barely able to contain themselves. Then Alex went over and hugged his grandmother. Dad and Grandpa simply stared, unable to believe what they were seeing. How was this possible? It was as if they had dreamt the whole thing. Grandpa shook his head slightly in disbelief. Nana looked around at them once again, becoming irritated by the lack of an answer.

"Well?" she repeated. "Is anyone going to answer me or not?"

At this statement she placed her hands on her hips, while Alex continued his hug and the others just stared with open mouths. Finally, Valerie spoke up.

"I knew it would work; I told you it would work!" she said excitedly, practically jumping up and down as she spoke.

"I don't understand; how is this possible?" said Dad slowly. He looked at his mother in disbelief. It was as if the entire illness had never happened.

Nana simply shrugged, giving Valerie a quick wink and grinning slightly. Alex finally released his grip on his grandmother and smiled up at her, and then at the rest of the group.

"She's better," he said simply.

Everyone in the room continued to stare in sheer disbelief, amazed at what they were seeing before them. Valerie stepped forward with her brother toward Nana and took hold of her grandmother's hand.

"It was the Heart of the Raven; it worked!" she said. "It really does heal sickness and hurt!"

Nana only smiled down at her. But the children could easily see the difference in her. The lines of pain and fatigue had disappeared from her face, making her look years younger, and there was almost a glow in her eyes, as if Nana's strength and energy had been renewed. Even her stance seemed slightly straighter.

"Where is the Heart, anyway?" asked Nana. "I would like to get a good look at it now that I feel better!"

Alex suddenly stiffened as he realized that he did not have his precious backpack attached to him. During all this commotion, he had left it in the television room. Without a word, he turned on his heel and darted out of the room and down the hall. Valerie looked around, noticing that everyone else still seemed to be in a state of shock. She had a big grin on her face as she remembered the glow from the crystal as Nana had held it only hours before. Her thoughts drifted to Sparks the pug, the toad, and finally to Alex's injured knee. The Heart really could do what the stories said it could. She had seen all of it with her own eyes; watched the crystal glow with its strange fire, and then witnessed the results. The thoughts warmed her from inside, and she sighed slightly, knowing that her grandmother would be okay. Her musings were suddenly interrupted by her father's voice.

"This is unbelievable," he said with awe. "How is this possible?"

Dad remembered what Nana had been like in years past, when he and his brother were younger, and their mother would tell them stories about the area or legends that were too strange to believe. She would take them on hikes and teach them how to identify plants in the forests just north of the family home. Halloween had always been a fun time, with Nana dressing up in a flamboyant witch's costume each year to scare local children who came to their door for tricks or treats. His mother pulled out all the stops at Christmas as well, insisting on having a huge, real tree to decorate each season, much to Grandpa's apparent aggravation. Christmas at home held warm memories for Dad, filled with decorations and the sweet smells of baked goods as Nana toiled for endless hours in the kitchen. Standing before him now, she looked every bit as healthy as she had years ago, instead of like the frail, coughing old woman from recent days.

Alex suddenly burst back into the room with a look of sheer panic on his round face. He looked at Valerie with both hope and terror, as if she might be able to magically fix whatever the unspoken problem was. Her little brother was on the verge of an explosion, and whatever the situation was, it could not be good.

"Someone took my backpack!" he exclaimed breathlessly.

Valerie's jaw dropped open in disbelief as the suddenly obvious thought flooded her brain. The Heart of the Raven was in there.

17

Ms. Stone wheeled herself down the hallway quickly, but not quickly enough to attract unwanted attention. To anyone passing by, she looked like any other patient wheeling along with a well-worn backpack on her lap. It had taken a little while to get used to the wheelchair. She was breathing in short, quick breaths, and trying to remain calm and focused as she headed for the elevator.

She had it. An evil grin formed on her thin lips. She would not lose it this time. Her goal was very close now, and she rolled toward it, trying to stay unnoticed and pretending in her own mind to be invisible. Soon she would meet the buyer. She could envision it: handing the crystal bird over for a large amount of cash, an exchange that would transform her life. Ms. Stone knew that within the tattered backpack lay her salvation, and no matter what happened, she had to get out of here with it.

It had been a combination of perfect timing and blind luck that the young boy had forgotten his pack in the television room while she had watched from a nook down the hallway. It had been easy to wait for everybody to leave the room, roll by, and grab it off the end table, before zipping it open to see that her prize was inside and exiting without anyone being the wiser.

She rolled forward, her hands now more comfortable on the hard rubber wheels of the chair. Dodging a gurney, she kept moving, closing the distance to the elevator. Suddenly, her chair was hit from the side, and she spun around as a frantic nurse tried to stop the bed she was rolling from one of the rooms.

"I'm sorry, are you all right?" asked the nurse in a startled voice.

"I'm fine. It's okay," replied Ms. Stone, keeping her head down.

She was facing the opposite direction now, back toward the television room - the scene of her crime. There were two things she did not want to see; two things that could ruin everything, could destroy all her hard work and planning for a better life. These two things now came into view, rounding the corner at the end of the hall and looking straight at her. Valerie and Alex. She tried to drop her head and avoid their gazes, but it was too late. They recognized her, and she knew it.

Panic set in and she spun the chair around, clattering against the bed that had hit her and speeding forward. She could hear the children shouting and running behind her and cursed under her breath as she pushed hard to spin the wheels of the chair. She considered ditching the wheelchair for a moment, and just running with her prize. But she pushed forward, and people leapt out of her way. She quickly realized that it might be an advantage to have the chair, and she pushed harder on the wheels, surging ahead.

The elevator was close now, and as she sailed past the nurse's station, the familiar "bing" sounded and the doors opened. An old man in a gown, steadying himself on an IV unit, emerged from the elevator. He barely had time to clear the doors and move quickly aside as Ms. Stone wheeled in, almost spinning to a stop in the small space inside. As she hit the button for the main lobby, she turned to face the two children, still too far away to prevent her escape. As the doors closed, she gave a slight grin and clutched Alex's backpack close to her.

The clunk of the doors seemed to solidify her escape, and she breathed heavily, trying to settle herself down a bit. They were just children, after all; what could they really do to her? Especially if she could pass off the patient-in-a-chair idea when she reached the lobby. If they were to make any move there, she would simply holler that they were accosting her, and security would certainly grab the children first. Her mind raced as she watched the lighted numbers descend. Gripping the backpack firmly, Ms. Stone readied herself to launch out of the elevator the second the doors opened wide enough. Should she ditch the chair? No, appear as the helpless patient for now, and then run when you get outside, she thought feverishly.

The elevator seemed to move agonizingly slowly, and she knew that every second counted. Finally the loud "bing" sounded, and the elevator lurched to a stop at the main level, the doors clunking sluggishly open. Ms. Stone wasted no time, practically forcing the wheelchair out of the opening and wheeling forward into the lobby. The doorway from the stairwell down the main hall to her left burst open, but she barely waited long enough to see the two children's faces before wheeling to her right, away from them and toward the main entrance.

She could hear them behind her in pursuit as she pushed hard toward the glass doors that led outside. She knew she would make it; she had what she had come for, and the children would not stop her. They were just young and stupid, after all. No one would believe their crazy story anyway, and she would escape with her prize. She was almost there, almost free. The young boy behind her who was yelling at her to stop entered her consciousness as she drove ahead, cradling the backpack in her lap. The Heart was inside, she could sense it, feel it...

Valerie and Alex gave chase, dodging people as they ran down the main corridor toward the lobby. Unfortunately, as they passed the cafeteria, they came face to face with the security guard.

"Whoa, kids!" he commanded. "Slow down, there is no need to run here."

"That lady stole my backpack!" said Alex between large breaths.

"Really!" exclaimed Valerie upon seeing the guard raise an eyebrow after a quick glance toward the woman in the wheelchair. He turned back toward the lobby and the "patient" wheeling toward the main entrance.

"Ma'am!" he called toward her in a loud voice. She didn't respond, but continued toward the doors instead. The children watched as Ms. Stone kept rolling, despite the security guard's assertion to stop. Valerie thought feverishly about what to do, her mind racing as she ran toward the entrance, ignoring the shouts of the guard just as Ms. Stone was doing. Everything became a blur - a mess of shouts and motion in her senses.

Suddenly a point of focus materialized as a man stepped through the glass doors of the main entrance, right in front of the wheelchair rolling toward it. The man instinctively grabbed the arms on the chair to prevent Ms. Stone from slamming into him, stopping it suddenly and holding it firmly. Valerie gasped as she recognized the tall, dark figure who had stopped Ms. Stone in her tracks. It was Mr. Thatch. He glanced up at the children as they came to a screeching halt, the rubber of the soles of their running shoes squeaking against the polished floor of the lobby. He levelled his gaze at Valerie and held her eyes in his for what seemed like minutes. Then he turned his stare to Ms. Stone.

"You have something here that doesn't belong to you," he said in a serious tone.

"What are you talking about?" she stammered. "Let go of me, I haven't done anything wrong!"

She grabbed hold of the backpack on her lap, and her hand was caught and held firmly by his. He didn't change his expression, and held on as she fought to free herself from his grasp.

"You will give back what is not yours to possess," he said quietly, holding her gaze as well as her arm. She stared at him with anger burning in her eyes. He produced his cellphone from a pocket in his jacket and tilted the screen so she could see it. Her eyes widened as she read the text conversation on it and realized that it was her very own messages to the buyer for the Heart. There could be only one explanation, and she glared back up at him. He was the buyer. She began to fight harder to free herself from his grasp, pulling away and hitting at him with her free arm. The security guard, followed by the children, ran up and saw the commotion. Mr. Thatch remained very calm, despite the approach of security and the struggles of Ms. Stone.

"My sister suffers from dementia," he began smoothly, looking up at the guard. "She has had a brain injury that causes her to do and say very strange things."

Ms. Stone glared at him momentarily, wondering what he thought he was doing. She began to shout at him even though he still held her fast.

"Let me go, you idiot!" she yelled. "Guard, I don't know this man! Get him away from me!"

"Ma'am, do you have some ID that we can see? Is it in your room perhaps?" asked the security guard in a firm voice.

Mr. Thatch fought to control Ms. Stone and keep her from injuring herself or others. She struggled in the chair, still fighting against him.

Suddenly she stopped as she realized with horror that she had left all of her things out in the car, and to admit it would certainly get her in more trouble. She looked back up at Mr. Thatch, and then at the children. Valerie had the trace of a grin on her lips, and although it enraged her and she could feel the blood pounding in her ears, Ms. Stone did her best not to betray her emotions. She would have to be clever to escape this predicament. But she wasn't even given the chance. Mr. Thatch knew better than to allow her any time to think the situation through.

"Last time she did this, it caused a huge problem; there were old people injured, and it took several orderlies to subdue her and get her back to her room!"

The guard stepped forward, satisfied that he was being told the truth. He grabbed hold of the wheelchair, and instantly Ms. Stone began to fight harder, cursing at them and throwing herself back and forth in the chair in an attempt to get free. Valerie and Alex stepped back slightly as the two men fought to keep Ms. Stone still.

"I don't think she has been given her medication today," said Mr. Thatch calmly.

"Nurse!" called the security guard. "Nurse! We need some help here!"

Quickly several people rushed forward to help restrain the crazed woman in the wheelchair. A young nurse advanced, trying to calm the woman. This action only made Ms. Stone yell louder, spouting obscenities and fighting hard against her assailants. It was no use, however; despite her angry denials, the nurse, along with an orderly, managed to subdue her. Ms. Stone eventually sank back in the wheelchair with an angry look on her face.

Everyone calmed down, and Mr. Thatch lifted the tattered backpack off her lap as the orderlies began to wheel Ms. Stone away. He turned to Alex and Valerie with a subtle smile, holding the pack out for them. Alex took it from him gently and swung it up onto his shoulder. Valerie watched them thoughtfully.

"You're not here to take the Heart away, like everyone else?" she inquired.

"The story of what you carry has been in my people's history for a very long time," Mr. Thatch began. "But you two finding it fulfills a prophecy foretold by my ancestors a millennia ago."

Valerie looked up at him. There was a softness in his voice as he spoke again.

"I must trust that this prophecy will see you do what is right for all…"

~~~~

The Heart of the Raven sat glistening in its glass display case and illuminated brightly from above by halogen lighting. Immediately beside it sat the geode. The smooth globe of its outer surface rested on a pedestal for display, showing its insides of amethyst crystals, as if divined by nature itself to cradle and protect the Heart. The page from the book that Valerie had finally surrendered also rested here in the glass case, placed carefully back into the old history book and detailing the story and the riddle of the Heart's location. It all looked beautiful. In front, a large plaque told the story of the Heart, and the legend surrounding it. Around the room, various pieces of native art hung on the mahogany wall panels, lit from above.

Valerie and Alex stood nearby, dressed very well and practically beaming with pride. Valerie wore a navy blue dress, and Alex looked very handsome in a sport jacket and tie. The two glanced at each other with sheepish grins, doing their best to keep straight faces as the mayor of the city gave a brief speech. It was all a blur to the children, and they kept their eyes on Dad, Nana, and Grandpa in the front of the gathering to keep themselves from getting the giggles. They stood at the forefront of the new exhibit of the museum, proud but a little unnerved. After more speeches, the curator of the museum finally presented Valerie and Alex with an overly large pair of silver scissors, and together they cut in two a large red ribbon strung in front of the display.

Valerie wondered if anyone in the room really knew what they were looking at, what this ceremony was all about, and how important this ancient native artifact was. As people came forward to view the Heart in its case, she and Alex looked on, remembering what they had seen it do. They were surrounded by people who were busily moving around the room, and everyone was well dressed for the unveiling of this new exhibit. The children were overwhelmed with questions and congratulations. Dad came forward with Nana and stood behind them so that the two children felt a little more secure. Valerie stood looking at the Heart sitting in its display. It emitted nothing like the brilliant fire of pink and purple light that she had seen before. Suddenly she felt a sadness creep over her. Was this it? Was this the destiny of this artifact? She could not reason it out in her mind. If it could do so much good, why should it stay locked up in this dreary existence?

An old woman approached the display, hunched and crippled, and leaning heavily on her cane. Her son, a man in his forties himself, helped her. Valerie watched as the woman marvelled at the crystal, and then it began to glow. Valerie and Alex gasped, and the people gathered around the exhibit exclaimed in awe at the sight of the light that emanated from the Heart. The children realized quickly that these people thought that it was a trick put on by the museum to highlight the crystal bird in its display. They obviously thought it was all part of the act! All but one person.

Valerie turned her gaze back to the old woman, who straightened herself up as the pain disappeared from her expression. She had a look of surprise on her face as she caught Valerie's gaze. Valerie simply grinned slightly, now realizing why the Heart should be right where it was. It could still do good, but here, it was safe from those who only wanted to profit from it. She turned as she felt eyes upon her. Mr. Thatch. He stood quietly at the edge of the room, watching. He smiled at Valerie. It was a part of him too, she knew. She felt warm, and secure. The Heart of the Raven had been located, and had finally found a home where it could be seen, safe from harm. The ancient native prophecy had now come full circle. As the light from the Heart faded, Valerie and Alex looked back at Nana. She smiled at them and shot them a quick wink. The adventure was at its end, and the children had found what they had set out to uncover. The Heart of the Raven.

~~~~

A week later, the children were once again in Nana's studio, while Dad worked. Alex was back to the easel, while Valerie sat at the large drafting table. Nana had just completed the framing on her latest sketch, and held it up for them to see with a satisfied grin. The children loved this place, filled with art and books. It was a very relaxed spot for them, where they could create anything, and hear stories from history, or just explore something interesting that Nana had tucked away amongst the paintings and photos.

It was now much cooler outside, and the warmth of the studio was both inviting and comforting as the children relaxed and worked on their artwork. Grandpa was back in the living room watching television, and it was as if time had skipped back several weeks. The sun shone through the large front windows, throwing bright light onto the area rug on the concrete floor of the studio, warm and radiant despite the chill in the air outside. Fall was present, and the world outside was preparing for the approach of winter. The leaves had already begun to turn, and were displaying their changing colours.

Valerie sat with a fresh piece of paper in front of her and pastels of every colour at her side. The page was still completely blank, as Valerie was lost in thought about the Heart, their adventure, and all of the events that had led them to where they were today. She began to draw it, trying to recreate the vibrant glow of the crystal. Her hands moved quickly with the pastels as she sketched the bird-like artifact from her memory. She sighed slightly, not happy with it. There was no way she could make it look like the radiant object she had seen. She set down the pastel in her hand, her thoughts going back to the first time she had seen the crystal begin to glow. She turned and looked at what Alex was doing. He was slopping paint onto a large sheet of paper, but Valerie recognized instantly what he was trying to depict. It was the injured toad from the bushes they had found. Alex had surrounded it with pink and purple, as though it was being healed from its injury. Valerie smiled. It was quite an adventure they had been on. Her smile faded suddenly, as she realized that it was over.

Nana was watching Valerie without her knowledge. She grinned slightly to herself and went to one of the bookcases to retrieve her scrapbook. Valerie lifted her eyes to the old leather-bound book of pictures and newspaper clippings. Her grandmother set it on the table beside Valerie and opened the crinkling pages. Reaching into a drawer in the table, she pulled out a clipping that looked quite new compared to the yellowed pages of the scrapbook. It was a recent article, one with a picture of Valerie and Alex, telling the story of how the two children had followed the clues to discover an ancient native artifact called the Heart of the Raven. Valerie beamed when she saw it. Nana glued it onto a fresh page as Alex came closer to watch, too. It was a perfect end to an ancient story. Dad had also saved the article from the newspaper, and posted it on the fridge in the kitchen at home, where the kids could see it every day.

"So what are you going to draw today, Miss Valerie?" asked Nana, smoothing the new page out.

"Not sure," she said. "Maybe I'll do a sketch of a Raven in flight…"

"That would be very cool!" said Alex.

"It will keep me from thinking about the fact that the whole thing is pretty well over with," she said with a trace of sadness.

Nana grinned as she looked at her grandchildren over the tops of her glasses. She flipped back several pages and raised an eyebrow.

"Well…" she began slowly, her smile widening. "There is this other old story that I have here…"

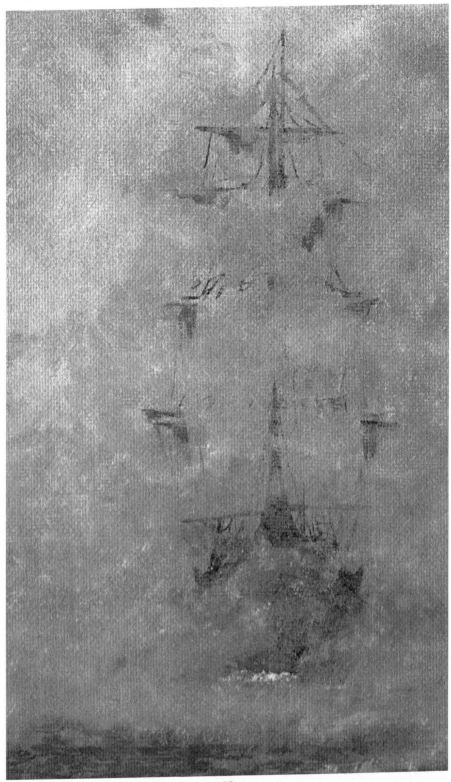

Part Two:
The Lost Channel

1

The rigging on the barge was near its breaking point, as cold waves broke over top of the bow, the spray icy and cold in the spring air. The river was always cold right up until late July or early August, and even then, swimmers found it only just bearable. Conrad wiped the moisture from his thin grey hair, his matching ice grey eyes narrowing against the rain. Steadying himself on the barge, he looked at the lines going down into the dark water off the bow, holding up a hand to shield his eyes against the wind and spray. His red Mustang rain suit was dripping with the constant assault of the river, and he wished that the weather would settle a little bit until he could retrieve his prize. His divers had found an old cannon and Conrad hoped it would be in good enough condition to determine which ship it had once belonged to. But the wind did not want to co-operate, making the retrieval risky and difficult.

Sixty feet below the surface, the cannon hung in the dimly lit waters, suspended on thick ropes from a crane on the deck of the barge. Everything swayed, straining in the rough waters. He couldn't remember how long he had been after the secrets of this hunt, but he had certainly invested a lot of time in research over the recent miserable winter.

Conrad cursed the lashing rain, wishing he could magically make it all go away, at least until after he had retrieved the cannon. The powers that be seemed to ignore his silent request, tossing the barge around in the river and pelting it with cold rain. If the treasure had been found in July, chances were good that the water would have been calm and smooth as a mirror! But, as fate would have it, the April weather and his first chance to resume the salvage of his prize had brought him and his crew to this struggle. He wanted that piece -the piece of the puzzle that could lead him to an ultimate payday. He would risk injury, both to himself or his men, to retrieve this prize that promised both fortune and fame.

Conrad Buell stared down into the dark waters, watching the taught ropes strain and groan against the weight they held. If he could just get this piece on the deck, he might at least know if he had followed the right path, found the right location in the river.

The wind suddenly gusted and he was forced to grab onto something to hold himself upright. The rigging strained and a line suddenly snapped. The operator in the crane tried to relieve the pressure by easing off, and Conrad, seeing the man's panic, screamed at him to hold the lines tight. He knew if the remaining lines went slack and then were jerked upward in these rough waters, they would surely snap under the pressure.

Rain continued to lash at his face and he wiped the water away from his eyes as he squinted to see the rigging off the bow. It stretched, giving off a creaking sound, as the main ropes began to stretch to their limits. Water droplets flew from the rigging. The barge surged upward in the waves and the first tether rope snapped. Conrad watched, helpless, as a chain reaction began. Each of the main ropes failed in turn as they took on the full load, and the deck heaved with the storm and strain of the massive cargo submerged in the waters. Conrad gritted his teeth, watching the chaos unfold. It was a nightmare to him, his dream was slipping away... again.

The final rope unraveled before his eyes, the last strand snapping under the strain. The arm of the crane lurched upward with the release of pressure, making the barge shift in the rough waters. Conrad and several of the men onboard fell to the deck, scrambling for some kind of handhold. There was a splash as several pieces of equipment fell over the side. Conrad watched as the final rope slid off the deck of the barge, disappearing into the dark waters of the river. The cannon was gone, and his prize was no closer. He screamed at the men on board who were simply trying to hold onto anything solid.

He stood up again and braced himself against the crane. The storm blew on, whitecaps rising on the waves in the channel for as far as the eye could see, the rain obscuring nearby islands, the pines only barely visible through the torrents of water and mist. Watching the black waters ahead of the barge, Conrad put a hand on his head, trying to block the thoughts of this failure. The rain hammered down on the deck, winds whipping the waves against the barge. It was over, and he would have to wait. Again.

~~~~

Nana was at it again. She showed Valerie and Alex a clipping in her scrapbook of a British Man o' War, referred to as a brig-sloop, which had become lost in the St. Lawrence River in an area of the Thousand Islands.

As the warship sailed into this channel, a force made up of French soldiers and Mohawk Indians had attacked it. The story told of 14 men being lowered from the ship into a longboat in order to go back and rendezvous with the other British ships and warn them about the waiting ambush. The incident occurred in August of 1760, when the country was first being settled, during the French and English Seven Year War. The article included a map of the narrow passage in the Thousand Islands where the warship was believed to have sunk, along with a pencil sketch of what the massive warship may have looked like. There was not much information about it, but one thing was certain - the longboat and warship were never seen again and its crew remained unaccounted for. Even the spot where it had been presumed they had disembarked the ship was never found again. For this reason, that particular passage of the Thousand Islands had earned the name The Lost Channel.

Valerie glanced over old paper clipping that had been glued roughly into the pages of Nana's scrapbook and traced a finger over the drawing of the old British ship. Imagine what it was like back then, she thought. Her eyes were wide as she looked at the old paper.

"Well, this is cool," said Valerie slowly. "But it really doesn't say much about it, other than the history stuff."

"Read it ALL, and you'll see," said Nana.

She did and there it was: the warship had been a payroll ship! It had been carrying chests of gold and silver coin to pay the wages of the British soldiers and local militia. It had also contained valuables in the form of gemstones and expensive jewelry to be given to Mohawk Indians further upriver In exchange for loyalty to the British crown. The coins had been increasingly rare at that time in history, and this payroll ship had been carrying the last large amount of them before the temporary introduction of paper notes designed to replace them. Valerie's eyes lit up as she read the words on the old paper. The payroll had never been recovered, presumed sunk with the lost warship, and was thought to be resting somewhere in the Lost Channel, awaiting discovery. Nana grinned as she observed Valerie's reaction. She had been waiting anxiously to reveal this story to the children, wanting to see their reaction to the great adventure she was laying out in front of them.

"This is really cool, Nana!" said Val.

Alex was looking at the clipping now, reading silently, his lips moving as he read. Valerie rolled the story around in her mind, examining each part of it mentally. This was different than their other 'adventures'. This one was a bit more serious. It wasn't just going on a hike or finding clues around town. It was much more complex - and it involved the river. She liked to swim, but Valerie knew that this idea would require some real work and skills they didn't have at their age. She frowned slightly as she turned back to Nana.

"You would need to be a diver to find the treasure!" said Valerie, stopping at the end of her sentence to look at Nana. As she finished the words, she already knew the answer. Alex already wore a grin; so did Nana. Their older sister, Jorden, was currently working on her scuba diving certification.

2

The pool water was clear and warm and the taste and smell of chlorine filled Jorden's senses as she surfaced, pulling her mask up. The regulator was heavy and she spit out the mouthpiece to breathe in 'real' air. She moved her feet, kicking with the flippers to stay at the surface. The gear was heavy and didn't exactly feel natural. She thought about what it felt like to swim when she was younger, how free it felt, how liberating the water was against her skin. This did not feel the same. She felt 'contained', as though she was wrapped in some sort of strange cocoon that allowed her to be in the water. Jorden, now 18 years old, had the same dark brown eyes as her younger sister and her father. She was almost as tall as her father and very slim. That was no surprise to anyone who knew Jorden, because all through school she had always been fairly athletic.

Her instructor surfaced a short distance away, followed by the two other students in the pool that day. Jorden turned in the water, moving so that she floated mostly on her back. It seemed much easier. She listened as the instructor spoke to them about dive time, decompression stops and nitrox. It was a lot to take in all at once and she tried to concentrate on what he was saying, despite trying to catch her breath.

The classes had been long and very complex. There was a lot more to it than she had originally thought. It wasn't easy, nothing like what she had imagined when she first wanted to be a diver. There was a ton of things to remember, a whole lot of precautions to remember, both before and during a dive.

She could feel the weight of the tank, the wetsuit and the dive weights. She remembered the first time she had done things wrong with the regulator and had inhaled a big breath of water instead of air! She had been a little embarrassed, but when two others in the class did the same thing that very same day, it had eased her mind.

The group of them bobbed in the warm water of the pool and Jorden realized suddenly how different the river would be - cold and dark - even during the warmest months of summer. Why had she chosen to try this? It sounded like fun in the beginning, but the more she got involved in scuba, the more it seemed like...well, work! It definitely was not easy, and, not only that, but it was expensive - a fact that her father kept mentioning on a weekly basis, until it nearly drove her crazy.

The instructor signaled them to submerge again, to pay attention to their breathing. Jorden snapped back to reality, squishing her mask back onto her face and popping the regulator back into her mouth, trying to ignore the taste of chlorine. Down she went, breathing through the aluminum body of the regulator, her eyes trained on the instructor in the underworld of the pool. She tried to breathe slowly, forcing air out of her lungs and watching the bubbles rise away from her face as the regulator performed its job. The instructor used a series of hand signals to get the group to perform the necessary objectives in their training. He had them swim laps around the outside edges of the pool, kicking their fins to move through the water, encouraging the group to get used to the weight of their equipment. Jorden had found it a challenge at first, but as the classes had gone on, it had become like second nature to her.

When this class was finally finished, the instructor informed them that their next session would be in the river, to complete their certification. The class cheered. Finally, thought Jorden. She liked the classes, but was anxious to see the underwater world of the river, to see the marine life and to possibly explore some of the nearby shipwrecks that local and visiting divers loved to visit.

She got out of her wetsuit, dried herself off and put on a warm, comfy pair of track pants and a t-shirt. The June weather was becoming warmer and warmer every day. She pulled her long, damp, sandy-blonde hair through an elastic band and grabbed her bag after storing the equipment in the designated lockers. The equipment belonged to the instructor and was supplied for the course. But for next week's foray into the river, she would need to use her own gear. Her father had promised to help her with the extra money she required to purchase this equipment, which meant one thing - she smiled at the thought - she needed to go shopping.

~~~~

The school year was almost over and summer break was just around the corner. The smell of spring lilac blooms had begun to fade and the night songs of amphibians were beginning to change to the chirping of crickets as the days became hotter. Another two days and they would be on summer holidays and Alex could hardly wait. He loved summertime because there was always something to do. He walked home, a short distance from the school, carrying his trusty backpack - it was a bit tattered and worn, but held everything he needed, a grand assortment of everything a young boy could ever require. Dad had offered to get him new one, but Alex had declined, saying that this particular backpack was lucky. He took it everywhere with him, never leaving it far out of reach. Valerie had joked with him that most kids have a favourite Teddy bear or stuffed animal of some sort, but he just had his pack. Alex ignored this, simply sticking his tongue out at her occasionally. What she had to say really didn't mean anything to him, but his backpack held his whole life in it.

Alex's sandy-coloured hair swung back and forth just above his grey-blue eyes as he trudged up the sidewalk to the new house. Well, it really wasn't new - just a different house. His father had sold their old home. He had met a lady a while ago and they had married last year and they'd all moved into the house that she owned - along with her family. Alex now had two step-brothers; Curtis, was three years younger than he was, the other, Tyler, was six years older than him. A smart boy, Tyler had dark brown wavy hair, which usually stuck out from under a ball cap. He loved to play video games with the younger boys, tormenting them with his skills.

At least boys still outnumbered girls, thought Alex. Jorden was practically almost out on her own anyway, so that just left Valerie and his stepmom, Pam, on the girls' side. Pam was a pretty lady, with blond hair in ringlets and hazel eyes. She was only a few inches shorter than Dad and loved being outside in her gardens. Having the other boys in the house to do things with was different to him, but he liked it just fine, and there was always plenty to do in the neighbourhood at this time of year. The creek was full of fish to catch, and it was just across the bicycle path, which ran right behind the hedge in the backyard. There were forts to build, trees to climb and a good game of 'guns' or hide-and-seek was always fun.

Curtis, who had caught up to him on the run from the nearby schoolyard, interrupted Alex's thoughts. Curtis was almost the same size as Alex, with curly brown hair and bright blue eyes. He had energy galore, from the first moment he awoke to the minute he laid down to sleep. He had no fear of anything and liked everyone he met. The two boys got along very well and Alex enjoyed playing with his little stepbrother.

The boys raced up the sidewalk and turned down the walkway to the house. A small black cat meowed a greeting to them as they came up the steps of the front porch. They rushed through the front door into the kitchen. Curtis kicked off his shoes and left his backpack and school work in a heap on the kitchen counter. Alex took off his shoes, too, but his backpack stayed on his back.

They ran past Val, who sat thumbing through a book at the breakfast counter and darted into the living room. Tyler was in the room lounging on the couch and playing a video game on the TV. The two younger boys looked at one another and jetted up the stairs toward the room they shared. Since video games were out of the question, it was LEGO time!

Both boys loved LEGO and would spend hours building unique and amazing constructions. They shared a huge plastic bin full of the small plastic bricks, pieces of varying colours and shapes. Today they were building spaceships and acting out their own make-believe adventures with their creations. It would be several hours yet before Dad or Pam called them down for dinner, but Alex always seemed to have a little snack of some sort within reach in his trusty backpack to tide him over. Today was no exception, and he pulled out a small bag of chips and shared them with his stepbrother as they continued with their constructions.

Their room wasn't very large, but it still had enough space for all of their stuff - Dad had been very creative and had built shelving and under-the-bed storage areas to house everything. Bunk beds also helped, as the boys each had dressers for their clothes that needed to fit in the room, too. It all seemed to work well though, with just enough room for a small aquarium on an end table. Several small tropical fish swam happily around in the tank, occasionally racing through the bubbles from the filter.

Today the room was brightly lit and the afternoon sun danced on the window curtains as the two boys played together. The sound of a vehicle door closing outside caught their attention. Pam was home from work. The sequence of events that would ultimately end with dinner being put on the table had begun, and the boys ripped themselves away from the bin of LEGO to race downstairs to find out what would be for dinner that night.

~~~~

Valerie and Jorden liked it when their father lit a small campfire down in the backyard at night. The smell of a campfire would be something they would always remember - especially the way Dad did it. He used fallen branches and timber from the bush behind the house - sweet smelling wood like apple, butternut and maple. It had a particular aroma, both fragrant and rich. The sounds of late spring were still in the night air. The peeper frogs' spring song filled the air less frequently as their mating season ended, and the chirp of crickets was just beginning.

It was a warm, starry night and the two girls sat in folding lawn chairs, watching the dancing flames. Dinner was long over, and, through the screens of the house's open windows, the clatter of plates going from sink to dishwasher could be heard. The warm glow from the kitchen lights shone out onto the cool grass of the back lawn, creating squares of light. Already the bioluminescent glow of fireflies could be seen, punctuating the dark shadows in the yard. The fire cracked and popped, throwing small sparks out onto the sand around the steel enclosure of the fireplace, which glowed momentarily before fading slowly away. The two girls simply sat in silence for a long period, staring into the fire, enjoying its quiet, flickering warmth. There was solace for them in this place, a peace that they would not fully realize at their ages. Looking back on it many years later, it would become a tangible thing - a refuge where they could take a break from everything that might be stressful, an oasis away from whatever chaos might be happening in their lives. But, for now, there were only the dancing flames.

Alex and Curtis appeared behind Valerie out of the shadows. Alex raised a finger to his lips as he looked toward his oldest sister, stealthily approaching his unsuspecting victim. Jorden simply grinned, knowing what was about to happen. Alex raised his arms up in his best horror movie style and jumped forward at Valerie with a piercing screech. Valerie nearly fell off her chair backward with the scare, grasping her chest as she steadied herself again.

"You creep!" she shouted at him as both boys laughed out loud.

Curtis produced a bag of marshmallows from behind his back and Alex climbed through the hedge at the back of the yard to locate some proper sticks to use to roast them. Jorden rose from her seat and set up two more folding chairs for the boys from a large plastic crate next to the fire pit where their father kept all the 'supplies'. She was still grinning at Valerie, who shot her an indignant glance.

Alex returned a few minutes later with several green branches that he had stripped of leaves. Curtis ripped open the plastic marshmallow bag, anxious to have a couple of the fresh, moist goodies inside. Everyone got comfy, chattering about the fire, the marshmallows and other things.

Curtis seemed mostly interested in watching his treat burst into flame on the end of the stick. Valerie was a little bit restless - a fact which Jorden could see, but she waited patiently for her sister to simply come out with it. Even Alex now looked at Valerie with a sideways glance, his curiosity aroused by her obvious fidgeting.

"What's up with you, did you poop your pants from us scaring you?" he inquired sarcastically with a large grin.

She looked at him with disgust, letting out a sigh that indicated that he was already trying her patience. It did nothing to diminish his grin, however.

"No, worm," she began. "I was thinking about the story Nana showed us about the Lost Channel."

"Ohhhhh," replied the two boys in a comical union.

Valerie rolled her eyes and Jorden grinned once again. The boys snickered, having fun at their sister's expense.

"If you'd shut up for a sec, I could tell the whole story!" sighed Valerie in exasperation.

After a couple more fake salutes and chuckles, the two troublemakers settled down, content to listen to Valerie and continue burning their now-empty roasting sticks. Even Jorden sat quietly listening as Valerie retold the whole story of the payroll ship and its lost treasure.

The story took the children back to the days of the first settlers in the New World, a land with a rugged wilderness and ongoing battles between the French and English. It described the Indian people who divided their loyalties to one group of the newcomers or the other. It also detailed mysteries of the early years of the country.

The location of the lost payroll, the treasure, from the British warship was, of course, one of those mysteries, comprised of local lore and legends wrapped up in the 'Gardens of the Great Spirit', the Thousand Islands.

"It could be on land, too, you know?" stated Jorden.

"Yes, but it probably would have been found by now if it was, don't you think?" Valerie replied.

"Maybe it was found already, or maybe it was never really lost. The French and the Mohawk may have plundered it from the ship, and then sunk it!" suggested Jorden, shrugging her shoulders.

Valerie considered all of this for a few moments. All of these statements made sense, but she didn't want to give up on the idea that it might be there somewhere, waiting to be found. She could visualize the treasure, in chests at the bottom of the river, with wisps of algae growing off of them, swaying in the current of the cold water.

"It's got to be there," she said quietly, looking into the flames again. "I just know it!"

Jorden let out a sigh, looking at her younger sister, feeling the anxious desire that Valerie had in her as she looked at the fire. She knew it would not be easy to pry Valerie away from this idea.

"Okay, I am almost finished my scuba course and I'll have my own diving gear next week. You find out as much as you can about this 'Lost Channel' stuff," Jorden stated, watching Valerie sit up straighter in her chair, her eyes brightening in the light from the fire.

"Even if we found it, how would we even get it out of the river?" asked Alex, who had been quietly listening in on the conversation.

"I'm not sure," replied Valerie slowly and thoughtfully. "But I'll figure something out long before we have to worry about it!"

"I guess it's time for another adventure," said Jorden as she turned her attention back to the fire.

Curtis simply cheered at the idea.

3

Conrad took off his glasses and rubbed his eyes. He'd put in several straight hours of reading maps and river charts and his eyes were tired and sore. The large square table in front of him was covered in large topographical maps and charts, old books and scraps of paper with various scrawled drawings and notes written on them. Dropping the pencil he had in his fingers gave him a bit of relief. He had been writing out notes and drawing grids on the maps long enough to make his hands stiff and sore.

Conrad's grey eyes swept the room, his gaze falling on certificates he'd received during his education and several awards in various glass frames that hung on the wall opposite his large table. A former history professor here at the college, he'd been retired for several years now, but remained a member of the alumni. As a bonus, he'd been granted the privilege to use this room, an extra off the back end of the Library, to conduct his 'research'. It wasn't very large, with plain white walls and only one small window looking out onto the back of the campus, but the large fluorescent fixtures over the table gave him good light - and it was essentially free of charge.

He hadn't managed to scrape up all of the funds necessary to put together another excursion with the salvage barge to rescue the cannon - but he was getting close - and time was ticking. The summers in this climate lasted only so long, and he had to use every available moment if he hoped to find anything. At least the barge crane had been repaired. As for the rest of the money he needed…funding these missions was always a problem.

Conrad gritted his teeth against the thought of having to 'panhandle' at local elite social functions looking for supporters to continue the search for the lost ship. Very few people in the area had any real understanding of the local history, and fewer still who would donate any money to such an undertaking - especially since Conrad had found very few things in the river to back up the legends of the Lost Channel. A couple of shards of pottery and the well-preserved remains of a musket were hardly enough to draw excitement from local sponsors with deep pockets. He was having a hard enough time keeping a few people around who could operate the barge and run the crane. Most of the time he tried to find younger qualified labourers who would donate their time in return for a share of whatever was ultimately found. Most gave up after a short time of it; some even refused to answer or return his calls after the first or second trip out.

Fortunately he had one man who could be counted on - his lead diver, Oscar, who had been a close friend for many years. Conrad knew that Oscar, a retired captain from the Coast Guard, would always help with the underwater side of his quest, even if he was only mildly optimistic that Conrad could lead them to the alleged treasure of the lost ship. He didn't have anything else on his agenda, even if he barely had enough in his pension to survive and fill his scuba tanks with air. But he was always happy to plunge into the cold waters of the river, searching the bottom relentlessly whenever Conrad could squeeze together the money to get them out to his next grid to search through the narrow passages of the Thousand Islands. Conrad lowered his head for a moment, breathing deeply and running his aching fingers through curls of mostly grey hair. He closed his ash grey eyes, trying to think of new ways to pay for the fuel and supplies he would need.

At that moment, Oscar tapped lightly and then opened the door to Conrad's 'office', entering quietly with a small cardboard tray containing two covered coffee cups. He was a large man with broad shoulders and a thick torso, with solid arms and legs that resembled tree trunks. Oscar had a full head of white hair, even though he was actually several years younger than his friend. He had piercing blue eyes and a thick moustache, which was also white. Conrad had always marvelled at the fact that there was a wetsuit made large enough to fit the man.

"Thought you might need one of these by now," Oscar stated in a gruff voice, setting the tray down on the edge of the map table and pulling out a chair for himself. The wood of the chair creaked and groaned as Oscar lowered his heft into it.

"I might as well. Maybe it will help my brain find a way to get some cash together!" Conrad sighed.

"You will. You always do. Maybe it's time to go back to the books?"

Conrad looked at Oscar, replacing his glasses, and picked up the coffee. He knew what his friend was talking about, of course. He meant another trip to the small local museum, another day or two of poking through old microfilms and drawers of dusty records. It also meant listening to that pencil-necked curator Mr. Thusk go on and on about local history, every word of it already common knowledge to Conrad!

"At least ONE of us is truly retired, I guess."

~~~~

The mist over the river was like a veil of lead, and the ship moved ahead slowly, with almost no wind to fill its mainsails. The British Man o' War Onondaga entered the labyrinth of fog-shrouded islands cautiously, her captain just as wary of shoals and hazards just beneath the calm surface as he was of attackers. There were 146 souls aboard the warship: 90 British infantrymen, 35 militia, ten women, three children and eight Algonquin Indians. It was August of 1760, and the captain and his officers tried in vain to part the mists blanketing the river that morning with their spyglasses, searching for a clear route through the maze of islands. The captain was a fairly tall man, his red British coat perfect with a red sash signifying his rank. He wore his sword on his left side, and everything about him told a story of sacrifice for his country. He was curt, but still polite to his crewmen and officers, and they respected him for it. As he gave his orders, every man aboard scrambled to his words. His piercing blue eyes stared out at the river. Everything was still and silent, except for the occasional call of a loon, and the tops of pitch pine growing on the islands were all that could be seen in the hovering fog. A slight breeze came along, billowing the sails slightly and shifting the Man o' War to starboard on her keel. It almost seemed as though the fog might lift, that the sun was trying to burn through it. The channel seemed wider now, and the captain breathed a slight sigh of relief, gazing down at the calm waters ahead of him. At least for the moment, he could see ahead through the channel, he relaxed a little at the thought that he could at least react in time if a rocky shoal came into view. He had only traversed this passage once, and the first time he had come through in clear, bright skies with a strong breeze and experienced men. This time he was not quite as comfortable with it, and some of the crew had come aboard for the first time when the warship had left York.

The ship was also carrying a far greater cargo this time. The new governor had entrusted the captain with the payrolls straight from Britain to pay the regulars in the New World and to buy the loyalty of the 'savages' in their war against the French: chests of coin and valuables, spared by noble and wealthy families and the government of Britain herself to ensure that the forces of the empire might be victorious.

The oak bulkheads of the warship creaked and groaned slightly as the ship pushed forward further into the channel. The flapping sounds of the mainsails filled the air and the mists began to dissipate, revealing the shores of the islands in the narrow passage. She was a heavy ship, but nonetheless, the captain was confident. She had 16 guns and the regulars aboard to help. The Onondaga had come through bad weather across the Great Lakes without a scratch. The opening of the river was a great relief to the captain, although the mists of the last few days had caused quite a bit of concern amongst the crew.

The ship glided into a wider spot in the channel and the mists seemed to disperse even more. To the north was an outcropping of granite topped by soft pines. Rocky shores lined the south of the channel, forming a line of impenetrable shallows. The air was quiet, with barely a sound, except for the lapping of the waves against the ships wooden hull. The captain stared forward, hoping that the channel would open further, that it would expose the wide breadth of the river he was more comfortable with. It didn't. Instead, the channel actually narrowed. He shouted commands to drop the sails to slow the ship so that they might manoeuvre in the tightened spaces of the river ahead. The men above followed the orders and furled the sails; the warship slowed her pace, walls of granite rising on either side of her. The current carried the vessel forward. The captain felt a sudden urgency to reach the open river again.

A sound came suddenly to the crew's ears, a cracking and splintering of wood, and the captain looked ahead over the bow in horror as he realized what was happening. A huge pine tree collapsed almost perfectly horizontally in front of them, between the walls lining the channel, at a level just 15 feet above the main deck. There would be no way to stop the ship in time. It was an ambush!

The masts of the ship met the huge tree trunk with a force they were unable to take, and they splintered and fell, a tangled mess of rigging and sails. The captain's horrified gaze fell upon the bluffs at the top of the granite walls. He could see the French uniforms and small artillery cannons. It was perfect, he realized; he would not be able to defend his ship against this surprise attack. His crew's guns could not hope to reach anywhere close to that kind of elevation in this narrow corridor. Regardless, they had to defend themselves, he thought. He shouted orders to the regulars to fire upon the bluffs, but he knew that their opponents had the high ground advantage.

Shots rang out and, as the first volley of cannon fire crashed down through the decks of the Man o' War, the captain already knew that their efforts would be futile. The wood shattered around him, and the artillery aiming down on the ship at such a sharp angle quickly breached the hull. The Onondaga began to take on water quickly.

The captain fought toward the starboard side of the main deck, tossing aside rigging and debris, shouting for the crew to lower one of the two longboats to attempt an escape to rescue. But these boats wouldn't be used for rescue today, he knew; he had to warn the rest of the British ships coming this way of the vile French awaiting in ambush.

Fourteen men scrambled aboard the longboat, struggling with the damaged rigging to lower the boat to the water. As soon as the boat settled on the water, the men shoved away from the sinking warship. As the captain glanced back toward the shore opposite him, a high, loud screeching noise arose from the pines lining the shore below the bluff and shapes swung from the trees out over the water toward the ship. Mohawk. They had made ropes high in the trees to gain access to the deck of the failing vessel. The attackers screamed at the ship's crewmen as they raised cruel blades toward them, firing pistols and muskets and causing chaos on the deck. He was finished, thought the captain as he took one last look back to see the longboat disappearing into the mist. As his attacker sank a knife into him, all he could hope for was that the souls aboard that small boat might escape to warn the others of their fate.

4

Valerie could hear the sound of a metal wrench hitting the concrete floor of the garage before she even arrived at the doorway. She was carrying her iPhone, along with a glass of milk and several cookies cradled in her other arm. It was a beautiful sunny summer day and Dad had been out tinkering in the garage again. It was a lazy Saturday for the kids and nobody seemed interested in doing anything but staying inside for now, playing with their favourite pieces of technology. Valerie had other ideas though, and loved being outside once it became warm in the spring. She stood just outside the garage on the front walkway, checking on her search in the window of her smartphone. The sun was already high in the sky and the leaves of the large maple tree in the front yard made shadows on the grass and walkway that shifted slightly in the light breeze.

The smell of freshly cut grass was in the air this day and children could be heard at a neighbour's house down the street, splashing and shouting in their pool. Birds sang and the cat lounged in the shade of one of Dad's sitting chairs, just outside the garage door next to the walkway.

Valerie had been trying to find more information on the British payroll ship from Nana's story about the Lost Channel, but there had been very little written about it. Her unsuccessful searches had frustrated her all morning and Valerie knew it would be difficult to find out the whole story. Still she had plugged away, combing for any information the Internet might offer up about it.

Suddenly, Valerie turned her attention back to her glass of milk, realizing that she was almost spilling it. Milk and Oreos were a favourite snack for her - almost comfort food. She chomped away on the cookies, chasing each bite with a little milk. Another tool hit the floor in the garage, which made Valerie a bit curious. She peeked inside, to see her father bent over some kind of strange looking cylindrical pod that had windows in the front, some of them facing downward on an angle. There were oddly short 'wings' on the side of it, with small propellers facing backward, along with two more facing upward into the air. The whole thing was yellow and there were lights fixed above the windows on it, tilted on a slight downward angle. It sat up about two and a half feet from the floor, supported on tubular legs, and was the weirdest looking vehicle Valerie had ever seen - that is, assuming it was a vehicle! Valerie also noted some sort of silver tanks affixed on top of the craft, with hoses leading off of them.

"What the heck was he building?" she thought.

Dad had a strange habit of simply deciding to build weird and wonderful things. He had built a remote control car with a video camera on it that he could drive around the sidewalks of the neighbourhood and see the sights on a TV in the garage. It was an amusing device, but the only practical thing it ended up doing was scaring the local cat and squirrel population half to death. He also had built an eight-foot long wooden powerboat for the two younger boys, complete with a steering wheel and an electric trolling motor for power. It ran on batteries and the boys could drive it up and down the creek in the summer when its current slowed. Of course, no powerboat was complete without flames painted on the body, much to the amusement of people walking by on the bicycle path beside the creek.

Yes, Dad had built many a strange contraption; he'd even joked about trying to build a plane once, until Pam reminded him about his fear of flying. Valerie grinned at her thoughts, but considered this new object the strangest thing he had ever come up with. He turned suddenly, realizing someone was there.

"Oh, hi there, sweetheart. I didn't see you there," he stated.

"What is THAT thing?" she asked, taking another gulp of milk.

"It's a submersible."

"A what??" she asked.

"You know, a submarine. Only small," he clarified, looking surprised that he would have to explain.

Valerie continued to look at it with raised eyebrows. She placed her glass on the nearest workbench. The garage was not so much a garage anymore, as it was Dad's personal retreat, complete with laminate flooring, recliners, TV and fridge. Not your typical storage and tools location, that's for sure. The workbench also contained one of Dad's computers, hooked up to the house's wireless Internet.

Valerie suddenly remembered laughing one day as Pam stood in the doorway of the garage, watching Dad sitting in the comfy recliner watching a movie on the TV. She simply stated that it would be nice if he would come in and watch a movie with her. Dad looked at her with a grin. She proceeded to remind him that the garage wasn't a recreation room. The next day, her father had arrived home with a two-person hot tub that he had bought from a neighbour down the street. When Pam arrived home from work, Dad had the bubbles all prepared in it, and Pam lounged in the hot, bubbling little oasis for a long time after a hard day at work delivering mail. Valerie hadn't remembered ever hearing her say anything negative about the garage again.

She examined the sub up close now, peering through the front windows of the strange vehicle. There was a cramped cockpit, with room to cram four people in small seats, and an array of odd gauges and crude levers sticking through what looked like a rough plywood control panel in front of what must have been the driver's seat. She could barely make out what look to be car batteries in the back of the small space, with wiring coming out to various different places inside. Outside the mini-sub, on top near the back end, were several air tanks that looked the same as the tank that Jorden had to strap on to go for her diving lessons. The entire vehicle looked like a miniature of the submarines that she had seen in history class from the Second World War. The only exception was the front windows that looked forward and down on a slight angle. The whole vehicle sat on a sturdy trailer. It was strange looking, almost a cartoon version of a real submarine.

"Go ahead, get in!" said her father, tinkering with a circuit board on the workbench.

"How?" asked Valerie.

"You can crawl in through the bottom at the back, see?" he replied, coming over and pointing up underneath the back half of the sub. "Don't worry, it's very safe."

Valerie crouched to look under where Dad had pointed, seeing up into the compartment where the seats were. She suddenly thought about a very obvious issue: a submarine with a hole in the bottom of it seemed a bit far-fetched, but she could not see any kind of hatch anywhere to seal up the entrance.

"Um, Dad. How does the water stay out?" she asked.

As she crawled up into the cramped space inside, she heard Dad explaining the intricacies of 'ambient pressure design', but as she sat down in the small driver's seat, the only thing she really understood as she looked at the gauges and control handles was his explanation of the idea of placing an empty coffee cup upside down in a sink of water and trapping the air underneath it.

"So this place inside holds the air in? Like the coffee cup?"

"Exactly!" said Dad enthusiastically. "The air is trapped inside and the sub doesn't leak it out, and fresh air is always pumped in slowly by the scuba tanks on top. The extra air simply escapes out the bottom..."

"Wow! That's kinda cool!" replied Valerie.

"Yep. Hey, I've sunk a lot of money into this sub - pardon the pun! I certainly don't want it to sink!" said Dad.

"Have you put it in the water yet?" she inquired, thoughtfully.

"Only twice, and I need to do a few more little things to make her perfect."

Dad saw a project, a mini-sub; Valerie saw a way of reaching the treasure in the river. She was unable to hide her grin. This could be the answer to finding the lost ship and its treasure, a vehicle that they could use to explore the river bottom and still stay completely dry. It was even better than the fact that Jorden would soon have her diving certification. Her thoughts rattled and raced around in her mind. All she would need now is to find out where the ship had actually sank, and convince Dad to launch the sub for a test run at that spot in the river.

Valerie gripped the control levers on the makeshift dashboard. She read the stickers on its black painted surface, seeing that each lever did something important: one controlled the up and down, another made it go forward and others were used to turn the vehicle. There were gauges for the battery power and the air in the tanks. It was all very cool.

"So, when are you gonna try it again?" she asked, trying to make it sound like an innocent question.

~~~~

The museum always seemed cold, no matter whether it was the heart of winter or the middle of a hot summer. It had that strange formaldehyde smell to it, as though one might see shelves of preserved animal carcasses suspended in jars and decanters. Mr. Thusk moved quickly down the main hallway, past displays of Indian artifacts and rocks and minerals from the local area. He was a very thin man of average height and almost totally bald, having begun to lose his hair fairly early in life; a few grey hairs still remained intact on his head just above his ears. It seemed that brown was the main part of his wardrobe - it was practically the only colour he wore.

He carried several file folders and a microfilm cartridge to one of the rear rooms of the museum. His lips moved as though he was speaking, even though he said nothing audible as he hurried forward down the hall. As he entered the room, he turned left in an almost robotic movement and continued towards a table where Conrad was sitting and waiting patiently.

The room was filled with records and old files, all held together in large binders on many bookshelves. Old framed photos hung on the dark wood of the walls, along with maps created long ago of the surrounding areas, some dating back to the very first settlements in the townships.

Conrad lifted his eyes from the pages of the binder he had in front of him as Mr. Thusk approached. The curator smiled briefly at Conrad, setting the folders and microfilm down on the end of the table.

"These are all I could find, and each contains a reference to your mystery ship," he chimed politely.

Conrad leafed through some of the folders, looking nonplussed.

"I am pretty sure I've reviewed all this material before, Mr. Thusk."

"Yes, but I thought maybe I would get them for you in case you, perhaps, missed something," Mr. Thusk replied.

This only agitated Conrad and he released a heavy sigh. It was frustrating enough to sift through all the old records stored here in the museum, but the last thing he needed today was for this annoying man to make him feel like some kind of idiot. He had been very thorough in his review of those folders and with his searches on the microfilm, and he didn't appreciate the curator stating that he may have 'missed' something. He hadn't. The problem was, there was simply nothing much written about the Onondaga or her cargo.

Conrad assumed that the British government had probably kept the ship and her payroll cargo as secret as possible for obvious reasons. It was simple precaution against the French raiding her -but raid her they had! The question was, what about the cargo? Had it simply sunk in the Lost Channel, and remained there waiting to be discovered, or had the French known about the riches she was carrying? Either way, finding the Onondaga or her lost payroll would not be an easy task. The current was swift through the Lost Channel and it was fairly deep as well, making it difficult to see without using sonar-imaging technologies. All of it would take time and cost a lot of money.

"I think I have exhausted this resource, my good man," Conrad stated curtly, placing both hands suddenly on the table and standing up abruptly, almost startling Mr. Thusk. The curator quickly took a step back and Conrad strode from the room and down the long hallway without another word.

Thoughts rolled through Conrad's mind as he walked toward the main entrance, shoving open the glass doors. He stood on the front steps momentarily, withdrawing his sunglasses and placing them over his eyes, shoving them up tight against his forehead in aggravation. It was a beautiful, warm and sunny day, but it did little for his mood. He would have to look for clues elsewhere and his options were running thin. Time was ticking.

5

Valerie awoke with a mission in her mind. She had dreamt in those last minutes before waking - dreamt of ships with sails, of muskets firing and the thousands of islands in the river nearby. She rolled out of bed, getting her bearings. It was early - very early. She could hear the birdsong that always marked the early hours of the morning: the distinctive calls of the cardinals and the chirps of the smaller wrens and chickadees. The house was silent inside. Everyone was still asleep, grasping those last few minutes of delicious slumber, snuggling down in their comfy beds, she presumed. But Valerie couldn't sleep any longer and she was anxious to tackle her new adventure.

It was a Sunday and typically a day where everyone in the family took it slow. Slow to wake, slow to emerge from their rooms to congregate anywhere. It was usually a quiet, non-eventful day, though not for Valerie - at least not today! She scrambled to get dressed quickly and headed downstairs in search of something to eat, as her stomach was reminding her of her need for breakfast. The cat greeted her as she entered the kitchen and the dog raised her head from the floor as she entered. The kitchen was neat and tidy, with everything in its place. Both Dad and Pam liked things that way and drove the children nuts with this fact on a daily basis.

Cereal, she decided. That would be quick and easy and she would be ready to rock. Ha, ha - ready to rock, she thought absently as she opened the fridge for the milk and searched the cupboards to find a bowl. It was a strange phrase, wasn't it? Personally, she loved rock music; so technically, she was always ready to rock! She dismissed the line of thought as she decided on which cereal to have this morning. As she shuffled the colourful boxes around in the cupboard, the dog stood, sauntering slowly over to her, tail wagging in expectation of a possible treat.

"Silly, this is not for dogs!" she stated factually in the animal's direction, only to see the dog's tail wagging even faster. It was clear to Valerie that the dog wasn't getting the message and she remembered that the Milk Bones were in the cupboard below the one she was in. Sighing, she quickly retrieved one and handed it off to the dog.

"There!" she said. The dog happily retreated back to her mat on the floor with her prize. But, before Valerie would ever make it to the table to eat her meal, she realized that she would have to feed the meowing feline as well. There was a definite price for being the first one to come downstairs in the morning!

The sun streamed through the kitchen windows and brightly illuminated the squares on the floor tiles as Valerie munched away on her cereal while pouring over the material she had searched through from Google on her smartphone. There was very little written about the Lost Channel and the British Man o' War that had vanished there in 1760. She wasn't really surprised at the lack of information. It would have been difficult to document anything at that early period in the settlement of the New World, let alone document something that the British would have wanted to be kept a secret.

Valerie put down her phone, drank the remaining milk in the bottom of her bowl as she rose from the table, and walked over to the kitchen sink. This was going to be a day of research, one where she would try to find any kind of puzzle piece to the story of the lost ship and its cargo. But she would need a little help. She rinsed the bowl carefully in the sink and placed it in the dishwasher along with her spoon, conscious of her father reminding her to do it countless times. Valerie headed back upstairs, trying to stay quiet.

She went over to Alex and Curtis's door. Pushing it open with light fingers, she cringed as the hinges gave out a slight squeal. Glimpsing inside the room, she saw that he two boys were still out cold, with their mouths opened wide - they looked almost comically comatose. She debated for a few seconds about whether or not to use the feather trick on them, but decided it would cause too much commotion in the end. Valerie preferred to keep it quiet this morning for some reason, and she stepped gingerly inside the room, approaching Alex's sleeping form.

As she reached forward to wake Alex, the cat jumped up onto the bed, meowing a greeting. Valerie hurriedly lifted the cat off of the bed and plopped her gently on the floor, shooing her back toward the doorway. Alex opened his eyes slowly. The sight of his sister standing over him and the obvious early morning chirping of the birds outside made him roll over away from her with a groan. Valerie grabbed his shoulder, rolling him back toward her, and raised a finger to her lips. Alex sat up slowly and yawned while rubbing one of his eyes.

Uh, oh! He could tell just by looking at her that this was one of 'those' times: times when Valerie urgently had to do something and wanted him to come along. Why? Why couldn't she just do it herself, whatever it might be today? He wanted to just sink back down in his bed for some more precious sleep. He became a little agitated as he saw her motioning for him to get out of bed and follow her out of the room.

"What the heck do you want?" he whispered, shrugging his shoulders.

"I want you to come with me; we need to go to the library," she replied quietly.

"We?"

"Yes. I think I know where to look for stuff about the Lost Channel!" she explained.

Alex rolled his eyes, remembering the many times she had landed them in trouble thanks to one of her 'missions'. Still, he knew very well that she would continue to bug him until he relented, so he rolled his legs off the bed, sat up on the edge and looked around his room. Curtis was still asleep.

"The library isn't even open yet!" he whispered coarsely.

"I know, but we can go get something at the store on our way. I have a couple of dollars," she said.

This seemed to motivate him ever so slightly and he grudgingly got up and moved toward his dresser. Not wanting to spoil the idea and make him change his mind, Valerie swiftly departed, shooing the cat out again as she went, and closed the door behind her.

Alex rummaged through the drawers of his dresser, pulled out the first pair of socks he found along with some shorts and a white t-shirt. He dressed quietly, even though he still was only half awake, not wanting to wake Curtis. Slinking silently out the door, he crept downstairs.

Valerie was already putting her shoes on, had her library card in her pocket and had scrawled a quick note to let her parents know where she and Alex were going. She was anxious to get going. Alex yawned, sat on the floor and began to pull on his shoes as well. He stood up and his eyes widened as his expression suddenly changed.

"What's wrong?" asked Valerie.

"Hold on a sec," Alex answered as he bolted back up the stairs. He returned momentarily, his trusty backpack slung over his shoulder.

"Whew! Almost jinxed us," he said with a grin and ran back to the kitchen to grab an apple from the fruit basket on the counter to eat as they walked.

The two of them exited the house quietly, closing the door gently behind them, barely making a sound. Outside, the birds continued to sing their happy morning songs and the morning air was still heavy with the smell of lilac blooms. There wasn't any trace of a breeze.

Alex and Valerie made their way down the street and stopped for their customary look over the railing on the bridge over Butler's Creek to survey the flowing water for minnows. The sun was warm on them and Alex was very glad he had worn shorts. He tossed his apple core beneath some bushes along the path. They continued on, walking along the sidewalk and jumping the cracks and seams in the sun-bleached concrete.

The library wasn't far from their home - it was usually only about a fifteen-minute walk - during which Alex talked Valerie's ear off! She had already tried in vain to quiet him twice, but it appeared that he had a lot on his mind today as well. Valerie was trying to focus on her important mission for the day and her thoughts drifted over to the history that she had read: the thousand islands, castles built by business tycoons, the United Empire Loyalists, battles that had been fought along the Canadian-American border between the French and English before the American Revolution, wooden warships and the Indian people who had lived here long before the white man's arrival in their lands.

As promised, they took a little detour to stop at the convenience store along the way and Valerie treated them to a Popsicle each, which they enjoyed as they dawdled and wasted time until the library opened.

The two children approached the library; its pink granite stones and large windows made it look like a huge castle. The nineteenth century style of the building fit well in this block. It was nestled amongst a neighbouring office building and the city's post office. There was a grand entrance to the library; large glass doors at the bottom of a set of several steps opened into a foyer beside the main desk. The entire floor of this level was covered with low, grey carpeting - very neat and tidy against the light-coloured wood and metal bookcases. They could smell the books and the old paper.

Valerie and Alex instinctively looked around, thinking of the grumpy woman who used to be the head librarian here, old 'Stoneface', Ms. Stone. But they both breathed a sigh of relief, remembering that Stoneface was probably in jail, or at least, far from here after an incident last year.

Valerie sat down at one of the catalogue computers and began her search. Alex plunked himself down beside her, pulling up a second chair for his backpack.

"Remind me again what we are looking for," he quietly said to his sister.

"A big book about local history. It will have the story of the Lost Channel in it."

"Perfect," he responded. "Then let's get it, so we can get down to the fun stuff!"

~~~~

The mist was just starting to burn off the river as Jorden got ready for her dive. The class was finally doing an excursion into the river to complete their certification. Curtis lifted Jorden's air tank off the picnic table that it had been resting on and held it upright while she wriggled into the rigging. Her mask sat up on her head, but other than that, she was ready. The class stood close to a stairway that led down into the water as they anxiously awaited the instructor's command to get in. Curtis stood nearby as well, ever helpful, watching as his sister flopped her fins in anticipation.

The sun was still fairly low on the water, its warm radiance reflected in the perfect stillness. Dad sat in his truck nearby, pretending to be engrossed in a newspaper, but Jorden had caught him looking over at her and the group several times, a look of concern on his face. He seemed happy to take her to her lesson and Curtis scrambled along with them in the truck, not wanting to miss anything. Pam had elected to have a well-deserved sleep-in session. Dad had seen the note left on the kitchen counter by Valerie and Alex about their venture to the library, and had scrawled a reply on the torn piece of paper that he and Curtis were taking Jorden to her class and that he would have his cell phone with him if they needed anything. They all communicated like this these days. He sighed, glad to at least know where everyone was on this particular Sunday and feeling as though everything was okay. He glanced up from his paper, took one more look at his daughter and smiled.

Jorden grinned to herself as the class turned their attention over to their instructor, who began to go over a few last minute instructions. Suddenly, a sound arose on the river and the entire group lifted their heads in unison and looked out across the water. Even Dad lowered his paper, scanning the islands in front of them. It sounded like a jet, and it emitted a shrill, hollow roar, like some kind of unleashed mechanical animal. A shape emerged from behind one of the nearby islands - a boat, long and sleek, its bright red paint reflecting the early morning sun. The dive class could only stare at it; even the instructor had fallen silent as they watched the monstrous machine tear the surface off the smooth morning waters, throwing a rooster tail of spray behind it into the air as it flew along like a bullet with butterfly wings. Only the very back end of the boat was in the water as it shot past them.

Dad squinted to see, raising a hand to get a full view of the 'rocket ship' as it glided effortlessly across the mirror-like waters. There was a name on the side, and Dad reached for his glasses quickly. He almost never wore them, refusing to acknowledge the fact that as he grew older his vision was getting worse. Plopping the glasses on his nose, he focused on the sleek machine as it sped down the river in front of them. 'My Way' was written in bold, white lettering on the side of the boat's bright red paint. Dad recalled seeing this huge powerboat on the river before, traveling at what must have been 200 miles per hour and powered by helicopter jet engines.

"The King of the Thousand Islands," he murmured under his breath with a slight grin, shielding his eyes against the morning radiance.

The class hooted and hollered, raising their arms and giving a small cheer at the awesome action scene they'd just witnessed. And just as suddenly as it had appeared, the boat was gone, blasting its way down river into the distance.

The instructor turned his attention back to his class and ushered them one by one down the stairs and into the cold river waters. Jorden was happy to finally get down to business and gave a brief wave to Curtis and her father before setting her mask in place and stepping down into the river.

The water was cold. Even through her wetsuit it took some time to adjust to the temperature, the layer of suit keeping a thin layer of water next to her that her body heat would eventually warm. Slowly she began to adapt to it, treading water and trying to listen to the instructor. After a final few reminders, the class submerged.

The world underwater was beautiful and colourful, a maze of brilliant green weed growth and many different kinds of fish, both large and small. The smaller fish curiously inspected the divers from a safe distance before darting off out of sight. Patches of sunlight danced on the rocky bottom in the shallow area where the class had gathered. Bright greens and blues refracted by the light of the sun above surrounded Jorden and her classmates, and the water was extremely clear, allowing them to see for quite a distance in the underwater world in which they now floated. A large bass silently observed the class from the safety of a clump of seaweed some distance away, while groups of bream and perch darted this way and that.

Jorden exhaled a cloud of bubbles through her regulator as she watched the instructor give hand signals for the exercises they were to perform. She lifted her mask, filling it with water, and then used her regulator to fill it with air until it was clear again, receiving a thumbs-up from the teacher. The class performed each of the simple tasks in turn, and then they were allowed to do as they pleased for the last few minutes of the dive.

Jorden examined some of the rocks and sticks on the bottom, sifting through the debris with a gloved hand, and shooed away an irritated crayfish in the process. It was a strange sensation to be floating along, she thought, free of the force of gravity and able to easily explore the river bottom.

Suddenly, through the silt and dirt she had stirred up in the water column, she could see something shiny. She reached down and lifted the object out of the sand, shaking it to clear the remaining dirt and detritus from its smooth, round surface. What it if was something valuable? Her thoughts turned to Valerie's story of the Lost Channel and her eyes widened in her mask - at that moment the whole idea of sunken treasure seemed a whole lot more real! She moved forward out of the cloud of dirt and held the object up to get a good look at it. It was a shiny, silver... pop can! Her instructor swam up and gave her another thumbs up, but Jorden felt disappointed.

Later, back on shore as she got out of her gear, she replayed the story of the ill-fated British warship again in her mind, imagining with a grin the possibility of finding the sunken cargo, the lost treasure. This could very well be a fun adventure that Valerie was cooking up after all!

6

Conrad pulled open the glass door of the library with an irritated yank, ignoring the old woman behind him who was almost struck by it as he stormed through into the main foyer. His travels today had brought him no luck, and certainly no new avenues to pursue in the hunt for the Onondaga. He paused for a few moments, removed his Ray-Bans and stuffed them into a shirt pocket and waited for his eyes to adjust to the indoor lighting after being out in the bright June sunshine.

Almost as if he were in a chain electronics store, a young library assistant came over to ask if she could assist him. Agitated by the interruption, he growled a curt response and stalked off to one of the catalogue computers. Sitting down, he hammered out several search strings, growing more and more irritated as the results came back without a match. He ran his fingers through his grey hair, bowing his head a moment in an attempt to regain his composure. Finally, he cupped his chin in his hands and thoughtfully looked at the flashing cursor on the screen. For long moments he contemplated. There must be some extra information somewhere, he thought. Desperate ideas swirled around in his mind as he continued to stare at the computer screen in front of him.

Then it hit him: he typed in a new search string, requesting a book on old British warships. A single title appeared on the screen, and he grabbed a little pencil and slip of paper from the box beside the monitor and jotted down the Dewey number. Luckily, the computer stated that the book was not already checked out.

Rising from his chair, Conrad strode through the rows of bookcases, heading for the history section. As he rounded a corner, he nearly slammed into two children coming the opposite way. The boy and girl dodged him, not even noticing his irritated look as they headed off. Conrad scanned through the rows of books, crouching down to search a lower shelf as he got closer to the number of the one he wanted. But he couldn't find it, and the numbers simply increased along the row. He looked again and again but it wasn't there, scanning the numbers to the left and right of the spot where it should have been. Clenching his teeth in frustration, he went back to the front desk to inquire about the missing book.

As he arrived at the low-slung wooden circulation desk, his agitation reached its peak. The two children he had nearly run over were here, checking out a book, and there only seemed to be one young woman working at the desk at the moment. He tried to remain calm, running and hand through his grey hair and straightening his shirt. The process seemed to take forever and Conrad took a peek around the children to check how many books they were actually signing out. Just one! As he looked at the cover absently, Conrad's eyes suddenly widened. The title jumped out at him: 'Historical Ships of the British Navy.' He thought he might faint. This pair of young kids had taken the exact book he was looking for, just moments before he would have picked it up himself. Blood pounded in his ears and he could feel frustrated anger building inside him. He would not be able to ask the young librarian anything about the book now - or about the children for that matter: it would certainly make her suspicious of his motives.

He overheard her telling the young girl that the book was due back in three weeks. He nearly passed out! He could not afford to wait that long. She called the girl and boy by name: Valerie and Alex. Mentally noting this, he quickly departed the library.

~~~~

Valerie retrieved the book and she and Alex happily walked out into the bright June sunshine. On the steps, Valerie stopped her brother and turned him around by pulling on his backpack.

"Hey!" he complained.

"Well, why should I carry this big book all the way home when I have you and your ratty old backpack with me?" she stated, laughing a little. She unzipped the main pouch, popped the book in and zipped it up securely.

"Oooh, one of these days!" Alex replied, squinting his eyes at her.

As they walked away from the library, they did not notice the agitated man stepping out from behind the end of the building, headed in their direction. He had replaced his sunglasses on his face to shield his eyes from the bright sun and stayed back just far enough not to look as though he was following them.

Valerie and Alex walked home along the sun-drenched sidewalks, waiting patiently for traffic to pass to cross the streets. The city was alive with activity, and everyone was out performing his or her daily routines. Several times the children yielded to passers-by, including a mother with a double stroller and an old man with a cane. The two chatted all the way, stopping briefly on occasion to watch a squirrel run along and climb the first available tree. It was getting late in the morning and the sun had become hot.

As they passed the schoolyard, they saw several younger children playing on the swings, kicking hard to make the swings to go as high as they dared. Valerie and Alex waved as they passed, approaching the bridge over the creek. They stopped once again, inspecting the gurgling creek below in hopes that they might see something new. This time they did. Alex pointed to a large snapping turtle lumbering its way around the rocky bottom, heading slowly downstream.

Conrad stood behind a tree, carefully keeping his distance. He wondered what he really would accomplish following these two kids, but he knew however, that the possibility of an important clue to the location of his sunken ship may well be in the book that they had with them. If only he had gone to the library sooner, none of this would have happened. He cursed quietly under his breath, impatient for the children to move on. He must at least find out where they lived. He certainly wasn't foolish enough to try to take the book away from them in broad daylight. No, better to remain out of sight, he thought, and keep tabs on them. He could feel the clock ticking inside his head; could feel his chance to find his prize slipping out of his grasp once again. Conrad gritted his teeth, trying to push the thoughts away.

Finally, Valerie and Alex moved on, the turtle having vanished from sight down the creek. They passed the entrance to the bicycle path, which ran diagonally across the street and down behind the back of their house, following the route of the creek. Up the hill and a quick turn to the left brought them to the walkway to the house situated between the house and the garage. As he watched them turn towards the house, Conrad chose to turn and walk along the bike path's shaded pavement.

A park bench beside the creek, nicely situated in a small, clear area directly behind the hedge at the back of their yard would make a good survey point, he thought. It was a bit cooler here because of the shade of several huge butternut trees and the brushy mixture of maples and birch that lined the edges of the path. He sat down and heard the slam of a screen door, and after a few minutes of quiet, he heard it again, the children obviously coming back out. He stood up from the bench, looking to ensure the hedge concealed the fact that he was there. It was thick and full; he was invisible to them, and he continued to watch the gurgling creek as he listened to them chattering as they came down into their backyard, but he couldn't quite catch their conversation. Conrad looked around, saw that no one was nearby and decided to creep closer to the hedge.

Alex sprinted down to the clubhouse at the back of the yard, throwing open its wooden door and pitching his backpack inside. Valerie followed, although she did not bother to hurry, clutching the book to her chest. They both entered the small wooden house and plopped down on the floor. Valerie had grabbed a small bag of salt and vinegar chips as she'd left the house, which she proceeded to rip open, slapping away her younger brother's eager hand with a grin. She relented, holding out the bag, and Alex immediately dug his hand in and pulled out a bunch of chips to crunch on loudly.

Valerie opened the book on her lap and thumbed through its old pages as she also chewed on chips. It was a very thick, old book and Valerie eyed the pictures of old wooden warships, dating back centuries. The images came alive in her mind as she thought again of the story she had read from Nana's newspaper clippings. The illustrations showed large wooden British warships, which had been involved in battles against the French during the time of Napoleon, along with other vessels that had been built and had sailed in the New World.

Valerie turned another page. A sketch of a large British Man o' War jumped out at her. The pencil drawing of the ship, half constructed and sitting in dry dock, caught her attention immediately. It was the Onondaga. She read the passage underneath the picture quickly, half skimming in her excitement, her hand frozen above the opening of the bag of chips. Alex suddenly realized that she had found something and leaned forward to look at the page.

"This is it!" she exclaimed, grabbing the book in both hands and laying it flat on the clubhouse floor.

She read aloud about the warship being constructed on Carleton Island, near the mouth of Lake Ontario, to defend against American ships entering the Thousand Islands and Lower Canada. It and another great ship, the HMS Ontario, were the largest brig sloops ever to sail in the New World. Even after the loss of the Ontario in a huge hurricane like no storm ever seen before in Canada, the British kept the 197 souls lost aboard the Ontario a secret from George Washington's American forces to the south, fearing the possibility of an invasion. The Onondaga remained however, until it was lost to a French and Mohawk ambush in the Lost Channel, a narrow passage near the modern international bridge in the heart of the Thousand Islands. The paragraphs detailed that she was lost while carrying a large payroll from Fort Niagara, to be dispersed amongst British infantry and militia defending Upper Canada in 1760.

"The ship has to be there!" Valerie practically shouted as she finally reached into the bag for another handful of chips.

"Looks like it's only half finished in the picture," Alex said thoughtfully.

"Yeah, but just imagine what she would look like sailing in the Thousand Islands at full sail!"

"Would have been way cool!"

"Now all we have to do is look at Dad's river charts and find the spot!" she said with determination.

"Oh yeah!" exclaimed Alex sarcastically and waved his arms. "That'll be easy!!!"

Valerie swatted him and gathered up the book.

"C'mon, let's go check it out!" she urged, ducking as she stood up and headed out the small wooden door.

Conrad cursed again to himself from behind of the hedge, realizing that the children had beat him in his pursuit to find vital clues to locate the wreck. His mind raced as he paced back and forth along the bicycle path. He had to get that book. As he headed back the way he came, he chuckled to himself. Ha, he mused, how would two kids ever have a hope of finding the Onondaga before he did?

~~~~

The whole family had a spaghetti dinner on the patio that night, and Valerie continued chattering about the discoveries she and Alex had made that day, talking about the treasure and the lost ship. Dad rolled his eyes slightly as he twirled his fork in the noodles, but he listened nonetheless to the excitement in her voice. Even Curtis and Tyler were engrossed in Valerie's tales of the lost warship. The children ate their load of pasta, everyone enjoying the view of the gardens from their spot on the patio. Birds sang in the evening air and the distant sound of lawn mower could be heard as they talked. Pam brought out a container of Parmesan cheese and sat down.

"Really," began Valerie again. "This could be the adventure of a lifetime!"

She spooled spaghetti noodles onto her fork, barely taking a breath between eating and retelling the story. Curtis was already halfway through his meal, and Dad and Pam knew that the growing boy would be asking for another plateful again very shortly!

Jorden was even interested. She remembered her diving class and the brief excitement she'd felt of pulling something from the river bottom with her own hands.

Tyler enjoyed the idea of the treasure hunt and suggested ideas to Valerie even while he ate. Dad could see what was coming and he sighed as he scooped up another forkful of spaghetti. He knew that there would be no changing his daughter's mind on the matter. She would be obsessed with the idea until it either reached the point where she found what she was looking for or it became totally impossible. He knew the person that he had to thank for the spark of the idea for this latest 'adventure' - but he also knew that Nana had the children's best interests at heart. It was their thing, he knew, and as much as he might worry about their adventures, he realized that they were learning something with each one as well.

He remembered it well: all the holes in the backyard at the old house, when they were searching for buried treasure; feeling worried sick when they arrived back at home after looking for some ghostly apparition from one of Nana's stories...

His thoughts switched to the work at hand; he had been tinkering on the mini-sub again. It was nearly ready for another test run, needed only a few minor adjustments. He wasn't even sure what he would use it for in the end, besides giving tours for a fee or renting it out for salvage or marine construction jobs. But it had been fun to build and it had given him something to do when he wasn't working or spending time with the family. He had the odd day off of work, times when the children were at school and Pam was at work, where he felt completely idle and the sub project had definitely filled that void. And it worked - it worked very well.

Dad suddenly realized that all of his family members were all looking at him. He stopped eating and his deep thoughts vanished.

"I'm sorry," he began. "What was that?"

"I was wondering where and when you might want to try your sub again?" inquired Valerie patiently.

"I hadn't really thought about it yet to be quite honest. There are still some things I need to finish."

Dad could tell what Valerie was up to, and he eyed her warily across the table. She pretended to be engrossed in her meal.

"You have a place in mind?" he asked, raising his eyebrows at her.

"Well, as a matter of fact," she replied. "I might!"

"And where would this lovely place be, to do a test run?"

"I saw a spot on your river charts, near Ivy Lea, in the Thousand Islands..."

"The Lost Channel."

"I think that's it. Hmmm, yes," Valerie replied, sucking up a strand of spaghetti.

Dad thought about it momentarily and noticed that everyone at the table seemed to be waiting for his response.

"That's eighty feet of water, with a fairly strong current," he noted, ignoring the concerned look from Pam and watching his daughter's reaction.

"The water starts getting dark around forty feet," he continued, still watching Valerie eat, although she was trying to retain an innocent posture. Alex grinned slightly, as did the rest of the children at the table, looking down into their plates, but hanging on every word.

Dad knew exactly what she was after - but the idea actually intrigued him - and it would be a great spot for the next test of the mini sub. He purposely hesitated on responding for another minute. The children had all fallen silent, waiting for the verdict, anticipating what he would say. He took a final bite of his meal, placed his fork on his plate and rose from his seat at the patio table. He could feel Valerie's eyes on him, but still he said nothing. The safety of this run would have to be his primary concern, especially since the kids would want to tag along, to search for this missing 'treasure'.

"That was fabulous dear," he said, leaning over and kissing Pam on the forehead as he gathered his plate to take inside to the sink. He turned taking a few steps from the table toward the house. Valerie's facial expression saddened slightly with disappointment as she assumed that her father was about to say 'no' to her idea. He paused at the patio steps and turned towards her.

"I guess I had better get her ready then, eh?"

He turned back around and walked up the steps to the house, wondering if her smile was as big as his grin.

~~~~

"I think you are overestimating those children's possible chances at locating the wreck," said Oscar, giving Conrad a cool look over the chart table.

"The point is, they now have a clue from that book because they beat me to it!" his friend replied, tossing a chart across the surface in front of him.

Oscar gave Conrad another look, furrowing his bushy, white eyebrows at him.

"They're children! What are they going to do; strap on scuba gear and bring the ship up themselves?"

Conrad cast his gaze down on the table, realizing that Oscar was right, of course, but still unable to shake the panic from his mind over their obvious discovery, which he had just narrowly missed. He drew a deep breath and exhaled heavily as he ran his fingers through his grey hair.

His frustration was obvious to his large friend, who simply shook his head slightly. Conrad had been working on this project forever, hoping that he could recover the Onondaga and her cargo, to make himself rich and acknowledged by his peers. Many times Oscar had dove under the river in search of Conrad's prize, only to return to the surface empty-handed. He had gone into the river in early spring, when the water was frigid and clear, and in the summer, when the waters warmed, but were cloudier. The results had always been the same - except for the odd small piece of unidentifiable metal, which would spark Conrad's interest. But the idea of two young children finding the wreck was a bit much for him. No diving skills, no equipment - how would they ever hope to accomplish anything more than visit close by on the shore? There was simply no way for them to beat his friend to the prize without massive amounts of help.

"Relax, my friend. They may have this book, but they have zero ability to dive," Oscar stated again. "Just wait for them to return it to the library and in a couple of weeks you will have your clues."

Conrad looked over at his friend and Oscar simply shrugged at him sympathetically. He was probably right, Conrad realized. What hope did they have? It was probably some school project that they were taking an interest in over the summer. Maybe they just wanted to look at the pictures. But as much as he tried to convince himself that Oscar was right, there was still a sliver in his brain about the whole thing. There was something about those two kids...

7

Jorden and Valerie were in Nana's studio, looking through artwork and her scrapbook. It was a rainy day and streams of water trickled down the large bay window at the front of the room, tracing light shadows on the carpet of the studio.

Nana entered, carrying a tray of teacups for her and the two girls. She set it down on a nearby table, pausing to see what they were so interested in.

"The Lost Channel...you like that story, hmm?" she asked, trying to hide a knowing grin. Valerie turned, holding up the clipping with a smile for her Grandmother to see.

"It's a really cool story, Nana, a lost ship and a sunken treasure. What could be more cool? And it's right here in the Thousand Islands!"

Nana simply smiled, walking over to the table where the girls were looking through everything. She flipped several pages in the scrapbook and listened as the girls recounted the story back to her and told her about the book from the library and Dad's mini-sub. Nana smiled at their excitement.

"Sounds like you might be able to find it...if it's there," she encouraged, still flipping through her scrapbook.

"Well, Jorden can dive now. She finished her course!" said Val.

"You girls have to be careful," cautioned Nana. "The river is no place to mess around. Promise me you won't do anything without your father there."

They both promised and Nana turned away from the book and walked over to the other table where she set the teacups out and poured tea into each.

"Okay, let's have some tea," she said.

The two girls sat with their grandmother and listened to her talk about art and the last few days' events. But even as she spoke, Jorden and Valerie noticed that Nana kept her gaze on the still-opened scrapbook. Something about the story had her captivated, too!

They enjoyed having tea with Nana; it was something that they had done since they were young. Nana also told them that 'English Tea' was the way that she had taught Dad and their Uncle Jay proper manners when they were young. The two girls sipped properly from their cups and listened attentively. The rain beat against the windows. It was very cozy in Nana's studio and both girls liked spending time there. Grandpa called out from his chair in the living room, informing them that Dad would soon be arriving to pick the girls up. They acknowledged him and then were quiet for a moment as they drank the last bit of tea.

"There might be someone who could direct you to where the lost treasure might be," said Nana so quietly that it was almost a whisper.

Both girls instantly perked up and looked questioningly at their Grandmother. Nana simply nodded toward her scrapbook. Valerie and Jorden got up, not noticing the sheepish grin Nana wore as she sipped the last of her tea. On the page was another clipping, one about a woman who had lived in the area long ago. She had been called 'Mother Barnes' and was a woman who had told fortunes by reading tealeaves. The first Prime Minister of the country had even consulted her. Their eyes flew through the lines of text. The headline of the clipping had referred to her as 'The Witch of Plum Hollow'…but she had died long ago.

Valerie turned back to her Grandmother, who was watching the girls intently.

"How could she help us find the Onondaga, Nana? She is long gone."

"No," replied Nana, placing her teacup back on the tray and looking Valerie straight in the eye. "Not necessarily her…there are others…"

~~~~

Curtis and Alex sat on the cool concrete of the garage floor and watched as Dad worked on the mini-sub. Every once in a while, he would drop the wrench he was working with, and would twist his body and mutter something incoherent as he reached to pick it up again. He lay underneath the contraption and was working up under the front nose area, wires hanging down. The area was illuminated by a flashlight that dangled crazily as Dad toiled. The boys exchanged funny looks as they each munched on sandwiches that Pam had made them for lunch.

It was fairly cool in the garage with the help of a large fan Dad had plugged in. It was certainly cooler than outside where the hot summer sun was baking the neighbourhood.

The cat entered the garage, flicking her tail as she made a quick observation of the activities. Pam followed her inside and folded her arms as she looked at the strange contraption with great concern. Alex nudged Curtis and motioned for him to follow as he stood up. It was obvious that Pam had something to discuss with Dad and, from the look on her face, it wouldn't be something they wanted to be involved in. The two boys ran outside, content to go and find their own adventure in the backyard. Pam sat down on a nearby chair as she continued to watch Dad mess about underneath his creation.

"Yes dear?" he chimed, sensing correctly that she was there.

Pam was quiet for a few moments before she spoke.

"I am worried about what you plan to do here," she began as she observed the strange vehicle from end to end.

"It's completely safe, my love," Dad assured her. "I have built and tested it myself. The design is the safest possible of any type of mini-sub there is. Even if it lost power and sank to the bottom, we're still able to get out by swimming through the bottom at the rear."

He went on to explain all the other safety features that he had designed for it, although to Pam's ears, the technological jargon was mostly 'Greek' to her. She was highly intelligent and was not fooled by the subdued tone - or the 'Geek Speak'!

"But you were talking about the Lost Channel, in eighty feet of swift water, where it's dark!"

Hearing the worry in Pam's voice, Dad finally slid himself out from under the mini-sub, fresh blotches of grease on his nose and cheek. He gave her a quick look with an expression that said that she was worrying needlessly. The cat sat alongside her, watching him as well, and flicked her tail in obvious disapproval. Dad wiped his face and hands with a clean rag from the workbench and then wiped down the wrench he was holding. He looked at Pam with a slight smirk as he waited for her to question him again. She didn't say a word, just stared at him. He reached over and turned on a small radio that sat on the workbench. A tune from 'The Trews' filled the silence with a familiar East Coast cadence.

"What?" she inquired. "What is that look for?"

"I've already taken her below eighty feet...in good current."

"What?!?"

Dad gave her the smirk again, but knew that this information would not please Pam. As he'd anticipated, she shot him a look that instantly told him he was in trouble, yet he grinned at both her and the cat.

"The sub works awesome. It will go to depths that any diver could reach, but I stay dry!" he said. "And it has the best possible safety features built in."

This seemed to do nothing to diminish the look he was getting. Pam was definitely not happy, and wore a look that the cat seemed to mirror as she continued to flick her tail at him. He could only smile at them, proud of his project, and how well it seemed to work. His wife knew that he had always tinkered with seemingly impossible things, from running the garage on solar power to heating the house with the woodstove in his little hideaway through heat pipes, but this was a touch too much. It seemed dangerous to her. She continued to look at Dad with that look. And so did the cat.

"Hey, I feel like I'm being ganged up on here," he said, still wearing his grin, motioning at the two of them.

"Well, I'm sorry but this is all a bit extreme, you have to admit. You have had other projects, but this is really out there!"

Dad thought for a few moments. Despite his joking around, he didn't wish to upset her. She was clearly concerned about it and he searched for a way to allay her fears.

"Even if it loses power and reserve air, we can simply land it on the bottom, and swim out. Seriously, honey, it's a very safe design," he reassured her again.

"Well, I don't like this. It sounds dangerous," Pam said again, resignedly.

"Well, blame my mother! This is another one of her great adventure ideas."

~~~~

Conrad could not believe his ears. To be denied a loan by the bank he had dealt with for over thirty years was something new. He continued to look at the loan manager, a man he had known for some time and had thought of as a friend, in disbelief. He rested his elbows on the pressboard desk, running his hands through his grey hair, searching for something in his brain he could tell this man that might change the outcome. Without a new loan, he would be unable to afford another expedition to find the Onondaga. Without money, he could not hope to find the chests laden with riches that would set him free. If he was to have a true retirement and get out of here to some tropical beach, he needed the resources to make it happen. It angered and frustrated him, and he found himself biting down on his tongue to refrain from saying something bad, which would surely end this meeting.

Suddenly the man across the desk stopped typing things into his computer, paused for just a moment and straightened his tie abruptly. He looked at Conrad soberly and cleared his throat with a little cough.

"Okay. I can probably get you an additional two thousand dollars, but you would have to let the bank go on title with your house," he said slowly.

Conrad lay back in the chair, pondering the offer as he looked at the perfection of the grid of ceiling tiles.

Two thousand, he thought. Was it worth putting his home on the line? He needed fuel for the barge and payroll for the few people who would be helping him. He knew that his mission would be impossible without financial aid. This loan, despite the risk involved, would keep him in the game for at least one more try. Oscar would be there, regardless, but he needed the money for the rest of the venture. For a moment he considered the depth of the situation, but he knew that he must act immediately if he was to have any chance of finding the Onondaga. Immortality awaited; he pictured his name in the history books as the victor who had solved the two hundred year old mystery. Those meddling children entered his brain along with their discovery of the library book in their grasp. They may only be children, he thought, but they seem to be on the very same course as me. He couldn't afford to stand by and let them reach the finish line first, even if they were only young and foolish, with no idea of the immensity of the quest. Time was ticking away, a constant thought in his mind, and this measly sum would at least partially fund one more trip on the river to continue his search.

Conrad gathered his thoughts together, sat upright, placed his hand on the desk and looked soberly at the loan manager. He could feel the cool surface of the desk under his clenched hands.

"Ok, whatever you need. Let's get this done," he said gruffly.

8

Nana had stopped by to visit and walked around the back gardens perusing each flower with keen eyes. The children were out playing on this sun-filled July day, making the most of the warmth of summer. Pam walked with Nana, pointing to various plants and noting how well they were growing. The yard had become a living thing, alive with the sounds of the children's laughter, tweets and twitters of birds and buzzing and chirruping of insects. A gentle, whispering breeze stirred the gardens.

"So beautiful," said Nana, impressed with the sights.

"Well, we've been working hard this year," explained Pam. "We hope to maybe enter it in next year's 'Communities in Bloom' contest."

"Well, I'm sure you will do well," Nana stated. "This is amazing."

She wandered with Pam, through the jungle of the gardens, pausing to look down at the fish lazing in the pond. She gazed at the brilliant flowers surrounding this pool of water that was dappled with water lilies as an occasional frog dove into the water to avoid their disturbing presence. It was like being immersed into another world for Nana, an escape from the real world. The tiger lilies swayed in the breeze, guided by an unseen symphony conductor. They paused in the shade of a large apple tree. The entire scene made them both stop and sigh as they breathed in the fresh air.

"Wow! This is something else," said Nana.

"I love it out here," Pam said. "It's like our own little paradise."

The two women stood quietly, looking at what Mother Nature was offering in front of their eyes. They drank it in, watching the bees and the occasional hummingbird enter the scene. It was perfection. The children came down into the yard to play. Alex and Curtis were kicking a soccer ball back and forth, but this distraction did nothing to diminish the moment. Nana looked out over the gardens, nodding in satisfaction.

"You have an amazing little piece of heaven here."

"Well, we have been working on it forever, so thank you," Pam replied.

The two women finally turned around to meander up to the garage, where Dad was working while the boys continued playing their game. Pam motioned graciously to her mother-in-law at the entrance, as if to say that she entered at her own risk. Nana simply grinned and stepped inside to see what was going on.

There was the smell of oil and electricity in the garage. Dad was again underneath his contraption, tweaking this and that, swapping tools occasionally. Music played on the radio and the clink of tools could be heard as Dad worked away. The mini-sub sat there, resembling a character from some obscure old film.

"That's some ship you have there!" exclaimed Nana, startling Dad to the point that a loud smack was heard, followed by a groan that indicated that he had hit his head on the underside of the vessel in his sudden surprise.

"Whoops, sorry!" said Nana, as she nudged Pam and gave her a slight grin.

Pam bit her lip in an attempt to keep from giggling.

Dad struggled to get out from under the mini-sub, stood up and rubbed his forehead.

"Yeah, she's almost ready," he said.

"Well, we don't want to keep you from your important work, son. Pam was just giving me a tour of the gardens."

"Yes, she has them looking great this year," he replied.

The two women left, leaving Dad to crawl back under his machine. Out on the walkway, Valerie and Alex, bounding up the steps from the patio, intercepted them.

"Well, hello you two!" Nana chimed.

"Hi, Nana!" said Alex, short of breath.

Valerie reminded Nana about the book that they had found at the library and of her searches on the Internet, which had turned up little else.

"There isn't going to be much written about it, but that's what makes it such a great mystery," encouraged Nana.

"I know, but that makes it so frustrating!" said Val. "It's nearly impossible to find anything out about it, because it's such an old story!"

"There is one place you may have missed checking," said Nana evenly.

Valerie's eyes brightened as she anticipated the next thing her Grandmother would say, waiting several seconds while Nana grinned at her.

"Where would people keep very old or interesting things with any historical purpose?" asked Nana.

Valerie paused for a second and thought. Alex whacked her lightly on the arm.

"Duh," he laughed. "The museum!"

Valerie's eyes opened wide as she realized that she had forgotten all about the local museum and its eccentric old curator, Mr. Thusk. She grabbed hold of Alex's arm and dragged him towards the sidewalk at a half run. Nana and Pam laughed out loud and Alex managed to break free from Valerie's grip just long enough to run over and grab his trusty backpack from the front porch. As the two excited kids took off down the street, Pam called quickly after them, "Be home for dinner at six!"

~~~~

Jorden was concentrating on checking her diving tank and regulator. The greenhouse was hot, but she didn't seem to mind as she intensely focused on the task at hand. She could hardly wait for tomorrow, when they would begin this adventure out on the water. It was the chance to finally test her newly acquired skills, to go on a real dive and actually search for real treasure. At least, it might be real!

Valerie had kept Jorden awake late the night before with talk of the Onondaga, until Jorden had finally, reluctantly drifted off to sleep. The story fascinated her as much as it did her sister, but she had been tired. Her fatigue hadn't stopped her from dreaming of shiny gold and jewels that could be waiting for them at the bottom of the channel, though. Visions of the underwater world had swirled in her mind even as she'd slept. She had awakened with fresh excitement and was busy ensuring that she would be completely ready.

Jorden had borrowed a wrench from Dad's garage to use to make sure that the fittings for her airlines were tight. The sun beat down into the greenhouse and she wiped sweat from her forehead and scooped some strands of her sandy blonde hair back over her ear.

What if they really found something from the cargo of the lost ship? It would be epic!

She glanced over at her mask and fins. Her wetsuit hung neatly nearby on a hanger in the rafters of the greenhouse. She didn't need to check much with those items, she thought. Jorden glanced around her, feeling the humidity and looked at Dad and Pam's collection of tropical plants. It was a veritable jungle of palms and citrus trees, small sensitive plants from the tropical regions of the world. They seemed to flourish in the oppressive heat and moisture in the small room.

Her thoughts were interrupted by Curtis bursting into the greenhouse to see her.

"What are ya doing?" he asked innocently, still breathing heavy from running around the yard.

"Just making sure everything is ready for my next dive in the river."

Curtis looked at the tank and the line leading off it.

"So this lets you breathe underwater?" he asked.

"Yep."

He thought for a second as he traced a finger over the cool metal of the aluminum of the tank.

"Maybe I could help. I can hold my breath under water for a long time!"

Jorden chuckled slightly.

"Well," she began. "It is a long way down to the bottom of the channel. I really don't think you could hold your breath that long!"

Curtis made a comically sad face.

"Tell ya what," she said. "Maybe you could help me carry my fins and stuff up to the garage, because I'm all set, I think."

The young boy's face brightened suddenly, happy to be included with what was obviously an important job. Jorden grabbed her tank in one hand and reached for the wet suit with the other. Curtis snapped up the mask and fins and headed quickly out the door ahead of her. Jorden took the lead as they made their way up to the patio and then up the steps to the walkway between the house and garage.

As they entered the garage, Jorden paused for a moment to let her eyes adjust to the darkened space. Her father was there, relaxing by leaning up against the workbench with a glass of what appeared to be lemonade. He wore a large grin. Jorden set her things in the corner and hung up her suit as Curtis followed.

"Well?" asked Jorden, curious about her Dad's amused look.

Dad nodded toward the strange vehicle that took up most of the floor space of the room. "She's all ready."

~~~~

Oscar sat on the edge of the barge as he coiled ropes and cables for the crane. He loved to dive in the depths of the river and his friend Conrad had given him a purpose to use his talents. Now that his friend had secured some cash, they could resume the hunt for their treasure. He hoped, for Conrad's sake, that they at least found something of worth on this trip, as his friend was going deeper and deeper into debt with this project. It worried Oscar a little. Normally Conrad was very straightforward and conservative about historical research, but this particular subject was proving to be an obsession.

Oscar got up and organized the lines, then sat on the edge of the barge once again to sharpen his dive knife. His huge hands worked skillfully as he turned the blade on a whetstone and dragged it along its length. The sound it made pleased him, especially amongst the sounds of gulls squawking overhead and the water lapping against the metal sides of the rusted old barge. There was barely a breeze, even down here on the river and the sun shone hot against his leathery, tanned skin. His bright white hair and moustache stood out in stark contrast to his weathered skin and, although he could feel the harsh rays of the sun seeping into his pores, he continued his work on the knife. He had always loved the river and the Thousand Islands; he felt at home and comfortable in the presence of the flowing waters.

The ominous tone of a lonely bell reverberated from a tugboat floating in the water by the docks behind him. The river was like something alive and Oscar knew from experience that its mood could change from a calm serenity to a boiling, thrashing fury in a very short time.

As he made the last stroke with the knife against the whetstone, Conrad's small black BMW pulled up at the dock. Oscar had always teased his friend about driving such a lavish foreign car on a retirement income, but as his friend emerged from the driver's side door, he could tell by his expression that this would be no time for jokes. It saddened Oscar to see his friend in this state. He was obviously stressed and not thinking clearly.

As Conrad walked toward the barge, carrying a box of charts and notes, Oscar could tell that his friend's mind was heavy with the lack of progress that they'd made. He also knew that Conrad was preoccupied with the fact that the children he had spoken about might have vital clues in their possession that he had missed. He barely acknowledged Oscar as he stepped aboard and carried the box into the barge's small wheelhouse. Conrad cleared a spot to place the box by shifting old papers and debris off of a small table into an empty wooden crate. Cursing slightly under his breath, he emerged once again, kicking a few pieces of loose rigging out of his way.

"Can't those guys even keep this boat a little bit tidy?" he asked, irritated.

"I'm surprised they're even sober when they do show up for work," Oscar replied.

Conrad let out a deep sigh and looked around at the mess onboard. Oscar finally sheathed his knife and placed the sharpening stone on the deck beside him.

"Relax, my friend," he urged. "We should be glad to have them show up at all. It's not like you're paying them a huge wage to do this."

"Yes, I know."

"And at least you will get another try at it tomorrow," Oscar said, trying to sound optimistic.

Conrad turned, not responding to his friend's comment. He looked westward, up the river to the dotted islands. Oscar was right, of course. At least with this small loan he had one more shot to find the wreck and claim his prize. Summer would be over soon enough and he would be prohibited from any future excursions if he could not show something for his efforts this time. He would be without any funds after this. What investor would step up to bankroll a search like this without something to tantalize their imagination that the treasure was actually there? He knew that this was it: it was now or never!

The river had a slight chop to it this day, even though the breeze was minimal. The islands in the distance rose from the waters, dark green with pitch pines and hard maple, surrounded by the dark blue of the river. Even though he could feel little wind here at the docks, he could see the trees on the island nearest to him swaying slightly. Soaring clouds, high in the sky, made a puzzle of shadow and light on the surface of the water. The river was hiding what he sought and he gritted his teeth as he imagined finding the ship, perfectly preserved, sitting upright on the bottom in the depths. He had to find it…before the money ran out!

"Will the crew be ready in the morning?" he asked as he stared out at the water.

"Three confirmed," replied the big man.

"Okay. I'll see you at six."

9

Valerie and Alex made their way downtown towards the museum. The sidewalks baked in the summer sun and the traffic on the streets flowed with the afternoon bustle. They passed retail storefronts displaying all types of wares along with offices and apartment buildings. The city was alive with people and cars, moving in all directions. The children cut down from the main street onto a side street lined with older homes, which led down to the street that ran parallel with the river. As they passed by their favourite fish and chip shop, the aroma of deep fried goodness wafted by - a smell that could make anyone hungry again, even if they had only just eaten! The parking lot of the small shop was busy today, filled with people waiting in line for the chance to indulge in fresh cut French fries and fish, hot out of the fryers. The smell was intoxicating, but Valerie and Alex pushed on towards the museum's stone hulk of a building.

Like many other old buildings in town, the museum shared the unique nineteenth century architecture that made the small city a charm. It was not a very large building compared to some of the others in the city, but it was beautified by lush gardens surrounding its stone facade. Flowers and well-tended rock gardens enveloped the entire building. Valerie stopped briefly at the walkway to the front door to look around at the gardens.

"Wow. They really keep this place nice," she observed, as Alex trotted up behind, his backpack slung over a shoulder.

They went up the walkway and Valerie pulled open the large glass door and held it while her little brother stepped in behind her. They were met with cool, filtered air. The lobby of the museum was much cooler than outside and had that 'old' smell, like ancient paper and ancient wood. But it also felt clean and preserved, like suddenly stepping back in time to a simpler place.

There was a guest book open on a pulpit to the side of the entryway and Valerie stepped up to take a look at it. The illegible scrawls and signatures in the book alongside handwritten dates made it plain to her that very few people visited the museum; either that or very few had taken time to sign the book! The white lined pages reflected the building's story of solitude, of history stored in its dark, quiet lodgings.

Valerie picked up the pen next to the book, adding her name and Alex's into the ledger along with the date. She stepped back and looked down the hallway. She could see dimly lit glass display cases detailing local prominent families from the city's beginnings, along with carefully preserved old vehicles and flags. Alex moved closer to his sister as she stepped forward and began to walk down the hall. Their footsteps echoed as they emerged from the carpeted lobby onto the hardwood flooring of the hallway. The wooden floor creaked and groaned as they exited the hall and entered the large main room of the museum.

All around them were cases filled with historical artifacts - including ancient Indian artifacts, crafts, and paintings - as well as old manuscripts and maps. The two curious young sleuths stopped abruptly, both looking across the room at a large glass case on the far wall. At its centre was a large pedestal holding a crystal geode and beside it was a purple amethyst crystal shaped like a bird. A Raven. Both of them glanced at each other, grinning.

Just then Mr. Thusk entered the room, noticed the children and smiled widely at them.

"Well, hello, Valerie. Hello Alex. It's very nice to see you once again!" he stated with a slightly formal, but enthusiastic tone.

"Hi, Mr. Thusk," returned Valerie.

"Making a visit to view your discoveries today?" he asked, nodding at the crystal glistening behind the glass of the display case.

"Actually, we were hoping you could help us with a new discovery," explained Valerie.

With this information, Mr. Thusk straightened himself up and clasped his hands together with a look of utter glee.

"How perfect, I would love to help any way that I can!"

The two children glanced at each other, trying not to laugh.

Mr. Thusk had always been very nice to the two of them and often made them giggle at his odd mannerisms. He was the perfect person to be the curator of the museum. He was polite, funny and very knowledgeable about the history of the city and the Thousand Islands region. Valerie and Alex knew that if anyone could help them find the Onondaga, it would be

Mr. Thusk!

"We are looking for information about the HMS Onondaga," she continued. "That's the ship that disappeared in-"

"The ghost ship of the Lost Channel!" Mr. Thusk interrupted, his eyes brightening.

"Yes!"

"Follow me, kids!" he exclaimed as he spun on his heel and practically bolted down the corridor.

Valerie and Alex shrugged at each other and followed Mr. Thusk down the hallways. The shuffled after the old curator as he led them into a small room in the back of the museum that contained bookcases full of binders and file folders, maps and boxes full of old papers. He politely pulled out two chairs from an old wood table sitting in the centre of the room and indicated that they should be seated. Alex plunked his backpack down and sat in the first chair and Valerie followed suit.

Mr. Thusk quickly scanned the bookcases, with a hand on his chin letting loose a loud, almost comical sigh. The children grinned at one another again as the old man darted here and there and rummaged through piles of papers and folders in his search for the information they sought. Suddenly he stopped, grabbed a box and yanked it out onto the table.

"Here it is!" he exclaimed.

He lifted the lid slowly, as thought he was some kind of magician about to reveal a magic trick. Inside were old papers with words delicately scribed in real ink. Mr. Thusk pulled a bunch of them out and laid them flat on the old table. The pages even smelled old. Valerie's eyes lit up as she read. These were original pages from the captain's log from the Onondaga! It detailed the voyage route and the precious cargo that had been intended for the enlisted loyalists to the British Crown, the men and their families who had been fighting the French and their Indian allies for control of the colonies of the New World.

Then, there it was, right in front of her: the captain's last entry dated August fourteenth, 1760.

"We sail through the myriad islands which lead us to home today. Our enemies know not what we are sought to deliver as it is well hidden in the bowels of our great vessel. With luck, and the wind filling our sails, we shall see home and our brethren by day's end."

"They had it hidden!" Valerie practically shouted.

"Yes, and it was never recovered. There is nothing more of the ship or its crew or cargo ever recorded in our history," explained Mr. Thusk quietly.

"But how is it that these pages survived?" asked Val.

"They were found on shore, here!" The curator grabbed a river chart and from the top of a bookcase and unrolled it on the table. Indicating to the kids to hold down the curled corners, he used his index finger to point out a spot on the mainland shore of the channel. An 'X' practically marked the spot.

Valerie looked up at the old man. A thousand questions flooded her brain.

"Who else has seen this?" she asked quietly.

"No one, young lady. I have been saving this for someone who had the ability to seek it out for the experience and the joy of discovery - and not just for sheer profit!"

Valerie considered this for a moment.

"But if the French or Mohawk warriors read this, they would know!" she contemplated and looked up at Mr. Thusk once again. The old man put a hand on her shoulder and leaned down to speak to her quietly.

"Apparently...their English was not that good!"

~~~~

The sun was barely up, painting the clouds pink and orange in the early morning light and the children were all awake. They could hear something going on outside, some clanging and clinking of machinery. Valerie got out of bed quickly, dressing so fast she barely knew what she was putting on. Her older sister was right behind her, struggling into a bathing suit with faded jogging pants and a plain white t-shirt over top. The girls raced for the bathroom and almost trampled Alex in the hallway. He waved a hand at them in annoyance as he retreated back into the bedroom that he and Curtis shared. The youngest boy was already awake as well, jumping from his bed to throw clothing on.

In no time at all they were all downstairs and had formed a stampede into the kitchen to grab something to eat before they began the day. Before they could even root through the cupboards, Valerie too a look out the window and gasped in her excitement. Alex shoved in to get a look, too. Tyler was already outside assisting Dad. The sub was perched on top of a trailer behind the truck and they both were working together to strap it down securely. Valerie watched her father step back from the arrangement and clap his hands together in approval of their efforts.

The children's attention was brought back to the kitchen, as a yawning Pam walked in. She was still wearing her housecoat.

"Anyone for waffles?" she chimed as she noted the excitement on their faces.

This drew shouts and hoots and she pulled the toaster from the cupboard as they helped with plates, cutlery and syrup. In the kitchen chaos, breakfast was eventually served, along with juice and coffee and whatever else this 'crew' could find to fill their bellies. Dad and Tyler entered to see the feeding frenzy in progress.

"Whoa!" said Tyler as he took a look at the rest of the bunch gorging themselves with the meal.

"Yep, be careful! And for God's sake, don't make eye contact!" Dad joked with Tyler.

As they waded into the fray, Pam sighed slightly and handed them each a drink and plate topped with a waffle. Dad leaned in and gave her a kiss on his way past her. The children chattered as they stuffed themselves, talking about the ship and the treasure they hoped to find. They gobbled up everything in front of them, then raced their dishes to the sink and sped off to grab those last few things they would need on their venture.

Alex reappeared with his backpack. Valerie came back into the kitchen with her charts and the book from the library. They both darted outside. Jorden was already stowing her diving gear in the back of the truck and Tyler had just gone outside to help her. Curtis simply ran around the front lawn, waving and shouting in excitement.

Pam began to make sandwiches to pack for a lunch as Dad leisurely leaned against the kitchen counter and savoured his coffee.

Pam looked up from the sandwiches she was stuffing into zip-lock bags to cast a glance towards her husband. He took a long sip from his coffee, and sighed, waiting with a smile on his face for her reaction. Pam knew exactly what he was up to.

"Don't do that!" she smirked at him.

"What?" he said and grinned as he took another sip of his coffee.

"You know, you silly man! Don't make them wait!"

"Let me have a little fun, will ya?" he continued to grin.

Almost on cue, they could hear the impatient shouts and hollers for him to come outside. Pam gave him the look.

"Oh, all right" he said to her quietly and stole another kiss.

"And be careful, for the love of God!"

He simply winked and turned toward the door.

~~~~

It was a bright, windless morning as they drove down the parkway towards the islands and the children all chattered with pent up excitement. Valerie went over the details of the story again as they drove, as Alex rolled his eyes in exasperation. The sub rode along strapped to its trailer behind them and Dad kept an eye on it in the rear view mirrors. It was only about 20 kilometres to the launch and Dad knew it would probably take the slow little sub at least a half hour to get to the channel from the marina. He turned up the radio and drowned out the chatter of the children as a tune from 'The Trews' came on. Dad loved their music and routinely blared it from the garage while he was tinkering away.

His thoughts turned to the time in February when he had fooled Pam into going to the band's concert and had wound up proposing to her on stage under the guise of her winning some fictitious contest. It had been a night to remember for the both of them.

The music continued to play as Dad drove down the parkway - a fitting soundtrack to their adventure as they neared the marina. Even with the music playing, the children continued their conversation until Dad made the turn into the marina. The parking lot was fairly full, with families running up and down the docks, preparing for a day out on the water.

People stopped and stared as the strange craft, perched on top of its trailer, entered the boat launch area. The ramp was free, so Dad expertly backed down it. The children jumped out of the vehicle excitedly as it came to a stop just before entering the river. Dad stepped out and hopped up onto the trailer to loosen the tie-down straps that held his creation in place. The sub's yellow paint job gleamed in the warm summer sun and a small crowd gathered to witness its launch as the children collected the ropes that Dad tossed them. Dad resumed his position in the truck and backed the trailer into the water as the children manned the dock beside the ramp.

The water bubbled and gurgled as the sub was launched. Its front windows bobbed as the sub lifted buoyantly off the trailer and began to float on its own. Jorden and Tyler pulled the ropes and brought the craft towards the dock, being careful not to bang it up against the old wood. Dad looked back to check to see if everything was alright and then pulled the truck and empty trailer out of the launch area and parked up in the parking lot. A few moments later he came down to the dock and assisted Jorden and Tyler with tying the sub directly alongside the dock. It was ready. He stood up for a moment and gave a satisfied nod to his crew. The bottom hatch was sealed. He reached over and opened the top of the sub as the craft bobbed lightly in the shallow waters of the boat launch.

"Okay. Let's get her ready, crew!" he said. "Jorden, you can ride on top with your gear until we get there, I guess."

Jorden nodded and headed up to the truck to get her diving equipment as Valerie, Alex and Curtis waited impatiently on the dock. Dad began turning the valves on for the tanks mounted on the back of the sub.

"What are you going to do, Ty?" he asked.

Tyler stood still and looked at the little ship floating in the water.

"I think I would rather stay on dry land!" he stated. "I was going to go over and look at some of the boats they have over here." He pointed in the direction of the marina.

"Okay. We'll be gone for a good while," Dad said and handed Tyler a twenty-dollar bill. "Here's some money to get yourself some lunch at the restaurant." Tyler happily accepted the money and headed off to explore, passing Jorden as she returned to the dock, hauling her gear. Dad helped her piled it on top of the backside of the sub between the air tanks where there was a depression in the hull to accommodate such things.

People watched as Dad climbed into the strange ship and sat down in one of the front seats, turning on switches and powering everything up. He checked on all the systems, making sure not to forget anything. Air pressure in the tanks: check. Battery and reserve battery power: check. Homemade GPS made out of an older tablet computer working: check. When he was sure they were ready, he gave a slight nudge on the joysticks that controlled the motors to make sure that they were functioning; check. He climbed back out slowly through the hatch, carefully choosing his footing, and emerged back out onto the dock. He smiled at his crew and extended a welcoming gesture to the sub hatch.

"Well, daylight is burning. Let's get this show on the road!" he exclaimed with a broad grin.

The children smiled and Curtis cheered. Valerie, Alex, and then Curtis climbed nimbly into the hatch, shuffling around in the tiny ship to get into a seat, and marveled at the sights of the dock area through the mini sub's small windows. Small fish scooted by and the children looked in awe at the underwater world in the shallows of the boat launch.

Dad held the last rope, as Jorden climbed onto the sub and perched herself between the air tanks with her diving gear. She would have to ride on top until they arrived at their destination, but she didn't mind at all.

Dad gave one final small shove to the craft as he boarded, taking off the rope and passing it to Valerie to stow away through the hatch. He made his way inside, took his seat and thrust the motors forward, making the sub slowly leave the marina. Curious people continued to watch the strange vehicle as it set off on its voyage.

As they maneuvered through the marina's docks and boats, Curtis poked his head up through the hatch to take a peek. He gave Jorden a quick thumbs-up with a big smile and ducked back inside.

10

The channel was quiet and fairly calm as Conrad watched Oscar ready his scuba tank. He motioned to the crewmen at the wheelhouse to stop and moved to the forward end of the barge to lower the anchor. The barge surged in the water slightly as the engines reversed and slowed the large vessel almost to a stop. Conrad hit the winch release and the huge anchor splashed into the water and disappeared into the depths. He watched it drop, the steel cable spinning off the winch quickly for what seemed like a long time. Finally it stopped. He secured it and had the man in the wheelhouse reverse the engines slowly. After a few seconds, the barge lurched slightly, the cable from the winch grew taught suddenly and the machine groaned slightly. The anchor was set. Conrad motioned again and the engines were shut off.

Oscar pulled on his tank and checked his regulator. His face stuck out through the hood of his wetsuit, his broad white moustache bristling off his bronzed skin in stark contrast to the dark rubber of the suit. Conrad often wondered how he could keep his mask water tight with all that hair! The big man produced his mask then, spat into it and rinsed it over the side of the barge before sliding it onto his head and wiggling it around to ensure a tight fit. Conrad was always repulsed by this action, despite the fact that his friend had explained that it kept his mask from fogging up.

Oscar shot one more bit of air through the regulator and placed it in his mouth. He looked up at Conrad briefly with a motion that everything was good - resembling some kind of huge owl looking at him through the mask - and slid over the side of the barge and into the waters of the channel. He disappeared almost as quickly as the anchor had, moving like some kind of huge strange fish.

Conrad watched the water for a moment and then moved over to another spot on the front of the barge where he'd placed the sonar imaging equipment. He dropped a torpedo-like device into the water and its rubber cable followed it down. Switching it on, he moved quickly toward the wheelhouse as his mind ran down the tasks to bring the sonar online. He stepped inside the small room, ignoring the man at the wheel, and pulled open the screen on a laptop that sat on one of the side benches within the wheelhouse. The screen came to life and Conrad deftly hit the combination of keys to start the program. A new screen popped up and an image started to appear that showed a rough outline of the channel's bottom. Collies streamed by as he watched, tracing the layout of the rock and sand along the river floor. A blotch appeared, just off the bottom. Oscar, he realized. He hit another button that saved the data and pulled his glasses from a jacket pocket.

Sitting down to get comfortable, he pulled open a nearby notebook to get reacquainted with their previous searches from his notes. He stared at the pages long and hard, only breaking his attention for the laptop screen and the updated images coming through. Would this be the day? Would he have some luck and turn the money pit of searching around? He dismissed these thoughts, trying to keep his focus.

The blotch on the screen moved here and there, close to the bottom and Conrad took some comfort in the fact that Oscar was diligently searching for some shred of something that might lead him to his prize. He imagined chests full of old British payroll, gold and silver coin and God knows what else! He would be set for life! It would be a discovery that would garner him immeasurable fame and fortune. He would have the money to retire, comfortable and secure, with more money than he could ever hope to spend. Conrad conjured up black tie events, where he was in the spotlight, detailing how they had located and salvaged this lost treasure.

He shook his head, trying not to think of the financial pressures or the flights of fancy that his brain was bringing forth. He ran a hand through his grey hair and rubbed his forehead for a moment. His thoughts were interrupted by a bleep from the laptop that indicated something from the sonar. He riveted his eyes on the screen, watching intently. Oscar had found something!

His heart began to race slightly as he remained glued to the screen. The blotch changed shape and became distorted as he watched. He noted the barge's position on the GPS at the helm beside him and jotted it in his notebook frantically as he tried to maintain his attention on the laptop and its images. He began to get a warm feeling, that maybe his one last attempt financially could pay off big, that this might be the moment he had been waiting for.

One of the other crewmen hollered and indicated that something was on the crane. Oscar had secured whatever it was he had found to the cable of the crane, and finally Conrad felt that he might actually see something, anything that would confirm his discovery of the Onondaga at last.

He stood up and tossed the notebook aside as he rushed out onto the deck to get a glimpse of what was coming up from the depths. The cable was reeling up onto the crane, squeaking and squawking as the large winch powered up whatever was being brought to the surface. The man operating the crane expertly worked the control and kept the cable straight and taught as he reeled in their catch. Conrad began to see a shape emerging through the dark water and his heart began to race. What had Oscar found?

The shape became clearer. The colour of rusted metal could be seen as the hulking object neared the surface. A cannon? Perhaps it was one of the old Man o' War's 22 six pound guns, disturbed from over 250 years of slumber in the depths of the river. The water churned as the object came to the surface beside the barge and Conrad made a slashing motion to the crane operator to stop. He placed his glasses on his face to get a better look as Oscar suddenly broke the surface nearby.

Squatting down on the edge of the barge, Conrad quickly examined the long cylindrical iron of the object tied to the crane cable. Silt and mud floated in the water as well, making it difficult to see. He stood, grabbed the cable and motioned absently behind him for the crewman operating the crane to lift it carefully. The winch ground into motion again as it raised the object from the water and swung it onto the deck under Conrad's guidance. Perhaps 10 to 12 feet long, it was perfectly cylindrical and definitely not the varying shape of a cannon. He released the cable to allow the operator to free the crane from their catch.

Conrad squatted next to the object and examined it closely. It was covered with muck and weeds. He wiped a hand along its smooth surface to uncover the metal. Oscar climbed out of the water onto the deck and eagerly pulled his mask up onto his forehead. Conrad cursed quietly as anger filled his face. This was definitely not the same object that they had found - and lost - before. Clearly stamped into the metal were three words, three measly words that twisted Conrad's face into a vicious snarl: 'MADE IN USA'.

Oscar shrugged. "Probably a leftover from the construction of the International Bridge years ago," he offered.

Conrad gritted his teeth and gave the steel cylinder a hard shove with the heel of his boot. It rolled and splashed back into the water.

"I'm sorry, Conrad," said Oscar, attempting to apologize. "It's murky down there today, and my eyes aren't what they used to be."

Conrad said nothing, choosing to keep his mouth shut, instead of possibly upsetting his friend with an angry retort. The sun was becoming hot now, and he wiped the sweat from his forehead as he considered his next move. Frustrated, he stalked back to the wheelhouse to consult the GPS and his grid chart. Oscar cleared his throat, removed his mask and flippers and sat down with a heavy sigh on a crate at the edge of the deck.

Just as Conrad reached the door of the wheelhouse, a distant splash upriver caught his attention. Reeling around, he raised a hand to shade his eyes. There was some kind of floating vehicle ahead of them, several hundred yards upriver. His face began to flush with anger as he made out the diver-down flag flying on a buoy nearby. This was all he needed. It was perfectly obvious why they were there: they were looking for the Onondaga as well! He fought the sudden urge to scream out. Rage filled him, as he watched two children emerge momentarily from the vehicle's open hatch. His breath caught suddenly in his throat and his grey eyes widened despite the bright sun. It was the two kids from the library! They appeared to be talking to a diver bobbing in the water beside the strange craft.

His mind raced uncontrollably. If these meddling children found the lost ship before he did, he would be finished! He would have no treasure, no money left and he could even lose his home to the bank. His brain felt like it was on fire as he watched the children vanish into the vessel, closing the hatch over them. Then he watched vessel slowly submerge in the still waters of the channel. He stepped into the wheelhouse and waved aside the man who ran the controls to the barge.

"Get out," he stated roughly. "I'll take it from here!"

Conrad hit the control lever for the anchor winch viciously, raised the anchor a few feet from the bottom and then stopped it again suddenly. Then he grabbed the large steering wheel and cranked the diesel engines of the barge to life. He pushed the throttle levers ahead and the large vessel lurched forward, plowing water ahead of the bow.

Oscar stood up from the crate he was sitting on and looked in the direction that they were heading. After a moment he looked back to the wheelhouse and raised his arms questioningly. Conrad simply stared ahead, anger twisting his face and gave the barge slightly more throttle.

~~~~

Jorden tapped on one of the side windows of the sub as she swam alongside and waved at its passengers inside. She could feel the current in the channel and paddled her fins a little harder to keep moving down at the same rate as the sub. As they went deeper, she began to be able to distinguish the bottom below - a combination of rock and sand, punctuated by small patches of vine-like weeds. It slowly became darker the deeper they went, and suddenly the lights mounted on the front and sides of the sub came on as Dad piloted the craft expertly toward the bottom.

Jorden swam ahead of the sub and marveled at the fish swimming around her, as others hid in the weeds as she approached. The sub came slowly to a stop and remained still just above the riverbed to illuminate the area with its lights. It hovered effortlessly, as Jorden began to search around for any trace the depths would reveal of the missing warship.

Inside, Dad kept his hands on the joystick that controlled the sub and watched as Jorden searched the bottom. Valerie sat beside him in the front, examining a photocopy of the map Mr. Thusk had made for her at the museum. The two boys sat in the back seats, pasted to the porthole windows, gasping and pointing at every fish they saw swim past. A curious sunfish swam right in front of Alex's window and he and Curtis laughed as they watched him watching them through the window, his mouth and gills opening and closing rapidly as he peered at them with large eyes. Finally the small fish darted away, and the boys watched Jorden whenever she came into their view.

The quiet hiss of the air tanks and the occasional bubbling sound from the open bottom hatch were the only other sounds in the sub's small compartment and both boys occasionally gave the water in the open hatch a nervous glance.

"Are you sure the water won't come up in here?" Curtis asked.

"It's perfectly safe, Curtie. This is an ambient pressure sub," explained Valerie, barely taking her eyes off the map she was holding.

"A what?" he asked, puzzled.

"You know, like, when you hold a cup upside down underwater, the air gets trapped underneath and stays there."

"Oohh, I get it!" he replied, still giving the gaping hole between them all a nervous glance.

Dad simply grinned, kept his eyes on Jorden and turned the sub slightly to shine the lights on a new search area.

"We should be right on the spot where the note washed up on shore according to this," Valerie stated, pointing to a mark on her map.

"Yes, but the note may have drifted down the channel for quite a way before washing up on the shore," said Dad. "I think we should search upriver from here if we don't find anything."

"I think you could be right," replied Val.

Dad nudged the sub forward slowly, directing Jorden on a course into the current. She swam ahead, scanning the bottom, stopping here and there to investigate closer. Fish swam away as she paddled upriver and tried to stay just far enough off bottom to get the widest view. Her bubbles rose from the regulator in steady streams as she worked against the current. A quick check on her dive watch told her she had about ten more minutes, and then she would have to surface and switch out her scuba tank. They had brought a spare that was strapped to the top of the sub. No sense only searching for twenty minutes, her father had said.

Just then, Jorden heard a loud thud, even underwater, and turned quickly to look back at the sub. She had to paddle herself quickly aside, startled as a large object plowed through the water directly toward her. An anchor! She watched it disappear and looked above her. She spotted a large square shadow on the surface of the water that was moving rapidly upriver. She looked back at the sub. It spun slowly, one of its motors sheared clean off the side! It wobbled suddenly to one side, but righted itself again, and Jorden realized in sudden terror that Dad was fighting to control the small vessel because it had been hit.

She dared not get too close to it and watched helplessly as it wobbled and spun. Suddenly, the other motor stopped, and the sub hung in the water, leaning slightly to one side. Jorden approached the front windows, but she could see Dad waving her away from the vessel and the frightened expression on the other children's faces. He made a motion for her to surface, but she lingered a few more moments, afraid to leave them. She knew that if the sub faltered too far onto its side, the air inside the cockpit would escape, flooding it. Dad motioned again, much more directly, and with one last frightened look, she paddled upward through the water.

The children were scared stiff and hung on to their seats with terrified screams. Dad shushed them gently - he knew that they were afraid.

"Everybody remember where their mini-tank is?" he asked calmly.

The children fumbled under their seats for their small breathing tanks, each one with a miniature regulator and mouthpiece attached to the top of it. Dad had installed them in case of an emergency, and he was certainly glad that he had spent the extra money. He spoke calmly to the kids, reassuring them that they were ok, even if he was a little worried himself.

"Now, it's all right, guys. When I pop this lever, we will bring this baby up to the surface in no time, so hang in there!"

Dad pulled the lever and instantly they heard the hiss of air rushing into open chambers at the front and back of the sub. The children grabbed their seats again with a gasp as the sub suddenly lurched upward, straightening itself up as it climbed quickly toward the surface.

With a jolt and a big splash the craft burst up out of the water, bubbling and bobbing. The kids let out a cheer and Dad closed the bottom hatch, sealing it shut. A little bit of a puddle sloshed around in the bottom of the compartment and Dad drew a deep sigh of relief. He opened the top hatch to let the children climb out on the top. He craned his neck around in the windows to try to survey the damage.

The port side wing, which normally held the motors that operated the vessel, was completely gone and he cursed slightly under his breath realizing that they would only spin in a circle if he tried moving forward. Out on top, Valerie was recounting the entire drama to Jorden, who had climbed up onto the sub herself. Dad emerged from the hatch and rested his elbows on the sides as he looked around at the rest of his contraption.

"Everyone okay?" he asked. He tried to lighten the mood as he glanced over at each of their white faces, still frightened from the ordeal.

"That was quite a ride, huh?"

"That was crazy!" said Alex.

Curtis simply grinned a little as he realized that they would be fine.

"Those idiots with the barge were the ones who clipped you - and almost got me," said Jorden, pointing upriver where the insolent vessel had all but disappeared.

"What the heck hit us?" asked Valerie.

"It was their anchor," stated Jorden flatly. "You would think the losers would have seen our dive buoy."

Dad looked around as they bobbed along in the current.

"How the heck are we gonna get back to shore?" Alex asked nervously.

"With this." Dad raised what looked like a small orange gun and, lifting it high in the air, pulled the trigger. A bright red ball of fire flew up into the air and soared in a high arc.

"Cool!" exclaimed Curtis. "Fireworks!!"

~~~~

Tyler knew at once that something was amiss from his seat at the patio of the marina restaurant. He munched on French fries as he watched a strange boat pull into one of the far docks. It was square and flat and the men aboard seemed to be having a heated argument as they tied up. The yelling and pointing continued, and Tyler wondered what could have caused such a ruckus. He grabbed his cell phone out of his shorts pocket and videoed their battle.

A grey haired man stood on the deck, his hands clasped into tight fists, hollering and swearing at the other few men who were quickly departing. One large fellow stayed on the dock, yelling back at the man on the boat. He was huge, with white hair pulled back into a ponytail and a large white moustache. He was not happy. In the end, he turned and waved a hand at the man in a disgusted, dismissing fashion.

Tyler zoomed in on the angry man still standing on the deck of the boat, a look of absolute rage on his weathered face. The huge fellow had stalked off down the docks and had headed for the parking lot. Tyler stopped taking the video and took a slurp of his Pepsi as he watched the man on the boat angrily fling some ropes aside and head inside the small cabin on his vessel.

By the time Tyler finished his meal, the angry man had also departed, carrying two briefcases and a laptop computer off of his vessel. I guess the day didn't go well for them, he thought. He wondered what the heck that crew had been doing anyway. And furthermore, where were the others? His family had been gone for several hours with no word from any of them. Tyler had attempted to text Jorden and Valerie, to no avail. He'd had some fun looking around the marina at all the boats and it was nice to have lunch here at the restaurant overlooking the marina, but he was starting to get bored. He could be at home on his PlayStation or chatting with some of his friends on Facebook. The argument between these men had been the only interesting thing to really happen in hours. His video would be good material for YouTube, he surmised.

He got up, took a final sip of his drink and took his bill inside to the counter to pay. It was cool inside, the air conditioning a welcome break from the heat of the summer sun on the patio. Tyler collected the change, leaving a tip for the young lady who had come to serve him and headed back to the parking lot, curious to see if any of those men would still be there. His video could have a part two if they were...

11

Pam was sitting in the kitchen playing a game on her computer when the truck rolled up outside. It had been a quiet day and she had done a little gardening, a smaller amount of housework and had even reserved herself time for a nap. The cat had followed her everywhere that afternoon, keeping vigil while she weeded the flowerbeds and had curled up on the end of the bed while she slept for an hour.

The familiar sound of their vehicle outside diverted her attention from the game in front of her. The cat pawed at the kitchen door, having heard the children's voices and the sound of the truck. Pam got up from her chair at the breakfast counter and walked across the kitchen to let the cat out. She looked out the door. What she saw immediately disturbed her. She noticed wide scrape marks down the side of the sub and something - although she could not really place it - was missing. Even though everyone was present and accounted for, she instantly began to worry, seeing the obvious damage to Dad's strange vessel.

Dad emerged from the truck and waved off the children's excited chatter as they jumped around on the sidewalk. Jorden carried her diving gear toward the garage as Dad and Tyler checked the straps on the trailer holding the sub. Pam watched her exhausted husband walk up the walkway toward the house. She could see that he was trying to look like everything was fine, but Pam could sense that something had gone very wrong.

"What happened?" she asked as she stood there propping the door open.

"Nothing major. We didn't find any lost gold, anyway," he replied calmly.

"Why is half of your sub missing?"

He looked up at her from the bottom of the porch. He knew she wouldn't be fooled by a lackluster answer, just as he knew that the children, now safe and sound at home again, would recount the entire adventure many times with each other - and with Pam! There was no hiding this from her!

"Well, we had a little incident. Some idiots on a barge dragged their anchor across us while we were under water. They tore off the port side motors and the wing, too." He braced himself for her response, for the inevitable 'I told you so'. But it didn't come. She simply shook her head slowly and placed a hand on her forehead. He tried to explain that they had never been in any danger, that the sub's safety systems had worked perfectly, but she leveled a look at him that told him his words were falling on deaf ears.

"If you insist on using that crazy contraption, I would prefer it if the children remained on dry land!"

She turned away from the kitchen doorway without another word and headed to the counter to begin supper. Dad went to the garage, thinking it better to leave the situation alone. The younger children went down to the backyard to play for a while as the sun began to set.

As Dad entered the garage, he met Tyler and Jorden.

"So, what now?" asked Jorden as she hung up her wetsuit to dry.

"Well, it will take me a couple days to get new parts and re-construct the wing."

"Who the heck were those people on that boat that hit us anyway?" she continued.

"Not sure, but I wish I knew. We had a dive buoy out and everything. They must not have been paying very good attention." Dad leaned up against the workbench, thinking.

"What did the boat look like?" asked Tyler, remembering the argument at the marina.

"When I came up, I saw it heading away. It was wide and flat with a little box on top in the middle," recounted Jorden.

Tyler grinned and pulled his phone from a pocket. He played around with it for a moment and then showed Jorden the video he had recorded.

"Is this the boat?"

"Yeah, it sure looks like it!" she responded, watching the small screen.

Dad stepped over to take a look.

"It's a construction barge."

The three of them watched the men arguing and gesturing in the video. Although it was slightly fuzzy with the bright summer sun, Dad could see the images well enough to get the idea.

"Looks like whatever they were doing out there didn't go well. If they were doing that when they hit us, it may explain why they didn't see the buoy

- and why they hadn't pulled their anchor up all the way," said Dad.

"Maybe they were fighting about that!" said Jorden.

"About what?" asked Tyler.

"About the anchor not being up all the way."

"It's possible. I guess we will never really know," said Dad with a sigh. "All I know is that it was a close call and it will take me a while to fix her up!"

Valerie, Alex and Curtis suddenly interrupted their conversation when they charged into the garage.

"Dinner's ready!"

~~~~

Conrad sat at his desk at home staring at the river chart in front of him, his fist supporting his chin, his glasses tipped onto his forehead. Oscar had not returned his calls for a week now. He felt genuinely bad about it all. His phone rang. He barely had the energy to glance at the call display, hoping that it might be his friend. It wasn't. A strange 800 number glowed on the screen, which meant that it was either a telemarketer or a bill collector. His mind sank into that black abyss of worry, that feeling that at any moment his electricity would be shut off or he might be removed from his home by the bank. He let it ring and ring. Finally it stopped and he looked back at the chart. He must find it, he thought. It was out there, waiting. He could not let these amateurs beat him to the prize that was his to claim. He had worked hard, had sifted through historical accounts for years. There had to be some clue that he had missed. Was it in the book that the children had borrowed? He sank his chin into his hands as he stared at the chart and waited for some kind of revelation - one that would not come despite how badly he wanted it. Once again he visualized actually finding the wreck, finding the gleaming chests of gold and silver that would etch his name into the history books. He was definitely close, but were they closer? His mind raced as he tried to calm his ever-present feelings of anger and frustration.

He dropped his glasses back onto his face, took a deep breath and flipped through his notes once again. It did him no good. The very thought of losing everything he owned because of a couple of curious children was almost more than he could bear. And without Oscar and the money to continue his search, he was lost. He thought of his friend again, how he had treated him and disregarded his advice and opinion, and this filled him with a deep sadness. Oscar had always been like a quiet older brother to him and he could feel a twinge of guilt for acting the way he had. His friend had been very upset at what he had done in the name of greed and glory and the fact that he had intentionally put children's lives in danger.

Conrad replayed the scene in his mind, how he'd blindly made the decisions in his refusal and resistance to let someone else take his moment in the spotlight away from him. Oscar obviously didn't understand him and his deep need to be a victor in this quest. Emotionally, success would mean that he would be respected as an intellectual and a historian. Financially, it would mean that he would never have to worry about money again. He wanted the freedom that would bring; wanted it more than anything. If it meant that he would be separated from his dear friend to have it, then so be it. Since he had already risked everything to continue the search this far, it seemed insane to abandon it now. He would have to find out what these children knew and why they had chosen to look in that particular spot in the channel. He knew that it would be difficult and that he just might have to stoop to fairly unscrupulous methods. He decided that this was fine with him: it was either fight for the prize or let them beat him to it! He looked up at the clock and tried to calm his storm of thoughts. Time was still ticking, after all...

~~~~

Nana had convinced her. Valerie sat at the table in the art studio, looking over the map and flipping pages in the book from the library that she'd placed beside it. There was still a major clue missing and it was the clue she needed to find the Onondaga once and for all.

Nana came in, carrying two cups of tea, sat beside her at the table and set out the hot beverages carefully for them.

"I just can't see it Nana. We looked and looked. We haven't found anything."

"Remember, some clues you can't find on paper, my dear," began her Grandmother. "Sometimes the clue you need is out there, but you can't read about it or see it on a map. You have to lay your hands on it, somewhere out there."

Valerie was silent, drinking in what Nana had said just as she did with her tea.

"You said yourself that your search was cut short with the business that happened to Dad's submarine. Maybe you would have found it, maybe you wouldn't have, but the river is a very big place to search."

"I think Pam's mad about what happened," said Valerie.

"Pam is just worried for your safety, sweetie-heart."

"I think Dad will want to try again. He is already working on fixing it."

"Your father has always had a talent for finding solutions to a problem, my dear. He always loved adventures when he was a boy, even though he acts like I shouldn't tell you kids about one or two!"

Nana's warm smile reassured Valerie and she took a sip of tea and listened as Alex and Grandpa played a video game on the television in the living room. Her thoughts began to wander, and she thought about the long-lost ship, its captain and the mysterious payroll chests that could be waiting somewhere in the deep to be found. Nana was right. There was something missing!

"Perhaps you should start on the shore, before looking down deep?" Nana said, as if she'd been channeling Valerie's thoughts.

"So, we should look around on land?" Valerie asked.

"Sometimes the places you least expect hold the greatest answers."

Valerie's eyes brightened. There was a campground not far away from the channel. It had hiking trails that led through the rough limestone and granite alongside it and through the thick forest that lined the river. Maybe Nana was right. It would be fun, too, a camping trip. They certainly couldn't do much in the river itself until Dad fixed the sub, so why not? Valerie grinned at her grandmother and took another sip of tea. Her Nana grinned back. Maybe this was the solution - a hike along the shore of the channel might reveal something that could bring them closer to finding the lost warship.

Valerie loved the idea of a camping trip and Dad had a dome tent with sleeping bags that had only been used twice by her count. It would be great fun, especially since the sub was sidelined. Valerie took another sip of her tea and glanced at the pencil drawn picture of the Onondaga. It was out there somewhere - just waiting to be discovered.

12

Dad dragged the tent bag down from the rafters of the garage, dusting it off. The camping idea would probably be good for the kids; it would occupy them this weekend and give them something else to do besides coming in and bugging him every hour about the sub. He had brought the damaged sub inside and had been working tirelessly to rebuild the wing and motors. It was delicate work to run the electrical wiring through the hull and he also had to make sure that everything was sealed well. The two youngest boys were constantly interrupting him, wanting to sit inside and pretend that they were on an underwater adventure. Sometimes, though, their curiosity and presence in the garage worked out to Dad's advantage, as he could feed the wiring through small holes in the craft while the boys pulled it through to the inside. They enjoyed helping out and thought that, with their help, the sub would actually be ready for another ride quicker!

Dad grabbed a blue Coleman cooler from up above so that the children would have somewhere to keep their food while they were off camping. He felt better with the knowledge that Jorden would be with them. Jorden and Valerie had their own phones, which was a comfort to him. Dad was glad that the kids had chosen to do something active and outdoorsy instead of lazing around inside watching TV or playing video games. It would do them some good to get out and explore and it certainly wasn't very expensive. They would have some fun and they would be safe. And they weren't too far away from home either - just a short drive up the scenic highway that ran along the river. Tyler, not much of a fan of the great outdoors, had already asked if he could spend the weekend at his friend's house and had been picked up earlier that day.

Dad put the tent bag just outside the door of the garage and headed towards the kitchen door, cooler in hand, to see what was on for lunch. As he entered, he could sense the commotion. The children were running around and putting together things that they thought they'd need to go camping. Pam was standing at the stove, stirring a pot of Kraft Dinner as she reminded them to pack certain items. She gave Dad a stern glance - a 'help me with this' look - and Dad grinned as he walked past her into the living room. The children had been gathering everything but the kitchen sink and had placed it all in piles on the couch and love seat. They'd collected mounds of clothing, backpacks, pillows and books. Wow, he thought. They were only going camping for two nights!

Pam shuffled food to the table and told children that they needed to eat before their grand adventure. The kids ran to the table like a herd of animals and gorged on the meal on their plates, barely taking a breath. Both Dad and Pam watched in fascination the scene unfolding in front of them as they quietly and civilly ate their own lunch. Then they turned around to toss some food in the cooler Dad had brought inside.

Soon enough the children were bugging Dad to go. He couldn't help but wonder why they were in such a rush. They crowded around him waiting for him to move, eager to begin their expedition. Finally, he relented and set down the iced tea that he'd been drinking on the kitchen counter. He gave Pam a quick peck on the cheek, as did the children, and they grabbed everything and ran out the door. Dad grinned, shook his head and walked outside carrying the cooler. He watched the crew load their stuff into the back of the truck.

Jorden grabbed the tent bag and tossed it in the bed of the truck. Dad rearranged the food in the cooler, taking more time than he should have. The kids were already in the truck as he fiddled away. He waited to see how long it would take them to complain. It didn't take very long before Dad was flooded with calls and shouts to get going. He loaded the cooler into the truck, hopped into the driver's seat and revved the engine. Pam stood on the porch and watched as they left. She had told Dad that she wasn't sure about all of this, but had been assured that the children would be safe - and that they'd have some fun for the weekend. Dad waved as they pulled away.

~~~~

It was mid-afternoon when they pulled into the campground. Dad paid the young man at the check-in gate and was handed the tag for the site that he had reserved for the kids. They rolled down through the campground, until they arrived at the marker for their spot. As soon as the truck stopped, the children hopped out and grabbed their stuff. Dad watched them set up the tent, grinning as they put everything together. He helped them unload the cooler and reminded them to listen to their oldest sister. Jorden grabbed an extra flashlight from the toolbox in the back of the truck. Alex was checking over the site, his trusty backpack slung over one arm. Curtis was searching for sticks suitable for a marshmallow roast. Valerie was already relaxed in a folding chair, looking at her book and map. Dad let out a sigh, seeing that they were pretty well set. He climbed back behind the wheel of the truck, gave Jorden a final pointer about safety as far as campfires were concerned and reminded them all to call home if they needed something. He turned on the vehicle, took one more look around at the junior campers and then gave a wave as he pulled out of sight.

Jorden went to help Curtis search for firewood and they scrounged around in the bush behind the tent. Their campsite was perfect, close to the beach area, but still surrounded by enough trees to make them feel like they were in the wilderness.

"This is gonna be cool!" exclaimed Alex, as he rummaged through his backpack for a pocket knife to shave down the sticks for the marshmallows. The fun had begun!

~~~~

When it grew dark, Valerie resorted to a flashlight to read by and Jorden started a small campfire, using some dry grass and the sticks and deadfall she and Curtis had collected earlier. They roasted the marshmallows - Curtis once again enjoying his well burnt. While the firelight danced on the children's attentive faces, Valerie recounted half a dozen legends and ghost stories that she had read.

As it got later, the sounds of crickets and loons rivaled the crackling of the fire. Jorden set up the spare flashlight she had in the tent and, soon enough, the yawns started. Valerie was the first to be ready and she crawled into the tent to curl up in a warm sleeping bag. The boys, however, seemed to be eager to stay up all night, and Jorden had to do quite a bit of convincing to get them to retire for the evening.

Once they finally got comfy inside, and after a bit of chatter and laughter between the two boys, they fell asleep quickly. Jorden lingered by the dying fire for a moment or two, mesmerized by the flames. Fatigue finally got the better of her, and she doused the remaining embers with a jug of water she had kept nearby. With the fire extinguished and the rest of the children asleep, Jorden stretched and yawned, then unzipped the tent and crawled inside, zipping the door closed quietly behind her.

In the darkness, though, there was someone watching. A lone figure stood a short distance away in the trees, silent and still.

~~~~

Pam looked up from her game on the tablet as Dad cursed quietly over a dropped tool from under the sub. He had worked all evening on finalizing the repairs and was almost finished, with the exception of a few minor items. He had added a few little things as well. The sub was now equipped with a marine VHF radio and a newly modified handheld GPS. Dad had run the antenna wiring up the dive buoy cable so that the devices would work even when the sub was underwater.

Pam looked at the strange ship and wondered what fuelled her husband's obsession over it. She worried about both his and the children's safety in that weird device when it was down deep under the surface of the river. Her thoughts were interrupted as Dad slid out from under the thing, sat up and looked at her with a smile.

"Got it!" he stated.

"All fixed up?"

"Yep. Why is it, that the last bolt or nut is always the one that is the pain in the butt?" he mused.

"Well, I know you would never give up until you got it!" she replied. She took a sip of tea from the cup she'd placed on the workbench and looked again at her husband's creation.

"Why would anyone want to invest so much time and effort into something like this?" she thought, shaking her head.

She looked at the lines and hoses snaking across the hull of the thing, thinking that it resembled an alien spaceship more than it did a mini-sub. Still, it had a certain charm and cartoonish look to it that only Dad could create. And it seemed to work well, she reasoned.

Dad got up, brushed himself off and placed several wrenches on the workbench with a satisfied grin.

"Do you think the kids are okay?" she asked as she put down her tablet.

"They'll be just fine. You don't remember going camping as a kid?" he said.

"I just get worried about them out there by themselves."

"Relax. Jorden and Valerie both have their phones if they have a problem or need something."

"I guess." Pam still seemed unconvinced. Dad simply raised his hands.

"Besides, look what amazing blissful peace and quiet there is around here tonight!"

She gave him a look that told him that his sarcasm was not exactly what she wanted to hear. He relented and shrugged his shoulders.

"Seriously, what if a wild animal comes around or they get cold?" Pam continued.

"Darling," he began in exasperation. "It's the middle of summer and there are at least a hundred other people camping at that park..."

She still looked at him. She was their mother and stepmother and she would still worry a little, he knew, no matter what he told her. He knew they would be fine - and probably have a lot of fun. He took a sip from the tall glass of iced tea that Pam had brought out for him and watched her quietly, trying without success to hide a smirk. She gave him that look again.

"They'll be fine!" he stated firmly, still grinning.

~~~~

Valerie was the first one up the next day and she quietly crawled out of the tent into the cool morning air. The sun was up, tracing shafts of light through the leaves, and it was warm already. The birds sang and there was not a trace of wind. She stepped out of the grove and looked at the stillness of the river. It was like a mirror, reflecting the trees of each island dotting the vista in front of her. Very few people were up yet and the campground was still fairly quiet. She stood there and took a deep breath of the fresh morning air. She was instantly glad for this little adventure, as she watched two cardinals flit from tree to tree, singing their early morning song. There wasn't a ripple on the water and she could see its edges lapping at the beach, sparkling in the sun like a thousand diamonds were laid out on it.

Alex poked his head out of the tent, followed shortly by Curtis, bright eyed and ready to go. Jorden was still slumbering, preferring to enjoy the morning in the comfort of her sleeping bag. The boys yawned and stretched, emerging from their cocoons ready to tackle the day!

Leaves painted shadows on the floor of the grove of trees. They barely moved in the steadily increasing heat of the morning. Not a cloud was in the sky as the two boys began to look around the campsite for something of interest. Predictably, they both inquired about something to eat and Valerie went to the cooler and got out some cereal packs for them that Dad and Pam had packed. She felt the grumbling of her own belly and picked out one for herself and they sat around the remnants of the previous night's fire enjoying their simple breakfast.

Perhaps it was the crinkling of the packages, or a rumble of hunger in her own tummy, but Jorden finally emerged from the tent, still looking tired. Once she saw the others plowing through breakfast, like a match strike she was awake.

"Well, good morning, guys."

"Mornin'," was all they could manage as they stuffed their faces with cereal.

Jorden wandered over to the cooler herself and elected some fresh fruit as opposed to the cereal. Once the group had filled their bellies, they packed the dishes back into the cooler, eager to get on with their day.

"So, what are we gonna do?" asked Curtis as he wiped milk from his face.

"Well, the channel is just over here," Valerie stated pointing to the east.

"You guys can do whatever you want, but I'm going swimming and tanning down on that awesome beach!" said Jorden immediately.

"Yay!" cheered Curtis. "Can I do that, too?"

"Yep! Get your suit on and grab your towel!"

Valerie knew that they wanted to go have fun, but her thoughts were still on the channel. "I'm going to hike the trail along the channel, to see if I can find any clues."

Alex grabbed his backpack without saying a word, already deciding that he was going with Valerie.

"Okay, you guy's won't get lost, right?" asked Jorden, expecting her sister to roll her eyes at her.

Instead, Valerie gave her a simple answer. "Nope. We will be back in an hour or so."

The two adventurers set off for the trail, leaving their siblings to their day at the beach. They found the nature trail that led through the thick trees and along the banks of the river. Alex followed Valerie, his trusty pack slung over his shoulder as they made their way along the winding dirt path through the forest of pines and maple. They saw many small animals: chipmunks chattered as they ran out of the way, their tails straight up like flags; black and grey squirrels darted to and fro; and even a small rabbit hopped across the trail in front of them. And, of course, there was the ever increasing complaining of seagulls searching for their morning meal.

The forest canopy became thicker and darker as they walked along. The children finally arrived at a point overlooking the river, the dead end of the trail, where a plaque had been erected that detailed the islands of the Lost Channel. Alex and Valerie took a moment to survey the river in front of them and then read words written on the historical plaque. It described the channel, but left out the story of the lost warship. The two children looked at its weathered surface and wondered why this important fact was not mentioned.

"It doesn't tell us anything!" said Alex, pointing out the obvious.

"I can see that," said Valerie. "Whoever wrote this didn't hear the story, I guess."

Suddenly, they could sense someone else in their vicinity. As Valerie and Alex turned around to look towards the trees behind them, their breath froze in their throats. Alex gripped his backpack tighter. Valerie gasped slightly and froze in place.

Before them stood a tall man dressed in clothing they had never seen before except in old textbooks in school. His piercing blue eyes were looking into the distance, not focused on them, but on the river. His long brown hair was pulled back into a ponytail under a strange triangular hat and his skin was very pale. The red coat he was wearing seemed tattered and rather too heavy for the kind of weather that day. And he wore a sword at his side. Valerie felt a chill run through her as she realized that the man standing in the shadow of the trees was dressed like a British soldier from long ago. She forced herself to say something, even as her brother grabbed for her arm.

"Are you from one of those battle re-enactments?" she stammered. "Like from the war of 1812?"

He simply stared ahead, watching the mirror-like waters of the channel. But his eyes stayed in her mind, piercing blue and alive. His gaze suddenly shifted to her - or did it? He seemed to look right through her, as though searching for something that wasn't there. When he began to speak, a chill ran deeper through the two of them.

"You have not gone far enough," he said with a voice as cold as winter. "What you seek lies further."

He raised his arm and pointed to a point beyond the end of the trail. Valerie and Alex turned and looked deep into the trees that lined the riverbank to the east of them. The line of rock and earth here rose along the banks and formed a cliff. The forest was thick and dark and it did not look as though it would be easy to traverse.

When Valerie turned back to question him further, her gaze fell on nothing but the trees and underbrush. He had simply vanished. The hairs rose on the back of her neck and Alex grasped her arm once again, even tighter this time. There was nothing there! They both took a breath and tried to relax, to make sense of what had just happened. But could not. For long moments the two children just stood there, trying to shake the cold feeling that had taken hold of them.

Slowly, the warmth of the dappled sun on their backs seemed to bring them back to reality and shake the surreal sense of the other presence that had stood in the trees with them. Alex released his grip on his sister's arm, revealing almost white knuckles. Valerie took a deep breath.

"Ahhh", she thought to herself as she realized that this was exactly what Nana had been talking about the other day with her over their teacups. "There might be someone who could direct you to where the lost treasure might be," she recalled her grandmother's exact words.

"Okay," she whispered. "I'd say that was a definite clue."

"Yeah!" Alex agreed.

They both looked toward the east again and wondering how - or why - they should continue. It was much darker through the forest, with no real path to follow, and Valerie felt a twinge of foreboding. She swallowed hard and remembered the whole idea of what Nana had said to her. They had to go, they had to follow through.

As she took a last look around the small clearing, Valerie noticed something buried in the fallen leaves and moss. It was red. She stepped closer and was very close to standing in the spot where they had seen the strange man. Almost completely covered by the forest floor was a tattered, old piece of cloth. She pulled it from its resting place and examined it closely. Dirt clung to the fragment; it was so old that moss roots were growing right through the fabric. A sash or scarf of some kind, she thought, and very old. She brushed the dirt away as gently as she could and tucked the find into Alex's pack, despite his grumblings about it.

"Let's go! You heard the man!" she exclaimed, regaining her resolve.

13

Jorden had a vague feeling that someone was watching as she read her book on the beach. She kept a careful eye on Curtis as he splashed in the shallows of the beach. It was turning into another hot, cloudless summer day and she was anxious to soak in every bit of it. Occasionally her mind would feel a little tug that there was something wrong, a slight nag on her psyche that they were being watched. She made a quick check behind her, but all she could see were the trees and other campers enjoying the beach area. She tried to banish these thoughts and turned her attention back to reading her book.

Eventually, her thoughts lingered between the book and Valerie and Alex. She figured that they had been gone for over two hours, but that wasn't an unusual thing for them. Whenever Valerie got an adventure of some kind in her brain, she would disappear until she found whatever it was she was looking for. Curtis dove in the water. It was a beautiful summer day, and Jorden tried to convince herself that the two others would be back soon. Still, the feeling remained, a niggling, uncomfortable intrusion into her mind that something was amiss. It was like a shadow over her, despite the rays and heat of the summer sun. She looked behind her again. Nothing.

Jorden swept her sandy blond hair off of her face and tried to focus on her surroundings. Everything seemed hunky-dory! She forced herself to dismiss the feeling and turned over to sun her back. She would be able to keep an eye on everything now, she thought as a slight breeze blew over her, cooling, but light. She propped up her book and finally settled down to reading again. She turned her head for a quick check on Curtis, who was fine and starting to build a sand castle on the beach behind her. She could feel the heat of the sun radiating off her back and made a mental note to put more sunscreen on both herself and Curtis shortly - it would not do well for them to return home with bad sunburns. She knew that Dad and Pam were counting on her to look after her siblings and she certainly didn't want to disappoint them. Her eyes caught movement in the trees just up off the beach and she lowered her book to get a better look. There was nothing there. Perhaps she was just imagining it, she told herself. Nobody was there and nobody was watching her! Hopefully, Valerie and Alex would be back soon.

~~~~

Valerie fought her way throughout the dark undergrowth, continually checking to see that her brother was keeping up. He seemed to be doing well, only occasionally getting hung up, usually because of his backpack. It was a slow-going process as they followed the river's edge, traipsing along the tops of its tall cliffs. Valerie wiped sweat from her forehead and forged ahead through the trees. The ground was getting rockier, but the trees in the forest here were still tall, consisted mostly of pines, and blocked out most of the sun. It also got much darker as they made their way forward.

When they got higher on the cliffs, Valerie reminded her brother to stay well away from the edge. He was quite fine with that idea! They decided to take a rest near the top of the cliff and found a moss-covered log to sit on and look out over the channel while they caught their breath.

But as they peered through the trees, they noticed that the river had suddenly become covered with a dense mist, despite the warm summer sun, and the nearby islands had been veiled with fog. It was very odd for a mist like this to rise in the middle of the day, Valerie thought. The water was hard to make out through the strange haze that had crept into this part of the channel, and she stood up, trying to find the islands she had seen in front of them only moments before. A strange chill gripped her again. It had been sunny and clear when they began their hike - what had happened?

As Valerie and Alex looked down from the cliff towards the river, their eyes widened in utter disbelief. A ship drifted slowly through the fog. It was a very old and very large vessel, with three masts standing at least sixty feet off of the main deck. It had sails, but they were all torn and hanging lifelessly in the still air of the channel. As it emerged from the fog, they could identify it as a huge wooden warship, with at least a dozen cannon ports on the side closest to them, but Valerie and Alex could see no signs of life on board the hulk. Its movement slowed and they could hear a faint echoing sound of the ship's massive wooden sides creaking.

Both children were taking short and quick breaths and an icy feeling had crept up their spines. They were rooted there, frozen to the spot, unable to break their eyes away from this apparition in the mist. All that they could do was watch the ghostly ship come closer.

"Could it actually be the Onondaga?" thought Valerie. "It had to be! But how was this possible?" Valerie's mind raced despite her fear and she tried to explain to herself what she and her brother were witnessing. She could not.

The ship suddenly rocked, and its main mast wobbled and then fell down across the deck without any sound. The two children watched in horrified fascination as the boat seemed to sink down through the mist directly in front of them in total silence. Then, as quickly as it had appeared, it was gone!

Slowly the mist parted and rays of sunshine shone brightly down onto the river. In what seemed like a mere minute or two, things were as they should be on a beautiful summer day, and, with the departure of the mysterious grey mists, Valerie and Alex relaxed once again. Each of them took a deep breath. They looked at one another, wondering if they had really seen the ghostly ship. Valerie shook her head and tried to clear the jumble of her thoughts. This was it! This was what Nana had been talking about: the final clue. "Sometimes the clue you need is out there, but you can't read about it or see it on a map," she'd told Valerie and Jorden on that rainy day. And now they knew the exact spot where the ship rested. But how would they find it again? Valerie yanked Alex around and delved into his backpack.

"Hey!" protested her brother at the sudden jarring.

"Hold on! I have to mark this place."

"With what? A neon sign?!"

"Just you watch!" she exclaimed excitedly.

Valerie withdrew the tattered red sash, brushing it off once more. She stepped forward toward the cliff edge to find a suitable tree, one that they would be able to see from the river below. Valerie tied the fabric around the tree, as high as she could reach.

"That's actually a great idea," chimed Alex, impressed at her resourcefulness.

"Yep. Now, let's get the heck out of here!" she said as she headed back through the trees to start their trek back along the cliffs towards the campground.

"Absolutely!" Alex agreed, having had quite enough adventure for the day.

~~~~

Exasperated, Jorden stood looking at their ransacked campsite, scarcely able to believe what she was seeing. Their food was still here, the cooler undisturbed, but the tent, their sleeping bags and all the small personal belongings they had brought were strewn all around the site.

"Why would someone do this?" she pondered angrily.

Valerie and Alex arrived back at the site, still very pale from their strange encounter, and Valerie could tell instantly when she looked at Jorden and Curtis that something was wrong. Confused, she looked around and immediately saw what was wrong: the place was a wreck!

"What happened?!" asked Valerie.

"I don't know. Some jerk ransacked the tent!" began Jorden. "Curtie and I were at the beach, and when we came back a little while ago, this is what we found."

The kids looked around at their trashed campsite and wondered what the culprit could possibly have been looking for. They cleaned up the mess and straightened out the tent and their supplies. No food was missing and even the firewood they had gathered was still here. It took about half an hour to get everything back to normal.

"My library book is missing! And the map!!" exclaimed Val.

"Why in the heck would somebody do all this just for that stuff?" Alex lamented.

Jorden got a thoughtful expression on her face, as everyone finished tidying up.

"Someone who is looking for the same thing we are," she said.

"It's okay, really. They don't know what we know now," replied Valerie, quietly.

Jorden looked at her with a questioning expression, curious as to why she would say that. Valerie recounted what had happened when Alex and she were on their hike. As she spoke, Valerie watched her sister's eyes widen and saw her raise an eyebrow to show her skepticism. Valerie dropped her hands to her sides, realizing that it was a strange and unbelievable tale, even as she told it.

"I'm serious!" she argued. "Alex, is that not what we saw?" she asked him to try to get him to reinforce her incredible story.

"Yeah, and it was really weird!" Alex nodded as he helped her out.

It was the pale, scared expression on her little brother's face that sold Jorden on the fact that they had indeed witnessed something very strange. There was no hesitation in their voices and Jorden realized that Valerie was telling them the truth.

"So, you're telling me you saw a ghost?" she asked.

"Two!!" corrected Alex. "A person and a ship."

Jorden thought for long moments and finally understood that the two of them firmly believed exactly what they were saying. This was no joke. Furthermore, the state of their campsite, the missing book and map, along with the strange vibes she'd had while down at the beach all combined into nothing but bad news. She suddenly felt like they should retreat to the safety of home, because whoever had ransacked their campsite could still very well be lurking nearby.

"We should probably just go home," she suggested.

Curtis did not seem to like that idea at all - and neither did Alex or Valerie.

"I don't wanna!" said Curtis and he stubbornly folded his arms.

"Would you rather be out here in the dark tonight with some lunatic running around?" she replied with a frown.

The threat of danger seemed to dawn on the three younger children and uncertainty crept into their faces. Jorden was right. It would be hard to relax and have fun if they were constantly wondering if someone might be watching them. If this person had been willing to steal from them, they might also be willing to hurt them. It had already been quite an ordeal out here with ghosts and crazy thieves!

The children all had the same uneasy feeling now and Alex gripped his backpack straps a little tighter. Dad and Pam would keep them safe; maybe they should go home. They all sat down for a moment and looked around at each another. It would be risky to stay another night. Even if the person who had done this to their site had left, they now had the book and the map in their possession. Valerie felt like a race was on to find the Onondaga - and the treasure! And they, alone, had the answer to the sunken ship's final resting place. It would be a full on sprint to the finish - to beat this mystery person to it.

"Yeah, maybe we should go home, but we can't tell Dad about this!" she stated.

"Why not?" asked Alex and Jorden in unison.

"Don't you see? If we tell him what happened, he might say that the treasure is too risky to go after. He'll be worried about us and he won't want to continue with the search!"

They sat and contemplated this fact for a while. What Valerie had said was true - Dad would be upset about someone messing with their things and stealing from them, and he might decide that it was better to just forget the whole thing.

"We'll call him, but nobody can tell him about this!" Valerie said. "He might not want to keep going to find the ship!"

Heads nodded. Valerie and Jorden made them promise to keep quiet about it and Jorden pulled out her cell phone. She messaged their father, stating simply that they were bored and wondered if he could come and pick them up. He answered quickly, curiously asking what was wrong. They assured him that they simply had run out of things to do. He messaged back that he would be there within the hour, and the children felt safer already.

They began to pack everything up and worked together to fold the tent and fit it back into its carrying bag. Before long, they saw the truck as it headed down the gravel road towards them. The familiar sight of it - and Dad's warm smile - made them forget instantly about the entire ordeal. He helped them stow everything in the bed of the truck while he asked hundreds of questions about whether they had had fun, did they swim, how was their sleep in the tent, and so on, just like an eager kid. He noticed that the children were fairly quiet for such an adventurous night in the outdoors, but dismissed it. Maybe they missed their TV and video games, or maybe they were just tired, he thought.

14

Conrad threw the book across the table. It was a useless piece of junk - all it contained was a short piece about the ship and a pencil sketch of what it had looked like. He'd gone to all this trouble for absolutely nothing!

The map was different, though he didn't have a clue where it had come from. It indicated the location of a note that was found after the ship sank. He figured that this note could have drifted down the channel for a while before washing up on shore where the map had said it had been found. Useless! He tried to restrain his anger and frustration and sat back down to look out the window of his den at home. It was pitch black outside. He felt the end of his game closing in. He had already done things that he knew were wrong - things that he would normally never do - and his old friend Oscar had clearly spelled it out to him as he left the dock that day. The words had stung and Conrad had felt sorry for it despite his desperation.

Things were definitely not going well for him. At any time now he could receive a demand of payment from the bank or a notification that his electricity or water would be shut off. The thoughts swirled in his mind, until he felt nauseous from it all. He couldn't help thinking that his whole world could come crashing down at any moment that everything he'd worked for would prove to be insignificant. It was almost more than he could stand.

He got up again and headed towards the kitchen. He needed a Tylenol for the headache that had surfaced. He set his glasses on the counter and reached into the cupboard above the stove for the bottle of pain medication. He poured a glass of water from the tap and swallowed the red tablet, grimacing as he washed the pill down. Why did they make them so large, he thought? Now he just needed to try to relax and wait for his headache to subside.

He looked out the kitchen window, trying to control his restless storm of thoughts - but they kept nagging at him, refusing to let him rest. There must be something he could do, one last thing that he hadn't tried yet. There had to be a way to uncover the final clue that would allow him to beat these meddlesome kids to the treasure. He had stolen their clues, but even though they had seemed useless to him, those kids still seemed to persist.

"Why was that?" he wondered. Had they learned something from this material that would lead them to the Onondaga before he could find it? He wished that Oscar had not left. That man had been his eyes in the realm beneath the surface of the river. Not having Oscar's help and support had become a huge handicap. And he certainly didn't have the funds to pay another crew. So that was it - it had come down to him, alone. How could he ever hope to find the ship by himself? Even with the sidescan sonar, the GPS equipment and all that technology had to offer these days?

The thoughts were racing in his brain and he looked out his kitchen window into the darkness of the night. The headache began to subside after a while, and he took a deep breath and rubbed a hand over his forehead. His eyes met something outside. He straightened and focused his attention out the window. The faint glow from the streetlights reflected off of a silver shard in the next-door neighbour's yard: a fishing boat! Conrad had seen the old man next-door hook up the trailer and boat to his SUV many early mornings and head out sometimes before sunrise.

A thought suddenly struck him like lightning and he worked the idea around in his mind. If he couldn't afford another run with the barge, perhaps he could use other means to try to locate the wreck. There were bonuses, too - no crew to pay, very little fuel required and he could basically launch something that size on his own! It was large enough that he could fit all of his techno gear in it and small enough to operate totally on his own. It would be perfect. He could do this for as long as he needed - as long as he could convince his neighbour to rent it to him. It would work. It had to - after all his options were running thin.

He left the kitchen. His headache was already beginning to disappear and his brain was running wild with ideas. Back in his den, he put his glasses back on and sat back down to review his charts and grids, reveling in the possibility of resuming his search alone. All he had to do was convince his neighbour to let him use his boat. If not, well someone in the city surely would. Slightly revitalized and with new enthusiasm, Conrad sat at the table making new notes and drawing grids on the charts where he hadn't yet searched.

After an hour, he could feel fatigue gripping at him and he rose from his seat to return to the kitchen to make a pot of hot coffee. Sipping from his cup, he attacked his new plan with vigour, downloading satellite maps of the channel on his laptop. When he finally decided to retire for the evening, it was late. He climbed the stairs to his bedroom and sank into his bed with a feeling of renewed hope. There were still obstacles, he knew, but with a good sleep, the solutions would present themselves...

~~~~

Dad watched the children carefully. They had been fairly quiet since returning from the campground and he suspected something was bothering them. They were having tacos, one of the family's favourites, but they seemed rather unenthusiastic about it. He glanced silently at Pam with a raised eyebrow and she returned the same to him. Tyler had returned from his friend's house in time for supper and even he looked around at the others, surprised by the silence at dinner. The only sound was the crunching of the hard taco shells as everyone ate.

"So, how was the camping?" asked Dad, trying to break the ice.

The children simply nodded as they munched away, without making any comments about their venture. This only served to arouse Dad's curiosity further. He was not easily fooled.

"Well? What did you guys do?" he persisted.

This prompted them to let out a quick stream of comments about swimming and hiking, the campfire and roasting marshmallows. Their father listened, watching each of them as they spoke. Although they made it sound like they enjoyed camping last night, there was something they were leaving out, he thought, something they weren't telling him...and they could tell that he knew it! The children attempted to hide their glances at one another, as they chowed down on the messy taco meal. Even Tyler had picked up on the situation at this point, but he remained remaining silent, observing them all.

After a few more moments consisting only of the sounds of crunching tacos, Dad pushed his plate forward and wiped his face with a napkin, looking at the children. They began to squirm in their seats as they continued to eat. Dad folded his arms on the table and cleared his throat loudly. Pam tried hard to suppress a grin as she ate - she knew well his familiar tactic with the children.

He sat there, motionless and silent, simply watching them. They could obviously sense it, because they squirmed even more, trying everything to shake his stare. Finally, their composure began to break. Curtis fled the table stating that he needed to go to the washroom. Jorden got up and took her plate to the kitchen sink. Valerie and Alex remained focused on finishing as quickly as possible, both worried that they might be at the focal point of an interrogation. Dad continued to watch them. They were acting strange and he felt the need to find out why. Pam waited in her chair and watched Dad's expression, feeling a little worried about the silence herself.

Valerie felt Dad's piercing stare as she crunched down the last of her tacos, and knew full well that he was on to them. She didn't like keeping things from him and a guilty feeling welled up in her stomach. After another few minutes of feeling like she was under some kind of spotlight, she gave in.

"Some weird stuff happened." she said simply.

"What stuff?" asked Dad, half-relieved to hear her begin to open up to him.

"We saw some really strange stuff on our hike, and we got back and somebody had gone through our things at the campsite. They stole my book and map about the channel."

Dad listened as Valerie unfolded the entire story. Jorden sat back down at the table, realizing that there would be questions she would have to answer. Valerie spilled it all: the strange ghostly ship, the fellow dressed in old British war clothing and the ransacked campsite. Dad and Pam listened intently and tried to filter all of the information that they were given. Tyler listened, scarcely able to believe the story. It was quite unbelievable to be quite honest, he thought.

As Valerie finished speaking, Alex watched for his father's reaction to the story. Even Alex realized how hard it would be to believe it all. Dad sat there for a few moments as he took it all in. Minutes passed. The children remained still until Curtis poked his head around the corner into the dining room to see what was happening.

Jorden suddenly felt the need to weigh in. "Someone was there Dad, watching us, and it was weird, just like when you guys were in the sub. Maybe it's the same people that dragged the anchor past us! They must have seen our dive buoy. Maybe it was intentional."

The more they thought about it, the more it began to make sense; someone seemed to be working against them - and Tyler's video of the men on the barge at the docks fit right into place in their story.

"Well," began Dad slowly, still considering the fabulous tale. "If what you say is true, then it looks like someone is trying to beat you guys to the finish."

Pam hid her grin behind her hand, knowing exactly where her husband was going with this. Although she was concerned about the children's safety on this little 'adventure', she didn't want to see the kids robbed of their fun. She knew that Dad had their best interests at heart and would die before allowing anything bad to happen to them.

Dad sat up straight in his chair. He looked around at the children. They were silent as they waited to see what Dad would say next. Was he angry? Would he tell them to give up, that they were in danger? He leaned forward slowly and looked directly at Valerie.

"Sounds to me like we'd better get at it, before someone else finds that ship before you guys do!"

~~~~

The man sat on a park bench down the street from the house where the children lived, far enough away not to be noticed, but close enough to keep an eye on it. It was early and the sun was just beginning to peek over the trees. The morning dew was still thick on the grass. Suddenly he heard the chattering of excited children as they emerged from the house. A man and an older boy came out of the garage and began loading the refurbished sub onto the trailer. They maneuvered it into place and strapped it down, as the children stood around watching the whole operation. So, he thought, they're going to try again...

~~~~

It was quite a job to load the mini sub and Dad directed Tyler as they winched it up onto its trailer. It was slow work and Dad was being very careful not to risk damaging his unique little contraption. Tyler wasn't a very patient person, though, and he had to be reminded to take it slow. Dad was in no rush.

Finally, the machine was up on the trailer, and they finished strapping it down. Valerie bugged her father to hurry. She was excited to take another look underwater, especially after the events that had occurred at the campground. Pam sat on the front porch alongside the cat with a mug of tea in her hands as she quietly watched everything. The little black cat flicked her tail as if in disapproval as she sat like a statue next to Pam. Jorden was busy checking her diving gear in the back bed of the truck - with Alex's help - and Curtis was happily playing with a stick in the front yard. At last, everything was secured and ready and the children piled into the truck with Dad. With a wave to Pam and the obviously annoyed cat, they were off. Dad cranked up the radio as they headed down the street and all of them were happy to get this part of their adventure underway.

~~~~

It took about half an hour for them to arrive at the marina and it was very busy there. Several trucks were lined up to launch their boats and Dad pulled up in line and shifted the truck into park.

"Well, you guys may as well get out and mess around for a bit. It looks like it will be a while before it's our turn," he said.

The children obliged and scooted off down to the docks to have a look around. Boats moved slowly about, docking or heading out to the river. Some were getting fuel at the marina's gas pumps. Families walked up and down the docks, heading towards the restaurant or carrying things out to their boats in preparation to leave. The dock boards creaked with all the foot traffic going here and there and the sun was already hot as the kids went out to look over the sides of the docks for fish. They watched sunfish dart about in small schools and pointed out to each other areas where thick weeds grew in areas of the marina where boats didn't churn up the bottom of the shallows.

Alex grabbed a small bag of chips from his trusty backpack, opened it up and tossed a few into the water. The kids laughed as they watched the sunfish stir up the surface of the water as they congregated in a miniature feeding frenzy.

After a half an hour of roaming about the marina, they heard Dad whistle and scurried up to the boat ramp where their father was waiting to launch the sub. Once again people gathered to see the strange little craft settle into its native environment. It bobbed alongside the dock as Tyler and Jorden secured the ropes to hold it in place.

Dad took over once he had moved the truck and Jorden proceeded to load her scuba equipment in its place on the back of the sub. They were ready. Tyler had decided that he would walk up the trail past the campground to follow them and keep watch. The others piled into and onto the vessel and Dad climbed in and turned on everything inside. Everything functioning well, he guided the sub forward and past the docks of the marina. Onlookers gazed in wonder at the vehicle as it glided along silently, half-submerged. Jorden waved to the gathered crowd as they headed out into the river.

It was hot. Valerie and Alex poked their heads up through the open hatch as they cruised along, eagerly anticipating reaching their destination in the channel. It was quite a distance, but Dad had fully charged the batteries that powered the motors and before long they could see the location of their target.

The water was very calm today - this would make things pretty easy, thought Valerie. All she had to do was locate the sash that she had tied around a tree high on the cliff, and they would be right at the spot where they had seen the ghost ship. This was it, she realized. Whoever had stolen her map and book must already be trying to find the ship too, so their time was running out. She had no more clues to uncover, no more searching for extra information. It all came down to this. It was today or never.

15

Conrad squinted in the bright sun, wiped the sweat off of his forehead and tried to shade his laptop screen with a piece of folded cardboard. The small boat rocked gently back and forth in the calm waters and the river lapped at the aluminum with a hollow sound. Other than the call of the occasional seagull, it was silent out in the channel.

He had made it back out. His neighbour had grudgingly agreed to let him rent his boat, a ramshackle aluminum fishing boat with only the bare necessities. At least it had a trolling motor, which allowed Conrad to change his position slowly. He had bought a camera and television system - called 'Fish TV' - from the local hardware store with some of the last of his money. It was crude, but it served the purpose of viewing the bottom of the river. He had duct-taped an LED flashlight to the camera - that was actually shaped like a fish! - which he'd dropped in the water to descend below the boat to the river bottom on a cable. The point of the gadget was to transmit the images back to the small battery powered TV to show the viewer the underwater world below as they were fishing. But to Conrad, this device would be his eyes as it searched the depths of the channel for his prize.

He found it difficult to maneuver. He had to roll the cable in his fingers to make it turn, and he couldn't do this with a lot of precision. It was slow, aggravating work. He had attached a hook to a crude heavy rope in case he actually found something. So far, he hadn't had to worry about using it. He toiled away, trying to work the outboard motor and the camera at the same time. He wished that he had better light - the images from the camera were fairly dark and low resolution due to the depths he was searching. It was hot, tiresome work and he cursed every time the occasional boater passed anywhere nearby and waved to him. Idiots! They had no idea how much even the slightest wake affected his ability to keep the camera steady below. But at least he was here, able to continue his quest for the ship and its riches.

Conrad took a break. He pulled out a chart he had laminated to protect it against water damage and marked another 'x' on one of his grids he was searching. Maybe the next one, he thought. Where was this blasted ship? Had he spent everything, all his time and money, searching for a myth, something that truly didn't exist? He shook away the pounding thoughts in his head and tried to keep his concentration on the small monitor.

He moved the boat ahead and searched another area of his grids. Surely this methodical way of exploring the river bottom would eventually pay off. He sighed and told himself to be patient. He had only been out for three hours and this type of search could take forever. He kept hoping that something interesting would show up on his screen, other than rocky, sandy bottom and the occasional curious fish.

He inched the boat forward by using the foot pedal that controlled the trolling motor. He almost needed an extra set of hands to do it right, but it was working, at least. Suddenly, as he watched the sonar, an image appeared. It looked like it could be a pile of sunken wood and his heart raced as he moved the boat over top of the spot. The camera moved through the depths on its cable, shining its weak light over the area. Conrad squinted hard at the monitor as he gingerly rolled the cable in his fingers, making the camera pan around. There was definitely something there.

He set the cable down on the boat's railing, trying not to disturb his view below, and reached into a toolbox behind him. Lifting the lid, he withdrew several half sticks of dynamite that were equipped with long, waterproof fuses. He eased back from the spot and pulled up the camera. He picked up one of the explosives, lit the fuse and quickly dropped it into the river, keeping his eyes fixated on the spot.

Seconds passed and Conrad could visualize the charge dropping to the bottom. There was a slight 'thud' and the surface boiled, stirring up weeds and dirt. Several fish floated to the surface on their sides, stunned and gasping for breath. After a few minutes, Conrad dropped the camera back in the water and lowered it carefully for a look at the river bottom. It seemed to take forever and he waited, his heart still racing, to get a view of his efforts.

As the debris in the water began to dissipate, Conrad felt his heart sink. He looked closely at the TV screen. There was nothing except that pile of wood, which was probably deadfall from the trees that had been swept over time to this spot in the channel. There was no gleam of gold, no indication of the remains of that ship - or any ship for that matter! He panned the camera to look everywhere, but the charge had only exposed the rock and sand of the river bottom.

He slammed a hand down on the laptop in frustration. Breathing deep, he decided to continue along, moving the boat forward more, squinting at the image on the monitor. He was feeling the beginning of a headache and rubbed at his forehead. A sound arose upriver from him, a splash. He looked around, confused. The fish that he had stunned with the charge had all swum away and the waters around his boat were calm again.

Another splash. He looked up, shading his eyes against the sun. They were back. He gritted his teeth, as he watched the sub, bobbing in the river, the young lady swimming beside it in scuba gear. He slammed the laptop shut and watched as they prepared for a dive. He could not allow this. He had to stop them or he would lose everything. Anger flared inside him at the thought of failing yet again, of losing to a bunch of children.

He reached down to grab the remaining charges and revved the motor on the boat just as the submarine submerged. This would not be the end of his search - it would be the end of theirs!

~~~~

The bubbles floated upward in the shafts of light shining through the water as Jorden kicked hard to stay alongside the sub. It descended quickly, and she had a hard time keeping up. The water was very clear, and, as they went deeper, Jorden could see the rocky terrain of the channel's bottom come into focus. Then Dad switched on the lights, and what she observed through the mask almost made Jorden drop her regulator!

The remains of a giant ship sat upright on the bottom, several of its masts still attached and rising at least sixty feet above the main decks. It was remarkably well preserved in the cold waters of the channel. Jorden swam over to the windows of the sub and pointed at the discovery. She watched Valerie almost jumping up and down in her seat.

It was an amazing view - an ancient warship submerged in the depths looking as though it had only recently been sent to its watery grave. There were holes through the wooden hull, gaping dark wounds from French cannon fire. The sails were gone, of course, and the ghostly visage of the ship gave Jorden goose bumps, despite her wetsuit.

Inside, Valerie, Alex and Curtis could barely be contained, excited with their view in the sub's lights. Weeds swept alongside the massive wooden hull of the ship in the current and fish darted inside the wreck upon seeing

Jorden and the strange craft.

Dad moved the sub closer to one of the large holes in the hull. Jorden grabbed a flashlight from her belt and peered inside. It was dark in there and Jorden could feel the hairs on the back of her neck rise, along with her breath rate. She tried to calm down, knowing that she would deplete her air quicker if she was breathing too fast.

Valerie was already busy inside the cramped cockpit of the sub, preparing a rope that they had brought in case they actually found something. It appeared that the time had come, and Alex and Curtis stuffed themselves against the windows in the back seat to help give her some room. Dad expertly hovered the vessel just outside the shattered hull of the old ship and hit a button on the GPS to mark their position. He gave a wave to Jorden through the front windows, and she slowly ventured inside the dark wreckage.

She paddled her fins as she moved around slowly inside, shining her light around. There was no current down here and she floated in the lower deck with ease. The interior was dark, but the sub's lights shone through the gaping hole in the side of the wreck and gave her reassurance that she wasn't alone. A she swept her flashlight around, she could see rusted cannons, some still propped through small portholes, and plenty of debris scattered about the rotting floorboards. As she swam along, fish darted away from her. A startled eel slithered quickly out the stairway leading to the deck above. Jorden felt a slight touch of vertigo as she looked around - such a strange place in the depths of the river. It was like a room from the past, buried underwater in a veil of dark weed growth.

There was a gleam in the light from her flashlight. It sparkled against the gloom and Jorden moved slowly towards this shimmery object. This was no aluminum can! The reflection bouncing back to her from the glow of her light was bright and she fought her rising heart rate. With a gloved hand, she brushed aside weeds and dirt and the gleam became even brighter. Her eyes widened. It was coins! Coins of gold and silver, gemstones and jewelry were spilled out onto the floor from a ruined wooden chest. There was another dilapidated chest beside it, and, as Jorden lifted its lid, she was almost blinded. It was brimming with coins as well as precious stones, too. Another chest lay a few feet away and yet another beside that one. They had found it! They had discovered the lost treasure of the Onondaga! Jorden tried to keep her heart rate down as she grabbed a handful of the gleaming metal and gems and watched the pieces tumble slowly from her gloved hand. It was beautiful. She lifted the remains of the wooden chest from the floor, amazed at its weight. It took her several minutes to get it back near the hole in the hull where she had come into the ship. The light still streamed inside from the sub.

Jorden rested for a moment to preserve her air supply. "Wow," she thought, "Valerie is gonna freak out!"

~~~~

Tyler sat on the cliff, paying more attention to his smartphone than what the others were doing. He had done his job after all - he had waved to Valerie from the tree where she had tied the tattered sash and waited while they dove to investigate the river bottom. After that he'd played a bunch of games, took a few pictures and quickly checked his email. It was sunny and hot, but in the pine forest that surrounded him, he found it was the constant need to slap at mosquitoes that was the most bothersome thing about being out here.

The sound of a boat motor finally tore his thoughts away and made him look up from his phone and out to the river below. It was just a small fishing boat, he thought, and turned his attention back to the screen. When boat motor stopped, though, Tyler again focused on the river below. There was a single man in the boat. He was an older man with grey hair and he seemed to have an awful lot of high-tech gear with him for just a fishing trip. Tyler stood up and watched the man fumble around in the boat. What was he doing? Tyler kept his eyes on him and saw the man light something and toss it over the side. The small flame of whatever it was disappeared in the waters of the channel and a few moments later, the surface boiled with what was obviously some kind of underwater explosion.

Tyler's pulse quickened at the thought of this man endangering his family and he turned around to search for a large rock to hurl down at the man in the boat. He found one, large and rough, and hoisted it, guessing at the distance between him and his target. He stopped suddenly, arm in midair. If he threw it and missed, it could sink and hit the sub or Jorden. He hesitated, wanting with all his being to stop the man in the boat, but not wanting to be a danger to his family in the depths below. He dropped the rock and lifted his phone. Surely he could get help here fast. He dialed 9-1-1.

16

Jorden emerged from the hull of the ship and paddled toward the sub with just a tiny amount of the massive treasure cupped in her gloved hands. She opened her hands to reveal the gleaming coins to the curious faces peering out from the craft's front windows. She could see Valerie, Alex, Dad and Curtis all smiling widely, practically rocking the vessel with their excitement. Jorden swam underneath the sub, reached up to pass the handful into its cavity and paddled up top to retrieve the netting that they had brought along. She freed it from the strapping on the top of the craft and headed back inside the wreck, as Dad held the sub and its lights steady.

The lights shone inside as she re-entered and paddled to the spot where the chests lay. It was tough work and she checked her dive watch. She had about ten minutes of air left. Jorden worked as quickly as she could, laying out the netting and anchoring it down with large pieces of debris, and then set the wooden chests on top of it. Then she tossed aside the net-holders, gathered the netting together as best as she could and swam back out to get the one end of the rope that Valerie was already pushing out the bottom of the sub. The other end of the rope was attached securely to the bottom of the sub with a large hook. Trailing it from the sub, Jorden took it inside the wreck and tied the netting to the rope to seal their find inside.

It took a lot of effort to shove the bundle out towards the hole and she had to make sure that it didn't become snagged on the aging wood. Finally, she got it to the opening and she looked over to the sub to see the others watching her through the windows and giving her a thumbs-up. Jorden tried to squeeze out through the hole, around the netting, but it was difficult. Just as she was close to being free, though, something drastic happened: a massive force slammed hard against her, throwing her back and almost knocking the regulator from her mouth.

She twirled, confused and disoriented. Her mind was blank and bubbles swirled around her, making it difficult to tell which way was up. The sub's lights didn't help, as they had seemed to go off in a different direction. Everything was hazy and Jorden fought to regain control of herself in the water column. She righted herself and realized that she was still inside the wreck. She paddled hard and reached the hole in the wooden hull and grasped at its edge, just as a second force of water exploded.

The water was cloudy; dirt and weeds flew all around her through the current. She held tight onto the edge of the hole and pulled herself out of the wreck, but as she tried to swim away, the rope became tangled around her leg. Jorden forced herself to remain calm, remembering her scuba instructor's training and advice. She looked around and saw the sub tilting from one side to the other - Dad was trying to keep it from turning upside down in all the chaos! The rope wrapped tighter around her leg. It was still attached to the sub through the bottom of its hull and was keeping it from rising. Jorden fought for control and pulled a small knife from a sheath on her leg. If she could cut the rope, they would be free and could get to safety.

The debris continued to churn in the water, making it hard to see, but Jorden grabbed the rope around her leg. She was about to saw into it when she felt a strong arm grab her around the middle. She fought against it, but it pulled her in tight and she felt the rope go slack and fall off of her leg. In her panic, she lost a flipper and her regulator fell out of her mouth. Jorden held her breath, still struggling against her attacker. She began to feel light-headed and consciousness began to slip away.

Seconds later, the regulator was forced back into her mouth and she breathed deeply. She lashed out to try to free herself again and realized that whoever had been holding her had let go, and she was free to make her way to the surface. But where was the sub? Jorden could barely formulate a thought as she swam towards the surface, but the thought of her family being in danger was unbearable. She stopped swimming and looked down into the murk below. She could still see the dim lights of the craft as it moved away from the ship.

A third explosion sounded below her. It rocked both the ship and the sub and Jorden felt it - like a heavy pulse in the water, it went through her like a shock wave. She looked up and could see a shadow on the surface. A boat.

~~~~

Dad fought to keep the sub upright. He reached instinctively for the new radio that he had installed and transmitted 'Mayday' three times as he tried to control the sub's swaying. The children were scared. They knew that the sub was still attached to the wreck of the old ship. Jorden had fastened the other end of it to the net that had been weighted down by their find. Everything became quiet for a moment and Dad pulled the joystick hard to move the sub away from the sunken ship. The rope went taut, straining.

Without a second thought, Valerie gathered her courage and reached down through the water in the floor hatch to grab the rope from below the hook in both hands. The rope was wet and slippery, but, determined, she got a good grip on it and gave it a strong tug. Alex and Curtis grabbed hold of the rope as best as they could to help their sister and, with all of their efforts, it pulled free.

The sub righted quickly and slowly began making its way upward towards the river's surface as Valerie continued to hold the rope. It was heavy to Valerie, almost dragging her toward the hatch, and in a flurry of sound she heard Dad holler to ask her if she was okay. She answered as she continued to grip the rope with both hands, steadying herself with a foot against the seats. Alex clutched his backpack and Curtis gripped his seat as they both watched with wide eyes as beads of water flew off the strained rope. The sub was suddenly rocked violently again and the children let out frightened screams. Dad tried to remain calm, slowly righted the sub again and told the kids to hang on. Valerie thought about letting go of the rope and reaching for the mini-tank, expecting the cramped cockpit to fill with water at any moment. Thankfully, it didn't happen and they all breathed a sigh of relief as they looked out to see the sunlight shining down through the water as they neared the surface.

The heaviness of the rope was exhausting and Valerie released her grip on it as they neared the surface. Dad was hollering again, telling them to shut the bottom hatch. Valerie let go of the rope, knowing that it was still attached by the hook below and hoping that it wouldn't pull them back down. Alex thrust his backpack into his seat and reached into the bottom of the sub almost to the sleeves of his t-shirt to try to slide the hatch closed.

Things began to happen quickly and Valerie felt the deja vu of their previous trip in the sub. Seeing him struggle, Valerie helped him slide the hatch closed and turned the hasp to seal it. They all fought to regain their seats, hoping that they would make it to the surface...

~~~~

Conrad threw another charge overboard, gripped by rage. He had to stop them from beating him to the treasure. He had to stop them from making him lose everything. This was his discovery, his prize and no one else's. As the water churned again, he grabbed another piece of dynamite. They would not take this away from him.

Suddenly there was a ripping sound of metal, and he looked down, horrified to see a blade sticking through the aluminum floor of the small boat. It was withdrawn quickly and water rushed in as a result. The blade appeared again in a different spot and punched another hole in the hull. It was a dive knife, he knew, and it disappeared again almost instantly. Water began to seep into the boat and Conrad sat up quickly and tried to put a hand over the holes to stop the flow. Once more the blade pierced the thin aluminum skin of the boat. There was no stopping the flow of water now. Conrad stood on top of the seat and watched the water rush in. How on earth could that young lady have the strength to puncture these holes in the boat?

Despite the questions in his mind, Conrad knew that he was doomed. He had to act fast, he thought, as the boat began to sink. Conrad scrambled to grab his laptop, forgetting the charts and other items now floating inside the aluminum hull. Trapped and with no other options, he grabbed his life jacket and threw it over his shoulders just as the back end of the boat submerged, the weight of the motor dragging it down.

He began to panic as his feet sank into the cold waters of the channel. His pants became wet and cold and stuck to his legs as the boat sank further. He could feel the water rising around him and he took a deep breath as he felt the chill of the water reach his chest. His charts floated away from him, drifting in the current. Whatever, he thought. They were useless now. The boat had disappeared beneath him and he kicked his legs and fought to keep himself upright in the life jacket as he bobbed up and down in the river holding the laptop above his head.

To his left, the young lady in the scuba gear broke the surface, coughing and spitting out water. She yanked her mask up onto her forehead and looked directly at him. Their eyes connected and he could see her anger flashing in them. He splashed uselessly in the cold water and finally released his grip on the laptop. She made no move to help him, seeing that the floatation jacket was doing its job and keeping him afloat.

She pulled her mask back on and dove face-first back into the water to locate the sub. There it was. She watched it rise through the murk, its lights brilliant in the water below her, and resurfaced.

Conrad splashed and kicked as he tried to turn around to face her. As he did this, another form burst forth from below the surface of the river. It was Oscar. "What was he doing here?"

The big man had suspected that Conrad was up to no good and had been following him for days just to keep an eye on things. This morning he had seen the family leave with the sub, and had foreseen this possible collision between the two parties. He gave Conrad a stern glance and then turned his attention to the young lady who had once again pulled off her mask.

"You all right?" he asked.

"Yeah, thanks," she replied and looked back down again to see the sub just off to the left beneath her.

It burst through the surface with a ton of bubbles and bobbed gently only a few metres away. She swam towards it and climbed aboard as the top hatch flew open. Valerie poked her head out and helped Jorden up onto its wet surface. Oscar swam over and grabbed hold of the side of the vessel. He looked up at the two girls and gave them a nod of affirmation that everything was okay. Dad emerged from the hatch and looked around in wonder at the scene before him. Conrad bobbed in the river, miserable and wet.

"Thanks again," said Jorden. "You saved us."

"No problem, little lady," Oscar replied and pulled up his mask. "That fellow doesn't deserve to be out here on the river."

Dad reached a hand out to Oscar and helped the big man up onto the sub as he kept a close eye on Conrad.

"You could have killed us!" shouted Valerie as she splashed water at the grey haired man bobbing in the water. His face remained grim.

"I don't think we'll have to worry about him," said Oscar and he pointed to a boat approaching their site. It bore the markings of the Coast Guard.

Valerie looked up to the cliff where Tyler was waving his phone with a grin she could see even from the distance that separated them. The Coast Guard boat came closer. The men on board were dressed in bright orange survival suits. They looked at the strange group floating in the channel. Conrad fought to keep upright in the life jacket and sloshed about clumsily in the water. He cursed quietly, knowing that there was no escape for him. It was all over…

The boat pulled in close, and Conrad was fished out of the water with a pole. The men dragged him aboard. He flopped onto the deck, sputtering, as the boat moved in towards the sub. Oscar wasted no time in describing the situation and the men on the boat listened intently. The captain of the vessel appeared on deck and looked at the group on the sub. His stern gaze told them that he was in charge of the entire situation.

"So this man was using explosives while you were diving?" he asked firmly.

"Yes, he was detonating these devices while all these people were down on bottom. They had a clear dive buoy deployed," replied Oscar.

"He could have killed us!" exclaimed Valerie and Dad shot her a glance as if to tell her to let others do the talking. The gentlemen from the Coast Guard looked at the yellow sub that bobbed in the water.

"We will deal with this fellow," said the man closest to the edge of the boat. "However, is that vessel licensed for the river?"

Dad dropped his gaze to the hull of the sub. He knew what they were asking, and no, it had never been certified or licensed to operate on the river, like any other boat.

"It's a home-built prototype," he offered, knowing that this statement could get him in trouble.

The men on the boat swapped glances. It was obvious that they were not very happy with Dad's answer.

"I suggest you take that vessel back to dry land and I hope we won't see you out here again without a proper hull number and licensing."

"Absolutely." Dad replied and ushered the younger kids quickly inside the sub. He hadn't expected that comment and wanted to get back to the docks before they changed their minds!

"What about him?" asked Oscar as he pointed to Conrad's wet, cold form huddled on the boat's deck.

"We will investigate this and deal with things accordingly," said the captain of the boat. "You will be contacted for your statement in this matter."

Since it was obvious that things had come to a close, Dad wasted no time in ducking back into the sub and steering it back to the marina. Jorden had climbed on board and they'd let Oscar hitch a ride with them. Tyler quickly left his post on shore to follow the sub back along the trails beside the river.

Despite all that had happened, Valerie shook with excitement and wondered what their cargo held. Several times during their return trip, Dad stopped the sub so that Oscar and Jorden could bring up the rope, along with the net containing their precious haul. Eventually it was secured to the bottom of the sub and the group arrived at the marina as the sun began its dip towards the horizon. The river was dead calm as they entered the docks and they were tired from the whole ordeal, but excited to reveal what they had brought back with them. Valerie and Alex had barely left the porthole windows the whole return trip as they tried to catch a glimpse of what the netting underneath held.

The sub's batteries were all but exhausted as they reached the dock. Oscar and Jorden tied the ropes off to hold the vessel in place. As the crew emerged from the small ship, people once again came down to look, curious. Dad stepped out onto the dock and its old wooden planks creaked slightly. He walked over to Oscar, shook his huge hand and thanked him for his help with everything.

"If it weren't for you, we might have all drowned," he stated factually.

"Well, I had a bad feeling that Conrad would not give up and might do something nasty," explained Oscar. "He was not always that way. He was a dear friend of mine, but I guess greed got the better of him. I'm just glad that you are all safe."

Oscar looked saddened at the thought of his former friend's actions. He knew that Conrad's desperate situation had prompted him to act the way he did, but when it came right down to it, he had endangered people's lives - and that was just wrong! Oscar hadn't wanted to see something bad happen and had acted correctly on his assumptions that concerned Conrad's behaviour. Dad shook hands with Oscar once more and thanked him again. The big man walked away from the family carrying his flippers but still clad in his diving gear.

~~~~

Jorden was down in the water, hoisting up the chests one by one as she untangled them from the netting. There were five in all and she struggled to lift each one up onto the dock, trying not to damage them. Tyler showed up just as Dad left to bring the truck down to pull the sub out. The children gathered around the old wooden chests on the dock.

Valerie was brimming with excitement and her eyes gleamed as she grinned at Alex and Jorden. Curtis bent down to inspect the one chest that was open, its shiny coins filling the decayed wooden box. Dad returned and backed the truck and trailer onto the boat ramp. Once the sub was safely on its trailer, the children loaded the chests into the bed of the truck. Onlookers continued to watch the commotion with curious gazes.

Dad closed the tailgate and turned to face the kids.

"Well! Congratulations, guys, you found it!" he began. "Now, we better all get home. Pam will be worried."

"I've already had three text messages from her!" exclaimed Valerie as she glanced at her phone's screen.

The group piled into o the truck read to head home, with both the sub and their cargo secure. As soon as they departed the marina, Curtis had drifted off to sleep.

"Do you think anyone will want to hear about this treasure?" Valerie asked her father as they drove down the highway.

Dad smiled at Valerie with a raised eyebrow. "Oh, I suspect this will be big news tomorrow," he replied with a knowing grin.

17

The garage was lit up and the sub was sitting in its place, water still beading on its surface. The chests had been placed on a large blanket on the floor, the decayed wood glistening in the fluorescent light overhead. Valerie stared at them. Alex and Jorden sat on one of Dad's stools at the workbench, while Curtis and Tyler checked out the sub. Dad came into the garage, carrying a tray of glasses filled with Pepsi. He set the tray down on the workbench and passed the refreshment out to the kids.

The police had been there earlier and had long since left after taking statements from all of them. They had listened in near disbelief at the events that the children and their father had recounted. Although the officers had not said much about the man who had attacked them, Dad was sure that he would be dealt with accordingly.

Valerie was beaming, unable to take her eyes off the chests. They had done it. They had found the Onondaga and its secret cargo. This was epic! They had taken the right steps and followed the clues, and in the end it had paid off. She was looking at a significant treasure that had been hidden from human eyes for over two hundred years. The cold waters combined with the depth of the wreck had kept the chests remarkably well preserved.

It was dark outside and the crickets were busy with their evening songs as the children admired the wooden boxes sitting on the floor of the garage.

"Well, you did it, guys!" said Dad with a big smile.

"Can we see it now?" asked Val, having used up her last shred of patience.

"I guess so! It's your discovery, after all!" replied Dad, knowing that they'd waited long enough for this moment.

Valerie and Alex opened the first chest; its hinged top screeched in rusty protest. The fluorescent lights above caused the gold and silver coins inside to sparkle in front of their eyes. There were coins of all sizes and most of them were stamped with the image of the King of England. There were gemstones in all the colours of the rainbow, some embedded in gold jewelry. This chest was filled almost to the brim with the loot. They opened the other chests to the same results. There was a ton of stuff, all of it glistening in the garage lights. Pam entered, holding a fresh mug of tea, and looked startled when her eyes fell on the glittering treasure.

"Wow! I guess it was a productive trip, eh, guys?"

Everyone nodded silently, still mesmerized by the sight on the floor and basking in the afterglow of a successful treasure hunt. It was so unbelievable. They had found the lost payroll and found actual proof about something that had been written about in history. And, if that wasn't enough of an accomplishment, Jorden had been able to use her newly acquired diving skills and had pulled something amazing from the river bottom with her own hands. One question remained, though, as the group stared at the open chests of loot. What would they do with it now?

It was a good thing that they had found it - the discovery of the ship and its treasure was extremely important historically. Valerie mulled over this thought. Now that they had it, what was next?

"Do we get to keep it?" asked Curtis. It was a simple and straightforward question and one that they'd all been thinking, too!

"No. In actual fact, it belongs to the British Government," replied Dad thoughtfully, as he sipped on his Pepsi.

"That's a lot of gold and silver," said Jorden.

Valerie continued to stare at their prize, hypnotized by the gleam. It was amazing. Nana would be proud of them, so happy that they'd successfully completed another one of her 'adventures', she thought. Nana had shown them the way, and she and Alex, along with the help of the rest of the family, had somehow managed to pull together and solve this mystery. Valerie felt satisfied and realized that she didn't really care what came next because they had done it - the lost payroll from the sunken Onondaga was sitting right in front of her. Pam was watching her expression.

"Well, looks like Nana gave you guys another great adventure, huh?"

Valerie looked away from the chests of gold, silver, coins and jewels. Her gaze rested on Pam.

"Yep, she is gonna love to see this!" Valerie replied.

Tyler took several pictures as he leaned on the hull of the sub with his phone, capturing images of their discovery. Jorden joined in, getting Alex and Valerie to squat down next to the open chests on the garage floor. Alex ran his hands through the coins, feeling their damp surfaces, and listened to the sounds of the clinking metal.

The wooden boards that made up the chests were ancient, waterlogged and spongy to the touch. Algae grew in small spots on the wood and gave it a slight greenish tinge. Droplets of river water still rolled off the sub.

"So, what do we do now?" asked Val.

"We should keep it all!" shouted Curtis.

Dad simply shook his head at the young boy.

"This doesn't belong to us. We need to get someone to help who knows what needs to be done. This is no small matter. "

Valerie shrugged her shoulders. She knew that he was right. The group all nodded in agreement.

"So?" asked Valerie again, a questioning look on her face.

"I think Mr. Thusk will probably be able to help," said Dad. "I think we'd better take this stuff to him in the morning."

~~~~

The excited museum curator rushed through the halls of the museum after receiving a call that the children would be there momentarily and would be bringing him their discovery. He bolted outside through the door and ran up to the truck as they pulled up in front of the building. He could barely believe his eyes!

Mr. Thusk simply stared at the wooden boxes loaded with coins and jewels that were sitting in the bed of the truck. They had actually done it, he thought. This was the single most amazing thing that had ever happened to the museum - and the city, he realized. It was even more incredible than the crystal bird that the children had discovered the year before.

Dad smiled and shook his hand before opened the tailgate of the truck and reached into its bed to pass the treasures over to the children to bring inside. As he did this, he noted to the curator that he had merely been the sub pilot and that it was the children who had made the whole discovery - and recovery - of the payroll.

The children brought all of the treasure inside the museum and placed the chests down carefully in a room where Mr. Thusk could examine and catalogue everything. The curator would have one of his assistants photograph each piece as he jotted down notes about them. After that, the items would be placed in a special room which was climate controlled and locked like a vault with a large key. It was such an unprecedented and marvelous discovery, that Mr. Thusk had decided not to take any chances, wanting to preserve the find as meticulously as he could.

He was jittery, excited. Here was history unfolding in front of him. He lingered over every chest, his eyes taking in every detail of the glimmering treasure. He listened attentively to the story of how they had found it - how the wreck of the Onondaga had been sitting on the river bottom in the Lost Channel just waiting to be discovered - his mouth agape. He had a lot of questions for Alex and Valerie and they happily answered his queries about the lost ship and its cargo. Mr. Thusk's hands flew as he scrawled their information in his notebook. He felt the need to capture all of the details, to log everything as it had happened. He beamed a huge smile at the children, almost ready to explode in his excitement.

~~~~

The next day, Mr. Thusk invited the children down to the museum again, where they sat with him and two other members of the museum staff and retold the entire story of how they had found the Onondaga and its cargo from start to finish. As they spoke, each telling their own parts of the story, the curator and his staff scribbled notes - they even used a tape recorder to record everything that was being said. When they finished, Mr. Thusk could tell that they were becoming tired, but furrowed his brow a little bit for a moment.

"So, this man who was dropping the explosives into the water, what did he look like?"

Valerie and Alex both began to excitedly describe the man and Mr. Thusk's curious expression changed to one of recognition, as though he knew what the answer would be before he had even asked the question.

"Well, it is fortunate that none of you were hurt, and I'm sure we won't be seeing him again any time soon!"

~~~~

One week later, everyone was back at the museum for a grand celebration and reveal of the Onondaga's Lost Treasure to the public. The children fussed with their dress clothes, unused to formal attire - and it was another hot day. They were bombarded with questions about how they found the shipwreck, were congratulated on their discovery and were greeted by so many people it was hard to keep track of them all. Pam and Dad even seemed uncomfortable, as there were reporters with cameras, television crews and important people from the city shaking their hands.

One of the librarians quickly approached Valerie and informed her that an anonymous person had returned the book about historical British Navy ships that she'd signed out and, in turn, they'd decided to donate the book to the museum to accompany the new display. As Valerie curiously pondered this information, her eyes locked on a guest standing in the corner of the room. Oscar had been watching her talking with the librarian, glowing with pride at the results of his actions from the week earlier. He'd also been relieved that he'd stopped his friend from making a final disastrous mistake. Without any hesitation, Oscar gave Valerie a knowing smile, a quick nod and a thumbs-up before he turned to walk to the exit of the building.

Mr. Thusk simply beamed at the entire entourage, reveling in the attention that the children's discovery had brought to the city - and to the museum.

Nana and Grandpa were also there. Nana shot Valerie and Alex a quick wink as she and their Grandfather looked at the old chests full of glistening gold and silver and colourful jewels. Valerie knew that they had Nana to thank once again for showing them the way to another great adventure.

The halls of the museum were brightly lit and packed with people coming to see the mysterious treasure from the Lost Channel. The displays included some of the finer pieces of jewelry and gems sparkling on small stands made of glass. Everyone gathered in the room looked with awe at the spectacle. Camera flashes punctuated the exclamations of the museum patrons.

Mr. Thusk emerged through the crowd to stand by Valerie and Alex. He was carrying some papers with him. He smiled widely at the children and asked them in his most polite way if all the family could gather together to see what he had brought.

The children flocked in closely, curious to see what the museum curator was holding. Mr. Thusk cleared his throat dramatically before he spoke.

"This letter arrived for you all yesterday," he began and put on a pair of thin reading glasses. He read from the letter:

"It is with great honour that I congratulate each of you on your immense discovery and thank you for your perseverance in bringing this lost piece of history to a final conclusion. The amazing feats you have accomplished speak volumes for your attention to detail and your abilities as young explorers. I extend my sincerest gratitude to you all, as you have uncovered a part of our, and your, history, which was previously thought lost."

Mr. Thusk removed his glasses and paused for effect.

"It is signed by Her Royal Majesty, Queen Elizabeth the second."

Valerie suddenly felt faint. Alex's mouth dropped open and the rest of children and their parents and grandparents looked around at each other in amazement. Flashes erupted from cameras all over the room as Mr. Thusk stood amongst the children and displayed the letter for all to see.

It was all crazy and the kids could only smile as throngs of people surrounded them, congratulated them and snapped photos. Dad and Pam, Nana and Grandpa had moved over to the side and watched as the children basked in the excitement and publicity of the occasion.

Eventually Mr. Thusk turned back to the kids and leaned down to speak to them privately.

"The British government is allowing the treasure to be displayed here for some time, but everything will eventually have to be returned to the United Kingdom. In addition, they have designated the site where the Onondaga sank as a British gravesite, which means that no one will be allowed near the wreck ever again."

The children nodded and tried to take everything in.

Mr. Thusk stood up tall again and straightened his brown suit jacket.

"You all should be very proud. You have accomplished something that is profound - and you completed an unfinished piece of history."

All the kids could do was smile, simply happy to have had another successful adventure.

Part Three:
The Last Train

Dedicated to those members of a brotherhood of railroaders with whom I have had the pleasure of working...

Foreword

I have been around the railroad all of my life, being a second-generation railroader myself. My father, Morley, worked for the same company for 37 years up until his retirement in 1994. I have remained there, with the possibility of retirement dangling in front of me 13 years from now... Although I vowed never to write anything pertaining to my work -- it would also be a conflict of interest -- I could not resist writing a story in such a way as to shed light on the rich history of the rail industry where I live, and the many fine people that I have come to know with my work.

As I plunge the characters of my family into another epic adventure, I also reflect on the 22 years I have spent with the rail company, the ups and downs, and many rewarding experiences as well. I would like to say that even though many parts of this story are fictional, many are not, and a few of the characters in the story are real people that I have had the pleasure to come to know and work with almost every day.

This will be the third and final book in the series, and I have enjoyed writing all of them. My children have always been big supporters of my writing, and it is with a real sense of deep satisfaction that I have finished this trilogy.

Dennis Stein

Dennis Stein

1

The sunset was beautiful over the train yard, the sky a kaleidoscope of pinks and oranges against the few clouds as the sun began to sink below the horizon. It was just beginning to get dark as the brakeman stepped up on the side of a grain car at the tail end of his train, keying the microphone on his radio.

"Shove for sixteen cars, 532," he commanded.

"Shove for sixteen," repeated the engineer, and the diesel locomotive at the other end of the train roared to life, pushing the rail cars down the track with a chorus of metallic 'clanks' and bangs. The steel of the wheels screeched along the rails, as the work train pushed its cargo into the dusty yard tracks. It was fall, and a light frost covered the track ties as evening came on. The air was cold, but very still, a fact that the train crew was grateful for.

"Eight now, 532...," said the brakeman into his handset.

"Eight," came the repeat.

The brakeman held onto the side of the car, watching attentively as the cars were pushed down into the train yard, keeping an eye out for anything that could be in their way, or a switch not properly lined for their route. They continued to roll down the track, the cars swaying and clanking as they met each joint in the rails.

"Four now, 532, four car lengths," he said.

"Four," replied the engineer.

As they slowed, the brakeman jumped off the car, his boots raising a small cloud of dust in the failing light.

"Ok to stop, 5-3-2."

"Stopping," came the reply.

The train gave a screech, the slack between the cars sounding a dull metallic smash as the train came to a halt. The brakeman produced and switched on a flashlight, as it was getting dark. It was cool and damp, even in the gathering darkness, but he wiped sweat from his brow with a gloved hand despite the chill fall air. He could hear the engine of the locomotive chugging at idle many cars behind him as he made his way to the last switch. It led down a spur track to one of the older factories in town, where his orders stated they had several boxcars to pick up. He removed the hook from the lock on the switch stand, throwing the handle with a quick grunt, lining the route for his train. Checking that the points of the switch had come completely over, he gave a satisfied grin and replaced the metal hook back into the locking clasp of the switch. It was only a few steps back to the last car on the train, and he stepped back up onto its side, grabbing the rusty handrail securely. Again he keyed the microphone on his radio.

"532, at least forty cars to the joint."

"Forty...pushing," came the reply as the locomotive again roared to life. The cars clanked down the track, through a narrow, thickly treed route along the outskirts of the city.

"Thirty cars, 532."

"Thirty," came the reply.

The brakeman held onto the side of the tail end car, keeping a close watch on the track ahead with his flashlight. The full moon had just begun to rise through the leafless trees, bathing the rails with its light. The chill in the air made his breath a steamy cloud as he listened to the cars ride over the steel trail, their wheels 'clacking' over the joints in the rails.

"Fifteen cars to a stop, 532," the brakeman said into the mic.

"Fifteen," repeated the engineer.

Through the gloom the brakeman could see the last switch, which would take the train down to the mill where they had to deliver several empty grain cars. As he squinted through the darkness, the illumination from his flashlight caught something. It wasn't right. The switch was lined the wrong way. He quickly grabbed the microphone clipped to his vest.

"Bring her to a stop, 532, stop."

"Stopping."

The group of cars gave a great yank, as the locomotive brakes were applied, the slack between them stretching out with a crash. The steel wheels screeched against the rail as the consist came to a halt -- just a single car length from the switch.

The brakeman jumped down, his boots crunching in the slag beside the track. *Just great*, he thought. *"Who left this switch lined that way? Probably kids".*

He stalked up to the switch stand, removed the hook and threw the switch the other way. He looked down the rails through the darkness with his light.

This portion of the track ended about a hundred yards down, and past that was a paved tree-lined walking and bicycle path that led to the city's waterfront. The railway had donated this land to the city for parkland. If they hadn't stopped in time, the train would have veered down to that area and it would have been a disaster. It was definitely no place for this train to go. With one last check on the switch, the brakeman replaced the hook into the switch stand, and walked back to mount the cars again.

"Okay to shove, 532. Fifteen cars to a stop," he said into the radio.

"Fifteen? What happened?" asked the engineer as the locomotive once again throttled up.

"Ah, looks like kids turned the last switch on us, but we're okay now. 10 to a stop," he responded. The radio crackled with some static as the reply came from the head end.

"Ten. Should have the train master lock that one up."

"Definitely! It's hard enough to see down through here, let alone have to worry about that switch. They should just straight-rail it. Five more, 532."

"Five," came the repeat. "We wouldn't want to go down the other way... Might meet up with the ghost of the tunnel!"

The brakeman grinned. Every rail man knew of the story of the ghost of the railway tunnel that ran underneath the city right down to the waterfront. It was an old urban legend about a train brakeman who had died in this tunnel while looking for his hand, which had been cut off by the wheels of the train he had been working. The story was that he had found gold buried between the rails, and as he had reached forward to claim it, his hand had been amputated by the train cars rolling forward. The poor soul had bled to death there beside the track, after wandering back toward the head-end of the train, seeking help. No one had ever found any gold, and the story was that his ghost continued to wander the tracks, searching for his hand -- and his gold!

The brakeman's thoughts were interrupted by the sight of the old stone mill coming into view out of the gloom.

"Two cars, 532."

"Two."

As the train slowed to a crawl, the brakeman dismounted from the tail end car again, walking to a spot where he could see the wall of the loading dock of the mill, and still be able to keep an eye on his train cars as well. The two boxcars stood silently on the track outside the loading dock, waiting to be coupled with this train. The brakeman shook off the chill as his breath steamed in the glow from his light.

"Something feels out of place", he thought as he glanced around for a moment. The air was dead calm, and all at once he could feel the hairs on the back of his neck stand up. His pulse quickened as he shone his flashlight around. The light caught something in the trees beside him. It was a man.

"Hey, you gave me quite a start! Can I help you with something?" he asked, his heart beating slightly faster.

The stranger didn't acknowledge him. He just stood there holding what looked like a lantern. His skin was as white as snow and his large, pale eyes stared towards the brakeman, not seeming to even notice him.

The brakeman's breath froze in his throat, his blood pounding as he looked at the grim visage. The man was dressed in striped overalls and wore a hat symbolic of the railway days of old. But it was the pale skin and the eerie eyes that enthralled him. There was no light coming from the lantern that was gripped in his hand -- it was as cold and dark as the leafless trees in the gloom of the cold night. Then the brakeman noticed the stranger's other arm: it ended where his wrist would be, the appendage covered in a tattered rag.

The brakeman's body began to tremble in fear as he watched the motionless stranger and he stumbled backwards, trying to put some space between him and apparition in the trees. Then he turned and started to run back towards his train, wanting nothing more than to be away from this 'thing'. As he sprinted, the train, with no instructions to stop, crashed into the boxcars and forced them forward through the stop blocks of the mill track. The two tail end cars jumped the track and toppled into the slag with a crash.

"What the heck was that? What's going on!" came the panicked voice of the engineer over the radio.

The brakeman fumbled for his radio as he turned back with his flashlight towards the trees, towards the thing he had seen. The leafless trees bore the resemblance of death in the still fall night, illuminated by the flashlight. But there was nothing else. An icy breeze stirred the bare branches of the trees, making them seem to come alive and dance before his eyes. His pulse was still beating hard as he tried to calm himself down. A final swoop of the flashlight confirmed that he was alone again, even though every nerve in his body felt alive and on fire.

"S-sorry, Mike..," he finally stammered, still barely able to take a breath. "I got distracted. Looks like we got a mess."

~~~~

Nana had been working in her studio for many days, trying to complete an oil painting. She'd finished her summer gardens to the best of her abilities and satisfaction. She routinely made the studio her escape as the colder weather approached. It was also a productive way for her to pass the many sunsets of winter. She didn't dislike the fall and winter, but as she grew older, she'd found that the warmth of the house was preferable to the cold air outside. She still liked a walk outside in the fall months, taking in the fresh crispness of the air and enjoying the songs of the birds as they gathered what food they could to last them through the winter months.

Outside the large bay window of her studio, the cool wind blew leaves across the frosted yard. The sun shone brightly, as if trying to hold off the advance of the inevitable winter ahead; the trees in the front yard already leafless skeletons, timeless reminders of Mother Nature's cycle.

Grandpa occasionally walked in quietly and watched her toil away at the large canvas. She was painting a picture of an old steam locomotive, surrounded by the smoke from its boiler and set against a mountain backdrop. It was coming along beautifully, full of rich detail from the stones alongside the track to the snow-capped mountains which made up the backdrop. The smell of the oil paint was thick in the air and combined with the aroma of many stacks of old papers and photos. Grandpa tried not to disturb her work, but his presence behind her did not go unnoticed, and she turned around, feeling his need to speak to her.

"Hi, what's up?" she asked.

"The children phoned a little earlier, asking if they could come and do some art with you," replied Grandpa.

"Valerie and Alex? Of course! That sounds like fun."

"Well, I knew you were busy working on this painting, so I didn't want to speak for you."

Nana put down her brush and observed her progress for a moment.

"Oh, I have lots of time for this," she said.

Nana loved to have the children over to do artwork and crafts in her studio. It was a Saturday, and she could think of nothing better than tea and artwork with her grandchildren.

Even though the leaves had fallen outside and the days were shorter and cooler, Nana's studio was alive with greenery. Plants of all types spread their green leaves across the bookcases and tables which housed several piece of artwork, some still in progress.

Grandpa watched as Nana picked up her brush once again, obsessed with the painting she was working on.

"Just promise me you aren't going to fill their heads with some crazy adventure," he said with a grimace.

Nana looked back at him, over her glasses.

"I haven't the faintest idea what you are talking about, my dear," she replied coolly.

Grandpa could sense her sarcasm and he shot her a look as he turned to head back into the house. She grinned to herself as he left and turned her attention back to her painting. As if she would EVER send the children on some crazy idea of an adventure!

The brush strokes came easy to her, as the painting developed on the canvas. *"It would be a great day"*, she mused, *"if the kids came out to visit...."* She stopped mid-thought and turned her attention to the bookcase beside her. There it was: her scrapbook -- a rough, tattered old binding of newspaper articles and pictures. It was thick with history, strange lore and tales of things that were mysteries in the local area. She had added to it many times over the years. The children simply loved it when she pulled the old book from the shelf to show them something new. Nana had a way of bringing the lost legends and stories of the local area to life for them, and they always sat and listened intently to whatever magical tale she would spin from the pages of that collection of clippings from the past.

Grandpa eventually reappeared in the doorway of the studio. "Okay, they are on their way," he informed her.

"Is Curtis coming as well?" she asked.

"I think he might be," he replied, shrugging slightly. "Your son has to work and so does Pam."

"Perfect. This will be a fun day," she responded, a little too enthusiastically.

Grandpa could sense the gleam in her eyes even though she had her back to him. He had seen the results of Nana's meddling in the past. Adventures! Crazy ideas! He was not fond of the idea of her sending the children off on some grand new quest resulting from a spark ignited by the stories in her scrapbook. Their Dad would probably not like it either! Every time Nana got out that book, it seemed to result in chaos. Grandpa liked things quiet, predictable. It would be nice if, just for once, the kids could come and spend time with them without some new craziness. He became concerned each time Nana conjured up some new adventure for the kids, wondering if the "missions" that she sent them on were safe. He knew that she would simply say that he worried too much. As though sensing his thoughts, she turned around to face him. She had that look in her eyes, combined with a slight, mischievous-looking grin that made Grandpa uneasy.

"What harm could come from some tea…and a little art?"

Grandpa gave her a look that told her that he was definitely not convinced!

2

Dad glimpsed at Valerie and Alex in the rear view mirror as they drove home from Nana's house. He knew something was up, because the children were normally talkative all the way back to the house, especially after a visit at their grandparents' home. Even Curtis was quiet, focusing on his iPod. They seemed engrossed in some papers that Valerie was holding onto and reading intently. He frowned slightly as he drove, continually checking on them in the rear view mirror. He had experienced this kind of 'quiet' before, after they had visited their Nana and Grandpa, and it always made him feel extra concerned when it happened.

Valerie focused on the pages that Nana had copied for them out of her famous scrapbook. It was an article about a trainman from long ago, and his futile search for treasure along the old railway lines not far from the children's home. Her dark brown hair hung over the pages as she read and Alex's sandy blond-head crowded close to read the pages, too. The sky had darkened as they drove home. Dad had picked them up on his way home from work. They were done school for the week and the children had jumped at the chance to hang out with Nana in her art studio at their house out in the country.

Valerie motioned to Alex, and, as if by some secret telepathy, he understood what she wanted. He pulled open his trusty backpack, rummaged around inside and, after a few moments, pulled out a small flashlight from it. He immediately clicked it on and handed it to his sister. Both the children's eyes were bright with interest as they continued to read by the light of the small torch. According to the article, over many years, several eye-witnessed had reported spotting a ghost in the area of the train tunnel in the downtown area. The article went on to tell about the legend of this ghost, how it was searching for both lost gold and its hand, which had been lost in an accident. Dad occasionally glanced at the rear view mirror, wondering what was up in the back seat.

"Did you have a nice visit with Nana and Grandpa?" he asked, breaking the silence of the drive.

"Oh yes! Nana was showing us a new painting she is working on," Valerie replied. Dad noticed that she didn't take her eyes off the page she was reading when she answered him.

"Watcha' got there?" he pressed, knowing he didn't really want to hear the answer. He knew full well that Nana had provided them with some new crazy adventure. He really didn't like it all that much when she filled their heads with such ideas. It had nearly resulted in disaster two or three times in the past.

"Oh, just a ghost story, about a trainman who lost his hand trying to find some lost gold," she grinned slightly as she said it, turning to wink slightly at her brother, who almost giggled out loud. They both knew that Dad would be unimpressed by this new story from Nana's book.

Dad sighed, realizing that Valerie had just confirmed his suspicions. *Great*, he thought. *"Just what we need: some new story that will have the kids traipsing all over the neighbourhood looking for some lost treasure again."* And he definitely did not like the idea that it could possibly involve the rail yard, all those tracks... and trains!

Every time the children got involved in these 'adventures' he worried about their safety. It was one thing to go on a treasure hunt of some kind. It was another matter altogether to allow the kids to risk their necks around railway tracks and trains. He made a mental note to speak to both of them when the subject arose again and the time was right. And they'd be talking about it again, soon! He knew that the two of them would be raring to dive into this latest 'quest' that their Grandmother had provided for them. He watched the road ahead as he drove, focusing more in the gathering darkness. They would be home soon, and he hoped, instead, that they would turn their attention to video games. Everyone would be safe that way!

"Well, that's kind of crazy," he said at last, as a way to dissuade them. "Everyone knows ghosts don't really exist...!"

~~~~

Harold looked down once more at his rough, hand-drawn map of the bicycle path, checked his handheld GPS, and marked a waypoint. It was a sunny fall Sunday, his only day off from the mundane cleaning job that he worked all week long. To his wife, this was his irritating hobby. To him, it could be his salvation from a life of TV dinners and never-ending work. He could almost hear the nagging life partner of almost thirty years telling him that he was wasting his time.

Harold's unkempt short hair was mostly black with a few streaks of grey through the sides, and he wore large, thick glasses that made his eyes look twice their size. He wasn't very tall, in fact, he was kind of stocky, and his potbelly stuck well out in front of him, ready to make the buttons on his plaid shirt burst.

He looked again at his map, muttering under his breath. His metal detector had picked up several items this particular day, an aluminum can, bottle caps, and the only thing that he had saved, an old copper penny. Maybe it was his lucky one. Perhaps it would help him in some way to find what he was seeking.

He made his way slowly down the bike path, sweeping the head of his metal detector as he went, listening through a pair of half-broken old headphones for any sign of a prize. A few joggers went by, concentrating on their breathing and not looking the strange man in the eye. He also paid them no attention -- not bicyclers, people walking their dogs or children heading home from school. He focused his senses on the task at hand and ignored the occasional strange glances he received from passersby. He didn't need -- or want -- to acknowledge anyone on this pass with a nod or a smile. He was busy. This was his chance to discover something important in the city's history, a chance to make his wife see that he wasn't wasting his time...and perhaps even his chance to be rich!

He walked for a long time along the grey asphalt of the path as the creek gurgled along beside him. Leaves covered the entire path in some areas and the trees' bare branches swayed slightly in the cool fall breeze. He stopped several times to check his map, and make a few sweeps with the metal detector, listening for any indication of a find. He frowned as he concentrated on his task, not hearing anything that would help him. It was a laborious task searching under the hidden areas of the path for valuables. He marked his GPS again and continued walking along until he reached a sidewalk, but he wasn't finished. He crossed a side street to continue on the pathway. This paved trail was part of the old railway line that had been donated to the city long ago to become a park-like walking and bicycling path that followed the creek through town. There were sitting benches along the pathway and large cement planters filled with lilies, hostas and other flowers. Memorial plaques stood silently in front of several bare trees as he walked along, reminders of someone's passing or of community groups who had contributed to the greenery along the path.

He came to a fork, and looked down the path's direction on the right where he saw a tunnel of bare tree branches and browned remnants of undergrowth. *"This is the way I have to go"*, he thought. *"It leads to the train tunnel."* He shuddered slightly, despite the sun on his back, and forced himself forward, slowly sweeping the detector along the dead grass beside the path as he went. He pulled off the headphones and slid them down around his neck as his pace slowed. A sudden strong wind swept through the tree branches, making them clatter together up above his head. Several clouds moved in quickly in to obscure the sun and the light on the asphalt of the path dimmed. Harold stopped for a moment, his senses now fully attuned to the sounds around him, and he noticed that the birds that he had been hearing all afternoon had stopped chirping their songs. There was only an eerie silence.

Harold forced his legs to continue on his route and he walked slowly as he rounded a bend in the path. He tried to focus his eyes through the skeleton-like trees on the old stonework of the tunnel entrance. It gaped wide, dark and hollow, the pavement of the path ending at its mouth. Old slag from the abandoned rail bed disappeared inside it in darkness. As he approached, Harold shuddered again, remembering the stories of the ancient train tunnel that led for almost two thousand feet under the city and emerged at the waterfront. The open maw of the tunnel seemed to breathe cold air on him from its depths, and he slowed his pace, trying hard to concentrate on his detector and his GPS, trying to break the mental grip that the huge stone entrance to darkness held on him.

The cold breeze picked up again, scattering dead leaves across the path in front of him and making the trees clatter even more. He stopped, unable to take his gaze away from the darkness in front of him. His pulse raced as he stared into the black abyss of the tunnel, its huge wooden doors swung wide, covered here and there in bits of moss and decay. He could not take another step. Harold could feel unknown icy fingers on his spine, sense a distant evil prying on his mind. He turned for a moment, wanting only to return to the sunshine that had lit up the path only a short while before.

He began to walk away, feeling the tug of the tunnel and its dark interior on his brain. As he put distance between himself and the gloom of the tunnel entrance, he felt a little more at ease. Although he wanted to find this lost treasure, he certainly wouldn't be venturing into the tunnel today...

~~~~

The location of the railway tunnel, although so far not disclosed in this story, is the first, and oldest in Canada. It runs directly under our City Hall, and has a total length exceeding 1700 ft. A railway company began construction of the tunnel in 1854, to provide access to the shipping port on the river and link it to the timber trade to the north. The railway ran to another city far to the north, and through the tunnel with special height-shortened diesel trains. It was completed in 1860, which is amazing considering the size of the project, and a lack of any major mechanized excavating equipment at the time. The railway was incorporated in 1853, and the company decided its rail line would not be complete without the tunnel. The first train made use of the tunnel in 1859, leaving the Grand Trunk Station almost a full year before the completion of the tunnel...

Restoration efforts have recently begun on the deteriorating north end of the tunnel, where it emerges in an overgrown ravine. Workers catalogue stones and place them in the open area behind the local coffee shop while they rebuild the structure and replace the original stonework. The city has budgeted funds for the work, and hopefully the fully restored tunnel entrance will be unveiled soon. The first 85 ft of the south end of the tunnel is open to visitors from spring to fall, complete with plaques to tell the story of the tunnel. Outside the tunnel sits a refurbished Canadian Pacific Railway caboose, which was donated to the city in 1987. CP Rail owned the tunnel after amalgamating with other smaller railways, and turned over the tunnel after it was no longer used to the city. Great oak doors cover the tunnel's 14 ft. wide by 14ft. high mouths at either end, and brickwork covers the inside ceiling. Although the rail and ties are long gone, sold off after the tunnel stopped being used in the 1970's, one can still imagine the roar of locomotives emerging from the tunnel, carrying goods from ships docked at the river...

3

Valerie awoke with the fall sun on her face, squinting as she opened her brown eyes. Her thoughts came flooding back to her from the night before, and she smiled slightly, remembering that it was a Saturday. She rolled herself quickly out of bed, stretched, pulled her hair back from her face as she looked out her window into the backyard and stretched again. There was a male cardinal at the bird feeder, singing his morning song as he ate. The sun shone strong on the yard, but Valerie could still sense the crispness of the morning air through the screen of the window. The grass was still very green, she noticed, though, and that promised a lengthy wait for the full embrace of winter. Valerie liked the snow as well, but she loved the fall -- even though most of the leaves had already fallen and had created a bright-coloured mosaic on the backyard lawn. The warmth of the sun pouring in through her window told her that it would be a very nice day indeed.

She finally got dressed, remembering that Nana was going to pick her and Alex up today to go and have tea. They were going to visit an old friend of Nana's, a lady that Nana had told her was a direct descendant of Mother Barnes, otherwise known in local lore as the Witch of Plum Hollow. Elizabeth Barnes had been the seventh daughter of a seventh daughter, and she had made extra money by telling people's futures by reading their tea leaves. Her abilities had been renowned in the area; in fact, she had even told a young lawyer from a nearby town that he would become the first Prime Minister of the newly settled country -- and she'd been right! Although she had passed away long ago, her children and grandchildren were still alive, and one particular relative still lived in the area. This lady was a friend of Nana's and Valerie was excited to meet her. If anyone could tell her the story about the trainman's gold, it would be her!

She got dressed and hurried from her bedroom to the bathroom. After a quick brushing of her teeth and a few sweeps of a brush through her brown hair, which she then drew back into a ponytail, she felt ready for the day. First of course, she had to wake up her brother, who was a chronic late sleeper on the weekends.

She made her way to Alex's room and pushed open the door. His room was sunlit and warm. As she expected, he was dozing under his blankets, the cat lying alongside his sleeping form. With a slight purr, the cat looked at Valerie as if to tell her in some secret language to go away and not disturb them, that Alex was still asleep and comfortable!

"Ha, not for long," Valerie thought to herself, a sly grin creeping onto her face. She raised her arms high in the air and spread her fingers wide overhead, as if stretching. Then she let out a long, loud holler.

Alex bolted upright in bed; the cat bolted from the room at the sudden loud noise. Looking around his room in confusion, he rubbed his blue-grey eyes and then focused on his sister. She still held her arms high while she laughed out loud. He grabbed his pillow and swung it in an arc at her. She easily took the brunt of the pillow, still laughing.

"Hey, it's time to get up!" she said cheerily.

"Ohhh, would you leave me alone!?" he complained back.

"C'mon sleepy! Nana's coming, remember?"

"Awww! I just wanted a few more minutes!"

Valerie completed agitating him by ripping his covers off the bed.

"You're such a dork!" he retorted, now fully awake.

Valerie was still grinning, satisfied by the torment. She left the room quickly and headed downstairs for some breakfast. Alex dressed himself groggily, and grabbed his trusty, tattered backpack, which held all of his important possessions. After a deep sigh, he headed downstairs as well, dragging his backpack behind him.

Down in the kitchen, Dad had already made some bacon and eggs. The smell of the sizzling bacon filled the entire main floor of the house with the promise of goodness. Pam, their step-mom, was engrossed in a game on the computer at the breakfast nook when the kids came down.

This was the time of morning that Dad and Pam loved, the quiet of the house on a weekend when the children slept in. Their oldest, Jorden, was once again away at college, and the next in line, Tyler, had decided to try living on his own. He had a good job and was renting an apartment not far away. Their youngest, Curtis, was at home, still sleeping in his bed upstairs.

So it had become a party of five of them now, a bit of a relief from the chaos of seven individuals living in one small house!

Alex and Valerie gobbled down their breakfasts along with a glass of orange juice and quickly tidied up their plates and placed them in the dishwasher. The dog let out a few barks to announce that a vehicle had pulled up out front. It was Nana. Dad scooted out the front door as the children put on their shoes -- he intended to have a word or two with Nana before the children disappeared with her. He stepped down off the front porch and over to the window of the silver minivan that Nana was driving.

"Now Mom, let's try to keep it from getting out of hand this time, shall we?" he said, sensing that she was about to escort the kids on some grand new adventure.

"Of course! We are only going for tea with Ms. Bitterman!" she replied with an innocent expression on her face.

"Yeah, I know, and I know who she is!" Dad said back, giving Nana a look.

He knew very well that Nana's friend was supposedly a descendant of The Witch of Plum Hollow and he'd even heard the stories of the early years of the country, when the famed fortune-teller would divulge the secrets of people's future for a few cents by using tea leaves. The whole thing made him uneasy.

"Relax son, I am simply taking them out to tea, so that my grandchildren learn proper table manners. I did it with you and your brother, too, you remember?!"

"Uh-huh!" Dad was not fooled by her attempt to disguise the matter.

"I just don't want any craziness this time."

She simply replied with a comical grin and fluttered her eyebrows at him.

Valerie and Alex ran down the front porch to greet Nana, and Dad cut the conversation short, still giving her the look. Nana simply smiled widely as the children piled into the van.

"Have fun with Pam and Curtis. We won't be too long!" sang Nana as she pulled away, still grinning.

Dad put his hands on his hips and watched the van disappear down the street, sure that Nana had not paid any heed to a single word he had said.

~~~~

Harold sat at the table as his wife placed an aluminum plate of oven-heated frozen breakfast in front of him. It was pancake day. He suppressed a slight groan as he looked at it, the fake-looking eggs and prefab pancakes, along with something that only vaguely resembled bacon. The television played its colourful ads as he stuck his fork into the bland meal, trying to keep a happy expression on his face. His wife had been talking steadily since he sat down, like machinegun fire. He caught only certain parts of her dialogue, as she prattled on about what the neighbours had just bought. *"Something shiny and new, no doubt,"* he mused. Her words trailed off in the background as he ate, filler for a lack-luster day off. Even as he tried to pay a tiny bit of attention, his thoughts drifted back to the train tunnel. He wondered if he was on the right path to finding the trainman's gold -- he hadn't much to go on except for inconclusive stories and a couple of very old newspaper clippings. If only he had some magical way of divining its location. *If it even existed at all,* he thought.

The sound of the furnace kicking on broke his train of thought. It would be cool for the next few days according to the weather forecast he had seen in the paper earlier. Great, he thought. *"Even more money to be spent on the heating bills."* Harold and his wife did not have much, but he somehow managed to keep the bills paid fairly regularly, even on his meager income. His cleaning job didn't give him big pay cheques, but it kept them sufficiently stable in their small two-bedroom home with the essentials they needed.

They had bought the house many years earlier, with the idea of starting a family, but, although he and his wife had tried, they had never been able to have children. Many doctors' visits later, the sad news came to them that they would probably never have children. Harold loved kids, and his wife had been heartbroken, but they loved each other very much and had decided to take a chance on a waiting list to adopt. A child in the house would make their lives complete, even if they didn't have much.

His hours at work this year had been cut back, however, making their budget a lot tighter. His wife had found a little work in her field of accounting, which basically meant that she was preparing people's taxes from their small home office. It had helped to balance things out. He dreamed of the day that they could retire with a small pension, one that his wife was also helping them to save for. The mortgage and the utility bills were their biggest obstacles. The latest two-week pay period for him had been one of the worst: after paying the bills that had come due, they'd had to roll change from their spare change bowl in the kitchen to get the very frozen dinners they were eating at the moment. Thank goodness tomorrow was payday! But, he figured, by the next weekend, they would probably be almost broke again, as he had to pay the electricity bill before they were cut off. After that, the remainder would be spent on groceries to carry them through the next two weeks. Living from pay cheque to pay cheque seemed to be the unending cycle of their existence.

After his 'gourmet' breakfast, he tossed the aluminum tray into the garbage can and retreated to their home office. It was time for him to do some more research about his hobby on the Internet. Even though his wife thought that he was wasting his time, she realized that it seemed to be the one thing that brought him some small amount of pleasure. Because everyone needed a hobby, she didn't seem to mind. She generally left him alone about it, usually with a huge sigh as she watched one of her television shows. After all, she reasoned, they still had what they really needed, and weren't living on the street.

Harold began to pour through his notes and maps as he pulled up the browser on their ancient home computer. What might Google tell him this morning? On a small map of the city spread out before him, he had made squares of the areas that he had already searched. Most of these squares were in the area near the train tunnel or on or alongside the bicycle path that led up to it. He reread the notes that he'd jotted down about those areas in an old notebook that he had pressed into service for his hobby. It was a police officer's style of notebook and he had a large paper clip attached to it to hold the page of his most recent notes.

The computer screen glowed with its soft light in the small, darkened room, illuminating Harold's round face. He turned his attention toward it and navigated to Wikipedia. It was usually a fount of knowledge, but there seemed to be very little written about the tunnel or the mysterious trainman. What was he missing?

~~~~

Valerie and Alex sat next to Nana at old Ms. Bitterman's dining room table. The room itself felt like a living jungle with tropical plants filling shelves and windowsills everywhere. Old pictures and framed documents lined the walls and, in one corner, a massive bookcase rose from floor to ceiling. The birds sang outside, despite the cool day, and there was a palpable magical feeling to the room in which they sat. A cat appeared in the doorway between the dining room and kitchen, surveying the small gathering before licking a paw and turning its back on the group to go and find something more amusing.

Margaret Bitterman brought out a large teapot from her kitchen and placed it carefully on a small towel in the centre of the dining room table. *"She would have to be in her eighties at least,"* Valerie guessed. Sporting short white hair, Margaret was scarcely as tall as Valerie, but seemed to still have a very sharp mind the way she chatted with Nana. She hobbled around the table and took a seat opposite them.

"So, you two young ones are here to find out something from me. I can always tell. Especially you!" she said, pointing a bony, old finger in Valerie's direction.

Valerie smiled, blushing slightly.

"They are looking for anything you can tell them about an old legend here in town," Nana explained to her friend.

"Well, please don't tell me about it. I always find the best answers from the tea leaves," she replied in a matter-of-fact tone.

Nana simply nodded.

The children sat quietly while Margaret poured tea for everyone. The old woman had an ageless quality about her and Valerie watched her intently as she poured tea into each cup, being careful not to spill it.

"I have milk and sugar here, kids. Make your tea as you like it."

Valerie picked up a small, old silver milk creamer and poured some of the cooling liquid into her cup. When she saw the tea reach the colour she liked, she stopped and passed the creamer over to Alex. He did the same, remaining quiet as Valerie moved to the sugar, taking some from the similar small, old silver bowl. Nana took a little sugar, but no milk.

They all sat quietly for a few moments as they sipped their tea. Margaret watched the children intently, reading their faces. Nana saw what she was doing and grinned to herself slightly.

Valerie glanced over the old woman as she drank and tried hard not to stare. She recalled Nana's conversation with her and Alex about how this lady was related to the Witch of Plum Hollow and tried to imagine what life might have been like for Margaret's grandmother in the early history of this country. Nana had told her that Mother Barnes had been consulted by many people who had wanted to know their futures, including some very important people, and others who had been seeking the location of hidden treasures. Had Margaret truly inherited Mother Barnes' gift of foresight? Could she tell them about the ghost of the train tunnel? Valerie had averted her gaze, but could still feel the old woman watching her. She shifted nervously in her chair.

"The tea is very good, thank you," she said politely, her eyes still downcast.

"You are very welcome, my young lady," Margaret replied.

An old wooden cuckoo clock hung on the wall in the room. Its small pendulum swung back and forth slowly and its intricate gears clicked quietly inside.

The wallpaper in the small dining room looked very old, with flowers and thin burgundy stripes against a cream coloured background, but there wasn't a seam or imperfection anywhere to be found. Valerie felt that the entire house a that sense of oldness about it, like stepping back in time to the earlier parts of the century.

When they finished drinking, Margaret spread a linen tea towel on top of the table next to the teapot. She poured the remainder of it onto the towel -- a tiny bit of liquid, followed by the leaves of tea from the bottom of the pot. They fell upon the towel, the points of their leaves resting in a small heap upon the tea stained fabric. Margaret looked at them fixedly and used a single finger to move the leaves around on the towel. She contemplated them for long moments. The children were aware that she was doing something and sat still and quiet, not making any movement as the old woman stared at the tea leaves.

"You seek the trainman," she said finally, a piercing gaze rising toward Valerie and Alex.

Valerie nodded slowly and kept her eyes locked with the old woman.

"His body was never found...and his soul has not rested. You seek a story which is not yet finished."

"Yes, we want to find his treasure," said Valerie quietly.

Margaret looked at the two children closely as she ran her fingers idly through the tea leaves.

"The spirit of the trainman is unable to leave this world," she explained. "It may be that he remains to guard his treasure, or that he seeks something which was lost."

Alex could feel the hairs on the back of his neck beginning to stand up as he listened. He wasn't sure if it was what the old woman was saying in her quiet tone or if it was the sequential ticking of the old cuckoo clock on the wall, with each tick marking the progression of time in a way that suddenly made him uncomfortable.

"There are others who seek the treasure as well, real people who have become obsessed with it. They have let greed cloud their minds, and could be dangerous if you cross their path."

Valerie nodded slowly and gulped, wishing that she could have another small sip of tea. Nana sat quietly and watched her grandchildren's reactions as she listened to her friend talk. Alex subconsciously gripped his trusty backpack. The tiny old woman leaned in closer and her eyes widened at the children.

"The train tunnel. The spirit of the trainman is there, and if you find his resting place, you may surely find what it is you seek," she concluded.

Teatime was over. Margaret escorted Nana and the children to the front door and Nana thanked her in the doorway as the children scrambled to get in the van that was parked out at the sidewalk.

"Thank you again, my dear. It's always nice to see you. You certainly spiced up that story well for them!" she said with a chuckle.

Margaret's expression suddenly turned more serious.

"Remember, some sugar and spice is not always so nice..."

4

Valerie gathered her things. A notebook, a couple of pencils and a couple of plastic baggies full of cookies and chips for snacks. She had also snagged two water bottles as well. She stuffed everything into Alex's backpack as he sat at the kitchen table watching her.

"I get to haul everything again?" he asked with a frustrated sigh.

"Well, yeah. You always have your backpack anyway!" she replied, simply.

He frowned slightly, knowing her logic was not quite right. "Maybe YOU should buy one!" he retorted.

She ignored the statement and zipped his backpack shut.

"C'mon, we better move it, it's supposed to rain later today."

"So now you're a weatherman?"

"Weatherwoman," she shot back. "No, Dad told me this morning."

The faint sound of the furnace kicking on in the basement below made her conscious of the cold. "We'd better grab a sweater, too," she added.

After quickly grabbing a couple of hooded sweatshirts -- and getting a warning from their father to be back in time for dinner -- the Valerie and Alex flew out the front door and ran down the stairs of the front porch ready to head out on a mission. Pam waved at them from the gardens, having decided to spend the day outdoors herself.

They made their way down to the entrance of the bicycle path, right at the end of their property. It was lined with flowerbeds and two park benches invited walkers to stop and take a rest. Valerie and Alex hurried down the asphalt of the path, as the creek gurgled along beside them.

It was very cool today, but at least there was no wind. The sun shone through the bare branches of the trees above as they walked along, chattering about where to start their mission. Squirrels darted across the path in front of them, busy gathering food for the coming winter, and birds chirped away, enjoying the sunshine on this cool fall day. They crossed several streets and two wooden bridges that spanned the creek. They stopped several times because Alex insisted on feeding several families of ducks that swam in the creek. He tossed them some of the chips Valerie had brought with them. As they rambled over a third bridge, Valerie and Alex both paused to watch small fish swimming in the waters below. They were getting closer and closer to the railway tunnel.

Once a bustling cargo transfer location, and a centre that had provided both jobs and provisions for the people, the tunnel was all but abandoned now and was mostly boarded up to protect it against squatters and graffiti. But Valerie knew that the chains holding the doors shut were loose enough to let them squeeze through: they had done it before…

As they walked along, Valerie and Alex both noticed that the sound of birds and crickets had stopped. The atmosphere around them had become dead silent, other than the light sounds of their footsteps along the asphalt. The massive doors of the tunnel entrance emerged into view and the two children subconsciously slowed their pace.

As they came closer, the dark, thick wood of the doors loomed in front of them. They stepped off the path, moving even slower, and stepped towards the tunnel through a grove of bare trees. A large cloud moved swiftly across the sun's face and cast a shadow on the grove and the massive doors momentarily, as if a curtain had been drawn closed. Alex felt a cold shiver grip him as he looked up at the ancient wooden doors.

"Maybe we should come back tomorrow," he said, trying to conceal his growing fear from his sister.

"What? No way! You're not scared, are you?" asked his sister.

"No. But if someone catches us, we could get in trouble."

"No one will see us. Once we are inside, we're fine."

With that she unzipped his backpack and rummaged around to find a small flashlight that she knew would be amongst his "collection". She retrieved it and zipped his backpack up again.

Valerie stepped forward to the darkened opening between the huge doors. Alex followed right behind her. A slight breeze stirred the tree branches around them, causing a clattering amongst the bare wood that made Alex shiver again. Valerie ignored it, squeezed herself sideways through the gap between the doors and disappeared into the darkness inside. Alex hesitantly took one last look around him and, with a deep breath, squeezed through to follow her.

There was the musty smell of something old and damp in the gloom of the tunnel. The sound of an occasional drop of water falling from the curved stonework of the ceiling high above reverberated in the hollow emptiness. As Valerie illuminated their way with the small flashlight, the children slowly ventured forward. On the ground, they could make out the rusted and ancient-looking steel rails in the dim light. As they shuffled forward, Valerie swept the light around in an attempt to avoid tripping on anything. Alex held firmly to the straps of his backpack and walked carefully in his sister's steps.

Their eyes eventually adjusted somewhat to the gloom and they could begin to make out the rotted wood ties underneath the narrow track, some of them crumbled and covered in reddish dust from the rust everywhere. The air was moist and cold as they continued forward, their breath a fog in the still darkness of the tunnel. There was a sudden high-pitched chirp from somewhere ahead of them -- a sound that both of the children recognized. Bats! Alex cringed, waiting for the rush of the winged creatures that they had probably disturbed. But nothing happened; the bats didn't come swooping at them!

"Did you hear that?" he asked Valerie.

"Yep," she whispered back. "Hopefully there is only a couple."

They moved slower, trying not to disturb the night creatures that they figured were probably suspended from the ceiling above and around them. A shape emerged slowly in the illuminated area of the tiny flashlight. Eventually, whatever it was, it filled the space in front of them. They moved cautiously forward towards their discovery. It was massive and steel -- and covered in rust. Valerie pointed the light up, then down and swept it from side to side. A giant triangular piece of steel jutted out from the front of the hulking object, down near the rails, underneath its bullet-shaped nose. It was a locomotive!

Valerie and Alex crept closer. In the dim glow of the flashlight, they could see the long steel cylinder, sitting atop massive steel wheels, its number plates discoloured from age on either side of where its headlamp should have been. The broken socket of the headlight resembled some kind of strange eye, empty and lifeless in the gloom. Valerie stepped to the side and pointed the beam ahead of them. There were several cars on the track behind the locomotive that disappeared into the darkness, equally covered in rust and barely visible with the small light.

"Whoa," said Valerie quietly.

"Yeah, that's old!" said Alex in awe.

"It's a steam locomotive!" said Valerie.

There was a sudden fluttering above as several bats sped past, awakened early from their slumber. Dust trickled through the light of the flashlight and the children ducked instinctively. A few moments later, the silence returned and Valerie tentatively placed her hand against the thick steel of the locomotive. It was rough, bubbled by rust and cold.

"This is it," she stated simply.

"This is what? It's a train!" replied Alex.

Valerie looked back at him with an expression that told him that his statement was obvious.

"It's not just *a* train... It's the *last* train!"

Her voice echoed down the tunnel, as the two children turned back to look at the locomotive again. Valerie recounted the story of this train to her brother, reminded him that this was the final train to come from the waterfront docks hauling lumber from the shipyard, halted by the terrible accident with the brakeman who had worked it. After the brakeman had been found and his body carried away to be put in his final resting place, the rest of the trainmen had tried to move the giant forward again to complete their task, but it broke down and was abandoned. The rail company who had owned the train had fallen into bankruptcy and the train had been simply left there, entombed in the tunnel.

"So, it will be here forever?" asked Alex.

"Maybe. It wouldn't be an easy thing to get out of here."

They stood silently for a few moments, looking up at the huge steel vehicle in front of them in the gloom. Valerie stepped across the rails and moved to the side of the tunnel, shining the light down the length of the ancient looking machine. Alex followed her. The children could make out the numbers on the side of the steel: 1542. The engineer's compartment was an empty black hole in the back end of the steel plating and was covered in cobwebs.

Suddenly, another light emerged from the darkness, further down the tunnel along the side of the train. It floated in the gloom as it moved slowly towards them. The sheer sight of it made the children shiver. Who or what could be in here with them? Alex backed up a step and held firm on the straps of his backpack. Valerie kept her eyes in the direction of the light, but also backed up close beside her brother. Their hearts started to pound and they both felt the rush of blood pounding in their ears. The light swayed hypnotically back and forth and grew brighter and brighter as it came towards them. It wasn't a flashlight though, they realized; it was a small flame burning inside a glass lantern! Valerie and Alex stepped back toward the doors that they knew were behind them. Alex's eyes grew wider as he tried to see what was coming at them. Valerie held the flashlight in her shaking hands as she retreated another step. Their minds raced to try to process what they were seeing in the darkness in front of them.

The lantern reflected its light off of the rusted steel of the train, still advancing. As it came closer, Valerie recognized that it was an old oil lantern. It was covered thickly in cobwebs that waved gently from the heat of the light. But, Valerie felt confused -- there was a problem with what her eyes were seeing, and Alex gasped slightly as the realization hit them both at the same time: there was no one holding this floating lamp in the darkness! It seemed to float and bob slightly, like someone was carrying it, but there was absolutely no one there!

Their breath froze as they watched in horrible fascination for just a moment more, but that was it: Alex was the first to turn and run, nearly tripping over the rails in his haste. Valerie was right behind him, nearly running him over. Their shoes crunched loudly on the gravel as they sped toward the sliver of daylight streaming in through the tunnel's doors. After quickly squeezing through the opening, they continued to run -- they didn't even dare to look behind them.

The sunlight hit them as they darted through the grove of trees at the entrance, but they didn't stop running, even when they hit the asphalt of the bicycle path. Finally they slowed down, their lungs on fire, but they still walked quickly in the direction towards home. Finally they glanced back nervously at the huge wooden doors, hoping that they would not see anything following.

"That was scary!" exclaimed Alex, trying to catch his breath.

"Yeah, I'm glad we are the heck out of there!" panted Valerie.

They made their way home, not talking much as they walked, both of them barely able to believe what they had just witnessed. Valerie was deeply lost in her thoughts as she walked. This was certainly a different kind of adventure than they had ever been on before...

~~~~

The first few days back at school after that weekend had been a disaster for Valerie -- she hadn't been able to shake what they had witnessed in the tunnel from her memory. Her math class had been the worst and her teacher had spoken to her several times during those days and had advised her to pay attention. Her inability to concentrate had resulted in a phone-call home. As a result, she had been faced with 'The Wrath' from her father over it.

So by Thursday morning, on her way to school, Valerie had challenged herself to stop dwelling on the memory of the ghastly lantern floating in the dark of the train tunnel and to instead focus on her classes. She would have the whole weekend coming up to try to make some sense out of it. The last thing she wanted was to annoy her father with their little adventure. He didn't like it already; she sensed that from the first day she and Alex had come home from Nana's. Dad didn't like it when he wasn't sure what was going on -- even if he had his suspicions. Her mission was to keep everything calm, routine and on an even keel, regardless of the scare that she and Alex had been given. School seemed so boring to her, but she tried her best to keep focused on it for the last two days of the week in order to turn things around.

As she and Alex walked up to the front walkway on their return home from school on Thursday afternoon, they could smell the aroma of something delicious drifting in the air out of the kitchen. Curtis joined them at the curb and the three children headed into the house to see what was happening. Pam was in the kitchen and the smell of something yummy was everywhere.

"Some banana bread for dessert tonight!" Pam said to them as they came in through the front door.

She pulled the loaf pan from the oven with thick oven mitts as the children put away their school things.

Valerie immediately sensed that Pam was up to something -- maybe she was trying to smooth over something that had yet to happened. *Something's not right*, she thought as she glanced over at Alex. He had the same look of bewilderment on his face. They usually ate dinner later, so the change of pace felt out of place. Curtis simply cheered, oblivious to anything that might be strange about the situation.

Dad was nowhere to be seen. As Valerie put her things away, she glanced out the door toward the garage. Its side door was open and she could hear music playing from inside.

"Where's Dad?" she asked, looking back at Pam.

Pam placed the hot dish on a potholder on top of the stove and didn't return her stepdaughter's gaze.

"Oh, he's in the garage, working on something."

"This definitely means trouble!" Valerie's mind registered the thought

immediately. *"Something's going on here."*

Valerie's mind raced as she mulled over what had happened in the last day or two, trying to retrieve from her memory any actions or conversations that might have agitated her father. Everything had been good. Alex knew better than to ask Valerie what was wrong, and, when Curtis came around the corner of the kitchen, he took his opportunity to escape.

"Hey, wanna play some Xbox?" he asked Curtis immediately.

"Yeah!" came the quick response, and the boys disappeared without a moment's hesitation, leaving Valerie and Pam standing in the kitchen.

"So," Pam began. "How was school today?"

"Fine. Everything is fine," Valerie responded as she finished putting away her books and jacket. She was waiting for some invisible hammer to drop, even though she didn't know what it was exactly.

And then Pam hit her with it. "Maybe you should go out and see your Dad for a few minutes."

Valerie looked at her step-mom with eyes like a deer caught in the headlights of a car. Pam simply gave her a small smile, one that suggested to her that maybe nothing was wrong at all. It was obvious that whatever the big secret was, Valerie would have to find out for herself by going out to the garage.

She stepped to the doorway out to the front yard and looked across the walkway to the open garage door. She cast a doubtful look in Pam's direction, but she was met with the same small smile. She took a breath and swallowed. "Well, whatever's happening," she decided, *"might as well get it over with!"*

Valerie pushed open the door, and walked out onto the porch, keeping her eyes fixed on the garage. She hesitated for a moment. Was her Dad mad at her about something? She had tried to make sure everything had gone smoothly after their scare... She stepped down onto the walkway toward the garage, listening. She could hear music playing along with the occasional clink of a wrench against metal. Valerie walked to the open doorway of the garage and peered in. Dad was busily working on a small electric motor. There was wiring lying next to it and some pieces of large sheet metal that was shaped like long blades. As she watched, her father began to attach one of the blades to the motor, swapping his wrench for a screwdriver to fasten it to the motor. He finally noticed her standing in the doorway.

"Hey, what's going on?" he said simply and turned his gaze back to the job at hand.

"Not much," replied Valerie meekly as she stepped inside. "Pam said I should come out and see you?"

Dad put down the screwdriver on the workbench behind him and picked up a rag to start wiping off his hands.

"Yeah, um," her father began, but then he paused slightly as if searching for the right words. "You know I really don't like all this craziness that Nana fills you and Alex up with, right?"

Valerie looked at him with a blank expression, but remained silent as she waited for him to continue talking.

"But," he said, looking at her evenly. "If you really want to know more about this legend about the trainman, I might just happen to know a man who can tell you all about it."

A wide smile instantly spread over Valerie's face. She was relieved that she wasn't going to get some kind of trouble, and if Dad had planned on helping them out, like he had done before, things would probably turn out pretty good.

"Yeah?" she encouraged him, still smiling. "Who is this man?"

He paused for a few long seconds -- for dramatic effect, of course -- and finally tossed the rag back on his workbench.

"How would you like to ride on a real train?" he asked back.

5

Harold was at the library until it closed that evening, sifting through local history books and newspaper articles. It did him little good. There was not much to add to his notebook about the trainman or the missing gold. It was becoming clear to him that he would not find the magic answers he needed here. He stood up from the table he had been sitting at for hours, stretched and collected the books to put them back in their places on the shelves. He strolled slowly down the long bookcases and replaced the books as he thought about what he should try next. The library was definitely a dead end for him. Harold enjoyed the quiet though, and the rows upon rows of books with their particular smell. It was a comfort to him as he went from shelf to shelf. He rubbed his thumb along the spines of the old books, searching for something, anything that would give him some kind of new clue to the whereabouts of the treasure. Time was beginning to run short and Harold could sense it. Another winter would mean very little progress in his search.

He continued to scan the titles on the shelves and withdrew a book, only to look at its cover, and slide it back in place. There was nothing that could help him here. He let out a large sigh and took one last look down length of the bookcase. It was useless tonight. It seemed that the clues to the story would elude him for another day.

Harold headed towards the large glass doors at the library's entrance and bid the ladies behind the desk a polite farewell. He pushed open the doors. As he stepped out into the dark cold of the evening, his breath was released as a fog in the still air. He gathered his coat around him and shuddered slightly from the chill. It was a cloudless night and the moon had just begun to rise between the bare branches of the trees that lined the city street.

"Guess it's off home, with nothing to show for it," he thought to himself as he turned away from the library entrance and started to walk up the street. The night was cold but still as he walked along pondering what to do next.

The streetlights above him illuminated his breath, making it look like smoke billowing away. His footsteps echoed between the buildings as he walked along the sidewalks, the quiet of the night only punctuated by the occasional passing of a car on the street beside him.

His wife would likely be lounging in front of the TV watching one of her shows when he arrived home, but he had already been searching the Internet night after night. Without any other options to explore, he surmised that he would probably just watch television with her until it was time to go to bed. He would have some time in the morning before his cleaning job, so perhaps something would come to him in the meantime.

The library had nothing; the museum had nothing, except for a selection of photographs of the old railways in town and a few business documents about them. The Internet had come up dry as well. Where would he find the information he needed? Harold had even managed to find an obituary for the trainman, but it just detailed his life and the family who survived him, but made no mention of the legend of the lost gold. It frustrated him deeply, this lack of progress. Maybe he needed to think differently about his search, to find other avenues to search for information.

Harold stopped abruptly in his tracks and stood straight up as a realization hit him like a bolt of lightning. The old man at the train station, the one who issued the tickets for the passenger trains here in town! He must certainly know something of the story. He was at least eighty years old and still worked at the wicket in the train station. Surely he could share some scrap of information that might shed new light on his search! His mind began to race as he resumed walking, this time at a quickened pace. *"How could I approach him? What would I ask?"* he wondered as he walked. Obviously he would have to come up with a plan -- he'd have to befriend the old man in order to get any of the information that he might possess that would be useful. His thoughts swirled as he strode along the sidewalks and across city blocks on his way home.

What did he know about the old man? He had only seen him a few times, on the rare occasion when he had needed to take the train to go and visit his mother at her rest home. The old gentleman had helped him get his ticket for the train. He'd been very professional and polite.

He continued to walk as he rolled these thoughts over in his mind. He would have plenty of time to figure out a strategy as he watched television with his wife tonight.

~~~~

The children were up bright and early on Saturday morning, excited for their day to begin -- their father had arranged to get them a ride on one of the small local freight trains this morning. Dad and Pam prepared breakfast in the kitchen. Valerie, Alex and Curtis practically wolfed down their plates of scrambled eggs and pancakes almost as fast as Pam brought them to the table in the dining room. The children always loved when Dad made a big breakfast on the weekends, because the whole house would be filled with the aroma of the bacon sizzling on the stove as they awoke. Alex sat eating with his tattered old backpack beside him on the floor as Dad emerged from the kitchen.

"Do you really need that to go for a short train ride, buddy?" he asked.

Alex gave his father a look that implied that the answer should be obvious.

"Maybe we should get you a new one, because that one looks like it has seen better days," Dad teased, knowing full well that the old pack was Alex's favourite thing in the world. Alex continued to eat, while his father winked at Valerie.

"Quit that!" Pam said to him as she gave him a playful swipe in passing.

He shrugged away quickly as he chuckled at her.

As the kids got dressed to go, Dad continued his fun and pretended to be in no great hurry, even though he knew the three were bursting at the seams to get going.

"Come on!" said Valerie in an exasperated tone.

Pam shot Dad another glance that told him enough was enough. He sighed, grabbed a warm jacket and today's newspaper and proceeded out the door to start the truck to the cheers of the kids. They piled into the old pickup, jostling for position in the back seat, excited to be underway.

It was a short drive to the south train yard, where rows of tracks lined up, some filled with railcars waiting to be switched about to build a train. Dad had worked with the trains since before the children were born, so it was no mystery to them how he had arranged this little adventure for them.

The truck raised a small, scattered trail of dust as Dad pulled it down to a switch where two locomotives were hooked to several railcars. These were nothing like the ancient rusted vehicle that Alex and Valerie had seen in the tunnel. The two large diesel locomotives hummed deeply and occasionally spit out a burst of air as Dad parked. Heat waves rose off of the top of them and the smell of diesel fuel lingered in the cool fall air. As they all got out of the truck, a man in a bright orange vest emerged from the front door of the head locomotive. He was tall, of medium build and sported a head of grey hair. His eyes were hidden by dark safety glasses as he descended the ladder on the side of the train and stepped down onto the gravel in brown safety boots.

"Going on a short run today, Mike?" Dad asked the man as the group of them approached the train.

"Yep, just over to drop off some boxcars for the factory at the east end, then back into the yard!" replied the man with a smile. Dad and the man shook hands briefly.

"Kids, this is Mike, and he is the Locomotive Engineer. He drives the train!"

Mike said hello politely to the children and greeted them each with a warm smile. He explained to them that they would go be riding along as he did this small job and that way they would get to see how the train worked first hand. Dad said that he would wait for them in the truck and gave a nod to Mike before he turned to walk back over to the pickup to read his newspaper.

Mike helped the children up the steel ladder and ushered them inside the huge cabin of the locomotive. There were two seats on one side of the cab and the seat where Mike sat, so that the controls of the train were in front of him. The children piled onto the seats excitedly, while Mike sat down in the Engineer's chair.

"The conductor will be riding the tail end of the train, to uncouple the cars when we get where we are going," Mike explained as he grabbed the radio handset.

"532, ready to go, J.P.," he said on the radio.

"The dispatcher has given us a signal to go, so let's roll," came the reply.

"Ok kids, here we go," said Mike. He hit a lever to release the air brakes, and then pushed another lever and the locomotive came to life with a dull roar. The children watched out the front windows as the train lurched forward and stretched out the slack between the cars.

"Pulling, 532," Mike said into the radio handset as the huge vehicle began to roll forward, its steel wheels screeching slightly against the rail.

With the push of a button, the bell began to ring on the locomotive as it clicked and clacked over the joins in the track ahead. They weren't moving very fast at all, but the children were in awe of the size of the train as they sat high off the ground in the cab.

The train moved out of the yard through switches in the track, and pulled out onto the main line. Curtis looked out the side window as Mike blew the horn on the train. They were coming to a crossing where the train tracks intersected one of the streets in town. Valerie could see the lights come on at the crossing and the gates drop to stop the traffic for them to pass. The horn sounded again, and they crossed through. The children grinned as they saw the cars stopped at the gates to wait for the train to pass. Curtis waved at the people with a big grin as they rolled through.

The train moved along the track through town, going through several other crossings, until they arrived at the factory where the work needed to be done. Mike spoke into the radio to the brakeman.

"Let me know when you have the switch, J.P.," he said.

He explained to the kids that the brakeman was getting down off of the tail end of the train to throw a switch in the track so that they'd be able to back down into the track leading to the factory. The children nodded enthusiastically and continued to watch out the windows of the locomotive.

"Switch is reversed; shove for six cars, 532," came the voice over the radio.

Mike pushed one of the levers again, and the train lurched backward, and began moving slowly back down into the siding track to the factory.

"Three more," the brakeman announced.

"Three," repeated Mike.

The steel wheels of the train screeched against the rails and the train moved slowly into the factory yard. Valerie could see the brakeman on the ground at the rear of the train through the mirror on the outside of the cab. He was walking along to watch that the way was clear.

"That'll do Mike, whenever you get her stopped," the brakeman said.

"Stopping."

Mike turned to the children once the train was stopped.

"So, your Dad tells me you are looking to find out about the legend of the ghostly trainman of the tunnel?" he asked.

Valerie's eyes brightened a little.

"Yes, we want to find out all about it. We want to search for his lost gold!" exclaimed Valerie.

"Hmmmm. Well, I don't know about lost gold, but I do know a lot about the story of the trainman," explained Mike. "He was my great Grandfather."

Valerie could hardly contain herself at this point. What luck! She listened intently as Mike told the story of how his great Grandfather had worked down at the docks with the early steam locomotives and how he'd helped to bring lumber from the old shipyards to the mill. He talked about the accident that had caused his great Grandfather's hand to be cut off. He explained that his great Grandfather had had an accident with a large steel device that was down at the south entrance of the tunnel.

At that point of his story, Valerie squinted her eyes and looked confused. Mike paused and looked straight at her. "What's wrong?" he asked her.

"Umm. I thought that the train had run over his hand," she said.

"No, I don't think so. See, the tunnel is a big hill inside, and there was a big steel thing that goes over the top of the rail at the waterfront. We call it a "derail". It is there so that if something happens to the train, like maybe it loses power and rolls backward, it will come off the track instead of going back down into the shipyard out of control. That's how he lost his hand, he slipped with the heavy steel derail, and cut his hand off in it putting it back on the rail while the train was headed up the tunnel."

Valerie pondered Mike's words for a moment. This changed the entire story. Her mind raced to digest what Mike had said.

"See, back then, they didn't have radios like we have now, so the brakeman had to give hand signals to the engineer, and at night he used his lantern to give those signals. The accident happened when the train was already going up the tunnel, so he was still down at the tunnel entrance when it happened. Old steam locomotives didn't move very fast, so he would normally have had plenty of time to catch up to the tail end."

The realization hit Valerie like a hammer: *"we were looking at the wrong end of the tunnel!"* she thought. If there was any truth to the legend of the trainman's lost gold, then the treasure was down at the waterfront! She looked over at Alex and he nodded with a grin as he'd put it together for himself. Valerie turned back to Mike.

"But what about the ghost?" she asked. "We saw a lantern floating in the tunnel."

Mike glanced at her with a questioning look.

"I don't know anything about that," he replied. "There have been stories, but I haven't seen anything to make me believe there is a ghost."

There was a burst of air just then, and Mike turned his attention back to what he was doing.

"We have made the cut. Pull clear of the switch, 532," the brakeman said over the radio.

"Pulling," replied Mike into the radio.

With the pull of a lever, and another hiss of air, the train moved forward again out onto the main line. The brakeman threw back the switch and Valerie watched in the mirror as he mounted the tail end car.

"Back to the barn," came the voice on the radio.

The train roared to life again and the children watched out the windows as they moved backwards through town and back into the train yard. The crossing bells rang as they moved down the track. On their entire return journey Valerie thought about what Mike had said.

As they came to a stop in the train yard, the children could see Dad leaning against the truck, waiting. They thanked Mike for the fun ride as they climbed down the ladder of the locomotive. Mike followed behind them and locked down the train.

"So, was it fun?" asked Dad as the children approached, all of them wearing big smiles.

"Yep," replied Valerie instantly. "It was definitely an interesting ride!"

6

The city council meeting dragged on that evening, with everyone only paying half of his or her attention to the matters at hand. It was getting late and there were still numerous items on the agenda to discuss. The mayor tried to keep things focused as he read from a notepad of issues that needed to be brought up that evening. It was time to iron out the new yearly budget. It would proved to be a lengthy meeting to decide where the city would spend its money. The conversation, consisting of one councillor speaking at a time, was very dry.

Shaun Locke sat back in his chair, uninterested in most of the babble. He was councillor for one of the East wards of the city and had been on city council for many years. He played with a pen idly while the group went on to discuss an expansion to one of the parks down by the waterfront. None of this interested him. He waited patiently for the next item of business.

Shaun was a large man with graying hair and piercing hazel eyes. His heavyset build made him look massive in his chair. He neatened his grey suit, agitated by the lengthy conversations taking place in the council chamber. To him these discussions were a complete waste of time. He wanted to get to the issue that he had been thinking about since the meeting had convened. It was getting late and Shaun had become restless in his chair.

The stale discussions continued and made him want to scream out loud. He sat back heavily again, just waiting and trying to be patient.

Finally, that topic of conversation had concluded and the Mayor called for the next item of business. Shaun took his chance to speak.

"There is the matter of the renovations with the train tunnel," he began.

"Yes. We have heard a submission for funding from the city's Historical Society to gate off the south end of the tunnel, to preserve it and keep people from desecrating the interior of the tunnel until a solid plan can be made to restore it for tourism."

"Well, I object to that idea," pointed out Shaun as he looked across the table at the mayor.

Mayor Hilroy, an experienced man in the city's politics, gave Shaun a confused look and raised his eyebrows. "You don't think it is a good idea to keep the tunnel locked up to protect it?" he asked as he removed his glasses.

Shaun leaned forward, cleared his throat and pretended to review non-existent notes on the pad of paper in front of him. He realized that he had to word his response properly -- and keep suspicion away from his own plans.

"The tunnel has a deep historical impact on the community, and it was the very first one constructed in this country. We should not deny the people of this community the opportunities to explore their own history. Perhaps it just needs to be monitored better."

The mayor dropped his notepad on the boardroom table and several of the other councillors shifted uncomfortably in their seats. "I thought that this was settled, that simply securing the tunnel for the time being was already a done deal," he retorted, sounding rather aggravated by the sudden turn of events. "We have already set aside the funding for the gate."

Shaun straightened in his seat and felt all of the eyes around the room on him.

"I think it would be fiscally irresponsible of the city to fund this project. If the Historical Society wants to simply lock it up, then perhaps they should come up with the money to do it," he stated, knowing in his mind that the group had no money to accomplish the expensive task.

He kept his eyes on the table in front of him as he waited for a response. Without his vote on the situation, he knew the motion would not go through. It would allow him to continue with his own plans for the tunnel.

There was hushed discussion between the councillors and he could tell that, by making his statements, council was at a deadlock with the issue. He tried not to let a grin creep onto his face because he knew that the mayor was still observing him. If the Historical Society got their way and the tunnel was gated off and locked, he would not be able to continue his search for the lost gold that he had heard was buried somewhere inside. He had been looking for it for months, hoping that it would provide him with a nice fat retirement fund if he somehow managed to unearth it. Even though gating the tunnel off would keep out the idiots and vandals, it would make his mission almost impossible and this was something that he did not want to see happen.

One time his search had been interrupted by a couple of kids, but that was the only trouble he'd had so far in his quest. Shaun disliked children. They were nothing but a pain, and he gritted his teeth slightly at the thought of them messing with his quest for cash. He could deal with them though. This motion in council for the gating was something that he had to concentrate on flushing.

"Well, I guess this is one that we will have to throw back to the Historical Society then," the Mayor finally conceded. "I can see that we won't be able to vote on it, as it looks like Councillor Locke has his own position on this matter."

Shaun smiled to himself, despite of the looks he knew he was getting from some of the others assembled at the table. This would stop what he saw as a huge roadblock to his search. He had his own ways of keeping the curious locals at bay, and with no cumbersome gates blocking the tunnel, it would leave him relatively free to keep looking for the treasure.

The meeting continued, but Shaun didn't pay much attention to the rabble of conversation; he was just relieved that his blockade of the vote had worked. When the meeting finally concluded, the councillors filed out of the room to head home to their own lives. Shaun gathered his trench coat around him as he stepped out through the large glass doors of City Hall and onto the sidewalk of the main street that ran through the city. It was dark now and cold. The streetlights cast their glow onto the roads below them and colourful signs were glowing in front of the businesses lining either side of the road. Shaun was startled by a voice behind him.

"Nice job, Locke," commented one of the remaining councillors exiting City Hall on Shaun's heels. "You know that the Historical Society can't do that job by themselves, and in the meantime, the local kids are spraying more graffiti in that tunnel all the time."

"Yeah, well, I think that spending that amount of taxpayer's money on something like that is just nuts," Shaun replied sharply.

The councillor just shrugged and shook his head as he gave Shaun a troubled glance before he turned and left to find his car. Shaun stood still and watched him go, lingering a moment longer in front of City Hall. His thoughts turned back to the hunt of treasure, to the possibility of fortune that could be his if he could just locate the gold that was rumoured to be in the depths of the tunnel. It would be a profitable cinch if he found it...he'd actually been looking for a potential buyer on the Internet, so that he could liquidate the treasure for cash if he found it. *"Not if,"* he thought, *"when I find it!"*

Gathering up his coat once more against the cold he stalked off to his own car as he whistled to himself in satisfaction.

~~~~

It was Sunday morning and Mr. Thusk hurried down the main hallway of the museum with a file folder full of old photos. He was happy to see Valerie and Alex again. The children were on another mission, he knew, and as the curator of the museum, he felt it his personal obligation to help them as best he could. He was getting old and the thought of an adventure to find antiquities was well beyond his means. But these two children never seemed to fail to bring him into an adventure all the same.

The late fall sunshine poured in through the huge windows in the hallway and painted glowing squares of light on the hardwood floors and on the faces of the display cases lined up along the way. He paused as he passed one of the cases and gazed into it fondly. Nestled inside a perfect sphere of polished rock was an amethyst crystal in the shape of a bird. This was one of his favourite exhibits in the entire museum collection. He sighed contentedly and resumed his quick walk to the large photo room where the kids were seated and pouring over old photos.

"Here we are, kids!" he chimed as he walked into the room and placed the folder on the heavy wooden table in front of Valerie and Alex. Valerie instantly turned her attention to it and started flipping through the photos. Several pictures were of the old train station that had been on Church St., but which no longer existed. She continued to flip through the aged pictures. She stopped for a moment when she discovered a photo of the entrance to the south end of the train tunnel at the waterfront.

There it was, laid out on the table. It felt like she'd been thrown back in time to the scene on the photo in front of her. It showed the tracks leading away from the tunnel mouth and the docks that jutted out into the water. She could make out a strange metal-looking device clamped over the rails just outside the tunnel entrance. *The derail,* she recognized.

"This is it!" she exclaimed as she leaned in closer to get a better look.

Alex and Mr. Thusk both crowded in to look at the photo of the old tracks and the gaping opening to the tunnel.

"What?" asked Alex, confused at her excitement. "So what? It's the tunnel."

"Not just the tunnel!" Valerie replied and pointed at to her discovery on the photo. "The derail -- this is the spot!"

Alex looked at the photo again, but couldn't resist his next obvious statement. "Yeah, but none of that stuff is down there now."

Valerie sat back in her chair and gave Alex a look. It was obvious to her. And she figured that it should have been to Alex. But, even old Mr. Thusk gave her a questioning glance, unsure what she was trying to explain was a clue in the old photo.

"Don't you see?" she asked, exasperated with her companions. "The photo shows us what *was* there, and now we know the approximate location of the derail that cut off the trainman's hand...and *possibly,* the spot where the lost gold is!"

Mr. Thusk straightened up with a slight grin and raised his eyebrows. He knew that the clue Valerie had found was important, but he also knew that she had missed something rather important. Slightly confused, she looked up at him from her chair.

"What?" she asked quietly.

"My dear, perhaps what you are looking for is *not* gold," he stated simply.

She considered his words for a moment, not quite grasping where he was going with his statement.

"What do you mean?" she asked.

She knew that Mr. Thusk was a well-educated man, especially when it came to the history of the city...and the country for that matter! She waited patiently for him to give her an answer.

"In the early history of this country, during the War of 1812, General Isaac Brock came here, appointed to these lands by the crown of Britain. He led the British forces, and at the time, the Loyalists here had very little money. Coin was in very short supply from Britain. So General Brock devised a 'paper note' to replace coins, as there was nothing in place here to mint actual coin money."

Valerie was wide-eyed.

"So the money was all paper?" she asked, amazed with this information.

"Yes, indeed. Mostly."

Valerie sat quietly as she looked at the photo and pondered this new fact for a moment. Once again they had been thrown a curve ball. Finding metal, even if it was buried in the ground, was made fairly easy by using modern metal detectors. Their father had bought them one several years ago, which had resulted in a lot of small holes in the lawn in the backyard. But if what Mr. Thusk had told them was true -- and she never doubted his word -- then what they were looking for would be much more difficult to find. Or impossible. *"Which"*, she thought, *"is why it has never been found."*

Alex spoke up. "How would paper be protected from the rain, if he buried it?"

"Exactly! It wasn't like there were plastic containers or zip-lock bags back then!" said Valerie. She turned to her brother. "Good question, Alex!" she added and he beamed.

Both the children looked up at Mr. Thusk. The hoped that he would have some ray of light to shed on their problem. But he simply smiled and shrugged his shoulders.

"Great," breathed Valerie. She lounged back deeply in the chair with a big sigh. They had a whole new set of questions...and no answers!

~~~~

Harold arrived on the train station platform, carrying a cardboard tray with two large coffees in it. This was all he could think of to break the ice with the old man who worked the ticket counter. He heard the outside speakers on the station blare the imminent arrival of the next passenger train as he walked passed the small gathering of people waiting to board. It was a sunny morning, cold and crisp. There was a light frost covering the ground this morning and he watched his step on the platform as he carefully balanced the tray. The train crawled down slowly into the station, breathing heavily like a team of horses. It came to a halt and the doors opened to allow passengers to disembark before the new passengers climbed on board. A burst of air came out of the locomotive and the air smelled slightly of diesel fuel.

This was Harold's one chance at getting more information on the train tunnel, and he hoped that this man could help him. The man had worked at the station since Harold had been very young, but he knew very little about him. But, if anyone knew anything about the legend of the trainman, Harold figured that it would be him. As passengers boarded the train, he swung open the door to the station, hoping that he would be able to have a moment or two with the old man.

Inside the station it was quiet in definite contrast to the hustle and bustle of people out on the platform. It was well lit, with polished white floors and wooden columns from the floor to a high domed ceiling. Wooden benches lined the walls, along with several old train paintings and a train schedule board. At the far end of the room stood a lone vending machine next to a drinking fountain, both flanked by doors to the washrooms. At the other end of the room were the baggage area and the wicket, with its thick glass separating it from the rest of the room.

Harold looked over to the wicket. He could see the old man, busily shuffling things inside and getting ready for the next departure. He briefly rehearsed the scene in his mind -- how he might approach him, what he would say -- all the while wondering how the old fellow would possibly construe his request. He subconsciously neatened his hair with his free hand, and pushed his thick glasses up further on his face.

He finally approached the old man, who had a flash of white hair on his balding head and was fairly short and stocky. He wore a dark blue cardigan over a white shirt and tie, and had no nametag for Harold to use to call him by name.

Harold stepped toward the wicket, carrying his offering, but the old man was so engrossed in his paperwork that he did not notice him right away.

"Good morning," Harold said, clearing his throat slightly.

"Good morning," replied the old man without looking up. "Next train isn't until 11:30."

Harold paused for a moment. "Um, no. I'm not here to catch a train. I wondered if maybe you might like a nice hot coffee this morning," he said, raising the tray.

Now the old man looked up at him with piercing blue eyes, having been disturbed from his duties by something he was obviously not used to. He glanced suspiciously, first at Harold and then at cardboard tray.

"A coffee?" he asked.

Harold straightened up and placed the tray on the ticket counter, trying his best to look unassuming and innocent.

"I came here because I am doing research about the history of the railways in town, and I thought you would probably be my best bet to ask about some of it, seeing as you have worked here for so long. You must know a lot about the trains around here?" he prompted with a questioning tone.

The old man's expression softened a little and he put his papers aside for a moment.

"Well, thank you. I guess I could use a little refreshment this morning," he relented in a more friendly voice.

Harold relaxed slightly, handing him one of the styrofoam cups through the opening in the glass. The old man opened it and took a brief sip, as Harold in turn opened his.

"Mmmm. Just the way I like it!" smiled the old man.

Harold smiled back, relieved that the ice had been broken. *"Great, maybe the old fellow will share some of his fountain of knowledge"*, he thought excitedly. *"If anyone knows something about the trainman and the lost treasure, surely he would."*

"So what exactly are you researching?" asked the old man, happily sipping at the hot beverage.

"The train tunnel and the legends surrounding it," said Harold.

The old man looked up at the ceiling suddenly, as if he was trying to remember something.

"Oh, yes, the tunnel. Well, it was the very first railway tunnel ever built in this country, completed somewhere around 1860--," began the old man.

Harold listened politely, nodding every once in a while, even though he already knew the information that the old man was telling him. But he felt that it would be rude of him to try to skip ahead and so he continued to be patient while reminding himself to write down some notes when he left.

Long minutes passed as the old man described the whole story of how the railway had built the tunnel to provide access to the shipyards and haul lumber and other goods back and forth using a very special height-shortened steam locomotive. As he told the story, he took a few gulps of coffee, stopping only briefly to check his watch. For a moment, Harold was afraid that maybe the old man would cut his tale short to return to his work.

"I'm sorry!" The old man stopped talking suddenly and extended his hand through the glass. "I'm John Harper, the station attendant here."

The two shook hands and Harold took his turn in introducing himself. He breathed a sigh of relief as John continued with his story and described how the tunnel started at the waterfront and extended north under the city on an uphill slope some 1700 feet.

"It was a marvel of engineering and excavation at the time, as few of the tools for major construction work existed at the time," John explained proudly. "The last train to use the tunnel is still in there, near the crest of the hill at the north end."

"Yes, I have heard that. Why was it left there?" asked Harold quickly, wanting to focus the conversation on this fact.

"There was a horrible accident involving one of the crew members on that train. The brakeman lost his hand and bled to death before he could go far enough to get help, the poor soul," replied John. A sudden look of sadness crept onto his wrinkled old face.

"What happened?" asked Harold quietly.

"Well, the story goes that he was at the south end of the tunnel and the train was already heading through it. The brakeman was securing the derail at the south entrance, and it fell on his arm, severing his hand from his wrist down. He bled to death trying to signal the train to stop with his lantern in his good hand. Terrible."

Harold was ecstatic. Just like that, a big piece of the puzzle had fallen into his lap! If there was truth to the legend of the trainman's lost gold, then the treasure was most likely at the waterfront!

"After the accident there was a full investigation, and the train remained in the tunnel during the whole thing. Without being able to transport goods for that amount of time, the struggling railway fell into bankruptcy, and the train was left there, abandoned," John continued.

"What an incredible story," said Harold in awe. "I guess it really was the last train!"

"Yes, the last train," agreed John.

7

Valerie had dragged Alex all over the downtown streets that day and he was starting to get a bit tired. They had already been to the library and the museum, with very little to show for it. Mr. Thusk, the museum curator, had shown them the collection of old railway photos that dated back to a time when the very first photographs were available. They'd look at pictures of old steam locomotives, the old railway turntable that used to be behind the train station and both pictures and sketches of the tunnel and its train. But Mr. Thusk had also unloaded a real bomb on their brains! His sister seemed determined to walk the feet right off of him today, and his trusty backpack seemed to get heavier with each step.

"Can't we just stop for a while?" he complained to Valerie.

"We still have one more stop to make, now that we have this photo," replied Valerie, holding up the photocopy that Mr. Thusk had made for them of the end of the tunnel at the waterfront.

"Great," Alex said, his voice full of sarcasm.

"Oh, relax! We will be there soon and then you can take a break!" said Valerie.

"Yeah, well, you're not carrying all this stuff!" he replied sharply.

Valerie ignored the complaint and continued making strides down the street toward the waterfront. They turned down off the main street and headed towards the river. The afternoon sun hit them full in the face as they left the shade of the buildings. It was warm on their skin, despite the chill in the air and, as they approached the waterfront, they could see mist rising off the calm waters of the river.

The two children zipped their jackets up a little further as they came to the wharf area. The temperature was much cooler by the water. As they crossed the park and walked along the wooden boardwalk of the docks, Valerie spotted the historic plaque that marked the south entrance of the train tunnel. The entire area here was now covered in grass and several large pine trees were scattered about the landscape. All of the old tracks had been removed long ago except for a short piece supporting an old caboose. Mr. Thusk had explained to the kids that the caboose had been donated to the city for a display. It had been carefully brought back down from the train through the tunnel and restored for tourists to see. With its shiny new coat of paint, it looked just like it would have when it was used for the railway.

Valerie and Alex stopped in front of the plaque and looked over at the massive wooden doors of the tunnel that were swung wide open. During the summer months, the tunnel attracted many people interested in history. But the waterfront was pretty much abandoned at this time of year -- all the boats had been removed from the docks for winter storage and tourism had died off with the cold.

"Well, this certainly doesn't help with anything," said Valerie as she looked at the writing on the plaque.

Alex dumped his backpack to the ground and sat on a park bench a few feet away, relieved to finally have a break.

"Did you really think it would?" he asked with a grin.

Valerie shot her brother a quick frown. She turned back to look at the entrance of the tunnel and held up the photograph. As she looked at the past in the photo and then the present in front of her, she sighed deeply. She measured the scene with her eyes.

"The derail would have been right over there," she estimated and pointed over to her right several feet away.

Alex surveyed the green lawn in front of the tunnel, shaking his head slightly.

"So what do you want to do? Dig up the park?" he asked, raising his hands in a grand gesture.

Again Valerie looked at him with a frown as she exhaled deeply. He simply continued to grin, knowing that he was aggravating her. He got up and walked across the lawn to the area that she had pointed out. There was no sign of anything but the smooth, manicured grass.

"They would have dug all this up already, to get rid of all the old tracks and put in the grass," he surmised and looked at his sister with a more serious expression.

"I know," she replied and shifting her eyes back to the photo.

"Besides, the derail is only one possible place to look for it. Maybe the trainman hid it somewhere else. We just don't know for sure," he said.

Valerie's expression fell slightly and she rested her arms on the plaque and lowered her head a bit. Suddenly Alex's face brightened.

"Hey, if the treasure really is paper, like Mr. Thusk said, then he probably would have put it someplace to keep it out of the rain! And like you said before, it wasn't like he had a plastic box to put it in!"

Valerie lifted her head as she listened to her little brother's reasoning. Alex walked into the entrance to the tunnel and looked up and all around the stonework. Valerie watched him and eventually left the plaque to join him inside the opening.

The musty smell of the old tunnel met her nose. She looked up the passage, where the light died and it became dark. The rails were still in here -- they started about fifty feet inside the opening and disappeared into the darkness.

Alex interrupted her thoughts. "Look for loose brickwork," he suggested. "Maybe he hid it in the wall of the tunnel! You hear about people finding all kind of things in the walls of old homes, so why not in here?" he added.

Valerie's thoughts raced. He was right. Hiding paper notes inside the entrance would have kept them from being destroyed by the rain and snow. The two children searched the walls, looking for any irregularity in the masonry. As they progressed, however, it became harder to see in the gathering darkness.

"Hold on. I'll get my flashlight," Alex said and ran out into the daylight toward the bench and his backpack. Squinting, he reached for his trusty pack that was lying on the ground beside the bench. As he rifled through it and located his small light, he caught some movement by the caboose out of the corner of his eye. He looked over towards the relic and was startled to see a man holding what looked like a metal detector. Valerie had followed Alex out of the tunnel and she also spotted the man. The two of them froze for a moment, but not before the man turned and noticed them.

"Oh, hello there," the man said, offering the children a polite smile. He looked to be older than their father, of medium height with black hair and thick glasses. He stopped what he was doing with the detector and turned his attention towards them.

"Nice day, isn't it?" he said and pushed up his glasses with a smile still on his face.

"Yeah," replied Valerie slowly and she walked over to stand next to her little brother.

"You guys like trains?" he asked, then shook his head. "Oh, sorry. My name is Harold. I'm hunting for treasure!" he said by way of introduction.

The two children looked at one another momentarily, still not sure how to respond. This fellow was a stranger after all and their father had instilled caution in their minds about talking to strangers. But Valerie didn't see anything threatening about this man.

"The trainman's treasure," she said simply.

Harold's expression lightened even more. "Yes! You know about it?" he asked.

"Yes. We are here searching, too," stated Valerie, still cautious.

"That's amazing! Imagine that, we are on the same hunt for the same thing!" said Harold. His smile widened.

The children relaxed slightly when they saw the excitement in Harold's face. He began to tell them about what he had found out and describe some of the ideas that he had. They thought that he was talking as fast as a chipmunk might have. It was obvious to them that he meant no harm...and he seemed as interested in the missing treasure as they were.

When it was her turn to talk, Valerie explained to Harold what Mr. Thusk had told them about General Brock and the paper notes. Harold almost dropped his metal detector as he realized what she was saying.

"Of course!" he almost shouted. "That's why I haven't found anything by looking for metal! It all makes sense!"

Valerie and Alex described their assumption that perhaps the trainman had hidden his stash inside the tunnel, to keep it safe and out of the rain. Harold listened intently and was happy to show the children his notes and maps. Valerie and Alex could quickly see that, although he was a grown man, he thought exactly as they did as he excitedly talked about all that he had found out.

"Well, come on," Alex prompted as he waved his flashlight. "We are going back in to keep looking!"

The three of them went into the entrance of the tunnel as looked carefully as Alex shone his light on the brickwork. There was occasional graffiti here and there, colourful paint breaking the earth tones of the wall. Harold adjusted his glasses as he perused the walls. Valerie poked at some of the bricks, testing them to see if there were any that might be loose. The tunnel echoed with their voices as they searched the first hundred feet into the passage, exchanging ideas and making observations.

Harold stopped short. "Sorry, I didn't get your names?" he asked politely.

"I'm Valerie and this is my brother, Alex," Valerie replied.

"Very pleased to meet you both. You seem like very smart children. I hope we can all find something cool!" Harold said enthusiastically, as he resumed helping Valerie poke at the brickwork here and there.

"Well, if we all work together, we just might!" replied Valerie brightly.

Their steps crunched on the slag of the rail bed and Alex occasionally shone his light down onto the track, so that they wouldn't trip over the ancient wooden track ties. There was the odd drop of water from the ceiling and every sound seemed louder than it should be in the tunnel. It was very humid and their breath didn't fog like it would have outside in the cold air. The three of them continued their search, occasionally switching from one wall to another. It was slow work, especially with only Alex's small flashlight to illuminate the walls.

Suddenly, a sound rose up from the darkness ahead in the tunnel -- one long, hollow, morose moan. They all stopped in their tracks. The hair stood up on the children's necks. Alex nervously pointed his small flashlight beam up the passage into the darkness and they peered forward. The sound repeated, grew louder and quickly morphed into an echoing groan.

The three of them were frozen, barely breathing as they listened, mouths agape and eyes wide, as they tried to determine what was ahead of them. The air shifted slightly and all at once they could sense something coming towards them. Alex's flashlight shimmered on a wall of thick, white fog that was billowing towards them in the darkness. The moan grew louder along with it. With pulses beating like hammers, they watched in terror as this strange fog approached them.

That was enough! Alex was the first to move. Forgetting his task of lighting the way, he turned heel, screamed and bolted for the tunnel entrance -- his flashlight beam bounced and swerved erratically as he darted down the passage. Valerie and Harold didn't waste a moment in the dark and followed right behind him. The ghostly sound from behind spurred them on and they were nearly tripping over themselves in the loose gravel of the rail bed. It seemed like an impossibly long distance to the light of the entrance. Alex was already out, and Harold and Valerie raced ahead, wanting nothing more than the sun to hit them. The fog was still rolling right behind them -- they could feel its cold, moist fingers trying to envelop them as they ran. They finally reached the entrance and rushed headlong out into the sunshine, not daring to look back until they felt safe. Alex had already darted a distance away from the tunnel entrance. He stood panting by the side of the caboose, his backpack in hand, and was eager to move even farther away! Valerie and Harold ran towards the caboose. They stopped and finally turned around to look back at the gaping mouth of the tunnel. The thick fog rolled out and disappeared quickly as it met the sun.

The three of them tried to calm their breathing as they gasped in the fresh air.

"The trainman's ghost," whispered Alex as he continued to grip the straps of his backpack.

"That was crazy," said Harold simply, breathing heavily.

Valerie watched the fog disappear in the rays of the sun. Exhausted, she plopped down on the ground, leaned back against the side of the caboose and tried to regulate her breathing. Behind one of the steel wheels of the large railcar, something caught her eye: a small open paper bag and a roll of loose fishing line. She looked closer. The white paper on the bag read 'flour'. Her brain tried to make sense of it while she caught her breath. *"What an odd thing to be here,"* she thought.

"Let's get out of here!" said Alex, interrupting her thoughts.

Valerie looked back at the tunnel, as the final wisps of fog dissipated.

"Yeah," she agreed. "Something definitely doesn't want us in there!"

~~~~

Once again Valerie did her best to concentrate in school, but her thoughts kept turning back to the train tunnel and the inexplicable things that had happened there. She had awakened the night before with a nightmare of her and Alex being chased by the trainman, his one good hand reaching for them as they ran from him. It had terrified her. She had kept it all quiet, tried to keep her fears about their frightening adventure from her father. She knew very well that he would not like it if he'd heard what they'd done. Alex had been very quiet this week as well. Valerie could sense that he wanted this all to go away, that maybe this time they should just let it go. She struggled to keep things on an even keel, and not to think about the trainman or the strange things that had happened. She tried to keep her eyes on the prize, and concentrate only on the treasure.

She walked home from school, met Alex along the way, and the two of them were mostly silent during their walk home. Later that day, Dad and Pam exchanged glances at the dinner table; they knew that something was going on, because Curtis was the only one doing a lot of talking. But, thankfully, Valerie and Alex were spared any questioning for the moment and they relaxed a little as the family watched a movie that evening.

The week crept forward, and during this time the two children quietly reflected on the series of events that had taken place. Valerie sat in her bed late on Friday night, with her notes and the photos and sketches spread out in front of her. *"What could we do next?"* she pondered. They seemed to be at a dead end. The information that Harold had shared with them had done little to shed any new light on their search, and the fact that they could not get near the tunnel without something bad happening was certainly not a very good sign to Valerie.

There was a small knock at her bedroom door. Valerie shook herself from her thoughts and tried to quickly shove the papers that she had on the bed down into a corner. She reached over and slowly opened the door to her room. It was Alex. He came in and perched himself at the bottom of her bed, with a look on his face that told Valerie that he was worried.

"Maybe we should just forget about the trainman's treasure," he said quietly.

Valerie shook her head and Alex already knew what was coming.

"I've been thinking about it. There is really nothing for us to be scared of," she stated matter-of-factly.

"Yeah, well, it scared us pretty good the other day. Even Harold ran!" Alex pressed.

Valerie looked at him for a moment. She could not deny that it had been scary. There was nothing she could say that would dispel what they had seen in the tunnel. She replayed everything in her mind again: the floating lantern, the fog, the strange atmosphere and the eerie moaning. It sent a shiver up her spine just thinking about it. In her thoughts, however, logic kept coming back.

"Look, have you ever heard of a ghost killing someone? It's just nuts. There has to be something else going on here."

Alex did not seem so sure.

"Ghosts do kill people!" he exclaimed.

Valerie gave him a long, sarcastic look. "Only in the movies, silly."

It did seem a little crazy, but he had seen strange things over their bunch of little adventures, and this fit the bill for the seriously weird.

"I don't know, it just seems like we are messing with something that we shouldn't be," he said.

Although he was trying as hard as he could to convince his sister that they should give up, Alex could tell from the look on Valerie's face that she was paying his words little heed. She was deep in thought about the odd sight of the small open bag of flour and the fishing line that she'd glimpsed at the caboose. Her mind would not let go of it for some reason. What was it doing there? It was an odd combination of random things to be left where it was.

"Well, I think there is more happening in the tunnel than meets the eye," she said.

Alex let out a sigh, knowing that he had not dissuaded her from the quest in the least. The tunnel made him nervous now. Twice they had ventured inside with the same result, but this last time had really shaken him up more than he would admit.

"It's getting late. I'm going to bed," said Valerie, pulling her comforter up over her shoulders to indicate to Alex that she really didn't want to discuss their situation any more. He left quietly and closed the door behind him as Valerie switched off her bedroom light. She lay there for a few moments with her thoughts still racing. Eventually, however, her eyes became heavy and she fell asleep. She had no dreams that night.

8

Shaun Locke used thick gloves to pull the barbed wire tight around the opening in the north entrance of the tunnel. He was sweating profusely, even in the chill air, as he was not used to doing much in the form of exercise. The wire was tough to work with, but he had managed to loop it through openings in the large wooden slats that made up the doors.

When he finished, he stood back to admire his work. *"That ought to keep the riff-raff out,"* he thought with satisfaction. He tucked the sharp ends of the wire down inside the doors with a large pair of bolt cutters. There, that finished the job!

He had not seen those children for a few days, but he had seen them snooping around the week before. That time they had been with someone else, a man...and it annoyed him. He was not about to let his search for financial freedom get interrupted by a couple of kids. Shaun hated children and regarded them as nothing but a pain. His own childhood had not been great -- perhaps that was the reason that he disliked young people. Whatever the case might be, these two were a potential threat to his finding the gold, and he wasn't about to let it happen.

He threw the cutters into a plastic bag lying beside him next to the doors, gathered his gear up and headed back towards the bicycle path. Carrying an ordinary grocery bag, he would not look conspicuous to anyone else who happened to be out walking dogs, biking or jogging. He brushed off his jacket as he emerged onto the asphalt of the path and made his way to a side street that intersected it not far away. He quickened his pace. He just wanted to get back home without anyone even seeing him anywhere nearby the train tunnel. He glanced around him. No one was in the area. He came to the street where his grey BMW was parked and looked around again, feeling a bit like he had committed some unknown crime. He unlocked his car and pitched the bag with the cutters in it into the back seat. Once behind the wheel, he felt a little more comfortable, revved up his vehicle and drove away toward downtown.

The light in the western sky was beginning to fade, turning the few clouds into pink and purple puffs of cotton candy. As Shaun drove down the main street, he saw many people walking around downtown. The lights and business signs had begun to cast their fluorescent glow on the sidewalks and a familiar place came into view. He made a split decision and pulled the car over. After a perfect parallel parking job, he smiled to himself and stepped out into the cold air once again, pushing the lock key on his car remote. Night had fallen. From the sidewalk he looked up at the neon sign on the building in front of him. He stepped forward and pulled open the heavy wooden door of the pub.

The warmth inside hit him instantly as he walked in and the air was alive with conversation and music. The smell of alcohol was thick in the pub. Shaun he took off his trench coat, arranged it over the back of one of the stools at the bar, sat down, adjusted his heft on the chair and leaned forwards on the thick oak bar in front of him. The bartender came over to him immediately and offered a greeting. Shaun ordered a double of Cranberry juice, and turned his attention to a large TV mounted on the wall behind the bar. He did not drink, but still enjoyed the atmosphere of the pub. There was a hockey game on, and he watched it while he fumbled in his pocket for some money to give the bartender when he returned with his drink.

Tearing his eyes away from the TV screen, he scanned the room quickly to search for anyone he recognized. There wasn't a large crowd in the pub tonight. Two women sat farther down the bar from him and he smiled cordially to them. They ignored him and continued with their conversation. He frowned slightly and turned his attention back to the game on TV. Despite the fact that he was obviously alone, he enjoyed the ambience of the place, and he settled into the chair to enjoy the mindless entertainment on the television. The sounds of the place -- the clinking of glassware as the bartender organized clean glasses on the racks behind the surface of the bar and the general buzz of activity here and there -- made him feel less...lonely!

Shaun had never had much luck with women, but was quite content living alone. There was no one he had to explain anything to if he chose to stay out late by himself; no one to have to please by buying expensive gifts and baubles; and his apartment was his space alone, a beautifully appointed location overlooking the river. He felt completely at ease here, watching the television and enjoying his drink.

His solitude didn't last long, however, as someone sat down suddenly next to him, yanking his attention away from the game. It was Douglas Wynne, an avid local historian. Shaun groaned quietly to himself, knowing full well why this man had come to sit with him. He was an older fellow, thin and tall with a head of grey hair.

"I heard about the council meeting the other night Shaun," Doug began. "So, the city can't at least spend a few bucks to protect the train tunnel from further desecration?"

Shaun turned his chair slightly; he didn't really want to have this conversation, but he knew that he would not be able to avoid it.

"Look, Doug. I explained my point of view to council, based on what my constituents are telling me: that they don't think their tax dollars should be paying for this," he explained, following his carefully thought out response.

"Well, in all seriousness, it is the only way it will happen. You know very well that the Historical Society doesn't have that kind of money."

Shaun was becoming agitated by the man's words. He hadn't wanted to debate this topic again tonight. One thing that he hated was to be made to look stupid. All he had wanted to do was to sit quietly with his drink, watch some mindless TV at the bar and then go home. It angered him that he now had to explain his decision on the council vote once again. Shaun decided to cut the conversation short.

"It is simple in my mind," he said sarcastically and turned back again toward the television, taking a sip from his glass. "Maybe you guys should do some fund-raising."

~~~~

The children sat eating their breakfast in relative quiet the next morning, as Pam moved back and forth between the kitchen and the dining room, bringing plates of pancakes and bacon, eggs and hash browns. It was finally the weekend and everyone was relaxed without the morning hustle and bustle of getting ready for school or work.

Dad watched the kids intently as he sipped a glass of juice. The clinking of cutlery against the stoneware plates was the only sound, other than the occasional meow from the cat awaiting her food as Pam walked past her. The children remained quiet as they ate -- even Curtis was unusually silent. Dad continued to shift his eyes around the table at them. He knew that something was up because they were constantly avoiding his gaze.

"So what's the plan for today?" he finally asked, breaking the silence.

"No plan," said Valerie quietly, not looking up from her plate.

Dad decided to just wait them out. Whatever was going on would come to the surface eventually. They had been acting strange for more than a few days now, and he and Pam had noticed. They had come home from school, retreating to their rooms or outside, without much in the way of conversation. Something was definitely bothering them and Dad was getting a little concerned. *"Nana and her crazy adventures,"* he thought as he shook his head.

The children finished eating one by one and brought their plates into the kitchen to rinse them in the sink. The cat let out the occasional meow as it wandered between the children's legs for attention. They disappeared quickly, heading outside to play in the cool fall air. Dad, still sitting at the table, gave Pam a raised eyebrow. She returned his knowing look with a raised eyebrow of her own.

Eventually Dad got up from the table, brought his own plate into the kitchen, rinsed it off and then started to load up the dishwasher from the morning meal. Once the sinks and counter were cleared, he stood for a moment to look out the kitchen window. Pam came to stand beside him and took a sip from her fresh cup of tea.

"What's up with them today?" she asked as she stood there looking out the window as well.

"Not sure, but I'm sure we will know before the day is done," he replied quietly. A train whistle sounded from the train yard; it was the local switching train heading out to service the local industries. They could hear the sound of the bell from the road crossing just down around the corner, as they watched the children playing in the yard. Dad wrapped his arm around Pam and pulled her close to reassure her. They were both lost in thought as the sun streamed through the kitchen window. The cat slid herself between them and rubbed up against their legs. It was quiet, peaceful. The children chatted and giggled outside as they ran about the yard, and time seemed to slow for a moment as Dad and Pam watched.

The day was cool, but bright. A beautiful fall day, most of the leaves had fallen now to create a kaleidoscope of colour on the entire yard. The kids played in them, tossing the leaves into the air. Their father had meant to rake them up to prepare for the coming winter, but despite the almost bare tree limbs lining the yard, he had held off. As he watched them play amongst the blanket of colour, he was glad that he had. There was still plenty of time.

The quiet was suddenly punctuated by a light knock at the kitchen door, and both Dad and Pam turned, wrenching their thoughts back to the present. A man stood at the screen door, waving at them politely and sporting a slight smile. They did not recognize him.

"Hi, folks. Hope I'm not disturbing you?" he said cheerfully.

"No. Can I help you?" Dad asked, observing him carefully as he approached the door.

"Sorry. I know you folks have no idea who I am and I assure you that I am not trying to sell anything," the man said.

"It's no problem," replied Dad as he opened the door. "Come on in."

The man stepped inside. He understood that the two parents were both curious and cautious about him. He stood in the doorway as he searched to find the words he wanted.

"My name is Harold Baker," he began. "I have been looking for Valerie and Alex. They are helping me and I am helping them with a search for a lost treasure. I know this sounds crazy, but your children have figured out some important clues to a historical story here in the city, and I felt compelled to come and see them about it."

Harold paused. He was expecting these adults to react in a negative manner. He knew he'd taken a huge gamble on finding the two children, and would not be surprised if their parents were not thrilled with him just showing up at their home. He handed Dad a piece of paper of an old news clipping.

It was an article written long ago, the paper old and yellowed from the passage of time. Dad reached onto the kitchen counter for his glasses, slipped them on and began to read as Pam looked over his shoulder.

"It's the recounting of an old legend here in the city about a trainman long ago who hid gold along the old railway tracks down at the entrance to the train tunnel," explained Harold as he adjusted his own thick glasses on his face.

"Yes, this is the same story the children's grandmother showed them not long ago," Dad commented as he read.

"Well, they seem to be on the right track, pardon the pun, but I was with them the last time they were looking in the train tunnel, and we saw some very strange things," Harold continued and then cleared his throat.

Dad looked up from the old article and leveled his gaze on Harold.

"What strange things?" Dad asked as he raised an eyebrow.

"I'm not sure how much of the supernatural that I believe in, but some of the things I and your children have seen make me question everything," came the reply.

Harold stammered through the events of their visit to the train tunnel. He described the mysterious fog and then told them the children's story of the floating lantern and stories of the ghostly apparition of the trainman with only one hand, which had been heard from some of the local train crews. It spilled out of him at a mile a minute.

Dad and Pam looked at each other as the blanks began to get filled in. They knew the children had been acting strange and that something must have happened, but the kids had been secretive and tight lipped. Harold's news had answered their questions and told the story in full.

Dad got a look of concern on his face as he handed the piece of newspaper back to Harold. He took a moment to think of his response to all of this news. As Dad rolled all of this new information over in his mind, Pam took hold of his arm in an effort to remind him that she was there with him.

Harold fidgeted slightly as he waited for Dad to comment. He felt that he knew the thoughts that this man was wrestling with.

"I'm not sure I believe in the supernatural either, Harold, and I am glad that you have come to us with this. I am not a fan of my mother launching these children on a crazy adventure, but they have a love for this stuff, so I will help out in any way I can," he finally said, slowly and assuredly.

"I certainly didn't mean to come here and upset you folks with all of this. I just think the children are close to making a remarkable discovery, shedding light on this old legend, and I-I want to help them," Harold stammered.

Dad thought about this request for a moment more before he spoke.

"Maybe you are right, Harold, and maybe it is time for me to get involved in this. I can tell you one thing I see about it." He looked Harold straight in the eyes. "I believe that someone might be messing with you guys."

9

Shaun was running out of time to find the gold, and he knew it. He had searched everywhere in and around the tunnel. He had even searched the old locomotive and its consist of railcars. He had dug many small holes here and there -- all to no avail -- and had carefully covered them back up to erase any evidence of his search. Shaun was becoming increasingly frustrated at his lack of progress in locating the treasure, a prize he knew would easily secure his retirement and allow him to live in comfort somewhere warm in the winters. Those children were becoming a real concern to him, and he knew that he would have to scare them off permanently if he was to find the gold before they did. To add to the problem, the children had an adult helping them now, a man that Shaun knew nothing about. It gave him little comfort that this man had fled the tunnel as fast as the two kids the last time he had scared them off.

He was walking the tunnel once again, carefully retracing his steps as he looked for anything he might have missed. His agitation grew as he shone his light along the ancient brickwork of the tunnel's interior walls. His boots crunched over the gravel that lined the track. The sound echoed eerily up and down the damp space. His breath hovered like a steamy white cloud in the stillness.

"There must be something I've missed," he thought, some obscure clue that would help him find the resting place of his salvation.

His light began to trace over the tail end boxcar of the old train as its beam sliced through the gloom. He advanced alongside the cars, shining his light inside and underneath them. There were no disturbances in the gravel underneath or around the train, no loose brickwork on the walls. Shaun gritted his teeth in frustration as he replayed the story of the trainman in his mind. He knew that it made no sense for him to be searching around the train itself, but perhaps something had happened that had not been written about. He had to be sure.

He passed the old locomotive, a massive hulk of steel and iron, silently sitting at the head end. Again, there was no sign of anything that would make Shaun think that someone had been digging here.

A slit of light shone in the darkness ahead. Shaun recognized it as a slim ray of sunlight that was seeping through the narrow opening in the massive north doors of the tunnel. Shaun clicked off his light as he approached these old wooden doors both to save the battery and let his eyes adjust better. He focused his eyes through the slit in the doors. He could just make out the bare branches of the grove of trees outside, and felt a slight breeze of fresh fall air waft through the cracks towards him.

"Where is the gold?" he thought feverishly and gripped the handle of his flashlight. His thoughts turned once again to his competition -- those meddling children. Had they found out something that he didn't know? Could they possibly locate the gold before he could scare them away for good? He shook away the thought, determined to keep searching. He turned back, once again clicking the button on the flashlight to illuminate the tunnel. It was along walk back down past the train once again. His footsteps echoed in the dark dampness.

He chuckled to himself as he recalled how terrified the children and this man had been the last time he had scared them away from the tunnel. His thoughts quickly returned to seriousness, however, as he mused about how he would give them an even worse fright the next time they dared come near the place. Ghosts. It was amazing to him that at this day in age, some people still believed in the possibility that they actually existed. How easy it was to convince people that there might be truth to the legend of the trainman.

An icy breeze rose up in the gloom and whistled through the tunnel and a hollow howl sounded as the cold wind whipped past Shaun in the darkness. He shivered uncontrollably for a moment, and then stopped still in his tracks. The hair stood up suddenly on the back of his neck as he listened. Was it a voice he was hearing, or was it simply the cold air travelling down the tunnel?

It ceased as quickly as it had begun, leaving Shaun slightly shaken, despite his disbelief in ghosts. He started to walk again, quickening his pace sub-consciously, his ears now tuned in to every noise in the gloom. He breathed a little easier as he reached the waterfront entrance, and the sight of the sunshine on the grass out in front of the entrance was a welcome sight. As he stepped outside, Shaun felt the warmth of the fall sun on his face and exhaled deeply. *"It must have been a sudden breeze coming through the north doors,"* he thought as he tried to rationalize what had just happened. But his brain refused to let go of the eerie sounds that his ears had registered inside.

He clicked off his light and glanced around to see if anyone had seen him. The coast was clear. He walked away from the tunnel entrance and shook his head at the thoughts in his mind. Still, as he left, he gave one more glance over his shoulder at the gaping maw of the tunnel opening.

~~~~

Valerie and Alex sat in the train yard on an old pile of railroad ties, watching the local switching train as it moved back and forth, rolling cars from one track to another. It was cold this morning and the sky was a veil of looming grey. The train made an occasional loud 'bang' as it coupled onto some of the boxcars to pull them out onto another track.

As they watched, smoke billowed from the stacks on top of the locomotive and the steel wheels screeched against the rails as the train engine roared to life to pull forward. Occasionally, a passenger train would zip past on the far tracks, its horn blaring as it approached the street crossing a few blocks away. Two long blasts would be followed by a short blast and then one more long blast. It was always the same and it made Valerie wonder why the trains did it that way. They would hear the train bell as well, as the passenger trains slowed to pull into the train station, where people would disembark to head home or board to move on to their destinations.

In the cold grey of the day Valerie's thoughts kept flowing. She was frustrated by their lack of success in their quest, but she was also still a little frightened. This was not like any other adventure that Nana had offered them information about. It was another slice of past history from her scrapbook, with the promise of an amazing discovery, but in this case, it was also dark and scary.

She shivered slightly from the cold, pulled her jacket up around her shoulders and wrapped the hood around her dark brown hair. Alex sat close by. He was wearing a heavy blue sweater and simply watching the train as it moved back and forth.

The massive locomotive moved past them once again, but they knew that they were well out of harm's way sitting where they were. Their father had told them many times to stay well back from the train tracks.

Valerie and Alex could see Mike, sitting in the window of the locomotive and he gave them a quick wave as he worked the controls, stopped the train and slowly backed it into another track. The children could see the brakeman further down the yard as he threw the switches by hand at the tail end in order to bring the train where it needed to go.

Valerie continued to ponder their discoveries -- or lack thereof -- in this new challenge. She felt as though she needed to 'zero the clock' and start from the beginning again. All of their searching -- at the library, the museum and in the tunnel itself -- had turned up nothing.

"Maybe it's not even there anymore," Alex spoke up as though he had sensed her thoughts.

Valerie said nothing for a while, simply sat in silence with her cheeks in her hands and her brown hair falling in front of her face.

"It makes a bit of sense," continued Alex, defending his previous comment. "This story has been around for a long time. Someone else may have already found it and kept it for themselves."

Valerie sighed deeply. Her mind refused to give up on the idea that the treasure was still there and waiting to be found.

"Maybe, but I don't think so. If someone found it, they would have trouble keeping it quiet. If someone came into a bank with gold coins, or old paper notes, whatever the heck it is, I'm sure someone would take notice."

"I guess," Alex agreed reluctantly and shrugged. "But maybe they didn't take it to a bank; maybe they sold it to someone else who wanted it."

"I don't know, maybe," replied Valerie bleakly.

Alex picked up a few stones of gravel and pitched them toward the tracks one at a time out of boredom. As much as he didn't like being dragged around by his sister, at least it always seemed to lead to fun. He looked up at the lead-grey sky and watched for a moment as the thick groupings of cloud moved past overhead, ready to shower them with cold rain at any moment. He shivered slightly and pulled his thick sweater closer around him.

The children's thoughts were interrupted once again by the roar of the diesel locomotive that had pulled up across from them again on the nearest track. There was a loud hiss of air from it as it stopped and they could see Mike again in the window of the engine -- he was holding up his hand as if he wanted them to wait for a moment. He got up from his seat and disappeared for several moments from the window. Then the door on the front of the locomotive opened and he emerged onto the front platform, stepping down the ladder to the ground.

The kids perked up a bit as Mike approached, wearing a soft smile on his face.

"Hi guys," he said simply. "What's up today?"

"Not much," Alex answered.

"You guys look bored. No luck with finding the trainman's gold?" Mike prompted.

"No. We are starting to wonder if it even exists," said Valerie.

Mike paused for a moment as he ribbed his chin in thought. The locomotive behind him let out a sudden puff of air as the compressor kicked in.

"Oh, it exists," he ventured finally. "I haven't seen the trainman's ghost, but one of the other fellows who works with our train has. He had to take several days off afterwards!" he elaborated.

He snapped his fingers suddenly and his eyes brightened as he remembered something. "That's what I meant to ask you guys! Did you check the old caboose? It was originally a part of the train, left up in the tunnel, until it was given to the city for a display down at the waterfront. It was a real big job for the city workers to uncouple the caboose and bring it safely down the tunnel before the tracks were removed at the tunnel entrance."

Valerie's jaw dropped. There it was! They had pretty much ignored the old caboose that sat just outside the tunnel at the waterfront, and had been restored to its original condition. It was the one part of the whole story that the children had missed -- or subconsciously dismissed. The two children looked at each other with expressions of amazement as they realized that the old caboose had never even really entered their thoughts as a possible part of this quest.

"Wow!" said Alex.

"No kidding!" replied Valerie, astonished.

Mike smiled at the children's reactions. He had simply wanted to see if they had found anything regarding the legend. It made him happy to think he might be helping these young adventurers with their little quest.

"Well, I just wanted to ask you guys about that, because it came to mind," he stated with a huge grin.

"It's amazing! We didn't even think about it!" exclaimed Valerie. "Thank you!"

Mike smiled with a bit of satisfaction.

"Sounds like you won't be bored for the rest of the day!" said Mike.

"Exactly!" shouted Valerie as she jumped up off the pile of ties. Alex got up as well, happy with the turn of events in their day -- and their mission.

Just then, Mike turned his head to look to up the tracks. The children followed his gaze. There was a large steel bridge-like structure up the tracks mounted with lights. The lights were all red except for those that were lined up for the track that the locomotive and its cars were sitting on. They displayed a yellow light.

"Whoops! Gotta go, kids. That's our signal to head out! See ya...and good luck," said Mike as he turned and headed quickly back to the ladder on the side of the locomotive. He stepped up quickly, entered the door on the front and appeared once again in the window on its side.

Valerie and Alex watched the smoke roll out of the top of the stack on the train as it came to life and moved slowly out of the yard, heading off to deliver its cars. They waved at Mike and he waved back as the train departed.

As they walked with purpose out of the train yard, Valerie and Alex looked at each other once again when they heard the sound of the train fade into the distance.

"I can't believe we missed the caboose!" said Valerie.

Alex gave her a big thumbs-up. "Looks like we have something new to check out!" he replied.

10

Shaun sat behind the wheel of his BMW in the parking lot at the waterfront. He sipped on a coffee as he watched those two children poke around the old caboose. It infuriated him. *"Why won't they just go away?"* he thought angrily to himself. It had agitated him more and more as the days went by. It was cold and grey out today and Shaun had left the car running for the heat. He took another sip from his coffee and placed it back in the cup holder as he watched the kids climb up and down on the caboose and inspect it from end to end. He had already been down this road, had already gone over the caboose, even inside during the few times it had been open to the public. He wished that they would just give up. Their messing around was causing him delays in his own search and his time was running short. It wasn't enough that he had his own financial worries, but these kids were not making things easier for him.

He gripped the steering wheel tightly and watched the children continue to walk around the caboose. He had to get rid of them somehow. He had followed them and knew where they lived in the city. He also knew about the older fellow he had seen with them and had figured out where he lived as well. The fact that they were now working together greatly upset Shaun. He had invested a lot of time in his search for the treasure and was not about to let a pair of kids and some janitor ruin his dreams! This was going to be *his* retirement fund -- and would belong to *him* only! The small pension from the city would never be able to pay for the way he wanted to live when he retired next year, so this was his chance to get the money he needed to live someplace warm in the winters, with plenty of sun, sand and even those little umbrella drinks. His knuckles turned white on the steering wheel as he clutched it tightly in his anger. He released his hands slowly to take another sip of coffee and watch the two children clamour over and around the caboose.

The young boy reached into a tattered old backpack on the ground nearby and fished out a small flashlight. Then he crawled underneath the rail car and used the light to look up in the nooks and crannies on the caboose's underside. He could see the young lady, bent over, directing the boy. He gritted his teeth.

"Just go away," he thought. The outside compartments on the caboose had been welded shut anyway, most likely done when the caboose was restored, so there wasn't any place to hide the treasure on it. But Shaun knew that all it would take is a bit of dumb luck by these two, and his retirement fund would be gone. He was going to have to take care of this once and for all -- he would have to frighten them *good*...frighten them so much that they would never, ever want to return again! If he couldn't get rid of them, they would just keep pestering him and getting in his way and that was something that he simply could not tolerate.

As he watched them, the girl pointed up towards something underneath the caboose and the young boy aimed the light at different spots of the undercarriage. He heard the girl give a frustrated shout at the boy and then watched him crawl back out from under the caboose...and then the two of them had a bit of a hollering match. Shaun grinned. He guessed that it meant that they were becoming agitated by not finding anything. As he continued to watch, they gathered up their things, the girl her jacket and the boy his backpack, and stomped off down the street away from the waterfront, gesturing and arguing with one another the whole way out of his sight. Shaun let out a deep breath. Finally. Although he knew they would return eventually, at least they were gone again, empty-handed for today. And the next time that they returned, he would have a very nasty surprise waiting for them!

~~~~

When Valerie and Alex arrived back at the house at a run, the side door of the garage was open and a light column of smoke was rising from the chimney at the back. The children stopped for a moment on the walkway to catch their breath, too tired to argue anymore. It was pointless to argue... they were obviously just very frustrated by their lack of progress. They could hear music playing in the garage, along with voices talking. As their breathing slowed, they became curious. It was pretty rare for Pam to venture out to the garage when Dad was out there, and besides, the voices were men's voices. As they stepped closer, the children recognized that it was Harold and Dad speaking. The two kids looked at one another, confused as to why Harold would be at the house talking to their father. They walked slowly up to the doorway and peeked inside.

They could feel the warmth of the wood stove and the overhead lights welcomed them with an inviting glow as they stepped inside the garage. Harold was seated in one of Dad's comfy chairs while Dad stood leaning up against his workbench. The two men were chatting idly as the children entered.

"Well, hello there," said Dad.

"Hi," replied Valerie as she gave her father a confused look. "What's going on?" she asked cautiously.

Dad and Harold exchanged glances for a moment.

"Nothing, really. Your father and I were just discussing the ghost!" said Harold.

Valerie's faced flushed a little bit in embarrassment.

"Ghosts don't exist! Right Dad?" asked Alex.

"That's right, bud. But you guys have seen some weird things, and I think I can figure out what is going on down there around the tunnel," Dad replied.

"Oh, and what is that?" asked Valerie as she relaxed a bit and curiosity took over.

"Well, Harold filled me in on everything that you two have been keeping quiet about lately, including what you saw Valerie -- the fishing line and bag of flour."

Valerie's mouth dropped open and her eyes brightened suddenly as she remembered the strange items beneath the caboose, and how she had felt it odd that they had been there. She had told Harold about it as they had left that day.

"Yeah, it was kinda weird for that stuff to just randomly be there," she stated.

"Indeed," said Dad as he shared a momentary grin with Harold.

He stood up straight and raised a finger in the air.

"For example, the floating lantern," he pointed out first and wiggled his fingers at them creepily. "That's where the fishing line comes in. Watch this!"

Dad grabbed a piece of fishing line that hung close by and pulled on it lightly. From out of the far corner of the garage, a plastic camping lantern that their father had bought for one of their camping trips seemed to float forward towards them. As Valerie watched it moving closer, she squinted slightly and could just barely make out the fishing line that supported it. Another line had been tied to the side of the lamp to make it move when

Dad pulled it.

"See?" asked Dad. "In the dark of the tunnel, with dust floating around, you would never see the fishing line, even with your flashlight Alex!"

Valerie's mouth hung wide open after seeing this demonstration and realizing what her Dad was saying. Now the pieces all slid into place in her young mind.

"Now, you want to be able to see the line?" he asked. "Check this out."

He turned toward the workbench and picked up what looked like a small handheld fluorescent light. The cylindrical bulb was a dark purple, however, and only about as long as her hand. Dad flicked the switch on the end of it and the bulb began to glow with its strange purple light.

"This is what we call 'black light'. It is more accurately ultraviolet light," Dad explained. "Some things that normally can't be seen in regular light glow brightly when exposed to UV light. Alex, turn out the lights, would ya, bud?"

Alex switched off the garage lights, and suddenly, anything white or fluorescent colour, such as the labels on some of dad's fishing gear on the shelf above the workbench, glowed brightly in the strange purple light.

"Now look at the lamp," instructed Dad as he raised the UV light up.

The lamp was there, hard to make out in the dark, but the fishing line it was tied to glowed like brilliant purple thread, clearly visible!

"Cool!" exclaimed Alex.

After a few more moments, Valerie turned the lights back on and Dad turned off the UV light and handed it to her to examine.

"They use that same kind of light to look for counterfeit bills in stores," said Dad.

Valerie rolled it over in her hand. It was perfect, compact and ran on batteries just like Alex's flashlight. She thought about the tunnel and figured this was most likely exactly how someone had make the old lantern that they had seen seem to be floating in the darkness toward them.

"But what about the flour?" she asked.

Dad and Harold again exchanged a grin.

"Can you think of any better way of looking like a ghost than by sprinkling white flour all over your hair, skin and clothes?" replied their father, still grinning.

"But why would someone go to all this trouble to scare people away from the tunnel over this old legend?" asked Alex.

"Duh, because it means that someone else believes there is treasure there too!" exclaimed Valerie, her eyes wide.

"There you go," said Dad.

Valerie and Alex stood there, mulling over this interesting discovery and thinking about the UV light. It was obvious to them now that the strange occurrences in the tunnel had a fairly simple explanation. Someone else was also looking for the treasure, someone who wanted to scare everyone else away. And it also meant something else: that as far as the legend of the Last Train was concerned, they were still on the right track!

11

Valerie, Alex and Harold stood at the massive wooden doors of the train tunnel and stared into the gloom ahead of them. They had returned once again, this time ready for whatever they might face inside. Frost glistened everywhere on the ground this morning, and they could see the fog of their breath in the air. Alex was already fishing through his backpack for the flashlight, as Valerie kept watch up the dark opening of the tunnel, gripping the UV light that her father had given her. It would be a long job of checking the train again and the three of them wanted to get this done and over with quickly. Even Harold was a bit hesitant and he looked inside the tunnel opening nervously. Alex, however, felt ready to tackle this challenge: the pep talk from Dad had made complete sense in his young mind.

"There are no such things as ghosts. There are no such things as ghosts," he repeated over and over to himself in his head as his father had suggested. *"Yep, there's nothing to be afraid of in the tunnel. If the trainman had actually lived, he was gone long ago, and did not return every night looking to find his severed hand, or his gold, or whatever!"* He found the light, clicked it on and was the first one to head into the mouth of the tunnel, despite his sister's look of amazement.

He turned to the other two when he realized that they were not moving.

"Well?!" he prompted in exasperation and held up his arms and let them drop hard to his sides for theatrical effect. Valerie and Harold looked at one another, and then back at Alex.

"Since when did you become Mr. Brave, pal?" she asked sarcastically.

"Since you guys have obviously forgotten what we are doing here in the first place!" he replied.

Harold adjusted his thick glasses and cleared his throat. In the short time that he had known these children, he had come to realize that Alex occasionally enjoyed tormenting his sister. Although it seemed funny at the moment, he tried to maintain his composure -- and tried even harder not to grin.

"Sure. Like I forgot!" she shot back and started forward to follow him.

Even Harold resigned himself to the fact that they were indeed going to go through with their plan. He fell in line behind the two children and they entered the darkness of the tunnel once again. They took one last look at the bright daylight outside the tunnel entrance and then began to trek onward into the damp gloom.

It seemed mustier today for some reason and the three shone their flashlights up the rusty rails ahead of them. Everything glistened with moisture in their view as they crunched along the gravel, their footsteps echoing eerily in the darkness. They stopped suddenly, freezing as a noise rose up in front of them. The sound of wings. The children dropped to the ground quickly, having heard the noise before. Harold remained standing. His eyes widened in terror at the vision that entered the dim light from his flashlight: bats, many bats! They swarmed past the three of them. Harold, having had no time to duck, simply remained frozen in place, an arm raised to shield his face, while the cloud of winged animals flew past, chirping as they went. After a moment, everything returned to the quiet echo of the tunnel ahead, and they stood together again, happy that it was over. Harold left out a large breath.

"Wow! That was intense," he said.

"Next time you should duck!" advised Alex.

"They were just scared because we disturbed them," interjected Valerie.

They crunched onward along the old rails, heading upwards as they walked.

Valerie stopped abruptly as she remembered the black light. She flipped the switch on the hand-held lamp and the strange purple light lit up, making anything white glow brightly.

"Turn your flashlights off, guys!" she said.

Alex looked at her questioningly.

"Seriously!" she stated. "Those lights mess this one up!"

When they switched off their flashlights, the entire tunnel suddenly took on a strange new glow. Alex was not sure that he liked this very much. The black light made the tunnel seem twice as gloomy and foreboding. It was as if it were Hallowe'en, or they in some scary theme park ride. Small white clumps of mold and moss on the walls and ceiling glowed brilliantly as if lit from within.

"Ummm, this is kinda creepy!" whispered Alex as he moved slowly forwards.

"Well, this is how we will notice anything that might be kinda weird," replied Valerie.

"Kinda weird?" Alex exclaimed quietly. "Let me know when things are NOT weird, ok?!"

Valerie ignored him. She was far too busy examining the glowing items that her lamp was exposing.

Harold came along behind the kids and looked around in wonder at what Valerie's light was revealing. Cracks in the brickwork glowed brightly with the fungi growing there, along with other things that were not normally visible. Their breath formed little clouds in the cold air, as they progressed up the tunnel.

Finally, the last car of the train came into view in the darkness, slowly revealing in the black light of Valerie's lamp. She held it the light higher to try to illuminate more of the scene before them.

"Wow. Here we are again," said Harold and he swallowed hard.

Valerie stood still and looked at the tail end of the train in the eerie black light. Her breath came out like smoke, barely visible. She swept her dark brown hair out of her face.

"Yep. This time we are gonna find it," she said firmly.

She strode forwards again and inspected the tail end of the train, the ceiling, the ground around them, everything. The UV light shone its strange light over the scene, making certain things glow. Moisture dripped from the ceiling. Even their breathing seemed loud in the hollowness of the tunnel.

Alex climbed the ladder on the open top car and peered over the side into it. He clicked on his flashlight momentarily to survey the car's interior.

"Rotted old wood, that's all," he informed his companions glumly.

"Well, we should look at all of them on the train," said Valerie.

"Yes, we don't want to miss a thing this time," agreed Harold.

Alex climbed down again and headed to the next car on the train. It contained the same thing. A boxcar was next, but it was completely empty. Alex pushed himself back out through the rusted door, which was open only about a foot. He already had a few smudges of dirt and old rust on his face.

For the next two hours they progressed slowly as they checked each car thoroughly -- over, under and through -- to be sure that they had not missed anything. Valerie continued to shine the UV light around the area, trying to cover everything. She crossed over the train, between the cars, to check the other side. The walls were the same and, except for the odd glow from a piece of mold, there was nothing interesting.

As she shone the UV light up toward the ceiling, she stopped. There it was: the glowing thread of fishing line!

Suddenly, a loud boom sounded through the tunnel from the distance. Valerie knew what she had heard. The dull thud echoed up the tunnel. She looked in the direction that they had come -- the sliver of light where the entrance should have been was gone, replaced by darkness. Someone had closed the doors to the tunnel at the waterfront! They were trapped inside, unless they could squeeze out through the north end doors at the head of the train.

"Was that what I thought it was?" asked Alex with a stunned expression on his face.

"I think so," Valerie replied quickly.

"It might be the city staff doing some maintenance, maybe?" asked Alex.

"I don't know too many city people that would be working on a Sunday, except for an emergency," offered Harold.

The three of them stared down into the darkness, their breathing the only sound besides the occasional drip of moisture from the ceiling. Their ears strained in the gloom. Then came another sound, faint, but still there -- the unmistakable sound of crunching gravel. Their eyes all widened in horror as they looked at one another in the strange purple glow of the UV light. Something was in there with them!

~~~~

The afternoon wore on and Dad surveyed the yard as he stood on the patio behind the garage. The frost was long gone and the long shadows of the late afternoon promised a cold evening. He sighed. Although he loved the fall, winter's cold was something he wished he could skip. And no doubt it would be here soon. The leaves had all fallen now, and he had done all the raking he was going to do, regardless of the wind. He sipped on a hot coffee that Pam had made for him and kept his free hand in the warm pocket of his jacket.

Pamela appeared beside him, enjoying the sun on her face on the cold fall afternoon. She stood quietly beside him and looked over the backyard. Her gardens were finished until the spring and she'd covered the pond with a tarp. She sighed slightly as she pondered next year's planting in the spring.

"The kids have been gone a long time," she stated.

"Yes, they're probably still down at the waterfront at the tunnel again," he replied.

"Do you think it is safe?" she asked.

"Well, Harold is with them, and although we just met him, he seems honest and upstanding. I don't think we need to worry," Dad replied.

Pamela said nothing more. She simply wrapped her arm around his and stood beside him comfortably as she continued to look out across the yard.

The children had indeed been gone most of the day. Dad and Pam had ensured that they had dressed warm enough for the cold -- they knew that they would be heading out to try again at their adventure.

Dad checked his watch. *"At least there are no holes in the backyard this time,"* he thought to himself. Still, he always worried when the children got involved in one of Nana's adventures. It wasn't so much that their grandmother taught them about the history of the area and of the country, but it always seemed to involve some crazy legend about treasure. Along with ghosts. There *always* seemed to be ghosts. Just once he wished that Nana would share a normal story with the kids, without lost treasure or ghosts!

12

Whatever was coming up the tunnel toward the trio was getting closer. They could hear the footsteps in the gravel much clearer now and Valerie gripped the UV light as she kept her eyes glued down the tunnel into the darkness. Alex looked ready to bolt at any moment -- but the three of them had no place to go! The only possibility would be to try to escape through the tunnel's north doors. But Valerie knew that Harold would never be able to get through there, as he was much bigger than they were.

A light appeared down the tunnel, dim and flickering. A lantern. Valerie could feel the hair on the back of her neck stand up and her breath quickened. She glanced over quickly at Alex and Harold again. Alex had a terrified look upon his face, his skin pale and sweating slightly. Harold didn't look much better. Valerie hoped at that moment that her father was right about the fishing line and the flour, hoped that logic and rational thought would prevail over the frightening scene which was unfolding before her eyes. She fought to remain still, fought against the powerful urge to turn and run.

The lantern floated even closer to them. A noise rose in the darkness, an animal-like howl, followed by low moans that made Valerie's skin crawl. Alex finally turned and ran. Harold lasted only a second or two more before he followed suit, leaving Valerie alone with her UV light in hand.

The lantern bobbed in the gloom as it came closer. Valerie could hear the rapid crunching of the gravel behind her as Alex and Harold fled up the tunnel alongside the train cars. The sound subsided for a moment; only its echoes drifted through the dark space. She no longer heard any footsteps coming from that direction. The lantern approached her silently, floating on...

The glow of a fishing line holding the lantern suddenly lit up in bright purple in the beam of Valerie's UV light. She exhaled loudly. It was nothing but someone messing with them! She raised the light slightly and saw the glow of the lines that both supported the lantern and made it move. It wasn't ghostly in the least! In fact, it made her angry. Her brow furrowed slightly with the realization that someone was playing tricks.

"You can come out now, whoever you are. I can see your fishing line trick!" she shouted into the darkness.

Alex clicked on his small flashlight from on top of one of the railcars that he and Harold had retreated to and aimed the beam down the tunnel. It was too weak now to illuminate much, since they had been using it for a long time and the batteries were starting to die.

Valerie squinted to see down the tunnel.

"We're not afraid!" she shouted.

A low growl rose up in the gloom ahead of her. It changed quickly into a scream as a faint outline began to emerge from the murky blackness. The figure grew closer and the screams and ranting continued. Valerie retreated a step, again questioning what she was seeing in the gloom. It was a man -- a large man, ghostly white, dressed in the overalls and hat of an ancient trainman. Her breath froze in her throat as she looked at his arms. He appeared to only have one hand, and, as she watched in horror, the apparition raised that one good hand out toward her.

She cried out, fear taking over her courageous front, turned quickly and darted up the tunnel toward the north doors. The UV light barely lit the way. She could hear Alex and Harold running across the tops of the train cars as she ran past. All of them wanted nothing else but the sunshine and safety outside those tunnel doors!

Valerie ran past the steel and iron hulk of the locomotive while the other two scrambled down the ladder on the side of the cars to follow. She could see the narrow shaft of light from the gap in the massive wooden doors just ahead. But she realized then that the opening was small, far too small for her or even Alex to fit through. As she skidded to a stop in front of the doors, her shoes sprayed up some of the musty gravel on the tunnel floor. She shoved against the doors, hard. They didn't budge.

Alex and Harold nearly piled into the back of her as they reached the doors. Harold helped Valerie, trying to ram his heft into the ancient wood. It was no use. The doors were secure. There was no way out. They were really trapped inside.

The 'thing' let out another howl from the rear of the train and the trio could tell that it was getting closer. The sound of labored footsteps echoed behind them.

"W-what are we gonna do now?" stammered Alex fearfully.

Valerie looked around quickly and tried to calm her mind long enough to think.

"These doors sure aren't going to open!" said Harold and he gave them one more hopeful shove.

"Let's get aboard the locomotive!" exclaimed Valerie. "We can close up the engineer's cabin!"

Without waiting for a response, she darted off toward the locomotive again. Alex and Harold followed right behind her. Alex's light was fading badly now, which made it difficult to see through the gloom and only added to their terror.

They climbed up the side of the old locomotive and entered the cab compartment through an open side door. Once they were all inside, Harold strained against the door to force it closed on its rusted steel track. Valerie slid and locked an open window and the trio was closed inside. They caught their breath and tried to calm down their heartbeats. Alex shut off his light to save the batteries, as did Valerie with the UV light. They couldn't hear anything outside the cab of the locomotive -- it was as if the ghostly trainman had freakishly disappeared.

"Maybe he wants one of *our* hands!" Alex whispered shakily in the dark.

"I don't know what he wants…and I would rather not find out!" replied Valerie quietly.

~~~~

Officer Mark Quaid was tired and ready to head home when the call came in. He had been out since the early hours of the morning, patrolling in his police cruiser. A fight between two teenagers at a local convenience store, an investigation of stolen bicycles in the city's west end and an old man who had wandered away from his old age home had rounded out his day. Now this -- the report of the doors to the train tunnel being closed up on a Sunday and suspected vandalism. It was aggravating, but if it weren't for some of the young people's antics in this quiet little city, he might not have a job.

He pulled down the main street and turned off toward the waterfront. Officer Quaid knew that whatever was going on down there wouldn't be serious in any way -- the teenagers who were probably messing around would likely bolt when they saw the police car.

Officer Quaid had only been with the city's police force for three years.

He'd moved a long way to establish himself and his family from a remote town where he had been one of two trainee police officers. A young man of 30 years, he was tall and fit, with a shock of short cut black hair, brown eyes and a polite smile; but he was fairly serious when he was on the job.

He pulled down to the public parking area beside the tunnel and swung the cruiser around next to the entrance. Sure enough, the doors were closed. He put the car in park and radioed the station.

"4-9 to base," he said into his mike.

"Go ahead, Mark," said the female voice on the radio.

"Doors are closed. No one in sight. I'm going to take a closer look," he replied.

"Want us to send another unit your way?"

He chuckled before responding. "No, I think this one is just small time," he replied as he grinned to himself.

He stepped out of the cruiser and adjusted his belt. Everything was quiet. He looked around, scanning the area. There was no one around. So who could've closed the doors? *"Probably a bunch of teens, playing ghosts and goblins to impress their girlfriends, or getting ready for a party underneath the city,"* he thought. The last thing he needed was a headline about a massive bonfire and party in the tunnel that ran underneath City Hall.

He stepped up to the doors and gave a yank on each of them, to no avail. They were solid and appeared to be barred from the inside somehow. He shone his flashlight through the small gap between them. He couldn't see or hear anything from inside. He squinted through the gaps in the thick wood of the doors.

"It's an awfully quiet party," he mumbled under his breath.

13

The trio stood quietly in the locomotive cab and tried to peer through the gloom out of the dirty windows. They had finally slowed their breathing down. Maybe they could hide here until the 'thing' went away. It was so dark outside the windows, with only that tiny sliver of light leaking in through the north doors of the tunnel. It was impossible to see anything, especially through the layers of dust and grime that covered everything.

Alex sat down on the floor and leaned up against the side of the cab door. He was desperately wishing that this whole scenario would be all over with, that he would just wake up from this strange and horrifying nightmare. He held his backpack tightly against him and closed his eyes shut, not wanting to look out into the blackness.

A brief noise suddenly broke through the silence outside of their temporary shelter. Alex immediately tossed his backpack and jumped up to huddle against his sister. Valerie grabbed onto Harold's arm. The three of them stood still, not moving, not wanting to make a sound. Their ears strained as they listened. They could hear a scuffling of some kind, not far away, followed by an agitated growl. It was the trainman! He was looking for them!

Then there was the sound of something moving around in the gravel along with more grunts and scuffling movements. Valerie's blood chilled in her veins and she leaned forward to try to see out the back windows of the locomotive. The gloom was impenetrable.

Suddenly a pale face appeared outside the rear window of the cab. Valerie backed away quickly and the three of them caught their breaths and froze in terror at the sight. For seconds that seemed like eternity, in a scene which played as if in slow motion, the three watched in horror as the trainman looked inside the cab at the three of them in turn, grinning maliciously at them through the dirty glass. A second later he held up a lantern with his good hand and lifted his bandaged stump of the other had to rest against the window.

Alex finally lost his composure and began screaming at the top of his lungs. His terror filled the small cab with a deafening tone. He fell backwards, tripping over his backpack on the floor, and landed against a large lever that was sticking up from the floor. It moved backward with him and emitted a rusty screech as Alex tumbled to the floor with a resounding, "ouch". He scrambled up quickly to lean against the far wall, shielding his eyes from the horrid vision in front of them.

Valerie had stepped further back away from the window at the same time, fighting the urge to scream herself. The trainman continued to glare in at them with a cruel smile, his grim visage searing itself into her brain. She wanted out of there. She wanted to be anywhere other than the tunnel at that moment -- home in her bedroom, out in the backyard, even in a boring old classroom at school -- just anywhere but here! The trainman's bloodshot eyes were trained on her now, and she felt weak, still too scared even to cry out. She could only stand there, frozen in place, as she watched in horrible fascination.

The whole floor of the cab lurched underneath them, along with the groan of iron and steel. The sound filled the darkness with an echoing boom. It lurched again, harder this time and the three of them struggled to maintain their balance. Valerie straightened herself up just in time to see the trainman's face bounce off the dirty glass of the cab, his eyes now full of confusion. She looked behind her and flipped the switch on her UV light for a moment to look at the large metal handle that Alex had fallen against. Letters had been engraved deeply into the rusted steel, which she could barely make out in the weak light. "BRAKE".

Just for a second, as she and the trainman locked eyes again, Valerie saw something shift in his appearance. Something told her instantly that perhaps he wasn't as scary as she had first thought. His demeanor had quickly shifted to a look of utter uncertainty as the sounds of groaning steel and the scrape of the train's wheels woke them both up to one undeniable fact: the train was moving!

Valerie, Harold and Alex grasped hold of anything around them in the dark that might help keep them upright against the motion. And there was plenty of motion! The violence of the movement down the tunnel increased. As the train gathered momentum, the entire locomotive shifted roughly from side to side along the joints of the ancient track underneath it. It was impossible to tell how fast they were moving in the darkness, but the sounds and the shaking of the train around them told them that they were headed down the tunnel at an increasingly tremendous speed!

Valerie had tried to keep her eyes on the trainman, who was trying his best to keep his grip outside the window as the railcars moved even quicker downhill towards the south entrance doors. As he swerved to and fro, his eyes were now wide with a new emotion: fear. Valerie could tell suddenly that this 'thing' clinging to the back of the locomotive cab was definitely no ghost -- he was surely as alive as they were…and he was scared!

The dim flame inside the lantern he was holding abruptly extinguished in the wind as they continued to careen down the tunnel out of control. A sliver of light began to appear ahead of them in the dark. *"It must be the light through the south doors,"* Valerie's mind registered, and it was getting closer very quickly.

"Get down!" she hollered to her companions. She crouched down quickly and grabbed hold of something in the dark that hopefully would be strong enough to brace herself against the impact that she could sense coming. Alex and Harold wasted no time following what she had shouted and dropped down to the floor, paying no further heed to the trainman, the dark or anything else!

The last thing that Valerie saw before the crash, when she glimpsed quickly up towards the back window, was the trainman flying forward against the window -- its thick glass warped with the impact as the train became like an accordion and the slack between the cars slammed them together as the train burst through the massive south doors of the tunnel. Splinters and chunks of wood flew everywhere as the light of day blinded them. It was like a huge explosion -- a blast of light and timber and dust and iron!

The sound was deafening, and the three of them held on for dear life as the tail end cars of the train ran off the rails at the tunnel entrance, throwing grass and dirt high into the air. Still the train raged forward. Valerie, Alex and Harold were tossed relentlessly about the cab of the locomotive, powerless to stop the ride that they were on.

The tail end car impacted steel as it smashed into the caboose standing silently on its pair of rails for display and shoved it sideways onto the ground. This car, though, remained upright, and the train came to a violent halt, the dust and debris floating around it as it all came to a final rest.

Valerie quickly picked herself up off the floor of the locomotive and shielded her eyes against the late afternoon sun. As her vision adjusted to the light, she saw her brother shaking his head as he started to rise and helped him to his feet. Harold was already struggling to stand as well. They stood still for a moment and looked around them in bewilderment as they tried to gather composure and settle their quickly beating hearts.

One of the side windows of the compartment had shattered in the crash and there was broken glass and chunks of rust on the floor. The trainman had disappeared from view. Valerie could see the mess of train cars, all strewn out in front of the locomotive, along with the caboose sitting crazily off kilter.

Together they slid open one of the doors and, one by one, descended the ladder a bit shakily, glad to finally step on solid ground again. Valerie looked at the furrows that had been plowed into the manicured lawn by the train wheels, and cringed at the idea that they might just be getting themselves into a lot of trouble this time! After all, they had just managed to destroy a historically important tourist attraction! There would be a lot of people in the city who would not be very happy about it.

Just then something caught Valerie's eye. There was something fluttering slightly at the end of the caboose in the barely perceptible breeze of the fall air. It looked like a paper of some sort and it was sticking out of the damaged end of the rail car. She walked slowly towards it, keeping her eyes fixed on the flapping piece of paper. As she got closer, things came into sharp focus in the fading light of the fall afternoon, and she watched as the paper dropped silently to the ground.

She knelt down beside the torn open steel of one of the caboose's side compartments. The welds had burst open from the impact. Her mouth fell open as she lifted the worn piece of ancient-looking paper from the damaged grass. It had an official looking emblem in the top right hand corner and several numbers written along the top edge in ink. In the middle of the document, the words read:

"Army Bill Office, Quebec. The bearer hereof is entitled to receive on demand, the sum of twenty five dollars from the Army Bill Office."

The date was printed below --*1813* -- along with several signatures and a stamp, none of which were very legible. Alex and Harold had approached her and peered over Valerie's shoulder, wide-eyed at the find that she held in her hand.

"Wow," exclaimed Alex. "That looks old!"

Valerie stood up and looked carefully inside the ruptured compartment on the side of the caboose. Alex produced his flashlight and turned it on. Its weak batteries still had enough juice to cast a small beam of light that was good enough to illuminate the opening. All three of them gasped at their discovery: shimmering copper and shining silver coins nestled in the secret compartment...lots and lots of coins.

"It wasn't gold after all!" exclaimed Harold.

A second later they could hear sirens in the distance. Valerie knew that as the sound got closer, it would be for them, and the wreckage that they'd unintentionally caused at the waterfront. That feeling that she always got when she knew she was in deep trouble with her father crept into her mind and she began to look around, hoping that the sirens would go in another direction. They didn't.

Within moments, they could see the wash of the red and blue lights off of the buildings up the block from the waterfront and hear the blare of horns from a fire truck as well as it meandered through late Sunday afternoon traffic in the downtown area. Emergency vehicles of all kinds showed up in the parking area at the waterfront, their lights on full display. Valerie, Alex and Harold stood together, rooted in the spot in front of the caboose's smashed compartment, and caught in the headlights of the police cruisers. They stood still as several officers exited their vehicles and approached the scene cautiously.

Alex instinctively raised his arms in surrender, but Valerie quickly nudged him and looked down at him with a frown on her face. He lowered his arms as if in defeat.

Officer Mark Quaid carefully approached the three of them as he looked in awe at the mess around them. He whistled to himself and his gaze fell on the children and Harold.

"Perhaps someone can tell me exactly what is going on, and why there is a train sitting here in a heap of a mess outside the tunnel?" he asked as he removed a notebook from the pocket on his vest and clicked the end of his pen quickly for dramatic effect.

"We were trying to get away from the ghost of the trainman!" Alex burst out excitedly.

Another policeman stepped up beside Officer Quaid and raised his eyebrows when he heard Alex's statement.

Officer Quaid looked down at the wide-eyed boy. "I'm sorry, a ghost?" he asked.

"It wasn't a ghost," clarified Valerie, still clutching the paper note in her hand. "We don't know who he was, but a man was chasing after us in the train tunnel, and we tried to hide from him in the locomotive of the train..."

"It's true," Harold interjected and he quickly cleared his throat with a little cough. Then he continued his explanation. "The children and I were following the story of an old legend here in the tunnel, and this fellow was all dressed up like a ghost and tried to scare us away."

"Maybe we should just start with your names and addresses first, hmmm?" said Officer Quaid with a look of obvious disbelief on his face.

They each went through the process of giving their name and address and answered the officer's questions about why they were there and what they had been doing. The children even included a few comments about the help and encouragement that they'd received from the museum curator, Mr. Thusk. Valerie again felt the crushing fear that they were in serious trouble, and she glanced over at some of the other emergency people -- firefighters and a couple of paramedics -- who were inspecting the wreckage of the train cars.

"So where is this fellow you described? Where is the man who was chasing you?" Officer Quaid asked as he looked briefly at each of them.

"Everything happened so quickly! He simply disappeared when the train came out of the tunnel," explained Valerie.

As if on cue, they all looked towards the sound of a slight rustling noise coming from inside the railcar behind the police officers. It was followed by a barely audible groan. Then, two fat hands, as pale as paper, grabbed the rusted top edge of the car, and a man emerged, face first, and looked around him groggily.

"It's him!" shouted Alex.

"Yes, that's the man who was chasing us!" Valerie exclaimed and pointed at him.

All Officer Quaid needed was one look at the man peering over the side of the railcar to assemble the rest of the story in his mind. This was Shaun Locke, a city councillor, someone who worked for the city. A man who should be able to be trusted. Why would this man be dressed up in some kind of ghostly-looking garb, chasing two young children and an older man around in the train tunnel?

Then Officer Quaid spotted the paper that Valerie had clutched in her hand and noticed the shine of coins spilling out of the old caboose behind the children and Harold. The pieces of the puzzle rapidly fell into place. He nodded towards the groaning man who had untangled himself from the wreckage and was trying to climb out of the railcar to no success.

"Make sure he's all right and then get him out of here," said Officer Quaid to the other policeman standing with him.

A paramedic went over as well to help Shaun out of the railcar and the moment he was on the ground and his vital signs checked, handcuffs were fastened around his wrists, despite his vehement complaints.

"I did nothing wrong," he sputtered and shouted as the officer held firmly onto his arm to lead him over to the cruiser. "It was these kids! I am a city councilman. You can't do this to me!"

"I understand *exactly* what has been happening here Mr. Locke, and yes, I can," countered Officer Quaid as he jotted down a few more notes in his book.

Valerie breathed a slight sigh of relief, even though she knew that this was far from over. She waited for more questions. She was also imagining the trouble her father would likely give them.

"I guess you guys are free to go, if you're sure you're all right, but we may need to come by and ask you more questions. Oh, and this 'treasure' you found? You know that it is not really *yours*, right? It belongs to the city," explained Officer Quaid.

All three of them nodded, relieved that they too were not in handcuffs.

"What about all of this?" Valerie asked as she indicated the mess around them.

Officer Quaid put away his notebook and pen. His face softened into a polite smile.

"Well, the public has always been allowed to explore the tunnel -- that's something that we have no control over. As I understand it, Councillor Locke voted down an idea to gate off the tunnel. Even if he avoids criminal charges for what happened today, he will have to go back to council and explain all of this. I can't see him being re-elected. Have a good evening, guys," he said with a wink and added, "try to stay out of trouble, eh?!"

"Thank you, officer," said Harold.

"But what about the treasure?" Alex asked Officer Quaid. "What'll happen to it?"

"Well, I'm sure it will be turned over to your friend down at the museum, Mr. Thusk," he replied and gave them all a smile as he turned to leave.

~~~~

Valerie, Alex and Harold all watched as Mr. Thusk gently placed the thick glass over top of the display of coins and paper notes in the large hallway of the museum. It was a special case that had been made especially to house documents that were sensitive to moisture. When everything was finished, the case would be vacuum-sealed and the paper money that the children had found with the treasure would be preserved.

Mr. Thusk took his time, checking to make sure that all the joints in the glass were well sealed. Then he started a small compressor beside the case.

"This will remove all the air from inside the case," explained the curator. "It will ensure that everything in it is very well protected."

Once the process was finished, Mr. Thusk removed everything from around the display and polished the glass one last time with a cloth. He gave a satisfied nod to them three bystanders once everything was done with a broad smile upon his old face.

"There!" he said. "All ready for the unveiling tomorrow. You three will be here for that, of course?"

The children glanced at each other quickly and Alex rolled his eyes at the thought of standing there in dress clothes, having to smile all day while people from the city looked at the new find. He would rather fake sick for the day!

"Of course," replied Valerie politely. She simply ignored the desperate look from her younger brother. Harold just stood there and smiled, very happy to see all three of their names on a small document resting inside the display case.

"Very well, then. I will see you in the morning at ten," concluded Mr. Thusk and he turned and hurried off down the hall.

The three adventurers pushed open the heavy glass doors of the museum and stepped out into the cold fall air. The sky was overcast once again. They pulled their jackets up around them in response to the cold and paused for a moment on the front steps of the old building.

"That was fun, guys. Thanks for a great adventure!" said Harold. "Maybe I will write a book about it!" He practically bounced down the stairs in his delight, gave them a quick wave and headed down the street towards his home.

The children smiled at each other.

"Well," said Alex. "Another one of Nana's adventures done and over with."

He hoisted his tattered old backpack up on his shoulder, ready to start their walk home.

Valerie didn't say anything for a moment -- she just watched her breath float away as steam in the still, cold air.

"Yeah, let's go visit her again soon," she finally replied.

A Note from the Author

This concludes the third adventure story starring my children, and as I put this manuscript down, ready to send it forward for editing, I am reminded of how fast time passes. It seems like only yesterday when I began to write "The Heart of The Raven". But I look at the children now, and realize just how much time has indeed gone by. My daughter is now finished high school and is working here in the city, trying to find her way in life. My son is just entering his second year of high school. And, in the meantime, my oldest daughter and her boyfriend have brought me suddenly to terms with becoming a Grandfather.

I can no longer cast myself as Dad in these stories, as much as I have enjoyed writing them. Time moves forward -- the scenes and the characters are continually changing. I can only hope that the children have had as much fun reading these adventures, as I have enjoyed creating them.

About the Author

Dennis Stein lives in the small city of Brockville, Ontario, Canada, where he still works full time at a day job, juggling his time with career, family and writing. He has a fascination with nature, and many stories to tell of his home in the beautiful Thousand Islands area of Ontario. Stein enjoys writing in a wide variety of genres, and regularly writes historical and human interest articles for several local publications.

All of Stein's writing is done during his spare time, as he works for CN Rail in a full-time position where he has been employed for over twenty years.